THUNDERHEAD

By Douglas Preston and Lincoln Child

The Relic
Mount Dragon
Reliquary
Riptide

By Douglas Preston

Dinosaurs in the Attic
Cities of Gold
Jennie
Talking to the Ground

Edited by Lincoln Child

Dark Company
Dark Banquet
Tales of the Dark 1–3

DOUGLAS PRESTON & LINCOLN CHILD

THUNDERHEAD

WARNER BOOKS

A Time Warner Company

Copyright © 1999 by Lincoln Child and Splendide Mendax, Inc.
All rights reserved.

Warner Books, Inc. 1271 Avenue of the Americas, New York, NY 10020
Visit our Web site at www.warnerbooks.com
A Time Warner Company

Printed in the United States of America
First Printing: July 1999
10 9 8 7 6 5 4 3 2 1

Library of Congress Cataloging-in-Publication Data

Preston, Douglas J.
    Thunderhead / Douglas Preston and Lincoln Child.
        p. cm.
    ISBN 0-446-52337-2
    I. Child, Lincoln. II. Title.
PS3566. R3982T48 1999
813' .54—dc21   98-37557
                                                          CIP

Book design by Giorgetta Bell McRee

Lincoln Child dedicates this book to his daughter, Veronica,
and to the Company of Nine.

Douglas Preston dedicates this book
to Stuart Woods.

ACKNOWLEDGMENTS

Lincoln Child wishes to thank Bruce Swanson, Bry Benjamin, M.D., Lee Suckno, M.D., Irene Soderlund, Mary Ellen Mix, Bob Wincott, Sergio and Mila Nepomuceno, Jim Cush, Chris Yango, Jim Jenkins, Mark Mendel, Juliette Kvernland, Hartley Clark, and Denis Kelly, for their friendship and their assistance, both technical and otherwise. Thanks also to my wife, Luchie, for her love and unstinting support. And I would especially like to acknowledge as an inspiration my grandmother Nora Kubie. Artist, novelist, archaeologist, independent spirit, biographer of Nineveh excavator Austen Henry Layard, she instilled in me from a very early age twin loves for writing and archaeology. She worked on excavations as far away as Masada and Camelot, and as close as her own New Hampshire backyard. Although she passed away ten years ago, during the writing of *Thunderhead* in particular she was never far from my thoughts.

Douglas Preston would like to offer his appreciation to the following people: Walter Winings Nelson, horseback riding companion across a thousand miles of deserts, canyons, and mountains, seeking the Seven Cities of Gold; Larry Burke, captain of the *Emerald Sun,* for hosting a memorable expedition up Lake Powell; Forrest Fenn, who found his own lost city; the Cottonwood Gulch Foundation of New Mexico; and

Tim Maxwell, director of the Office of Archaeological Studies at the Museum of New Mexico. I would also like to thank my wife, Christine, and my children Selene, Aletheia, and Isaac. I want to thank once again those two who can never receive enough thanks, my mother and father, Dorothy and Jerome Preston.

We would like to thank Ron Blom and Diane Evans at NASA's Jet Propulsion Laboratory for their help with an article of Douglas Preston's explaining how space-borne radar is used in locating ancient trails. We offer them our apologies for creating the unpleasant and wholly fictitious character of Leland Watkins. No such persons as Leland Watkins or Peter Holroyd work, or have worked, at JPL. We would also like to express our great appreciation to Farouk El-Baz, director of the Center for Remote Sensing at Boston University, for his help with the technical aspects of remote sensing the earth from space; and we thank Juris Zarins, the archaeologist who discovered the lost city of Ubar in Saudi Arabia.

Our deep appreciation goes out to Bonnie Mauer, who read the manuscript not once but several times and offered excellent advice. Thanks also to Eric Simonoff, Lynn Nesbit, and Matthew Snyder, for their continued assistance, counsel, and encouragement. Special thanks to Mort Janklow for sharing a surprising and very moving personal anecdote in connection with our story. And to Clifford Irving, for his advice on the manuscript, as well as Kim Gattone, for so kindly assisting with some of the technical aspects of rock climbing. At Warner, we would like to thank Betsy Mitchell, Jaime Levine, Jimmy Franco, Maureen Egen, and Larry Kirshbaum for believing in us. Thanks also to Debi Elfenbein.

We hasten to add that any outrages committed in the name of anthropology and archaeology within the pages of *Thunderhead* are fictitious and exist wholly within the authors' imaginations.

THUNDERHEAD

1

THE FRESHLY PAVED ROAD LEFT SANTA FE and arrowed west through piñon trees. An amber-colored sun was sinking into a scrim of dirty clouds behind the snow-capped Jemez Mountains, drawing a counterpane of shade across the landscape. Nora Kelly guided the rattletrap Ford pickup along the road, down chamisa-covered hills and across the beds of dry washes. It was the third time she had been out here in as many months.

As she came up from Buckman's Wash into Jackrabbit Flats—what had *once* been Jackrabbit Flats—she saw a shining arc of light beyond the piñons. A moment later, her truck was speeding past manicured greens. A nearby sprinkler head winked and nodded in the sun, jetting water in a regular, palsied cadence. Beyond, on a rise, stood the new Fox Run clubhouse, a massive structure of fake adobe. Nora looked away.

The truck rattled over a cattle guard at the far end of Fox Run and suddenly, the road was washboard dirt. She bounced past a cluster of ancient mailboxes and the crude, weather-beaten sign that read RANCHO DE LAS CABRILLAS. For a moment, the memory of a summer day twenty years before passed through her mind: once again she was standing in the heat, holding a bucket, helping her father paint the sign.

Cabrillas, he'd said, was the Spanish word for waterbugs. But it was also their name for the constellation Pleiades, which he said looked like water skaters on the shining surface of a pond. "To hell with the cattle," she remembered him saying, swabbing thick letters with the paintbrush. "I bought this place for its stars."

The road turned to ascend a rise, and she slowed. The sun had now disappeared, and the light was draining fast out of the high desert sky. There in a grassy valley stood the old ranch house, windows boarded up. And beside it, the frowsy outlines of the barn and corrals that were once the Kelly family ranch. No one had lived here in five years. It was no great loss, Nora told herself: the house was a mid-fifties prefab, already falling apart when she was growing up. Her father had spent all his money on the land.

Pulling off the road just below the brow of the hill, she glanced toward the nearby arroyo. Somebody had surreptitiously dumped a load of broken cinderblocks. Maybe her brother was right and she should sell the place. Taxes were going up, and the house had long ago passed the point of no return. Why was she holding on to it? She couldn't afford to build her own place there—not on an assistant professor's salary, anyway.

She could see the lights coming on in the Gonzales ranch house, a quarter mile away. It was a real working ranch, not like her father's hobby ranchito. Teresa Gonzales, a girl she'd grown up with, now ran the place by herself. A big, smart, fearless woman. In recent years, she'd taken it upon herself to look after the Kelly ranch, too. Every time kids came out to party, or drunken hunters decided to take potshots at the place, Teresa rousted them and left a message on the answering machine at Nora's townhouse. This time, for the past three or four nights, Teresa had seen dim lights in and around the house just after sunset, and—she thought—large animals slinking about.

Nora waited a few minutes, looking for signs of life, but the ranch was quiet and empty. Perhaps Teresa had imagined the lights. In any case, whoever or whatever it was seemed to have left.

She eased the truck through the inner gate and down the last two hundred yards of road, parked around back, and killed the engine. Pulling a flashlight out of the glove compartment, she stepped lightly onto the dirt. The door of the house hung open, held precariously by a single hinge screw, its lock cut off long ago with bolt cutters. A gust swept through the yard, picking up skeins of dust and moving the door with a restless whisper.

She flicked on the flashlight and stepped onto the portal. The door moved aside at her push, then swung back stubbornly. She gave it an annoyed kick and it fell to the porch with a clatter, loud in the listening silence. She stepped inside.

The boarded windows made the interior difficult to make out, yet even so it was clearly a sad echo of her memory of the house she grew up in. Beer bottles and broken glass lay strewn across the floor, and some gang member had spray-painted a tagline on the wall. Some of the boards covering the windows had been pried away. The carpet had been ripped up, and sofa cushions sliced in half and tossed about the room. Holes had been kicked in the drywall, along with liberal pepperings from a .22.

Perhaps it wasn't that much worse than the last time. The rips on the cushions were new, along with the ragged holes in the wall, but the rest she remembered from her previous visit. Her lawyer had warned her that in its present condition the place was a liability. If a city inspector ever managed to get out here, he would immediately condemn it. The only problem was, tearing the thing down would cost more than she had—unless, of course, she sold it.

She turned from the living room into the kitchen. Her flashlight beam swept over the old Frigidaire, still lying where it had been overturned. Drawers had recently been removed and strewn about the room. The linoleum was coming up in big curls, and someone had hastened the process, peeling off strips and even ripping up floorboards to expose the crawlspace underneath. *Vandalism is hard work,* she thought. As her eyes roved over the room again, something began to nag at the back of her mind. Something was different this time.

She left the kitchen and began to climb the stairs, kicking aside wads of mattress ticking, trying to bring the thought into focus. Sofa cushions sliced, holes punched in walls, carpeting and linoleum ripped up. Somehow, this fresh violence didn't seem quite as random as it had in the past. It was almost as if someone was looking for something. Halfway up the darkness of the stairwell, she stopped.

Was that the crunch of glass underfoot?

She waited, motionless in the dim light. There was no sound but the faint susurrus of wind. If a car had driven up, she'd have heard it. She continued up the stairs.

It was even darker up here, all the windowboards still in place. She turned right on the landing and shone the flashlight into her old bedroom. Again she felt the familiar pang as her eyes moved over the pink wallpaper, now hanging in strips and stained like an old map. The mattress was one giant packrat's nest, the music stand for her oboe broken and rusted, the floorboards sprung. A bat squeaked overhead, and Nora remembered the time she'd been caught trying to make a pet out of one of them. Her mother had never understood her childish fascination for the creatures.

She moved across the hall to her brother's room, also a wreck. *Not so different from his current place.* But over the smell of ruin, she thought she detected the faintest scent of crushed flowers in the night air. *Strange—the windows are all shuttered up here.* She moved down the hall toward her parents' bedroom.

This time, there was no mistaking it: the faint tinkle of broken glass from below. She stopped again. Was it a rat, scuttling across the living room floor?

She moved silently back to the top of the landing, then paused. There was another sound from below: a faint thud. As she waited in the darkness, she heard another crunch, sharper this time, as something heavy stepped on broken glass.

Nora exhaled slowly, a tight knot of muscle squeezing her chest. What had begun as an irritating errand now felt like something else entirely.

"Who is it?" she called out.

Only the wind answered.

She swung the flashlight beam into the empty stairwell. Usually, kids would run at the first sight of her truck. Not this time.

"This is private property!" she yelled in her steadiest voice. "And you're trespassing. The police are on their way."

In the ensuing silence, there came another footpad, closer to the stairwell.

"Teresa?" Nora called again, in a desperate hope.

And then she heard something else: a throaty, menacing sound that was almost a growl.

Dogs, she thought with a sudden flood of relief. There were feral dogs out there, and they'd been using the house as a shelter. She chose not to think about why this was somehow a comforting thought.

"Yah!" she cried, waving the light. "Get on out of here! Go home!"

Again, silence was the only reply.

Nora knew how to handle stray dogs. She stomped down the stairs, speaking loudly and firmly. Reaching the bottom, she swept the beam across the living room.

It was empty. The dogs must have run at the sound of her approach.

Nora took a deep breath. Even though she hadn't inspected her parent's bedroom, she decided it was time to go.

As she headed for the door, she heard another careful footstep, then another, excruciatingly slow and deliberate.

She flashed her light toward the sounds as something else registered: a faint, breathy wheeze, a low, monotonous purring mutter. That same scent of flowers wafted through the heavy air, this time stronger.

She stood motionless, paralyzed by the unfamiliar feeling of menace, wondering if she should switch off the flashlight and hide herself or simply make a run for it.

And then out of the corner of her eye she saw a huge, pelted form racing along the wall. She turned to confront it as a stunning blow landed across her back.

She fell sprawling, feeling coarse fur at the nape of her neck. There was a maniacal wet growling, like the slavered fighting of rabid hounds. She lashed into the figure with a vicious kick. The figure snarled but relaxed its grip slightly, giving Nora a moment to wrench free. Just as she jumped up, a second figure slammed into her and threw her to the ground, landing atop her. Nora twisted, feeling broken glass digging into her skin as the dark form pinned her to the ground. She glimpsed a naked belly, covered with glowing spots; jaguar stripes; claws of horn and hair; a midriff, dank and matted—wearing a belt of silver conchos. Narrow eyes, terrifyingly red and bright, stared at her from grimy slits in a buckskin mask.

"Where is it?" a voice rasped in her face, washing her in the cloyingly sweet stench of rotten meat.

She could not find the voice to reply.

"Where is it?" the voice repeated, crude, imperfect, like a beast aping human speech. Vicelike claws grasped her roughly around the neck and right arm.

"What—" she croaked.

"The letter," it said, claws tightening. "Or we rip your head off."

She jerked in sudden fevered struggle, but the grip on her neck grew stronger. She began to choke in pain and terror.

Suddenly, a flash of light and a deafening blast cut through the darkness. She felt the grip slacken, and in a frenzy she twisted free of the claws. She rolled over as a second blast ripped a hole in the ceiling overhead, showering her with bits of lathe and plaster. She scrambled desperately to her feet, shards of glass skittering across the floor. Her flashlight had rolled away, and she spun around, disoriented.

"Nora?" she heard. "That you, Nora?" Framed in the dim

light of the front door, a plump figure was standing, shotgun hanging forward.

"Teresa!" Nora sobbed. She stumbled toward the light.

"You okay?" Teresa asked, grabbing Nora's arm, steadying her.

"I don't know."

"Let's get the hell out of here."

Outside, Nora sank to the ground, gulping the cool twilight air and fighting down her pounding heart. "What happened?" she heard Teresa ask. "I heard noises, some kind of scuffle, saw your light."

Nora simply shook her head, gasping.

"Those were some hellacious-looking wild dogs. Big as wolves, almost."

Nora shook her head again. "No. Not dogs. One of them spoke to me."

Teresa peered at her more closely. "Hey, your arm looks bitten. Maybe you'd better let me drive you to the hospital."

"Absolutely not."

But Teresa was scanning the dim outlines of the house, eyebrows knitted. "They sure did leave in a hurry. First kids, now wild dogs. But what kind of dogs could vanish so—"

"Teresa, one of them *spoke* to me."

Teresa looked at her, more searchingly this time, a skeptical look creeping into her eyes. "Must've been pretty terrifying," she said at last. "You should've told me you were coming out. I'd have met you down here with Señor Winchester." She patted the gun fondly.

Nora looked at her solid figure, her rattled but capable face. She knew the woman didn't believe her, but she didn't have the energy to argue. "Next time I will," she said.

"I hope there won't be a next time," said Teresa gently. "You need to either tear this place down, or sell it and let someone else tear it down for you. It's becoming a problem, and not just for you."

"I know it's an eyesore. But I just hate to think of letting it go. I'm sorry it's caused trouble for you."

"I would've thought this might change your mind. Want to come in for a bite of something?"

"No thanks, Teresa," Nora said as firmly as she could. "I'm all right."

"Maybe," came the reply. "But you better get a rabies shot anyway."

Nora watched as her neighbor turned onto the narrow trail that headed back up the hill. Then she eased into the driver's seat of her truck and locked all the doors with a shaking hand. She sat quietly, feeling the air move in and out of her lungs, watching Teresa's dim form merge slowly with the dark bulk of the hillside. When at last she felt in full control of her limbs, she reached for the ignition, wincing at a sudden stab of pain in her neck.

She turned over the engine, unsuccessfully, and cursed. She needed a new vehicle, along with a new everything else in her life.

She tried it again, and after a sputtering protest the engine coughed into life. She punched off the headlights to conserve the battery and, slouching back against the seat, gently pumped the accelerator, waiting for the engine to clear.

To one side, a flash of silver winked briefly. She turned to see a huge shape, black and furred, bounding toward her against the last twilight in the western sky.

Nora slammed the old truck into gear, punched on the headlights, and gunned the engine. It roared in response and she went fishtailing out of the yard. As she careened through the inside gate, she saw with consummate horror that the thing was racing alongside her.

She jammed the accelerator to the floor as the truck slewed across the ranch road, spraying mad patterns of dirt, whacking a cholla. And then, the thing was gone. But she continued to accelerate down the road to the outer gate, wheels pounding the washboard. After an unbearably long moment, her headlights finally picked up the outer cattle guard looming from the darkness ahead, the row of old mailboxes nailed to a long horizontal board beside it. Too late, Nora jammed on the brakes; the truck struck the cattle guard and was airborne. She landed heavily and skidded in the sand, striking the old board. There was the crunch of splintering wood and the boxes were flung to the ground.

She sat in the truck, breathing hard, dust smoking up around her lights. She dropped into reverse and gunned the engine, feeling panic as the wheels dug into the deep sand. She rocked twice before the truck stalled.

In the glow of the headlights, she could see the damage. The row of ranch mailboxes had been a rickety affair to begin with, and they had recently been supplanted by a shiny new set of post office boxes that stood nearby. But she could not back up: there was no choice but to go forward.

She jumped out and, glancing around for any sign of the figure, moved around to the front of the truck, picked up the rotten, abandoned mailboxes, and dragged them aside into the brush. An envelope lay in the dirt, and she grabbed it. As she turned to step back into the truck, the headlights caught the front of the envelope. Nora froze for a moment, gasping in surprise.

Then she shoved it in her shirt pocket, jumped into the truck, and peeled back onto the road, careening toward the distant, welcoming lights of town.

2

THE SANTA FE ARCHAEOLOGICAL INSTI-
tute stood on a low mesa between the Sangre de Cristo
foothills and the town of Santa Fe itself. No affiliated museum opened its doors to the public, and classes were limited
to invitation-only graduate seminars and faculty colloquiums.
Visiting scholars and resident professors outnumbered students. The campus sprawled across thirty acres, its low adobe
buildings almost invisible among the walled gardens, apricot
trees, tulip beds, and rows of ancient, blossom-heavy lilacs.

The Institute was devoted almost exclusively to research,
excavation, and preservation, and it housed one of the finest
prehistoric southwestern Indian collections in the world.
Wealthy, reserved, and much wedded to its traditions, it was
looked on with both awe and envy by professional archaeologists across the country.

Nora watched the last of her students leave the low-
ceilinged adobe classroom, then gathered her notes and slot-
ted them into an oversized leather portfolio. It was the final
class of her seminar, "The Chaco Abandonment: Causes and
Conditions." Once again, she was struck by the unusual atti-
tude of students at the Institute: quiet, respectful, as if unable
to believe their good fortune in being granted a ten-week resident scholarship.

Stepping out of the cool darkness into the sunlight, she walked slowly along the graveled path. The Pueblo Revival buildings of the campus, with their organic sloping walls and projecting vigas, were painted a warm rust color by the morning light. A thunderhead was developing over the mountains, dark beneath but topped with a spreading crown of brilliant white. As she glanced up to look at it, a sharp pain lanced one side of her bruised neck. She reached to massage it as a dark shadow seemed to come across the sun.

Passing the parking lot, she traced a circuitous route toward the rear of the campus, turning at last down a flagstone walk columned with lombardy poplars and old Chinese elms. The walkway ended at a nondescript building whose small wooden sign read simply RECORDS.

Nora showed her badge to the guard, signed in, and went down the hall to a low doorway, stopping at the cement steps that led down into the gloom. Down to the Map Vault.

She tensed for a moment, the darkness of the stairs bringing back another unwanted memory of the evening before. Again, she felt the broken glass stabbing into her skin, the tightening claws, the sickly sweet smell . . .

She shook the memory away and started down the narrow steps.

The Institute's collections contained innumerable priceless artifacts. Yet nothing on campus, or in its extensive collections, was as valuable, or as guarded, as the contents of the Map Vault. Although the vault contained no treasure, it housed something far more valuable: the location of every known archaeological site in the Southwest. There were more than three hundred thousand such sites, from the most insignificant lithic scatter to huge ruins containing hundreds of rooms, all carefully marked on the Institute's U.S.G.S. topographical map collection. Nora knew that only the tiniest fraction of these sites had ever been excavated; the rest lay slumbering under the sand or hidden in caves. Each site number corresponded to an entry in the Institute's secure database, containing everything from detailed inventories to surveys to digitized sketches and letters—electronic treasure maps leading to millions of dollars worth of prehistoric artifacts.

How strange, Nora had always thought, that such a place would be guarded by Owen Smalls. Resplendent in beat-up leathers, heavily muscled, Smalls always looked like he had just returned from a harrowing expedition to the farthest corners of the earth. Very few who met the man realized he was an Eastern boy from a wealthy family, a summa cum laude graduate of Brown University, who if placed out in the desert would be dead or lost—or both—within the hour.

The steps ended at a metal door with a small casement window, a red light glowing above it. Nora dug into her bag, extracted her security card, and inserted it into the slot. When the light turned green, she heaved the door open and stepped inside.

Smalls occupied a fanatically neat little office outside the vault itself, overlooking the reading area. He rose as he saw her enter, placing a book carefully on his desk.

"Dr. Kelly," he said. "Nora, right?"

"Morning," Nora said as casually as possible.

"Haven't seen you around for a while," Smalls replied. "Too bad. Hey, what'd you do to your arm?"

Nora glanced briefly at the bandage. "Just a scratch. Owen, I need to look at a couple of maps."

Smalls squinted back. "Yeah?"

"In the C-3 and C-4 quadrants of Utah. Kaiparowits Plateau."

Smalls continued scrutinizing her, shifting his weight, sending a creak of leather echoing through the room. "Project number?"

"We don't have a project number yet. It's just a preliminary survey."

Smalls placed two giant, hairy hands on the desk and leaned over them, looking at her more intently. "Sorry, Dr. Kelly. You need an approved project number to look at anything."

"But it's just a preliminary survey."

"You know the rules," Smalls replied, with a disparaging grin.

Nora thought fast. There was no way that Blakewood, the Institute's president and her boss, would assign a project number based on the meager information she could give him. But she remembered working on a project in a different part of Utah, two years before. The project was still current, if a bit moribund—she had a bad habit of not finishing things up. What was the damn project number?

"It's J-40012," she said.

Small's bushy eyebrows raised.

"Sorry, I forgot it was just assigned. Look, if you don't believe me, call Professor Blakewood." She knew her boss was at a conference in Window Rock.

Smalls turned to the computer on his desk and rapped at the keys. After a moment, he looked up at Nora. "Seems to be approved. C-3 and C-4, you said?" He resumed his typing, the keys ludicrously small in his hands. Then he cleared the screen and stepped away from the desk.

Nora followed as he stepped up to the vault and swung the door open. "Wait here," he said.

"I know the routine." Nora watched as he stepped into the vault. Inside, bathed in pitiless fluorescent light, lay two rows of metal safes, locked doors across their tops. Smalls approached one, punched in a code, and lifted its door. Hanging within the safe were countless maps, sandwiched in layers of protective plastic.

"There are sixteen maps in those quadrants," Smalls called out. "Which ones do you want to see?"

"All of them, please."

Smalls paused. "All sixteen? That's eight hundred eighty square miles."

"As I said, it's a survey. You can always call President—"

"Okay, okay." Holding the maps by the edges of their metal rails, Smalls stepped out of the vault, nodding Nora toward the reading area. He waited until she sat down, then gently placed the maps on the scarred surface of the Formica table. "Use those," he said, indicating a box of disposable cotton gloves. "You've got two hours to complete your study. When you're done, let me know and I'll replace the maps and let you out." He waited while she donned a pair of gloves, then grinned and returned to the vault.

Nora sat at the table as he shut first the safe, then the vault, and returned to his office. *You'll know when I'm done,* she thought to herself. The "reading area" consisted of a large table with a single chair, placed in clear view of Smalls's glass-windowed office. It was a cramped, exposed space. Not at all suitable for what she had in mind.

She took a deep breath, flexed her white-gloved fingers. Then, carefully, she spread the maps out on the table, the plastic crackling as she aligned them along their edges. The sequence of 7.5-minute maps—the most detailed U.S. Geological Survey maps made—covered an exceedingly remote area of southern Utah, framed by Lake Powell to the south and west and Bryce Canyon to the east. It was almost entirely Bureau of Land Management country: federal land that, in effect, nobody had any use for. Nora had a good idea of what the area was like: slickrock sandstone country, bisected by a diagonal—trending maze of deep canyons and escarpments, sheer walls, and barren scabland.

It was into this desolate triangle, sixteen years before, that her father had disappeared.

She remembered with painful vividness how, as a twelve-year-old, she had pleaded to go along with the searchers. But her mother had given a brusque, dry-eyed refusal. And so she spent two tormented weeks, listening for news on the radio and poring over topographical maps. Maps just like this one. But no trace was ever found. Then her mother instituted proceedings to have him declared legally dead. And Nora had never looked at a map of the area since.

Another deep breath. This would be the hard part. Making sure her back was to Owen Smalls, Nora slid two fingers into her jacket and removed the letter—the letter she had never allowed from her person since she found it, just nightmarish hours before.

The envelope was discolored and brittle, addressed faintly in pencil. And there, as she had in the glow of the headlights the previous night, she read the name of her mother, dead six months, and the address of the ranch that had been abandoned for five years. Slowly, almost unwillingly, she moved her gaze to the return address. PADRAIC KELLY, it confirmed in the generous, loopy hand she remembered so well. *Somewhere west of the Kaiparowits.*

A letter from her dead father to her dead mother, written and stamped sixteen years ago.

Slowly and carefully, in the fluorescent silence of the Map Vault, she removed the three sheets of yellowed paper from the envelope and smoothed them beside the maps, shielding them from Small's view with her body. Again, she glanced at the strangest things of all: the fresh postmark and POSTAGE DUE stamp, showing the letter had been mailed from Escalante, Utah, only five weeks before.

She brushed her fingers along the soiled paper, over the red POSTAGE DUE notice and the badly faded ten-cent stamp. The envelope looked as if it had been wet, and then dried. Perhaps it had been found floating in Lake Powell, swept down the canyons in one of the flash floods the area was famous for.

For perhaps the hundredth time since she first read the letter the night before, she found herself forced to squash a surge of hope. There was no way her father could still be alive. Obviously, somebody had found the letter and mailed it.

But who? And why?

And, more frighteningly: was this the letter the creatures in the abandoned ranch house were after?

She swallowed, throat painfully dry. It *had* to be; there was no other answer.

A loud squeak shattered the silence as Smalls shifted in his chair. Nora started, then slipped the envelope beneath the nearest map. She turned to the letter.

Thursday, August 2 (I think), 1983

Dearest Liz,

Although I'm a hundred miles from the nearest post office, I couldn't wait to write you any longer. I'll mail this first thing when I hit civilization. Better yet, maybe I'll hand-deliver it, and a lot more besides.

I know you think I've been a bad husband and father, and maybe you're right. But please, please read this letter through. I know I've said it before, but now I can <u>promise</u> you that everything will change. We will be together again, Nora and Skip will have their father back. And we will be rich. I know, I <u>know</u>. But, dear heart, this time it's for real. I'm about to enter the lost city of Quivira.

Remember Nora's school report on Coronado, and his search for Quivira, the fabled city of gold? I helped her with the research. I read the reports, the legends of some Pueblo Indian tribes. And I got to thinking. What if all the stories Coronado heard were true? Look at Homer's Troy—archaeology is full of legends that have turned out to be fact. Maybe there was a real city out there, untouched, containing a fabulous treasure of gold and silver. I found some interesting documents that gave an unexpected hint. And I came out here.

I didn't really expect to find anything. You know me, always dreaming. But, Liz, I <u>did</u> find it.

Nora turned to the second page, the crucial page. The writing grew choppy, as if her father had grown breathless with excitement and could barely take the time to scribble the words.

Coming east from Old Paria, I hit Hardscrabble Wash past Ramey's Hole. I'm not sure which side canyon I took—on a whim, mostly—maybe it was Muleshoe. There I found the ghostly trace of an ancient Anasazi road, and I followed it. It was faint, fainter even than the roads to Chaco Canyon.

Nora glanced at the maps. Locating Old Paria beside the Paria River, she began sweeping the nearby canyon country with her eyes. There were dozens of washes and small canyons, many unnamed. After a few minutes her heart leaped: there was Hardscrabble, a short wash that ran into Scoop Canyon. Scanning the area quickly, she found Ramey's Hole, a large circular depression cut by a bend in the wash.

It went northeast. It exited Muleshoe Canyon, I'm not exactly sure where, on an old trail pecked into the sandstone, and I crossed maybe three more canyons in the same way, following ancient trails. I wish I had paid more attention, but I was so excited and it was getting late.

Nora traced an imaginary line northeast from Ramey's Hole, still following Muleshoe. Where had the trail jumped out of the canyon? She took a guess and counted three canyons over. This brought her to an unnamed canyon, very narrow and deep.

I traveled the next day upcanyon, veering northwest, sometimes losing the trail, sometimes finding it again. It was very tough going. The trail jumped to the next canyon through a kind of gap. This, Liz, was where I got lost.

Breathing quickly, Nora traced the unnamed canyon, traveling across a corner of the next map and into a third, miles of deadly desert travel for every inch her finger moved. How far would he have gone that day? There was no way of knowing until she saw the canyon herself. And where was this gap?

Her finger came to a stop amid a welter of canyons, spread over almost a thousand square miles. Frustration welled within her. The directions in the letter were so vague, he could have gone anywhere.

The canyon split, and split again, God knows how many times. Two days I went up. This is unbelievably remote canyon country, Liz, and when you're in the bottom of a canyon you can't see any landmarks to orient yourself. It's almost like hiking in a tunnel. Despite the maddening twists and turns, it somehow had the feel of an Anasazi road to me. But only when I reached what I call the Devil's Backbone, and the slot canyon beyond, was I sure.

She turned to the final page.

You see, I've found the city. I know it. There is a damn good reason why it remained unknown, when you see how fiendishly they hid it. The slot canyon led to a very deep, secret canyon beyond. There's a hand-and-toe trail leading up the rock face here to what must be a hidden alcove in the cliffs. It's weathered, but I can still see signs of use. I've seen trails like this below cliff dwellings at Mesa Verde and Betatakin, and I'm certain this one also leads to a cliff dwelling, and a big one. I'd try the trail now, but it's exceptionally steep and growing dark. If I can make it up the face without technical climbing gear, I'll try to reach the city tomorrow.

I have enough food for a few more days, and there is water here, thank God. I believe I must be the first human being in this canyon in eight hundred years.

It is all yours if you want it. The divorce can be reversed and the clock turned back. All that is past. I just want my family.

My darling Liz, I love you so much. Kiss Nora and Skip a million times for me.

Pat

That was it.

Nora carefully slipped the letter back into its envelope. It took longer than it should have, and she realized her hands were shaking.

She sat back, filled with conflicting feelings. She had always known her father was a pothunter of sorts, but it shamed her that he would consider looting such an extraordinary ruin for his own private gain.

And yet she knew her father wasn't a greedy man. He had little interest in money. What he loved was the hunt. And he had loved her and Skip, more than anything else in the world. She was sure of that, despite everything her mother had said.

She gazed once again over the expanse of maps. If the ruin was really as important as he made out, it must also be un-known. Because she could see from the maps that nothing re-motely like it had been marked. The closest human habitation seemed to be an extremely remote Indian village, marked NANKOWEAP, that was at least several days' journey away at the far edge of the tangle of canyons. According to the map, there weren't even any roads to the village; just a pack trail.

The archaeologist in her felt a surge of excitement. Find-ing Quivira would be a way to vindicate her father's life, and it would also be a way to learn, finally, what had happened to him. And, she thought a little ruefully, it wouldn't hurt her career, either.

She sat up. It was clearly impossible to determine where he had gone by looking at the maps. If she wanted to find Quivira, and perhaps solve the mystery of her father's disap-pearance, she would have to go into that country herself.

Smalls looked up from his book as she leaned into his of-fice. "I'm done, thank you."

"You're welcome," he replied. "Hey, it's lunchtime, and once I lock up I'm going to grab a burrito. Care to join me?"

Nora shook her head. "Got to get back to my office, thanks. I've got a lot of work to do this afternoon."

"I'll consider that a raincheck," Smalls said.

"Too bad we live in the desert." Nora went out the door to the sound of harsh laughter.

As she climbed the dark stairs, the bandage pulled against her arm, reminding her once again of the previous evening's attack. She knew that, logically, she should report it to the police. But when she thought of the investigation, the disbelief, the time it would all take, she couldn't bring herself to do it. Nothing, *nothing,* could interfere with what she had to do next.

3

MURRAY BLAKEWOOD, PRESIDENT OF the Santa Fe Archaeological Institute, turned his shaggy gray head toward Nora. As usual, his face bore a look of distant courtesy, hands loosely folded on the rosewood table, eyes steady and cool.

The lighting in the office was soft, and the walls were lined with discreetly lit glass cases, filled with artifacts from the museum's collection. Directly behind his desk was a seventeenth-century gilded Mexican *reredos,* and on the far wall was a first-phase Navajo chief's blanket, woven in the "Eyedazzler" pattern—perhaps one of only two of its kind still in existence. Normally, Nora could hardly tear her eyes from the priceless relics. Today she didn't spare them a glance.

"Here is a map of the area," she said, pulling a 30-by-60-minute quadrangle map of the Kaiparowits Plateau from her oversized portfolio and smoothing it in front of Blakewood. "See, I've marked the existing sites along here."

Blakewood nodded, and Nora took a deep breath. There was no easy way to do this.

In a rush she said, "Coronado's city of Quivira is right here. In these canyons west of the Kaiparowits Plateau."

There was a silence, then Blakewood leaned back in his

chair, speaking in a gently ironic tone. "There were a couple of steps missing there, Dr. Kelly, and you lost me."

Nora reached into her portfolio and brought out a photocopied page. "Let me read you this excerpt from one of the Coronado expedition reports, written around 1540." She cleared her throat.

The Cicuye Indians brought forward a slave to show the General, who they had captured in a distant land. The General questioned the slave through interpreters.

The slave told him about a distant city, called Quivira. It is a holy city, he said, where the rain priests live, who guard the records of their history from the beginning of time. He said it was a city of great wealth. Common table service was generally of the purest smoothed gold, and the pitchers, dishes and bowls were also made of gold, refined, polished and decorated. He called the gold "acochis." He said they despised all other materials.

The General questioned this man as to where the city lay. He replied that it was many weeks' travel, through the deepest canyons and over the highest mountains. There were vipers, floods, earthquakes and dust storms in that distant country, and none who traveled there ever returned. *Quivira* in their language means "The House of the Bloody Cliff."

She returned the sheet to her portfolio. "Elsewhere in the report, there's a reference to 'ancient ones.' Clearly that would be the Anasazi. The word *anasazi* means—"

"Ancient enemies," said Blakewood gently.

"Right," Nora nodded. "Anyway, 'House of the Bloody Cliff' would imply that it's some kind of cliff dwelling, undoubtedly in the redrock canyon country of southern Utah. Those cliffs shine just like blood when it rains." She tapped the map. "And where else could a large city be hidden except in those canyons? Moreover, this area is famous for its flash floods, which come up out of nowhere and scour the whole place clean. And it lies over the Kaibab Volcanic Field, which creates a lot of low-level seismic activity. Every other place has been carefully explored. This canyon country was a stronghold of the Anasazi. This has *got* to be the place, Dr. Blakewood. And I have this other narrative that says—" Nora stopped as she saw Blakewood beginning to frown.

"What evidence do you have?" he asked.

"This *is* my evidence."

"I see." Blakewood let out a sigh. "And you want to organize an expedition to explore this area, funded by the Institute."

"That's right. I would be happy to write the grants."

Blakewood looked at her. "Dr. Kelly, this"—he gestured to the map—"is not evidence. This is the sheerest kind of speculation."

"But—"

Blakewood held up his hand. "Let me finish. The area you describe is perhaps a thousand square miles. Even if it contained a large ruin, how do you propose to find it?"

Nora hesitated. How much should she tell him? "I have an old letter," she began, "that describes an Anasazi road in these canyons. I believe the road would lead to the ruin."

"A letter?" Blakewood's eyebrows elevated.

"Yes."

"Written by an archaeologist?"

"Right now, I'd rather not say."

A shadow of irritation crossed Blakewood's face. "Dr. Kelly—Nora—let me point out a few practical matters here. There's not enough evidence, even with this mysterious letter of yours, to justify a survey permit, let alone an excavation. And as you pointed out yourself, the area's known for extremely severe summer thunderstorms and flash floods. Even more to the point, the Kaiparowits Plateau and the country to its west encompasses the most complicated canyon system on the planet."

The perfect place to hide a city, Nora thought to herself.

Blakewood stared at her briefly. Then he cleared his throat. "Nora, I'd like to give you some professional advice."

Nora swallowed. This wasn't how she had envisioned the conversation developing.

"Archaeology today isn't like it was a hundred years ago. All the spectacular stuff has been found. Our job is to move more slowly, assemble the little details, analyze." He leaned toward her. "You always seem to be looking for the fabulous ruin, the oldest this or biggest that. None of that exists anymore, Nora, even around the Kaiparowits Plateau. There have been archaeological survey parties in that area at least half a dozen times since the Wetherills first explored those canyons."

Listening, Nora struggled to keep her own doubts at bay. She herself knew there was no way to be certain whether her father actually reached the city. But there was no mistaking the tone of certainty in his letter, or the high flood of his triumph. And there was something else: something always present now in the back of her mind. Somehow, those men—those creatures—that attacked her in the farmhouse had known about the letter. That meant they, too, had reason to believe in Quivira.

"There are many lost ruins in the Southwest," she heard herself say, "buried in sand or hidden under cliffs. Take the lost city of Senecú. That was a huge ruin seen by the Spanish that has since disappeared."

There was a pause as Blakewood tapped a pencil on the desktop. "Nora, there's something else I've been meaning to discuss with you," he said, the look of irritation more plain now. "You've been here, what, five years?"

"Five and a half, Dr. Blakewood."

"When you were hired as an assistant professor, you realized what the tenure process involved, correct?"

"Yes." Nora knew what was coming.

"You will be up for review in six months. And frankly, I'm not sure your tenure will be approved."

Nora said nothing.

"As I recall, your work in graduate school was brilliant.

That is why we brought you on board. But once you were hired, it took you three years to finish your dissertation."

"But Dr. Blakewood, don't you remember how I got tied up at the Rio Puerco site—?" She stopped as Blakewood raised his hand again.

"Yes. Like all of the better academic institutions, we have a scholarship requirement. A *publishing* requirement. Since you brought up the Rio Puerco site, may I ask where the report is?"

"Well, right after that, we found that unusual burned jacal on the Gallegos Divide—"

"Nora!" Blakewood interrupted, a little sharply. "The fact is," he went on in the ensuing silence, "you jump from project to project. You have two major excavations to write up in the next six months. You don't have time to go chasing some chimera of a city that existed only in the imagination of the Spanish conquistadors."

"But it *does* exist!" Nora cried. "My father found it!"

The look of astonishment that came across Blakewood did not sit well on his normally placid face. "Your father?"

"That's right. He found an ancient Anasazi road leading into that canyon country. He followed it to the site, to the very hand-and-toe trail leading up to the city. He documented the entire trip."

Blakewood sighed. "Now I understand your enthusiasm. I don't mean to criticize your father, but he wasn't exactly the most . . ." His voice trailed off, but Nora knew the next word was going to be *reliable*. She felt a prickling sensation move up her spine. *Careful,* she thought, *or you could lose your job right here and now.* She swallowed hard.

Blakewood's voice dropped. "Nora, were you aware that I knew your father?"

Nora shook her head. A lot of people had known her father: Santa Fe had been a small town, at least for archaeologists. Pat Kelly always had an uneasy relationship with them, sometimes providing valuable information, other times digging ruins himself.

"In many ways he was a remarkable man, a brilliant man. But he was a dreamer. He couldn't have been less interested in the facts."

"But he wrote that he *found* the city—"

"You said he found a prehistoric hand-and-toe trail," Blakewood broke in. "Which exist by the thousands in canyon country. Did he write that he actually found the city itself?"

Nora paused. "Not exactly, but—"

"Then I've said all I'm going to say on this expedition— and on your tenure review." He refolded his old hands, the fine pattern of wrinkles almost translucent against the burnished desktop. "Is there anything else?" he asked more gently.

"No," Nora said. "Nothing else." She swept her papers into the portfolio, spun on her heels, and left.

4

NORA SCANNED THE CLUTTERED APART-
ment with dismay. If anything, it was worse than she remembered. The dirty dishes in the sink looked as unwashed as
when she'd seen them a month before, tottering so precariously that no additional plates could be added, the lower
strata furred in green mold. Sink full, the apartment's occu-
pant had apparently taken to ordering pizzas and Chinese
food in disposable cartons: a tiny pyramid rose from the
wastebasket and trailed onto the nearby floor like a bridal veil.
A flood of magazines and old newspapers lay on and around
the scuffed furniture. Pink Floyd's "Comfortably Numb"
played from speakers barely visible behind piles of socks and
dirty sweatshirts. On one shelf stood a neglected goldfish
bowl, its water a murky brown. Nora glanced away, unwilling
to look too closely at the bowl's occupants.

There was a cough and a sniff from the apartment's inhab-
itant. Her brother, Skip, slouched on the decomposing orange couch, propped his dirty bare feet up on a nearby table
and looked over at her. He still had little bronze curls across
his forehead and a smooth, adolescent face. He'd be very
handsome, Nora thought, if it weren't for the petulant, im-
mature look to his face, his dirty clothes. It was hard—
painful, really—to think of him as grown up, his physics

degree from Stanford barely a year old, and doing absolutely nothing. Surely it was just last week she'd been babysitting this wild, happy-go-lucky kid with a brilliant knack for driving her crazy. He didn't drive her crazy anymore—just worried. Sometime after their mother's death six months ago, he'd switched from beer to tequila; half a dozen empty bottles lay scattered around the floor. Now he drained a fresh bottle into a mason jar, a sullen look on his inflamed face. A small yellow worm dropped from the upended bottle into the glass. Skip picked it out and tossed it into an ashtray, where several other similar worms lay, shriveled now to husks as the alcohol had evaporated.

"That's disgusting," Nora said.

"I'm sorry you don't value my collection of *Nadomonas sonoraii*," Skip replied. "If I'd appreciated the benefits of invertebrate biology earlier, I'd never have majored in physics." He reached over to the table, pulled open its drawer, and removed a long, flat sheet of plywood, handing it to Nora with a sniff. One side of the board had been set up in imitation of a lepidopterist's collection. But instead of butterflies, Nora saw thirty or forty mescal worms, pinned to its surface like oversized brown commas. Wordlessly, she handed it back.

"I see you've done some interior decorating since the last time I came by," Nora said. "For example, that crack is new." She nodded at a huge gash that traveled from floor to ceiling along one wall, exposing ribs of plaster and lath.

"My neighbor's foot," Skip said. "He doesn't like my taste in music, the philistine. You ought to bring your oboe over sometime, make him really mad. So anyway, what made you change your mind so fast? I thought you were going to hold on to that old ranch until hell froze over." He took a long sip from the mason jar.

"Something happened there last night." She reached over to turn down the music.

"Oh yeah?" Skip asked, looking vaguely interested. "Some kids trash the place or something?"

Nora looked at him steadily. "I was attacked."

The sullen look vanished and Skip sat up. "What? By who?"

"People dressed up as animals, I think. I'm not sure."

"They *attacked* you? Are you all right?" His face flushed with anger and concern. Even though he was the younger brother, resentful of her interference and ready to take offense, Skip was instinctively protective.

"Teresa and her shotgun came along. Except for this scratch on my arm, I'm fine."

Skip slouched back, the energy gone as quickly as it had arrived. "Did she drill the bastards with lead?"

"No. They got away."

"Too bad. Did you call the cops?"

"Nope. What could I say? If Teresa didn't believe me, they certainly wouldn't. They'd think I was nuts."

"Just as well, I guess." Skip had always distrusted policemen. "What do you suppose they wanted?"

Nora didn't reply immediately. Even as she'd knocked on his door, she'd still been debating whether or not to tell him about the letter. The fear of that night, the shock of the letter, remained with her constantly. How would he react?

"They wanted a letter," she said at last.

"What kind of letter?"

"I think it was this one." Carefully, she pulled the yellowed envelope from her breast pocket and laid it on the table. Skip bent over it, and then with a sharp exhalation picked it up. He read in silence. Nora could hear the clock ticking in the kitchen, the faint sound of a car horn, the rustle of something moving in the sink. She could also feel her own heart pounding.

Skip laid the letter down. "Where did you find this?" he asked, eyes and fingers still on the envelope.

"It was near our old mailbox. Mailed five weeks ago. They put up new mailboxes but our address wasn't included, so I guess the mailman just stuck it in the old box."

Skip turned his face to her. "Oh, my God," he said weakly, eyes filling with tears.

Nora felt a pang: this was what she'd been afraid of. It was a burden he didn't need right now. "I can't explain it. Somebody found it somewhere, maybe, and dropped it in the mail."

"But whoever found it would also have found Dad's body—" Skip swallowed and wiped his face. "You think he's alive?"

"No. Not a chance. He would never have abandoned us if he were alive. He *loved* us, Skip."

"But this letter—"

"Was written sixteen years ago. Skip, he's dead. We have to face that. But at least now we have a clue to where he might have died. Maybe we can find out what happened to him."

Skip had kept his fingers pressed to the envelope, as if unwilling to relinquish this unexpected new conduit to his father. But at these last words, he suddenly removed his hand and leaned back on the couch. "These guys who wanted the letter," he said. "Why didn't they look in the mailbox?"

"I actually found it in the sand. I think it might have blown out—the mailbox door was missing. And those old boxes looked like they hadn't been used for years. But I really don't know for sure. I kind of knocked them down with my truck."

Skip glanced back at the envelope. "If they knew about the farmhouse, you suppose they also know where we live?"

"I'm trying not to think about that," Nora replied. But she was. Constantly.

Skip, more composed now, finished the last of his drink. "How the hell did they find out about this letter?"

"Who knows? Lots of people have heard the legends of Quivira. And Dad had some pretty unsavory contacts—"

"So *Mom* said," he interrupted. "What are you planning to do?"

"I figured—" Nora paused. This was going to be the hard part. "I figured the way to find out what happened to him would be to find Quivira. And that will take money. Which is why I want to put Las Cabrillas on the market."

Skip shook his head and gave a wet laugh. "Jesus, Nora.

Here I've been living in this shithole, with no money, begging you to sell that place so I could get my feet on the ground. And now you want to blow what nest egg we've got looking for Dad. Even though he's dead."

"Skip, you could always get your feet on the ground by finding a *job*—" Nora began, then stopped. This wasn't why she came here. He sat on the sofa, shoulders hunched, and Nora found her heart melting. "Skip, it would mean a lot to me to know what happened to Dad."

"Look, go ahead and sell the place. I've been saying that for years. But don't use my share of the money. I've got other plans."

"To mount an archaeological expedition might take a little more than just my share."

Skip sat back. "I get it. So the Institute won't fund anything, right? Can't say I'm surprised. I mean, it says here he never *saw* the city! He's all worked up over a trail. There's a leap of faith in this letter, Nora. You know what Mom would say about this?"

"Yes! She'd say he was just dreaming again. Are you saying it, too?"

Skip winced. "No. I'm not siding with Mom." The scornful tone had been stung from his voice. "I just don't want to lose a sister the way I lost a father."

"Come on, Skip. That's not going to happen. In the letter, Dad says he was following an ancient road. If I can find that road, it would be the proof I need."

Skip pushed his feet to the floor, elbows on his knees, a scowl on his face. Suddenly he straightened up. "I've got an idea. A way that maybe you can find that road, without even going out there. I had a physics professor at Stanford, Leland Watkins. Now he works for JPL."

"JPL?"

"The Jet Propulsion Laboratory at Cal Tech. It's a branch of NASA."

"How's that going to help us?"

"This guy's been working on the shuttle program. I read

31

about this specialized radar system they have that can see through thirty feet of sand. They were using it to map ancient trails in the Sahara Desert. If they can map trails there, why not in Utah?"

Nora stared at her brother. "This radar can see old roads?"

"Right through the sand."

"And you took a class from this guy? You think he still remembers you?"

Skip's face suddenly became guarded. "Oh, yeah. He remembers me."

"Great! So call him up and—"

Skip's look stopped her. "I can't do that," he said.

"How come?"

"He doesn't like me."

"Why not?" Nora was discovering that a lot of people didn't like Skip.

"He had this really cute girlfriend, a graduate student, and I . . ." Skip's face colored.

Nora shook her head. "I don't want to hear about it."

Skip picked up the yellow mescal worm and rolled it between finger and thumb. "Sorry about that. If you want to talk to Watkins, I guess you're going to have to call him yourself."

5

Nora sat at a worktable in the Institute's Artifact Analysis Lab. Lined up in front of her, beneath the harsh fluorescent light, were six bags of heavy-mil plastic bulging with potsherds. Each was labeled RIO PUERCO, LEVEL I in black marker. In one of the nearby lockers, carefully padded to eliminate "bag wear," were four more bags marked LEVEL II and yet another marked LEVEL III: a total of one hundred and ten pounds of potsherds.

Nora sighed. She knew that, in order to publish the report on the Rio Puerco site, every sherd had to be sorted and classified. And after the sherds would come stone tools and flakes, bone fragments, charcoal, pollen samples, even hair samples; all patiently waiting in their metal cages around the lab. She opened the first bag and, using metal forceps, began placing artifacts on the white table. Glancing up at a buzzing light, she could see a corner of white cloud scud past the tiny barred window far above her head. *Like a damn prison,* she thought sourly. She glanced at the nearby terminal, blinking the data entry screen into focus.

SANTA FE ARCHAEOLOGICAL INSTITUTE
Context Recording / Artifact Database

Site No _____   Site Book Ref _____

Area/Section _____   Grid Square _____

Plan No _____   Context Code _____

Accession No _____   Lev/Stratum _____

Coord _____   Trinomial Desig _____

Provenance _____   Excav Date _____

Recorded by _____   Lev Bag _____ Of _____

Artifact Description (4096 chars max)

CONFIDENTIAL—DO NOT DUPLICATE

She understood precisely why this kind of statistical research was necessary. And yet she couldn't help but feel that the Institute, under Murray Blakewood's guidance, had become shackled by an obsession with typology. It was as if, for all its vast collections and reservoir of talent, the Institute was ignoring the new developments—ethnoarchaeology, contextual archaeology, molecular archaeology, cultural resource management—taking place outside its thick adobe walls.

She pulled out her handwritten field logs, tabulating the artifacts against the information she entered into the database. *46 Mesa Verde B/W, 23 Chaco/McElmo, 2 St. John's Poly, 1 Soccoro B/W* . . . Or was that another Mesa Verde B/W? She hunted in the drawer for a loup, rummaging unsuccessfully. *Hell with it,* she thought, placing it to one side and moving on.

Her hand closed over a small, polished piece of pottery, evidently the lip of a bowl. *Now this is more like it,* she thought. Despite its small size, the fragment was beautiful, and she still remembered its discovery. She'd been sitting beside a thicket of tamarisk, stabilizing a fragile basket with polyvinyl acetate, when her assistant Bruce Jenkins gave a sudden yelp. "Chaco

Black-on-Yellow Micaceous!" he'd screeched. "God *damn*!" She remembered the excitement, the envy, that the little fragment had generated. And here it was, sitting forlorn in an oversized Baggie. Why couldn't the Institute devote more energy to, say, learning why this fantastic style of pottery was so rare—why no complete pots had ever been found, why nobody knew where it came from or how it was made—instead of ceaselessly numbering and cross-tabulating, like accountants of prehistory?

She stared at the potsherds spread out in a dun-colored line. With a sudden movement, she pushed away from the desk and turned toward the phone, dialing information.

"Pasadena," she said into the phone. "The Jet Propulsion Laboratory." It took one external and two internal operators to learn that Leland Watkins's extension was 2330.

"Yes?" came the voice at last, high-pitched and impatient.

"Hello. This is Nora Kelly, at the Santa Fe Archaeological Institute."

"Yes?" the voice repeated.

"Am I speaking to Leland Watkins?"

"This is Dr. Watkins."

"I'd like a moment of your time," Nora said, talking quickly. "We're working on a project in southeastern Utah, looking at ancient Anasazi roads. Would it be possible for you—"

"We don't have any radar coverage in that area," interrupted Watkins.

Nora took a deep breath. "Is there any way we might cooperate in getting some radar coverage? You see—"

"No, there is no way," said Watkins, his voice growing nasal in irritation. "I've got a list a mile long of people waiting for radar coverage: geologists, rain forest biologists, agricultural scientists, you name it."

"I see," said Nora, trying to keep her voice even. "And what about the application process for such coverage?"

"We're backed up two years with applications. And I'm too

swamped to talk to you about it. The shuttle *Republic* is in orbit right now, as you probably know."

"It's rather important, Dr. Watkins. We believe—"

"Everything's important. Now, will you excuse me? Write if you want that application."

"And the address—?" Nora stopped as she realized she was talking to a dial tone.

"Arrogant prick!" she shouted. "I'm *glad* my brother boned your girlfriend!" She slammed the phone into its cradle.

Then she paused, staring speculatively at the phone. Dr. Watkins's extension had been 2330.

Reaching again, she slowly and deliberately dialed a long-distance number. "Yes," she said after a moment. "Give me extension 2331, please."

6

WITH A HEAVY SIGH, PETER HOLROYD settled himself on the old tractor-style seat, turned the right handgrip to retard the spark advance, and kicked the engine into ferocious life. He sat for a minute, letting the motorcycle warm up. Then he dropped into first, turned out of the complex into the California Boulevard traffic, and headed west toward Ambassador Auditorium. A thin haze hung over the San Gabriel Mountains. As usual, his eyes—raw from a long day of poring over massive computer screens and false-color images—smarted in the ozone. Free of the purified atmosphere of the complex, his nose began to run freely, and he hawked a generous blob of phlegm onto the blacktop. A small plastic image of the Michelin tire mascot had been glued to the gas tank, and he reached down to rub its fat belly. "O God of California traffic," he intoned, "grant me safe passage, free of rain, loose gravel, and tight drivers."

Ten blocks and twenty minutes later, he nosed the old motorcycle south, heading for Atlantic Boulevard and his Monterey Park neighborhood. Traffic was easier here, and he shifted into third for the first time since starting the engine, letting the wind blow away the heat of the cylinders beneath him. His thoughts returned once again to the persistent archaeologist who had kept him on the line for such a long time that morning. In his mind, he saw a dumpy, mousy-looking academic with chopped-off hair and no social graces. He had promised nothing except a meeting. A meeting far from JPL, of course—if Watkins got even a whiff of extracurricular dealings, he'd be in deep shit. But these hints of a lost city had intrigued him more than he wanted to admit. Holroyd hadn't had much luck with women, and the thought that one—mousy or not—was willing to drop everything and drive all the way from Santa Fe to meet with him was flattering. Besides, she'd promised to pay for dinner.

After a brief, easy run, the streets grew more congested and aggressively urban. Another three blocks, another three lights, and he nosed up onto the sidewalk beside a row of four-story buildings. Pulling a brown bag from beneath the bungee cord on the rear fender, he craned his neck up toward his apartment. Ancient yellow curtains twitched limply in the hot, fitful breeze. They were a bequest of a previous tenant and had never felt air conditioning. Snorting again, Holroyd angled across the street and headed toward the intersection, where the sign for Al's Pizza glowed against the gathering dusk.

He glanced around and slid into his usual booth, enjoying the chill air of the restaurant. The traffic had made him late, but the place was still empty. Holroyd tried to decide whether he felt disappointed or relieved.

Al himself came over, a small, impossibly hirsute man. "Good evening, professor!" he cried. "Nice night, eh?"

"Sure," said Holroyd. Over Al's hair-matted shoulder, he could see a small television, its grainy image struggling through a film of grease. It was always tuned to CNN, and the sound was always off. There was an image of the shuttle *Republic,* showing an astronaut floating upside down, tethered by a white cord, the magnificent blue orb of Earth as a backdrop. He felt a quick familiar feeling of longing and turned back to Al's cheerful face.

Al slapped the table with a floury hand. "What tonight?

We've got good anchovy pizza, coming out in five minutes. You like anchovy?"

Holroyd hesitated a moment. Probably she'd thought better of making such a long trip; after all, he hadn't exactly been encouraging on the telephone. "I love anchovies," he said. "Bring me two slices."

"Angelo! Two slices anchovy for the professor!" Al cried as he swept back behind the counter. Holroyd watched him walk away, then reached for the paper bag and dumped the contents onto the tabletop. A notebook, two blue highlighters, and paperback copies of *The White Nile, Aku Aku,* and Lansing's *Endurance* fell out. With a sigh, he fanned the pages of *Endurance,* located the paper clip, and settled back.

He heard the familiar squeal of the pizza parlor door and caught a glimpse of a young woman struggling through, lugging a large portfolio case. She had unusual bronze-colored hair that broke in waves over her shoulders, and penetrating hazel eyes. Her body was slim, and as she dragged the case through the door he couldn't help but notice a shapely rear. She turned and he looked up quickly, guiltily, only to be arrested by her face: smart, restless, impatient.

This couldn't be her.

The woman glanced up and the hazel eyes met his. He quickly shut the book and smoothed a hand over his hair, made unruly by the motorcycle ride. The woman walked straight toward him, dumped her portfolio on the table, and slid into the far side of the booth with a cool rustle of her long legs. She brushed back the copper-colored hair. Her skin was tan, and he noticed a scattering of freckles along the bridge of her nose.

"Hi," she said. "Are you Peter Holroyd?"

He nodded. And experienced a moment of panic. This was not the frowsy scholar he'd expected: this woman was lovely.

"I'm Nora Kelly." She extended her hand.

Holroyd hesitated a moment. Then he put the book down and shook the proffered hand. The fingers were cool and unexpectedly strong.

"Sorry to corner you like this. Thanks for meeting with me."

Holroyd tried a smile. "Well, your story was interesting. But a little vague. I'm interested in hearing more about this lost city in the desert."

"Well, I'm afraid it has to be vague for the time being. You can understand the need for secrecy."

"Then I'm not sure what I can do for you," Holroyd said. "It's like I told you on the phone. All those requests have to go through my boss." He hesitated. "I'm just here to learn a little more."

"Your boss would be Dr. Watkins. Yes, I talked to him, too. Real nice guy. Modest, too. I like that in a man. Too bad he couldn't spare me more than nine seconds."

Holroyd began to laugh, then quickly stifled himself. "So what's your position at the Institute?" he asked, shifting in the booth.

"I'm an assistant professor."

"Assistant professor," Holroyd repeated. "And you're the one in charge of the expedition? Or is there someone else?"

The woman gave him a penetrating look. "I'm kind of at the same level you are. Fairly low down on the totem pole, not really in control of my own destiny. This," she patted her portfolio, "could change all that."

Holroyd wasn't sure if he should be offended. "So when exactly do you need the data? It might speed things up if the Institute's president contacted my boss directly—he's always impressed by big names." He mentally kicked himself for sounding a disparaging note about his boss. You never knew when something like that might find its way back, and Watkins was not the forgiving type.

She leaned toward him. "Mr. Holroyd, I've got a confession to make. I'm not working right now with the complete support of the Institute. The fact is, they won't even consider an expedition to find this city until I bring them proof. That's why I need your help."

"Why are you so interested in finding this city?"

"Because it could be the greatest archaeological discovery of our time."

"And how do you know that?"

Al appeared, bearing two huge slices of pizza dense with anchovies. He slid them under Holroyd's nose. A salty aroma wafted upward.

"Not on the portfolio!" the woman cried. Taken aback by the sudden tone of command, Al scooped the slices onto a neighboring table, apologizing profusely as he backed away.

"And bring me an iced tea, please!" she called after him, then turned back to Holroyd. "Look, Peter—can I call you Peter?—I didn't drive all the way here to waste your time on some dime-a-dozen digsite." She drew closer, and Holroyd caught a faint clean scent of shampoo. "Ever hear of Coronado, the Spanish explorer? He came into the Southwest in 1540, looking for the Seven Cities of Gold. A friar had gone north years before, looking for souls to save, and he returned with a huge, drilled emerald crystal and stories of lost cities. But when Coronado himself came northward, he found only the mud pueblos of the Indian tribes of New Mexico, none of whom had gold or wealth. But at a place called Cicuye, the Indians told him about a city of priests, called Quivira, where they ate from plates of gold and drank from golden goblets. Of course, this drove Coronado and his men into a frenzy."

The tea came, and she cracked the plastic seal from the cap and took a sip. "Some of the natives told him Quivira was way to the east, in present-day Texas. Others said it was in Kansas. So Coronado and his army went eastward. But when he got to Kansas, the Indians said Quivira was far to the west, in the country of the Red Stones. Eventually, Coronado returned to Mexico, a broken man, convinced he'd been chasing a chimera."

"Interesting," Holroyd said. "But it doesn't prove anything."

"Coronado wasn't the only one to hear these stories. In 1776, two Spanish friars, Escalante and Dominguez, traveled westward from Santa Fe, trying to blaze an overland route to

California. I've got their report here somewhere." She dug into her portfolio, retrieved a creased sheet of paper, and began reading.

> Our Paiute guides took us through difficult country, by what seemed to us a perverse route, northward instead of westward. When we remarked upon this, the response was that the Paiutes never traveled through the country to the west. Asked the reason, they became sullen and silent. Halfway through our journey, near the Crossing of the Fathers on the Colorado River, half of them deserted. It was never clear from the rest exactly what lay to the west that caused such strong emotion. One spoke of a great city, destroyed because the priests there had enslaved the world, and tried to usurp the power of the sun itself. Others hinted darkly of a slumbering evil which they dared not awaken.

She replaced the sheet of paper. "And that's not all. In 1824, an American mountain man by the name of Josiah Blake was captured by Ute Indians. In those days, exceptionally brave captives were sometimes offered a choice between death or joining the tribe. Blake naturally joined the tribe. He later married a Ute woman. Utes are nomadic, and at certain times of the year they would venture deep into the Utah canyon country. Once, in a particularly remote area west of the Escalante, a Ute pointed toward the setting sun and mentioned that in that direction lay a ruined city of fabulous wealth. The Utes never ventured any closer, but they gave Blake an engraved turquoise disk that had supposedly come from the city. When he finally got back to white civilization ten years later, he swore that one day he would find this lost place. Eventually, he went back to look for it and was never seen again."

She took another sip of tea and placed the bottle carefully beside the portfolio. "Today, people assume these are all just myths, or maybe lies told by the Indians. But I don't think it was either a myth or a lie. The location of the lost city is too consistent across all of the stories. I believe the reason nobody has ever found this city is because it is hidden in the most remote section of the lower 48. Like other Anasazi cities, it was probably built high up on a cliff, in an alcove or under an overhang. Or perhaps it's simply been buried in drifting sand. And that's where you come in. You've got what I need, Peter. A radar system that can pinpoint the city."

Despite himself, Holroyd found himself drawn into the story and its promise of adventure. He cleared his throat, searching for a note of reasonableness. "Excuse me for saying it, but this is rather a long shot. First of all, if the city is hidden, no radar could see it."

"But I understand your Terrestrial Imager can see through sand as well as clouds and darkness."

"That's correct. But not rock. If it's under a ledge, forget it. Second—"

"But I don't want you to find the city itself. Just the road leading up to it. Here, look at this." She opened her portfolio and pulled out a small map of the Southwest, overlain with several thin, straight lines. "A thousand years ago, the Anasazi built this mysterious road system, connecting their large cities. These are the roads that have been mapped. Each one leads to or from a major city. Your radar could surely see those roads from space. Right?"

"Maybe."

"I have an old report—a letter, actually—that states there is a similar road leading into this warren of canyons. I'm certain it leads to the lost city of Quivira. If we could trace that road on a satellite image, we'd know where to look."

Holroyd spread his hands. "But it's not that simple. There's the waiting list. I'm sure Watkins must have told you about that, he loves to talk about it. There's two years' worth of applications for—"

"Yes, he told me all about that. But who actually *decides* what the radar examines?"

"Well, the imaging applications are prioritized by urgency and date of receipt. I take the pending jobs, and—"

"You." Nora nodded in satisfaction.

Holroyd fell silent.

"I'm sorry." Nora said suddenly. "Your dinner's getting cold." She replaced the map in her portfolio as Holroyd gathered up the congealing slices of pizza. "So it would be a simple matter to, say, push one of the applications to the top of the queue?"

"I suppose." Holroyd sank his teeth into the pizza, barely tasting it.

"See? I fill out an application, you move it to the top of the pile, and we get our images."

Holroyd swallowed hard. "And just what do you think Dr. Watkins, or the boys at NASA, would think of my ordering an orbit change for the space shuttle just so it could fly over your area? Why should I help you with this? I'd be risking my ass—I mean, my job."

Nora looked at him. "Because I think you're more than just some bean-counting drone. Because I think you've got the same kind of fire in your gut that I've got. To find something that's been lost for centuries." She gestured at the table. "Why else would you be reading these books? Each one of them is about discovering the unknown. Finding Quivira would be like discovering those cliff dwellings at Mesa Verde. Only greater."

Holroyd hesitated.

"I can't," he said after a moment, in a very quiet voice. "You're asking for the impossible." He realized with a thrill of fear that, for an instant, he'd actually been considering how he could help her. But the whole idea was crazy. This woman had no proof, no credentials, nothing.

And yet he found himself unaccountably drawn in by her, by her passion and excitement. He had been to Mesa Verde as a child. The memory of those vast silent ruins still haunted him. He looked around, trying to collect his thoughts. He glanced at Nora, gazing back at him expectantly. He'd never seen hair quite that color, a burnished coppery sheen, almost metallic. Then his view moved back to the little image on the television screen of the *Republic* floating in space.

"It's not impossible," Nora said in an undertone. "You give me the application, I fill it out, and you do what you have to do."

But Holroyd was still staring at the image: the shining ivory shuttle drifting through space, the stars hard as diamonds, the earth endless miles below. It was always like that. The excitement of discovery that he had longed for growing up, the chance to explore a new planet or fly to the moon— all those dreams had withered in a cubicle at JPL, while he watched someone else's adventure unfold on a dirty monitor.

Then he realized with a start that Nora had been staring at him. "When did you join JPL?" she asked, abruptly changing the subject.

"Eight years ago," he said, "right out of graduate school."

"Why?"

He stopped, surprised by the bluntness of the question. "Well," he said, "I always wanted to be part of the exploration of space."

"I bet you grew up wanting to be the first man on the moon."

Holroyd blushed. "I was a little late for that. But I did have dreams of going to Mars."

"And now they're up there, orbiting the earth, and you're sitting here in a greasy pizza parlor."

It was as if she had read his mind. Holroyd felt a surge of resentment. "Look, I'm doing just fine. Those guys wouldn't be up there if it weren't for me and others like me."

Nora nodded. "But it's not quite the same thing, is it?" she said softly.

Holroyd remained silent.

"What I'm offering is a chance for you to be part of what might be the greatest archaeological discovery since King Tut."

"Yeah," said Holroyd. "And my part would be to do for

you just what I do for Watkins: crunch some data and let someone else run with it. I'm sorry, but the answer is no."

But the woman never took her hazel eyes from his. She was silent, and it seemed to Holroyd that she was making some kind of private decision.

"Maybe I can offer you more than that," she said at last, her voice still low.

Holroyd frowned sharply. "Like what?"

"A place on the expedition."

Holroyd felt his heart accelerate. "What did you say?"

"I think you heard me. We'll need a remote sensing and computer specialist. Can you handle communications gear?"

Holroyd swallowed, his throat suddenly dry. Then he nodded. "I've got gear you've never even dreamed of."

"And how are you set for vacation? Could you take two, maybe three weeks off?"

"I've never taken a vacation," Holroyd heard himself say. "I've got so much time accrued, I could leave for six months and still get paid."

"Then that's it. You get me the data, and I get you on the expedition. I guarantee it, Peter, you won't be sorry. It's an adventure you'd remember for the rest of your life."

Holroyd glanced down at the woman's hands, tapered and beautiful, clasped together expectantly. He had never met anyone so passionate about something. He realized he was having a hard time catching his breath.

"I—" he began.

She leaned forward quickly. "Yes?"

He shook his head. "This is all too sudden. I have to think about this."

She looked at him, appraisingly. Then she nodded. "I know you do," she said softly. Reaching into her purse, she pulled out a piece of paper and handed it to him. "Here's the number of the friend's apartment where I'm staying. But, Peter, don't think too long. I can only stay a couple of days."

But Holroyd barely heard her. He was putting something together in his head. "I'm not necessarily saying I'll do it, you understand," he said in a lower tone. "But here's how it could work. You wouldn't need to put in a request. The shuttle's devoting the last three days of the mission to radar sweeps, sixty-five orbits at varying latitudes. There's this mineral exploration company that's been wanting a sweep of some areas of Utah and Colorado. We've put them off for a while now. I could fit them into the lineup. Then I'd extend their run slightly to get the areas you need. The only thing you'd have to do is put in a purchase request as soon as the data is downloaded from the shuttle. Normally the data is proprietary for a couple of years, but the right kind of academic requests can get around that. I'd lead you through the red tape when the time comes."

"A purchase request? You mean I have to pay?"

"It's very expensive," said Holroyd.

"What are we talking here? A couple of hundred bucks?"

"More like twenty thousand."

"Twenty thousand dollars! Are you crazy?"

"Sorry. That's something not even Watkins can control."

"Where the hell am I going to get twenty thousand dollars?" Nora exploded.

"Look, I'd be arranging an alteration in the orbit of a United States spacecraft for you. That's bad enough. What else do you want me to do, steal the damn data?"

There was a silence.

"Now there's an idea," said Nora.

7

IF NORA HAD EVER WALKED INTO A HOTTER, stuffier place than Peter Holroyd's apartment, she couldn't remember it. The air was not just dying here, she decided; it was dead and decomposing.

"Got any ice?" she asked.

Holroyd, who had walked down the four flights of stairs to retrieve his mail and open the door for her, shook his shaggy head. "Sorry. Freezer's busted."

Nora watched him sort through his mail. Below the mop of sandy hair, the very white skin of his face was stretched over two prominent cheekbones. As he moved, his limbs never seemed to be in the right place, and his legs seemed a little short for his narrow torso and bony arms. And yet the overall impression of melancholy was countered by a pair of intelligent green eyes that looked hopefully out on the world. His taste in clothes was questionable: striped brown polyester pants, topped by a V-neck short-sleeved checkered shirt.

Grimy yellow curtains flapped apathetically in the travesty of a breeze. Nora walked to the window, glancing south toward the dusky boulevards of East L.A. Then she looked down toward the nearby intersection and the front window of Al's Pizza. She'd spent the last two nights at a friend's house in Thousand Oaks. This was an ugly little corner of L.A., and she felt a sudden sympathy for Peter and his longing for adventure.

She took a step back. The apartment was so barren she was unable to determine what kind of housekeeper Holroyd was. A small bookcase, made up of plywood strips balanced on cinderblocks. Two elderly Adirondack chairs, festooned with back issues of *Old Bike Journal.* An ancient motorcycle helmet on the floor, scarred and scuffed. "Is that your bike I saw chained to the lamppost?" Nora asked.

"Yup. An old '46 Indian Chief. Mostly." He grinned. "Inherited a basket case from my great-uncle, and scrounged the rest of the parts here and there. You ride?"

"My dad had an old dirt bike I used to ride around the ranch. Rode my brother's Hog once or twice before he laid it down on Route 66." Nora looked back toward the window. There was a row of very strange-looking plants: black, crimson, a riot of drooping stalks and pendulous flowers. *Must be the only things around here that enjoy the heat,* she thought.

A small plant with dark purple flowers caught her attention. "Hey, what's this?" she asked, reaching out curiously.

Holroyd looked over, then dropped the mail. "Don't touch that!" he cried. Nora jerked her hand away.

"It's belladonna," Holroyd said, bending to pick up the scatter. "Deadly nightshade."

"You're kidding," Nora said. "And this?" She pointed to a neighboring plant, a small flower with exotic maroon spikes.

"Monkshood. It contains aconitine, which is a really terrific poison. In the tray there are the three deadliest mushrooms: the Death Cap, Fool's Mushroom, and *A. virosa,* the Destroying Angel. And in that pot on the sill—"

"I get the picture." Nora turned away from the Death Cap, its horrible mantle resembling plague-spotted skin, and gazed once again around the bare apartment. "Enemies bothering you?"

Holroyd tossed the mail into the garbage and barked a laugh, his green eyes suddenly catching the light. "Some people collect stamps. I collect botanical poisons."

Nora followed him into the kitchen, a small, cramped area almost as free of furniture as the rest of the apartment. A large wooden table had been pushed up against the old refrigerator. Sitting on the table were a keyboard, a three-button mouse, and the largest monitor she had ever seen.

Holroyd smiled at her appreciative glance. "Not a bad chunk of video real estate, is it? Just like the ones at the Lab. A few years ago Watkins bought these for all his top imaging staff. He assumes that no one who works for him has a social life. Pretty good assumption, at least as far as I'm concerned." He glanced at her.

Nora raised a speculative eyebrow at him. "So you *do* bring some homework with you, after all."

The smile vanished as he caught the implication. "Only declassified homework," he replied, as he reached into a rumpled Jiffy bag and pulled out a rewriteable DVD disk. "What you asked for doesn't exactly fit that category."

"Can I ask how you did it?"

"I took the raw data from the shuttle feed this morning and burned an extra copy onto the disk. I've always got a handful of disks in my backpack; nobody would know the difference." He waggled the disk and it flashed in the dim light, sending out a coruscation of color. "If you have the right clearance, stealing data isn't difficult. It's just that, if you get caught, the penalties are much stiffer. *Much* stiffer." He grimaced.

"I realize that," said Nora. "Thank you, Peter."

He looked at her. "You knew I'd help, didn't you? Even before you left the pizza parlor."

Nora returned the glance. It was true; once he'd described the way he could access the data, she felt certain he'd agree. But she did not want to hurt his pride. "I hoped you would," she replied. "But I wasn't really sure until you called the next morning. And I can't tell you how much I appreciate it."

Nora realized Holroyd was blushing. He quickly turned his back and opened the refrigerator door. Inside, Nora could see two cans of alcohol-free beer, some V8 juice, and a large computer CPU. Looking more closely, she noticed the computer was connected to the monitor by cables running through a small insulated hole in the back of the refrigerator.

"Too hot out here," Holroyd said, sliding the disk into the computer housing and closing the refrigerator door. "Put your topo over there, okay?"

Nora began to unroll the map, then paused. "You realize this won't be like crunching numbers all day long in an air-conditioned lab," she said. "On a small dig like this, everybody does double or triple duty. You'd be coming along as an assistant, specializing in image sensing. Only they're not called 'assistants' on archaeological digs. They're called 'diggers.' For a reason."

Holroyd blinked at her. "What are you trying to do? Talk me out of going?"

"I just want to make sure you know what you're getting into."

"You've seen the books I read. I know it won't be a picnic. That's part of the challenge, isn't it?" He sat down at the wooden table and pulled the keyboard toward him. "I'm risking a possible prison sentence, bringing you this data. You think I'm afraid of a little digging?"

Nora smiled. "Point taken." She pulled up a plastic chair. "Now how does this thing work, exactly?"

"Radar's just another kind of light. We shine it down on Earth from the shuttle, and it bounces back changed. The Terrestrial Imager simply takes digital photographs of what bounces back, and then combines them." Holroyd punched some keys. There was a brief pause, then a small window opened at the bottom of the screen, displaying scrolling messages as a complex program began to boot. Several other small windows flew open in corners of the screen, displaying various software tools. Then a large window appeared at the screen's center. Holroyd moused the cursor through several menus. Finally, an image began rolling down the large central screen, line by line, painted in artificial reds.

"Is that it?" Nora stared at the screen in disappointment.

This was the last thing she'd expected: confusing monochromatic patterns like no landscape she had ever seen.

"It's just the beginning. The Imager takes infrared emissions and radiometry into account, but that would take too long to explain. It also looks at the earth in three different radar bands and two polarizations. Each color represents a different band of radar, or a different polarization. I'm going to paint each color on to the screen, layering one on top of the other. This'll take a few minutes."

"And then we'll be able to see the road?"

Holroyd gave her an amused look. "If only it were that simple. We're going to have to beat the shit out of the data before we can see the road." He pointed. "This red is L-Band radar. It has a wavelength of twenty five centimeters and can penetrate five meters of dry sand. Next, I'll add C-Band."

A blue color scrolled down.

"This C-Band has a six-centimeter wavelength, and it can penetrate at most two meters. So what you see here is a little shallower." More key taps. "And here goes X-Band. That's three centimeters. Basically, it gives you the surface itself."

A neon green color rolled down the screen.

"I don't see how you can even begin to figure all this out," said Nora, gazing at the distorted swaths of colors.

"Now I'm going to paint in the polarizations. The outgoing radar beam is polarized either horizontally or vertically. Sometimes you send down a beam horizontally polarized, and it bounces back vertically polarized. That usually happens when the beam encounters a lot of vertical tree trunks."

Nora watched as another color was added to the screen. It was taking longer for the program to paint the image on the screen; obviously, the computational problem was becoming more complex.

"Looks like a de Kooning," said Nora.

"A what?"

Nora waved her hand. "Never mind."

Holroyd turned back to the screen. "What we've got is a composite image of the ground, from the surface to about fifteen feet deep. Now it's a matter of canceling out some of the wavelengths and multiplying others. This is where the real artistry comes in." Nora could hear a touch of pride in his voice.

He began typing again, more quickly this time. Nora watched as a new window opened on the screen, lines of computer code racing as routines were added and deleted. The remote desert vastness was suddenly covered by a thin web of tracks.

"My God!" Nora cried. "There they are! I had no idea the Anasazi—"

"Hold on a minute," interrupted Holroyd. "Those are modern trails."

"But this area isn't supposed to have any roads."

Holroyd shook his head. "Some of these are probably wild horse trails, deer trails, coyote trails, mountain lion trails, maybe even four-wheel-drive tracks. There was some prospecting for uranium in this area in the fifties. Most of these tracks you wouldn't be able to see on the ground."

Nora slumped back in her chair. "With all those trails, how can we ever find the Anasazi one?"

Holroyd grinned. "Be patient. The older the road, the deeper it tends to lie. Very old roads also tend to spread through erosion and wind. The pebbles ancient travelers turned up have been smoothed over time, while new roads are covered with sharper pebbles. The sharper pebbles backscatter more strongly than the smooth ones."

He continued to type. "No one knows why, but sometimes dramatic things happen if you multiply the values of two wavelengths together, or divide them by each other, or cube one and take the square root of another and subtract the cosine of your mother's age."

"Doesn't sound very scientific," said Nora.

Holroyd grinned. "No, but it's my favorite part. When data's buried as deeply as this, it takes real intuition and creativity to tease it out."

He worked with steady determination. Every few minutes

the image changed: sometimes dramatically, sometimes subtly. Once Nora asked a question, but Holroyd merely shook
his head, brow furrowed. At times, all the roads vanished;
Holroyd would curse, type a flurry of commands, and the
roads returned.

Time crawled by, and Holroyd grew increasingly frus-
trated. The sweat stood out on his brow, and his hands flew
across the keys, hitting them with greater force. Nora's back
began to ache, and she found herself shifting constantly in the
cheap chair, trying to find a comfortable position.

At last, Holroyd sat back with a muttered curse. "I've tried
all the methods, all the tricks. The data just won't put out."

"What do you mean?"

"Either I get a million roads and trails, or I get nothing."
He got up and went to the refrigerator. "Beer?"

"Sure." Nora glanced at the clock. It was seven, but the
apartment was still insufferably hot.

Holroyd sat down again, passing her the beer and propping a leg up on the computer table. A knobby ankle protruded from below the cuff, pale and hairless. "Is there
anything unusual about the Anasazi roads? Something that
might differentiate them from all these animal trails and modern stuff?"

Nora thought for a moment, then shook her head.

"What were the roads used for?"

"Actually, they weren't really roads at all."

Holroyd pulled his leg from the table and sat up. "What do
you mean?"

"They're still a deep archaeological mystery. The Anasazi
didn't know about the wheel and they didn't have any beasts
of burden. They had no use for a road. So why they would
take such trouble to build them has always puzzled archaeologists."

"Go on," Holroyd urged.

"Whenever archaeologists don't understand something,
they cop out by saying it served a religious purpose. That's
what they say about the roads. They think they might have

been spirit pathways, rather than roads for living beings to travel on. Roads to guide the spirits of the dead back to the underworld."

"What do these roads look like?" Holroyd took a swig of beer.

"Not much of anything," Nora said. "In fact, they're almost impossible to see from the ground."

Holroyd looked at her expectantly. "How were they built?"

"The roads were exactly thirty feet wide, surfaced with adobe. On the Great North Road it appears that pots were deliberately broken on the road surface to consecrate it. The roads were dotted with shrines called *herraduras,* but we have no idea—"

"Wait a minute," Holroyd interrupted. "You said they were surfaced with adobe. What exactly is adobe?"

"Mud, basically."

"Imported?"

"No, usually just the local dirt mixed with water, puddled and plastered."

"Too bad." The excitement left Holroyd's voice as quickly as it came.

"There's not much else. When the Great North Road was finally abandoned around 1250, it seems to have been ritually closed. The Anasazi piled brush on the road and set it on fire. They also burned all the shrines along the road. And they burned several large structures too, one of which I excavated a few years ago, called Burned Jacal. Seems it was some kind of lighthouse or signaling structure. God knows what they used it for."

Holroyd sat forward. "They burned *brush* on the road?"

"The Great North Road, anyway. Nobody has done much research on the other roads."

"How much brush?"

"A lot," said Nora. "We found large swaths of charcoal."

Holroyd slammed down the beer, swivelled in his chair, and began hitting keys once again. "Charcoal—carbon—has a very specific radar signature. Even tiny amounts of it absorb radar. It has an almost nonexistent backscatter."

The image on the screen began to shift. "So what we're going to look for," he murmured, "is just the opposite of what I've been searching for all this time. Instead of looking for a particular reflection, we're going to look for a shadow. A linear hole in the data." He punched a final key.

Nora watched as the image on the screen disappeared. And then—as a new image scrolled down the screen with maddening slowness—she saw a long, faint, sinuous black line etch itself across the landscape: broken in countless spots, yet unmistakable.

"There it is," said Holroyd quietly, sitting back and looking at her, his face shining with triumph.

"That's my road to Quivira?" Nora asked, her voice trembling.

"No. That's *our* road to Quivira."

8

NORA WORKED HER WAY THROUGH THE early evening traffic, struggling to keep the highway ahead from blurring into parallel images. She was tired, more tired than she could remember being since her marathon study sessions of graduate school. Though Holroyd had offered to put her up in his apartment the night before, she had instead opted to drive straight back to Santa Fe and the Institute. She had arrived a little after ten in the morning. The day had dragged as Nora, exhausted and distracted, tried to wrap up the end-of-term business. Again and again, her mind had turned back to Quivira and what her next step should be. She sensed it was pointless to approach Blakewood again, even with this startling discovery; there was little chance of him changing his mind. She had passed him in a hallway shortly after noon, and his greeting was decidedly cool.

She slowed, downshifting to second as she turned into Verde Estates, her townhouse development. The afternoon had ended on an unexpected note: a call from Ernest Goddard's office, requesting a meeting the following morning. Nora had never even spoken to the Institute's chairman of the board, and she could think of no reason—no good reason, anyway—why he would want to see her. She'd been absent from the Institute without notice for two days, and had made no headway on the Rio Puerco ceramics. Perhaps Blakewood had put a bug in his ear about the troublesome junior professor.

Nora switched on her headlights as she navigated through the curving lanes. Verde Estates might be a development, but it was older and it lacked the ludicrous Santa Fe–style pretensions of the newer condo complexes. There had been time for a good growth of fruit and fir trees, softening the edges of the buildings. A calm warmth began to flow into her tired limbs as she maneuvered into her parking space. She'd take half an hour to relax, then fix a light meal, take a shower, and fall into bed. Her favorite way to unwind had always been to work on her oboe reeds. Most people found reed-making a tiresome, endless nuisance, but she had always enjoyed the challenge.

Twisting the key out of the ignition, she grabbed her portfolio and bags and started across the blacktop toward her door. Already, she was mentally laying out the tools she'd need: jeweler's loup; a piece of good French cane; silk thread; sheets of fish skin to plug leaks. Mr. Roehm, her high-school oboe teacher, had said that making double reeds was like fly-tying: an art and a science in which a thousand things could go wrong, and in which the tinkering was never done.

She unlocked the front door and stepped inside. Dropping her things, she leaned back against the door and closed her eyes wearily, too exhausted for the moment to turn on the lights. She heard the low growl of the refrigerator, a dog barking hysterically in the distance. The place had a smell she didn't remember. *Odd,* she thought, *how things can grow unfamiliar in just two days.*

Something was missing: the familiar click-clack of nails on the linoleum, the friendly nuzzling of her ankles. Taking a deep breath, she pushed herself away from the door and snapped on the lights. Thurber, her ten-year-old basset hound, was nowhere in sight.

"Thurber?" she called. She thought of going outside to call for him, but changed her mind immediately: Thurber was the most domesticated animal on the planet, for whom the great outdoors was something to be avoided at all costs.

"Thurber?" she called again. Dropping her purse on the front table, her eyes fell on a note: *Nora, please call. Skip.* Reading this, Nora smirked. *Must need money,* she thought; Skip normally never used "please" in a sentence. And that explained Thurber's absence. She'd asked Skip to feed Thurber while she was in California, and no doubt he'd taken the pooch back to his apartment to save himself time.

Turning away, she started to take off her shoes, then changed her mind when she noticed a scattering of dust on the floor. *Gotta clean this damn place,* she thought as she headed for the stairs.

In the bathroom she shrugged off her blouse, washed her face and hands, dampened her hair, and then pulled on her favorite reed-making sweatshirt, a ragged thing from the University of Nevada at Las Vegas. Walking into her bedroom, she stopped to look around a moment. She'd been so quick to judge Holroyd's apartment, almost eccentric in its barrenness, its lack of personality. And yet, in its way, her own place was not that different. Somehow, she'd never had time to give much thought to decorating. If furnishings were a window into the soul, what did this jumble of rooms say about her? A woman who was too busy crawling around ruins to fix up her own place. Almost everything she had belonged to her parents; Skip had refused to take anything except her dad's book collection and old pistol.

With a smile and a shake of her head, she reached automatically for the brush on top of her dresser.

And found it gone.

She paused, hand outstretched, motionless with perplexity. Her brush was always in the same place: the archaeologist in her insisted on keeping her possessions *in situ*. Her damp hair felt cool on the back of her neck as she mentally went through the motions of three mornings before. She'd washed her hair as usual, dressed as usual, combed her hair as usual. And replaced the brush as usual.

But now it was missing. Nora stared at the strange, inexplicable gap between the comb and the box of tissue. *Goddamn Skip,* she thought suddenly, irritation mingling with relief. His own bathroom was a solid mass of mildew, and he liked to sneak showers at her place when she was away. He'd probably dumped it someplace, and . . .

Then she paused and took a breath. Something in her gut told her that this had nothing to do with Skip. The strange smell, the dust in the hall, the feeling that things were not right . . . She whirled around, searching for anything else that might be missing. But everything seemed to be in place.

Then she heard a faint scratching sound coming from outside. She looked over, but the black windows only reflected the interior. She turned off the lights with a quick brush of her hand. It was a clear, moonless night, the desert stars spread out like diamonds across the velvet blackness beyond her window. The scratching came again, louder this time.

With a surge of relief, she realized it must be Thurber, waiting at the back door. On top of everything else, Skip had managed to leave the dog outside. Shaking her head, Nora walked downstairs and through the kitchen. She twisted the deadbolt on the door and yanked it open, kneeling as she did so for the anticipated nuzzle.

Thurber was nowhere to be seen. A skein of dust swirled on the concrete step, flaring into sharp relief as the headlights of a car approached along the back alley. The headlights swept across the grass, past a stand of pines, and silhouetted a large presence, furred and dark, springing back into the protective darkness. As she stared, Nora realized she had seen that movement before—a few nights before, when the same object had raced alongside her truck with horrifying unnatural speed.

She stumbled backward into the kitchen in a rush of terror, face hot, gulping air. Then the moment of paralysis passed. Filled with sudden anger, she grabbed a heavy flashlight from the counter and dashed for the door. She stopped at the threshold, the flashlight revealing nothing but the peaceful desert night.

"Leave me the hell alone!" she cried into the blackness. There was no dark figure, no prints in the damp earth beyond the door; only the lost sigh of the wind, the crazed barking of a distant dog, and the rattle of the flashlight in her shaking hand.

9

NORA STOPPED OUTSIDE A CLOSED OAKEN door labeled CHAIRMAN OF THE BOARD, SANTA FE ARCHAEO-LOGICAL INSTITUTE. Clutching more tightly to the portfolio that now never left her side, she looked carefully down the hall in both directions. She was uncertain whether the nervousness she felt had to do with the events of the night before or with the impending meeting. Had word of her shenanigans at JPL somehow gotten out? No, that was impossible. But maybe this was going to be a dismissal anyway. Why else would Ernest Goddard want to see her? Her head ached from lack of sleep.

All she knew about the chairman was what she had read, along with the rare newspaper photo and even rarer glimpse of his striking figure around campus. Although Dr. Blakewood might have been prime mover and chief architect of the Institute's vision, Nora knew that Goddard was the real power and money behind Blakewood's throne. And unlike Blakewood, Goddard had an almost supernatural ability to cultivate the press, managing to get the occasional tasteful and laudatory article placed in just the right venue. She had heard several explanations for the man's tremendous wealth, from inheriting a motor oil fortune to discovering a submarine full of Nazi gold—none of which seemed credible.

She took a deep breath and grasped the doorknob firmly. Maybe a dismissal would be a good thing at this point. It would free her to pursue Quivira unhindered. The Institute, in the person of Dr. Blakewood, had already passed judgment on her proposed expedition. Holroyd had given her the ammunition she needed to take the idea somewhere else. If the Institute wasn't interested, she knew she would find a place that was.

A small, nervous secretary ushered her through the reception area to the inner office. The space was as cool and spare as a church, with whitewashed adobe walls and a Mexican tiled floor. Instead of the imposing power desk Nora had expected, there was a huge wooden worktable, badly scuffed and dented. She looked around in surprise; it was the exact opposite of Dr. Blakewood's office. Except for a row of pots on the worktable, lined up as if at attention, the room was devoid of ornamentation.

Behind the worktable stood Ernest Goddard, longish white hair haloing his gaunt face, a salt-and-pepper beard below lively blue eyes. One hand held a pencil. A rumpled cotton handkerchief drooped from his jacket pocket. His body was thin and frail, and his gray suit hung loosely on his bony frame. Nora would have thought he was ill, except that his eyes were clear, bright, and full of fire.

"Dr. Kelly," he said, laying down the pencil and coming around the worktable to shake her hand. "So good to meet you at last." His voice was unusual: low, dry, barely higher than a whisper. And yet it carried enormous authority.

"Please call me Nora," she replied guardedly. This cordial reception was the last thing she expected.

"I believe I will," Goddard paused to remove the handkerchief and cough into it with a delicate, almost feminine gesture. "Have a seat. Oh, but before you do, take a look at these ceramics, will you?" He poked the handkerchief back into his pocket.

Nora approached the table. She counted a dozen painted bowls, all peerless examples of ancient pottery from the Mimbres valley of New Mexico. Three were pure geometrics with vibrant rhythms, and two contained abstract insect designs: a stinkbug and a cricket. The rest were covered with anthropo-morphics—splendidly precise, geometric human figures. Each pot had a neat hole punched in the bottom.

"They're magnificent," Nora said.

Goddard seemed about to speak, then turned to cough. A buzzer sounded on the worktable. "Dr. Goddard, Mrs. Henigsbaugh to see you."

"Send her in," Goddard said.

Nora threw him a glance. "Shall I—"

"You stay right here," Goddard said, indicating the chair. "This will only take a minute."

The door opened and a woman of perhaps seventy swept into the room. Immediately, Nora recognized the type: Santa Fe society matron, rich, thin, tan, almost no makeup, in fab-ulous shape, wearing an exquisite but understated Navajo squash blossom necklace over a silk blouse, with a long vel-veteen skirt.

"Ernest, how delightful," she said.

"Wonderful to see you, Lily," Goddard replied. He waved a spotted hand at Nora. "This is Dr. Nora Kelly, an assistant professor here at the Institute."

The woman glanced from Nora to the worktable. "Ah, very good. These are the pots I told you about."

Goddard nodded.

"My appraiser says they're worth five hundred thousand if they're worth a penny. Extremely rare, he said, and in perfect condition. Harry collected them, you know. He wanted the Institute to have them when he died."

"They're very nice—"

"I should say they are!" the woman interrupted, patting her impeccable hair. "Now about their display. I realize, of course, that the Institute doesn't have a formal museum or anything of that sort. But in light of the value of these pots, obviously you'll want to create something special. In the ad-ministration building, I imagine. I've spoken to Simmons, my

architect, and he's drawn up plans for something we're calling the Henigsbaugh Alcove—"

"Lily." Goddard's whispery voice assumed a very subtle
edge of command. "As I was about to say, we're deeply appreciative of your late husband's bequest. But I'm afraid we
can't accept it."

There was a silence.

"I beg your pardon?" Mrs. Henigsbaugh asked, her voice
suddenly cold.

Goddard waved his handkerchief at the worktable. "These
bowls came from graves. We can't take them."

"What do you mean, from graves? Harry bought the pots
from reputable dealers. Didn't you get the papers I sent
along? There's nothing about *graves* in them."

"The papers are irrelevant. Our policy is not to accept
grave goods. Besides," Goddard added more gently, "these
are very beautiful, it's true, and we're honored by the gesture.
But we have better examples in the collection."

Better examples? thought Nora. She had never seen finer
Mimbres bowls, not even in the Smithsonian.

But Mrs. Henigsbaugh was still digesting the grosser in-
sult. "Grave goods! How dare you insinuate they were
looted—"

Goddard picked up a bowl and poked one finger through
the hole in its bottom. "This pot has been killed."

"Killed?"

"Yes. When the Mimbres buried a pot with their dead, they
punched a hole in the bottom to release the spirit of the pot,
so it could join the deceased in the underworld. Archaeologists call it killing the pot." He replaced the bowl on the
table. "All these pots have been killed. So you see they must
have come from graves, no matter what the provenience
says."

"You mean you're going to turn down a half-million-dollar
gift, just like that?" the woman cried.

"I'm afraid so. I'll have them carefully crated and returned to you." He coughed into his handkerchief. "I'm very sorry, Lily."

"I'm sure you are." The woman spun around and left the office abruptly, leaving a faint cloud of expensive perfume in her wake.

In the silence that followed, Goddard settled onto the edge of the table, a thoughtful look on his face. "You're familiar with Mimbres pottery?" he asked.

"Yes," Nora replied. She still could not believe he had turned down the gift.

"What do you think?"

"Other institutions have killed Mimbres pots in their collections."

"We are not *other* institutions," Goddard replied in his soft whisper. "These pots were buried by people who respected their dead, and we have an obligation to continue that respect. I doubt Mrs. Henigsbaugh would approve of us digging up her dear departed Harry." He settled into a chair behind the worktable. "I had a visit from Dr. Blakewood the other day, Nora."

She stiffened. This was it, then.

"He mentioned that you were behind in your projects, and that he felt your tenure review might go poorly. Care to tell me about it?"

"There's nothing to tell," Nora said. "I'll submit my resignation whenever."

To her surprise, Goddard grinned at this. "Resignation?" he asked. "Why on earth would you want to resign?"

She cleared her throat. "There's no way, in six months, I'm going to be able to write up the Rio Puerco and Gallegos Divide projects, and—" She stopped.

"And what?" Goddard asked.

"Do what I need to do," she finished. "So I might as well resign now, and save you the trouble."

"I see." Goddard's glittering eyes never left hers. "Do what you need to do, you say. Might that be searching for the lost city of Quivira?"

Nora looked sharply at him, and once again the chairman grinned. "Oh, yes. Blakewood mentioned that, too."

Nora remained silent.

"He also mentioned your sudden absence from the Institute. Did it have something to do with this idea of yours, this search for Quivira?"

"I was in California."

"I should have thought Quivira was somewhat east of there."

Nora sighed. "What I did was on my own time."

"Dr. Blakewood didn't think so. Did you find Quivira?"

"In a way, yes."

There was a silence in the room. Nora looked at Goddard's face. The grin was suddenly gone.

"Would you care to explain?"

"No," said Nora.

Goddard's surprise lasted only for a moment. "Why not?"

"Because this is my project," Nora said truculently.

"I see." Goddard eased himself off the table and leaned toward Nora. "The Institute might be able to help you and your project. Now tell me: what did you find in California?"

Nora moved in her chair, considering. "I have some radar images that show an ancient Anasazi road leading to what I believe is Quivira."

"Do you indeed?" Goddard's face expressed both astonishment and something else. "And just where did these images come from?"

"I have a contact inside the Jet Propulsion Laboratory. He was able to digitally manipulate radar images of the area, canceling out the modern tracks and leaving the ancient road. It leads straight into the heart of the redrock country mentioned in the early Spanish accounts."

Goddard nodded, his face curious and expectant. "This is extraordinary," he said. "Nora, you're a woman of many surprises."

Nora said nothing.

"Of course, Dr. Blakewood had reasons to say what he did.

But perhaps he spoke a little precipitously." He placed a hand lightly on her shoulder. "What if we make this search for Quivira *our* project?"

Nora paused. "I'm not sure I understand."

Goddard withdrew his hand, stood up, and walked slowly around the room, looking away from her. "What if the Institute were to fund this expedition of yours, roll back your tenure review? How would that sound?"

Nora gazed at the man's narrow back, absorbing what he had just said. "That would sound unlikely, if you don't mind my saying so," she answered.

Goddard began to laugh, only to be cut short by a series of coughs. He returned to the worktable. "Blakewood told me about your theories, about your father's letter. Some of the things he said were less than generous. But it happens that I, too, have long wondered about Quivira. No less than three early Spanish explorers in the Southwest heard these stories about a fabulous golden city: Cabeza de Vaca in the 1530s, Fray Marcos in 1538, and Coronado in 1540. Their stories are too similar to be fiction. And then in the 1770s, and again in the 1830s, more people came out of that wilderness, claiming to have heard of a lost city." He looked up at her. "There's never been a question in my mind that Quivira existed. The question was always exactly *where*."

He circled the table and came to rest on its corner once more. "I knew your father, Nora. If he said he found evidence for this lost city, I'd believe him."

Nora bit her lip against an unexpected well of emotion.

"I have the means to put the Institute squarely behind your expedition. But I need to see the evidence first. The letter *and* the data. If what you say is true, we'll back you."

Nora placed a hand on her portfolio. She could hardly believe the turnaround. And yet, she had seen too many young archaeologists lose credit to their older, more powerful colleagues. "You said this would be our project. I'd still like to keep it *my* project, if you don't mind."

"Well, perhaps I do mind. If I'm going to fund this expedition—through the Institute, of course—I would like control, particularly over the personnel."

"Who did you envision leading the expedition?" she asked.

There was the slightest of pauses while Goddard steadily met her gaze. "You would, of course. Aaron Black would go along as the geochronologist, and Enrique Aragon as the medical doctor and paleopathologist."

Nora sat back, surprised at the rapidity with which his mind worked. Not only was he thinking ahead to the expedition, but he was already peopling it with the best scientists in their fields. "If you can get them," she said.

"Oh, I'm reasonably sure I can get them. I know them both very well. And the discovery of Quivira would be a watershed in southwestern archaeology. It's the kind of gamble an archaeologist can't resist. And since I can't go along myself"—he waved his handkerchief in explanation—"I'd want to send my daughter in my stead. She got her undergraduate degree from Smith, just took her Ph.D. at Princeton in American archaeology, and she's anxious to do some fieldwork. She's young, and perhaps a little impetuous, but she has one of the finest archaeological minds I've ever encountered. And she's highly skilled at field photography."

Nora frowned. *Smith,* she thought to herself. "I'm not sure that's a good idea," she said. "It might muddy the chain of command. And this is going to be a difficult trip, particularly for a . . ." She paused. "A sorority girl."

"My daughter *must* go along," said Goddard quietly. "And she is no 'sorority girl,' as you shall discover." An odd, mirthless smile flashed briefly across his lips before disappearing.

Nora looked at the old man, realizing the point was non-negotiable. Quickly, she considered her options. She could take the information she had, sell the ranch, and head into the desert with people of her own choosing, gambling that she could find Quivira before her money ran out. Or she could take her data to another institution, where it would probably be a year or two before they could organize and fund a trip. Or she could share her discovery with a sympathetic backer uniquely qualified to outfit a professional expedition, leading the top archaeologists in the country. The price of admission was taking the backer's daughter along for the ride. *No contest there,* she thought.

"All right." She smiled. "But I've got a condition of my own. I need to take the JPL technician who assisted me along as a remote imaging specialist."

"I'm sorry, but I'd like to reserve the personnel decisions."

"It was the price of getting the data."

There was a silence. "Can you vouch for his credentials?"

"Yes. He's young, but he's got a lot of experience."

"Very well."

Nora was surprised at Goddard's ability to take a challenge, parry, and come to a decision. She found herself beginning to like him.

"I also think we have to keep this confidential," she continued. "The expedition has to be assembled very quickly and very secretly."

Goddard looked at her speculatively. "May I ask why?"

"Because . . . " Nora stopped. *Because I think I'm being shadowed by mysterious figures who will stop at nothing to find the location of Quivira.* But she couldn't say that to Goddard; he'd think her crazy, or worse, and rescind his offer in an instant. Any hint of a problem would complicate, maybe even wreck, the expedition. "Because this information is very sensitive. Think what would happen if pothunters learned about it and tried to loot the site before we could reach it. And on a practical matter, we have to move fast. The flash flood season will be on us soon."

After a moment, Goddard nodded slowly. "That makes sense," he said. "I'd like to include a journalist on the expedition, but I'm sure his discretion can be relied on."

"A journalist?" Nora burst out. "Why?"

"To chronicle what may be the most important find in twentieth-century American archaeology. Imagine the story the world would have lost if Howard Carter had not had the London *Times* covering his discovery. I actually have somebody in mind, a *New York Times* reporter with several books to his credit, including an excellent profile of the Boston Aquarium. I think he can be relied upon not only to be a good digger but to produce a highly favorable—and highly visible—account of you and your work." He glanced at Nora. "You have no objection to *ex post facto* publicity, certainly?"

Nora hesitated. This was all happening so fast: it was almost as if Goddard had worked it all out before even talking to her. As she thought back over their conversation, she realized he must have. It occurred to her that there might be a reason for his excitement that he was not sharing with her.

"No," she said, "I guess not."

"I didn't think so. Now let's see what you've got."

Goddard pushed away from the desk as Nora reached into her portfolio and removed a 30-by-60-minute U.S.G.S. topo. "The target area is this triangle just to the west of the Kaiparowits Plateau, here. As you can see, it contains dozens of canyon systems that all eventually drain into Lake Powell and the Grand Canyon, to the south and east. The closest human settlement is a small Nankoweap Indian encampment sixty miles to the north."

Then she handed Goddard a sheet of paper: a U.S.G.S. 7.5-minute topographic map, onto which Holroyd had over-printed in red the final image from his computer, properly scaled. "This is an image taken from last week's shuttle over-flight, digitally enhanced. The faint, broken black line across it is the ancient Anasazi road."

Goddard took the sheet into his thin pale hands. "Extraordinary," he murmured. "Last week's flight?" Again he looked at Nora, a curious admiration in his eyes.

"The dotted line shows a reconstruction of my father's route through this country, following what he thought to be that road. When we extrapolated the road from the shuttle radar image onto this map, it matched my father's route. The road seems to lead northwestward from Betatakin Ruin, through this maze of canyons, and over this huge ridge, which my father labeled the Devil's Backbone. It then appears to lead into a narrow slot canyon, ending up in this tiny, hidden canyon, here. It's somewhere in this canyon that we hope to find the city."

Goddard shook his head. "Amazing. But Nora, all the ancient Anasazi roads we know about, Chaco and the rest, run in absolutely straight lines. This road winds around like a broken spring."

"I thought of that, too," Nora said. "Everyone's always thought Chaco Canyon was the center of Anasazi culture, the fourteen Great Houses of Chaco with Pueblo Bonito at their hub. But look at this."

She pulled out another map, showing the entire Colorado Plateau and San Juan Basin. In the lower right-hand corner, an archaeological site diagram of Chaco Canyon had been overlaid, showing the huge ruin at Pueblo Bonito surrounded by a circle of outlying communities. A heavy red line had been drawn from Pueblo Bonito, through the circle, through a half dozen other major ruins, and running arrow-straight to the upper left hand corner of the map, terminating in an x.

"That x marks what I calculate to be the location of Quivira," Nora said quietly. "All these years we've believed that Chaco itself was the destination of the Anasazi roads. But what if Chaco *wasn't* the destination? What if, instead, it was the collecting point for a ritual journey to Quivira, the city of priests?"

Goddard shook his head slowly. "This is fascinating. There's more than enough evidence here to justify an expedition. Have you given any thought to how you might get in there? Helicopters, for example?"

"That was my first thought. But this isn't a typical remote site. Those canyons are too narrow and most are a thousand feet deep. There are high winds, beetling rimrock, and no flat areas to land. I've studied the maps carefully, and there's no place within fifty miles to safely land a helicopter. Jeeps are obviously out of the question. So we'll have to use horses. They're cheap and can pack a lot of gear."

Goddard grunted as he stared at the map. "Sounds good.

But I'm not sure I see a route in, even on horseback. All these canyons box up at their sources. Even if you used this Indian settlement far to the north as your jumping-off point, it would be one hell of a ride just to get to the village. And then, waterless country for the next sixty miles. Lake Powell blocks access to the south." He looked up. "Unless you . . ."

"Exactly. We'll float the expedition up the lake. I've already called the Wahweap Marina in Page, and they have a seventy-foot barge that will do the job. If we started at Wahweap, floated the horses up to the head of Serpentine Canyon, and rode in from there, we could be at Quivira in three or four days."

Goddard broke into a smile. "Nora, this is inspired. Let's make it happen."

"There's one other thing," Nora said, replacing the maps in her portfolio without looking up. "My brother needs a job. He'll do anything, really, and I know with the right supervision he'd be great at sorting and cataloging the Rio Puerco and Gallegos Divide material."

"We have a rule against nepotism—" Goddard began, then stopped as Nora, despite herself, began to smile. The old man looked at her steadily, and for a moment Nora thought he would erupt in anger. But then his face cleared. "Nora, you are your father's daughter," he said. "You don't trust anybody, and you're a damn good negotiator. Any other demands? You'd better present them now, or forever hold your peace."

"No, that covers it."

Silently, Goddard extended his hand.

10

THERE WAS AN ABRUPT HAMMERING SOUND; Nora almost dropped the artifact in her hands and looked up from her desk in a panic, heart galloping. Skip's scowling face was framed in the glass window of her office door. She slumped back in her chair and breathed out. Skip raised one hand, and, with an exaggerated gesture, pointed downward at the doorknob.

"You almost gave me a heart attack," she said as she let him in. Her fingers still trembled as she closed and relocked the door. "Not to mention the loss of two years of my salary if I'd dropped that Mogollon pot."

"Since when did you start locking your office?" Skip said, slouching into the only chair not covered with books and tugging a large satchel onto his knees. "Look, Nora, there's something—"

"First things first," Nora interrupted. "You got my message?" Skip nodded and passed over the satchel. Nora unlooped the leather straps and looked inside. Her father's old Ruger lay at the bottom, shoved into a battered holster.

"What do you want it for, anyway?" Skip asked. "Some academic rivalry that needs settling?"

Nora shook her head. "Skip, I want you to be serious for a

minute. The Institute's agreed to fund an expedition to Quivira. I'll be leaving in a couple of days."

Skip's eyes widened. "Fantastic! You don't waste any time, do you? When do we go?"

"You know perfectly well you're not going," said Nora. "But I've arranged a job for you, here at the Institute. You'll start work next Monday."

The eyes narrowed again. "A job? I don't know jack shit about archaeology."

"All that time you spent, crawling around the ranch on your hands and knees with Dad, looking for potsherds? Come on. Anyway, it's an easy assignment, first-year stuff. My associate Sonya Rowling will show you around, get you started, answer questions, keep you out of trouble."

"She cute?"

"She's married. Look, I'll be gone about three weeks. If you don't like it by the time I get back, you can quit. But it'll keep you occupied for the time being." *And maybe keep you in a safe place during the day,* she thought. "You won't mind looking after my place while I'm gone? And you'll leave my stuff alone, for a change?" She shook her head. "You use my shower, you steal my hairbrush . . . I ought to start charging rent."

"I didn't steal your hairbrush!" Skip protested. "I mean sure, I used it, but I put it back. I know how neurotic you are about that kind of thing."

"Not neurotic. Just neat." She glanced over. "Speaking of looking after my place, where's Thurber? Didn't you bring him?"

A funny look came over Skip. "That's what I wanted to tell you," he said in a low voice. "Thurber's missing."

Nora felt the air leave her lungs in a sudden rush. "Missing?" she repeated.

Skip looked down abjectly.

"What happened?"

Skip shook his head. "Don't know. It was the second night you were gone. He was fine the first night, or as fine as he ever gets. When I came in the second night and called for him, he was gone. It was weird. The door was locked, all the windows were shut. But there was this funny smell in the air, almost like flowers. There was some dog barking like mad outside, but it didn't sound like Thurber. I went outside anyway and looked around. He must have jumped the fence or something." He sighed deeply and looked at his sister. "I'm really sorry, Nora. I looked all over for him, I talked to the neighbors, I called the pound . . ."

"You didn't leave a door open?" Nora asked. The raw anger she'd felt the night before, the feeling of violation, was gone, leaving only a strange and terrible fear behind.

"No, I swear I didn't. Like I said, everything was locked up."

"Skip, I want you to listen to me," she said in a low voice. "When I got home last night, I could tell something wasn't right. Somebody had been in the apartment. The place was dirty. My hairbrush was missing. There was a strange smell, the same one you noticed. And then I heard some scratching, and went outside—" She stopped. How could she explain it: the humped, fur-covered figure, the strange lack of footprints, the feeling of utter alienness that had come across her as she stood in the dark, flashlight in hand? And now Thurber . . .

Skip's skeptical look changed suddenly to concern. "Hey, Nora, you've had quite a week," he said. "First that thing out at the ranch, then this expedition coming together out of nowhere, and Thurber disappearing. Why don't you go home and rest up?"

Nora looked into his eyes.

"What?" he asked. "Are you afraid to go home?"

"It isn't that," she replied. "I had the locksmith out this morning to install a second lock. It's just that . . ." She hesitated. "I just have to keep a low profile for the next day or two. I can take care of myself. Once I'm out of Santa Fe, there won't be any more problems. But, Skip, promise me you'll be very careful while I'm gone. I'll leave Dad's gun in the bedside table drawer in my apartment. I want you to have it after I leave. And don't go by the old place, okay?"

"You afraid the Creature from the Black Lagoon will get me?"

Nora rose quickly. "That's not funny, and you know it."

"All right, all right. I never visit that broken-down old shack anyway. Besides, after what happened, I'll bet Teresa's watching that place like a hawk, finger on the trigger."

Nora sighed. "Maybe you're right."

"I am right. You wait and see. Black Lagoon, zero. Winchester, one."

11

CALAVERAS MESA LAY SLUMBERING UNDER the midnight sky, a shadowy island rising out of an ocean of broken rock—the vast *El Malpaís* lava flow of central New Mexico. A screen of clouds had moved over the stars, and the mesa lay still underneath: silent, dark, uninhabited. The nearest settlement was Quemado, fifty miles away.

Calaveras Mesa had not always been uninhabited. In the fourteenth century, Anasazi Indians had moved into its south-facing cliffs and hollowed out caves in the soft volcanic tuff. But the site had proved uncongenial, and the caves had been abandoned for half a millennium. In this distant part of *El Malpaís,* there were no roads and no trails; the caves remained undisturbed and unexcavated.

Two dark forms moved among the silent broken rafts and blocks of frozen lava that lapped the sides of the mesa. They were covered with thick pelts of fur, and their movements had the combined swiftness and caution of a wolf. Both figures wore heavy silver jewelry: concho belts, squash blossom necklaces, turquoise disks, and old sand-cast bow guards. Beneath the heavy pelts, naked skin was daubed with thick paint.

They reached the talus slope below the caves and began to ascend, picking their way among boulders and rockfalls. At the bottom of the cliff itself they rapidly ascended a hand-and-toe trail and disappeared into the dark mouth of a cave.

Inside the cave, they paused. One figure remained at the mouth while the second moved swiftly to the back of the cave. He pushed aside a rock, revealing a narrow passage, and wriggled through into a smaller room. There was a faint scratching sound and the wavering light of a burning splinter revealed that this room was not empty: it was a small Anasazi burial chamber. In niches carved in the far wall lay three mummified corpses, a few pathetic broken pots left beside them as offerings. The figure placed a ball of wax with a bit of straw stuck into it on a high ledge, lighting it with an uncertain glow.

Then he moved to the central corpse: a gray, delicate form wrapped in a rotting buffalo hide. Its mummified lips had drawn back from its teeth and its mouth was open in a monstrous grimace of hilarity. The legs of the corpse were drawn up to the chest and the knees had been wrapped with woven cords; its eyes were two holes, webbed with shreds of tissue; its hands were balled up into shriveled fists, the fingernails hanging and broken, gnawed by rats.

The figure reached in and cradled the mummy with infinite gentleness, removed it from the niche, and laid it down in the thick layer of dust on the cave floor. Reaching into the pelt, he removed a small woven basket and a medicine bundle. Tugging open the bundle, he extracted something and held it up to the uncertain light: a pair of delicate bronze hairs.

The figure turned back to the mummy. Slowly, he placed the hairs in the mouth of the mummy, pushing them deep into the mummy's throat. There was a dry crackling noise. Then the figure leaned back; the candle snuffed out; and absolute darkness fell once again. There was a low sound, a mutter, then a name, intoned again and again in a slow, even voice: "*Kelly . . . Kelly . . . Kelly . . .*"

A long time passed. There was another scratch of a match, and the wax was relit. The figure reached into the basket, then bent over the corpse. A razor-sharp obsidian knife gleamed in the faint light. There was a faint, rhythmic scraping noise: the sound of stone cutting through crisp, dry flesh. The figure soon straightened up, holding a small round disk of scalp, dotted with the whorl of hair from the back of the mummy's head. The figure placed it reverently in the basket.

The figure bent once more. There was now a louder, digging noise. After a few minutes, there was a sharp rap. The figure held up a disk of skullbone, examined it, then placed it in the basket beside the scalp. Next, he moved the knife down the mummy until it reached the clenched, withered fists. He gently pulled aside the rotted tatters of buffalo hide from the hands, caressing them in his own. Then he worked the knife between the fingers, methodically prying them loose and breaking them off one at a time. Cupping each finger, he cut off the whorl of fingerprint and placed the desiccated chips of flesh into the basket. Then the figure moved down to the toes, breaking them off the body like breadsticks and quickly carving off the toe prints. Small showers of dust rained onto the cave floor.

The little basket filled with pieces of the corpse as the makeshift candle guttered. The figure quickly rewrapped the mummy and lifted it back into its niche in the wall as the light winked out. Picking up the basket, he left the chamber and rolled the rock back into place. Gingerly, he pulled a buckskin bag from the pelt, unwound the tight knot of leather that sealed it shut, and teased the bag open. Holding it away from himself, he carefully sprinkled a thin trail of some powdery substance along the base of the rock. Then he carefully sealed up the bag and rejoined his companion at the cave entrance. Swiftly and silently, they descended the cliff face and were once again swallowed up in the darkness of the great lava flow of *El Malpaís*.

12

THE HEADLIGHTS OF NORA'S TRUCK SWUNG across the predawn dark, scissoring through clouds of dust rising from the corrals, highlighting the wooden gates of the dude ranch. She came to a stop in a rutted parking area and killed the motor. Nearby, she could see two dark-colored vehicles, a pickup and a van, each bearing the Institute's seal. Two slant-load horse trailers had been backed up to nearby horse pens, and ranch hands were loading horses into them under electric lights.

Nora stepped out into the coolness of the early morning air and looked around. The sky would not begin to lighten for another half hour or so, but already Venus was rising, a sharp fleck of light against the velvet sky. The Institute vehicles were empty, and Nora knew everyone must already be at the fire circle, where Goddard planned to introduce the expedition to one another and say a brief farewell. In an hour, they would begin the long drive to Page, Arizona, at the end of Lake Powell. It was time she met the others.

But she lingered a moment. The air was filled with the sounds of her childhood: the slap of latigo, the whistles and shouts of the cowboys, the boom of prancing hooves in the trailers, the clang of stock gates. As the aroma of piñon smoke, horses, and dust drifted near, a tight knot that had been growing within her began to relax. Over the last three days she had been supremely cautious, supremely vigilant, and yet she had seen nothing more to alarm her. The expedition had come together with remarkable speed and smoothness. Not a word had leaked out. And here, away from Santa Fe, Nora found some of the tension that had kept her so painfully on edge begin to ebb. The mystery of who had mailed her father's letter was never far from her thoughts. But at least, once they were on the trail, she would leave her strange pursuers far behind.

A cowboy in a battered hat strode out of the corral, leading a horse in each hand. Nora turned to look at him. The man was barely five feet tall, skinny, barrel-chested and bandy-legged. He turned and shouted to some hands deeper in the dusty darkness, bracketing the orders with four letter words. *That must be Roscoe Swire,* she thought: the wrangler Goddard had hired. He seemed a sure enough hand, but as her father had always said, *he ain't a cowboy til you see him ride.* She again felt a momentary annoyance at how the Institute's chairman had taken over the hiring of all personnel, even the wrangler. But Goddard was paying the bills.

She pulled her saddle out of the back of her truck and stepped around. "Roscoe Swire?" she asked.

He turned and removed his hat in a gesture that managed to be both courtly and ironic. "At your service," he said in a surprisingly deep voice. He had a great overhanging mustache, droopy lips, and large, cow-sad eyes. But there was a certain scrappiness, even truculence, about his manner.

"I'm Nora Kelly," she said, shaking the small hand. It was so rough and scabby, it was like grasping a burr

"So you're the boss," said Swire with a grin. "Pleased." He glanced at the saddle. "What you got there?"

"It's my own. I figured you'd want to load it with the rest in the front of the trailer."

He slowly placed his hat back on his head. "Looks like it's been drug around a bit."

"I've had it since I was sixteen."

Swire broke into another smile. "An archaeologist who can ride."

"I can pack a set of panniers and throw a pretty good diamond hitch, too," said Nora.

At this, Swire took a small box of gingersnaps out of his pocket, placed one underneath his mustache, and began to chew. "Well, now," he said, when his mouth was full, "you ain't shy about your accomplishments." He took a closer look at her gear. "Valle Grande Saddlery, three-quarter-rigged with the Cheyenne roll. You ever want to sell this, you let me know."

Nora laughed.

"Look, the others just went up to the circle. What can you tell me about them? Buncha New Yorkers on vacation, or what?"

Nora found herself liking Swire and his sardonic tone. "Most of them I haven't met. It's a mixed group. People seem to think all archaeologists are like Indiana Jones, but I've met plenty who couldn't ride to save their lives, or who'd never ventured beyond the classroom and lab. It all depends on what kind of work they've done. I bet there'll be a couple of sore butts by the end of the first day." She thought about Sloane Goddard, the sorority girl, and wondered how she, Holroyd, and the rest were going to fare on horseback.

"Good," said Swire. "If they ain't sore, they ain't having fun." He pushed another gingersnap into his mouth, then pointed. "It's up that way."

The fire circle lay north of the corrals, hidden in a stand of scrub juniper and piñon. Nora followed the trail, quickly spotting the flickering fire through the trees. Huge ponderosa logs were arranged in broad rings, three deep. The circle lay at the base of a tall bluff, which was pockmarked here and there by caves, a pendulous overhang across its top. Light from the fire leaped and flickered, painting the sandstone bluff lurid colors against the dark. A fire circle before a long journey was an old Pueblo custom, Nora knew, and after witnessing the incident with the Mimbres pots, she wasn't particularly surprised Goddard had suggested it. It was another indication of his respect for Indian culture.

She stepped into the firelight. Several figures were seated on the ponderosa logs, murmuring quietly. They turned at her approach. She immediately recognized Aaron Black, the imposing geochronologist from the University of Pennsylvania: six-foot-five-inches tall or more, with a massive head and hands. He held his head erect, chin jutting forward, which both added to his stature and gave him a slightly pompous air.

But the look belied Black's towering reputation. She had seen him at numerous archaeological meetings, where he always seemed to be giving a paper debunking some other archaeologist's shaky but hopeful dating of a site; a man of intellectual rigor who clearly enjoyed his role as spoiler of his colleagues' theories. But he was the acknowledged master of archaeological dating, at once feared and sought after. It was said that he had never been proved wrong, and his arrogant face looked it.

"Dr. Black," Nora said, stepping forward. "I'm Nora Kelly."

"Oh," Black said, standing up and shaking hands. "Pleased to meet you." He looked a little nonplussed. *Probably doesn't like the idea of having a young woman for a boss,* she thought. Gone were the trademark bow tie and seersucker jacket of his archaeological conferences, replaced by a brand-new desert outfit that looked as if had been lifted straight out of the pages of Abercrombie & Fitch. *He's going to be one of the sore ones,* Nora thought. *If he doesn't get his ass killed first.*

Holroyd came over and shook her hand, gave her a quick awkward hug, and then, embarrassed, stepped back in confusion. He had the luminous face of a Boy Scout setting out on his first camping trip, his green eyes shining hopefully.

"Dr. Kelly?" came a voice from the darkness. Another figure stepped into the light toward her, a small, dark man in his middle fifties who radiated an unsettling, even caustic intensity. He had a striking face: dark olive skin, black hair combed back, veiled eyes, a long, hooked nose. "I'm Enrique

Aragon." He briefly took her hand; his fingers were long, sensitive, almost feminine. He spoke with a precise, dignified voice, in the faintest of Mexican accents. She had also seen him many times at conferences, a remote and private figure. He was widely considered to be the country's finest physical anthropologist, winner of the Hrdlička Medal; but he was also a medical doctor—a highly convenient combination, which had undoubtedly figured in Goddard's choice. It amazed her again that Goddard could have gotten professionals of the stature of Black and Aragon at such short notice. And it struck her even more forcefully that she would be directing these two men, very much her superior in both age and reputation. Nora shook off the sudden surge of doubt: if she was going to lead this expedition, she knew, she had better start thinking and acting like a leader, not an assistant professor always deferring to her senior colleagues.

"We've been making introductions," Aragon said with a brief smile. "This is Luigi Bonarotti, camp manager and cook." He stepped aside and indicated another figure who had come up behind him to meet Nora.

A man with dark Sicilian eyes leaned over and took her hand. He was impeccably dressed in pressed khakis, beautifully groomed, and Nora caught the faint whiff of an expensive aftershave. He took her hand and half-bowed with a kind of European restraint.

"Are we really going to have to ride horses all the way to the site?" Black asked.

"No," Nora said. "You'll get to walk some, too."

Black's face tightened with displeasure. "I should have thought helicopters would make more sense. I've always found them sufficient for my work."

"Not in this country," Nora said.

"And where's the journalist who's going to be documenting all this for posterity? Shouldn't he be here? I've been looking forward to meeting him."

"He's joining us at Wahweap Marina, along with Dr. Goddard's daughter."

The others began to range themselves around the fire and Nora settled down on a log, enjoying the warmth, inhaling the scent of cedar smoke, listening to the hiss and crackle taunt the surrounding darkness. As if from far away, she heard Black still muttering about having to ride a horse. The flames capered against the sandstone bluff, highlighting the black, ragged mouths of caves. She thought she saw a brief glow of light inside one of the caves, but it vanished as quickly as it had come. Some trick of the eye, perhaps. For some reason, she found herself thinking of Plato's parable of the cave. *And what would we look like,* she thought, *to those dwellers deep inside, gazing at shadows on the wall?*

She realized that the murmur of conversation around her had died away. Everyone was staring at the fire, absorbed in their own thoughts. Nora glanced at the excited Holroyd, pleased that the remote-sensing specialist wasn't having second thoughts. But Holroyd was no longer staring at the fire: he was staring beyond it, into the darkness of the cliff face.

Nora noticed Aragon look up, then Black. Following their gaze, she again saw a flash of light inside one of the caves beyond the fire, fitful but unmistakable. There was a faint clicking noise, and more yellow flashes. Then a lone figure resolved itself, gray on black, against the darkness of the cave. As it stepped forward out of the shadow of the sandstone bluff, Nora recognized the gaunt features of Ernest Goddard. He came silently toward the group, his white hair painted crimson by the fire, staring at them through the flames and smoke. He moved something within his hand, and the flashes returned yet again, flickering through his narrow fingers.

He stood for a long moment, holding each person in turn in his gaze. Then he slipped whatever was in his hand into a leather bag and tossed it over the flames to Aragon, closest on the circle. "Rub them together," he said, his whispery voice barely audible above the crackle of the campfire. "Then pass them around."

When Aragon handed her the bag, Nora reached inside and felt two smooth, hard stones. She drew them out and held them to the firelight: beautiful specimens of quartz, river-tumbled by the look of them, carved with the ritual spiral design that signified the *sipapu,* the Anasazi entrance to the underworld.

In that instant, she recognized them for what they were. Pulling them out of the glare of the fire, she rubbed them together, watching the miraculous internal sparks light up the hearts of the stones, flickering fiercely in the dark. Watching her, Goddard nodded.

"Anasazi lightning stones," he said in his quiet voice.

"Are they real?" asked Holroyd, taking them from Nora and holding them to the firelight.

"Of course," said Goddard. "They come from a medicine cache found in the great kiva at Keet Seel. We used to believe the Anasazi used them in rain ceremonies to symbolize the generation of lightning. But we aren't sure anymore. The carved spiral represents the *sipapu.* But then again, it might represent a water spring. Again, nobody knows for sure."

He coughed lightly. "And that's what I'm here to say to you. Back in the sixties, we thought we knew everything about the Anasazi. I remember when the great southwestern archaeologist Henry Ash urged his students to seek other venues. 'It's a sucked orange,' he said.

"But now, after three decades of mysterious and inexplicable discoveries, we realize that we know next to nothing about the Anasazi. We don't understand their culture, we don't understand their religion. We cannot read their petroglyphs and pictographs. We do not know what languages they might have spoken. We do not know why they covered the Southwest with lighthouses, shrines, roads, and signaling stations. We do not know why, in 1150, they suddenly abandoned Chaco Canyon, burned the roads, and retreated to the most remote, inaccessible canyons in the Southwest, building mighty fortresses in the cliff faces. What had happened? Who were they afraid of? A century later, they abandoned even those, leaving the entire Colorado Plateau and San Juan Basin, some fifty thousand square miles, uninhabited. Why?

The fact is, the more we discover, the more intractable these questions become. Some archaeologists now believe we will *never* know the answers."

His voice had dropped even further. Despite the warmth of the fire, Nora couldn't help shivering.

"But I have a feeling," he whispered, his voice weaker, hoarser. "I have a *conviction* that Quivira will contain answers to these mysteries."

He glanced at each of them again, in turn. "All of you are about to embark on the adventure of a lifetime. You're headed for a site that may prove to be the biggest archaeological discovery of the decade, perhaps even the century. But let's not fool ourselves. Quivira will be a place of mystery as well as revelation. It may well pose as many questions as it answers. And it will challenge you, physically and mentally, in ways you cannot yet imagine. There will be moments of triumph, moments of despair. But you must never forget that you are representing the Santa Fe Archaeological Institute. And what the Institute represents is the very highest standard of archaeological research and ethical conduct."

He fixed Nora with his gaze. "Nora Kelly has been with the Institute only five years, but she has proven herself an excellent field archaeologist. She is in charge, and I have put my complete trust in her. I don't want anyone to forget that. When my daughter joins you in Page, she will also report to Dr. Kelly; there can be no confusion of command."

He took a step away from the fire, back toward the darkness of the overhanging bluff. Nora leaned forward, straining to hear, as his whisper mingled with the muttering fire.

"There are some who do not believe the lost city of Quivira exists. They think this expedition is foolhardy, that I'm throwing my money away. There is even fear this will prove an embarrassment to the Institute."

He paused. "But the city is there. You know it, and I know it. Now go and find it."

13

THE EXPEDITION PASSED THROUGH PAGE, Arizona, at two o'clock that afternoon, the horse trailers followed by the pickup and the van, threading caravan-style down through town to the marina, where they edged into the gigantic asphalt parking lot facing Lake Powell. Page was one of the new Western boomtowns that had sprung up like a rash on the desert, built yesterday and already shabby. Its trailer parks and prefabs sprawled down toward the lakeshore through a barren landscape of greasewood and saltbush. Beyond the town rose the three surreal smokestacks of the coal-fired Navajo Generating Station, each climbing almost a quarter mile into the sky, issuing plumes of white steam.

Beyond the town lay the marina and Lake Powell itself, a green sinuosity worming its way into a fantastical wilderness of stone. It was huge: three hundred miles long, with thousands of miles of shoreline. The lake was a breathtaking sight, a sharp contrast to the banality of Page. To the east, the great dome of Navajo Mountain rose like a black skullcap, the ravines at its top still wedged with streaks of snow. Farther up the lake, the buttes, mesas, and canyons were layered one against the other, the lake itself forming a pathway into an infinity of sandstone and sky.

Staring at the sight, Nora shook her head. Thirty-five years before, this had been Glen Canyon, which John Wesley Powell had called the most beautiful canyon in the world. Then the Glen Canyon dam was built, and the waters of the Colorado River slowly rose to form Lake Powell. The once silent wilderness, at least around Page, was now filled with the roar of cigarette boats and jetskis, the sounds mingling with the smell of exhaust fumes, cigarette smoke, and gasoline. The place had the surreal air of a settlement perched at the end of the known world.

Beside her, Swire frowned out the window. They had talked horses most of the trip, and Nora had come to respect the cowboy. "I don't know how these horses are going to like floating on a barge," he said. "We might have ourselves a surprise swimming party."

"We'll be able to drive the trailers right onto the barge and unhook them," Nora replied. "They never have to be unloaded."

"Until the far side, you mean." Swire fingered the heavy mustache that drooped beneath his nose. "Don't see any sign of that Sloane gal, do you?"

Nora shrugged. Sloane Goddard was supposed to fly directly into Page and meet them at the marina, but there was no sign of any Seven Sisters sorority types among the fleshy, beer-bellied throngs milling around the docks. Perhaps she was waiting in the air-conditioned fastness of the manager's office.

The two trailers pulled up on the vast cement apron of West Boatramp. The van and the pickup came up behind and the company emerged into the sweltering heat, followed by the four Institute employees who would drive the vehicles back to Santa Fe.

Down here near the water, Nora could see Wahweap Marina in all its glory. Styrofoam cups, beer cans, plastic bags, and floating pieces of newspaper bobbed in the brown shallows at the bottom of the boatramp. SKI ONLY IN CLOCKWISE DIRECTION read one sign and nearby was another: LET'S ALL HAVE FUN TOGETHER! Endless ranks of moored houseboats

90

lined the shore in either direction, enormous floating metal-sided RVs. They were painted in garish colors—motel greens and yellows, polyester browns—and sported names like *Li'l Injun* and *Dad's Desire*.

"What a place," Holroyd said, stretching and looking around.

"It's so *hot*," Black said, wiping his brow.

As Swire went to help back the horsetrailers around, Nora noticed an incongruous sight: a black stretch limousine flying down the parking lot toward the docks. The crowds noticed it too, and there was a small stir. For a moment, Nora's heart sank. *Not Sloane Goddard,* she thought, *not in a limo.* She was relieved when the car came to a halt and a tall young man tumbled rather awkwardly out of the back, straightened up his skinny frame, and took in the marina through dark Ray-Bans.

Nora found herself staring at him. He was not particularly handsome, but there was something striking in the high cheekbones, aquiline nose, and especially in the bemused, confident way he surveyed the scene before him. His soft brown hair was wild, sticking out every which way, as if he had just climbed out of bed. *Who in the world can he be?* she wondered.

Several teenagers in the crowd instinctively moved toward him, and soon a crowd gathered. Nora could see the man was talking animatedly.

Black followed her stare. "Wonder who that guy is?" he asked.

Tearing her glance away, Nora left the group to gather up their gear and went in search of Ricky Briggs, one of the marina's managers. Her route to the marina headquarters took her past the limo, and she paused at the edge of the crowd, intrigued, glancing again at the man. He was dressed in starchy new jeans, a red bandanna, and expensive alligator cowboy boots. She could barely hear his voice over the hubbub of the crowd, making comments while he waved a paperback book in one hand. As she watched, he scribbled an autograph in it, then handed it to a particularly ripe-looking girl in a string bikini. The small crowd laughed and chattered and clamored for more books.

Nora turned to a woman standing at the fringe of the crowd. "Who is he?"

"Dunno," the woman said, "but he's gotta be famous."

As she was about to walk on, Nora heard, quite distinctly, the words *Nora Kelly*. She stopped.

"It's a confidential project," the man was saying in a nasal voice. "I can't talk about it, but you'll read about it soon enough—"

Nora began pushing through the crowd.

"—in the *New York Times* and in book form—"

She elbowed past a heavyset man in flowered trunks.

"—a fantastic expedition to the farthest corner of—"

"Hey!" Nora cried, bursting through the last of the crowd. The young man looked down at her, surprise and consternation on his face. Then he broke into a smile. "You must be—"

She grabbed his hand and began pulling him through the crowd.

"My luggage—" he said.

"Just shut the hell up," she retorted, dragging him through the stragglers at the edge of the crowd, who parted before her fury.

"Just hold on a minute—" the man began.

Nora continued to pull him across the tarmac toward the horse trailers, leaving the perplexed crowd behind to disperse.

"I'm Bill Smithback," the man said, trying to extend his hand as he skipped alongside of her.

"I know who you are. Just what the hell do you mean, making a spectacle of yourself?"

"A little advance publicity never hurt—"

"Publicity!" Nora cried. She stopped at the horse trailer and faced him, breathing hard.

"Did I do something wrong?" Smithback said, looking innocent, and holding a book up to his chest like a shield.

"Wrong? You arrive here in a limo, like some kind of movie star—"

"I got it cheap at the airport. And besides, it's hot as hell out here: limos have excellent air conditioning—"

"This expedition," Nora interrupted, "is supposed to be *confidential.*"

"But I didn't reveal anything," he protested. "I just signed a few books."

Nora felt herself beginning to boil over. "You may not have told them where Quivira is, but you sure as hell alerted them that something's going on. I wanted to get in and out of here as quietly as possible."

"I *am* here to write a book, after all, and—"

"One more stunt like that and there won't be a book."

Smithback fell silent.

Suddenly Black appeared out of nowhere with an ingratiating smile, hand extended. "Delighted to meet you, Mr. Smithback," he said. "Aaron Black. I'm looking forward to working with you."

Smithback shook the proffered hand.

Nora watched with irritation. She was seeing a side of Black that wasn't obvious from the SAA meetings. She turned to Smithback. "Go tell your *chauffeur* to bring your stuff and put it with the rest. And keep a low profile, okay?"

"He's not exactly my chauffeur—"

"Do you *understand?*"

"Hey, does that hole in your head have an off switch?" Smithback asked. "Because it's getting a little strident for my tender ears."

She glared at him.

"Okay! Okay. I understand."

Nora watched as he went shambling off toward the limousine, head drooping in mock embarrassment. Soon he was back, carrying a large duffel. He slung it on the pile and turned to Nora with a grin, bemused composure regained. "This place is perfect," he said, glancing around. "Central Station."

Nora looked at him.

"You know," he explained, "Central Station. That squalid little spot in *Heart of Darkness*. The last outpost of civilization where people stopped before heading off into the African interior."

Nora shook her head and walked toward a nearby complex of stuccoed buildings overlooking the water. She found Ricky Briggs ensconced in a messy office, a short, overweight man yelling into a telephone. "Goddamned Texican assholes," he said, slamming the phone into its cradle as Nora entered. He looked up, his gaze traveling slowly up and down her body. Nora felt herself bristling. "Well, now, what can I do for you, missy?" he asked in a different tone, leaning back in the chair.

"I'm Nora Kelly, from the Santa Fe Archaeological Institute," she said coldly. "You were supposed to have a barge here ready for us."

"Oh, yeah," he said, the smile vanishing. Picking up the phone again, he punched in a number. "They're here, the group with the horses. Bring the barge around." He replaced the phone, then turned and without another word charged for the door. As she scrambled to follow, she realized she was showing a little more bitchiness than was good for a leader of an expedition. She wondered what it was about Smithback that had suddenly made her flare up like that.

Nora followed Briggs around the side of the complex and down the blacktop to a long floating dock. Planting himself at the edge of the dock, Briggs began yelling at the nearby boaters to clear away their craft. Then he swivelled toward Nora. "Turn the horse trailers around and back 'em down to the water. Unload the rest of your gear and line it up on the dock."

After Nora gave the orders, Swire came around and jerked his head in the direction of Smithback. "Who's the mail-order cowboy?" he asked.

"He's our journalist," said Nora.

Swire fingered his mustache thoughtfully. "Journalist?"

"It was Goddard's idea," said Nora. "He thinks we need

someone along to write up the discovery." She stifled the comment that was about to come; it would do no good to badmouth either Goddard or Smithback. It puzzled her that Goddard, who had chosen so well with the rest of the expedition personnel, had picked someone like Smithback. She watched him hefting gear, his lean arms rippling with the effort, and felt a fresh stab of irritation. *I go to all this trouble to keep things quiet,* she thought, *and then this smug jerk comes along.*

As Nora returned to the ramp to help guide the trailers, a great barge hove into view, davits streaked with dirt, aluminum pontoons stoved and dented in countless places. LANDLOCKED LAURA was stenciled across the tiny pilothouse in rough black letters. The barge eased around a bend in the harbor, its engines churning in reverse as it approached the cement apron.

It took a half hour to load the trailers. Roscoe Swire had handled the horses with great skill, keeping them calm in spite of the chaos and noise. Bonarotti, the cook, was loading the last of his equipment, refusing to let anyone else lend a hand. Holroyd was checking the seals on the drysacks that held the electronics gear. Black was leaning against a davit, tugging at his collar and looking overheated.

Nora looked down at her watch. Sloane Goddard had still not shown up. They had to make the sixty-mile trip to the trailhead by nightfall: offloading the horses after dark would be too complicated and dangerous.

She jumped aboard and entered the tiny pilothouse. The barge's captain was fiddling with a sonar array. He looked like he might have just stepped off a porch in Appalachia: long white beard, dirty porkpie hat, and farmer's overalls. WILLARD HICKS was sewn in white letters on his vest pocket.

The man looked over at her and removed a corncob pipe from his mouth. "We need to shake a leg," he said. "We don't want to piss him off any more than he is already." He grinned and nodded out the window toward Briggs, who was already bawling to them, *Move out, for chrissakes, move out!*

Nora looked up the ramp toward the parking lot, shimmering in the heat. "Get ready to shove off, then," she said. "I'll give the word."

The expedition was gathering forward of the pilothouse, where some grimy lawn chairs had been arranged around an aluminum coffee table. A dilapidated gas grill stood nearby, coated in elderly grease.

She looked around at the people she would be spending the next several weeks with: the expedition to discover Quivira. Despite impressive credentials, they were a pretty diverse bunch. Enrique Aragon, his dark face lowering with some emotion he seemed unwilling to share; Peter Holroyd, with his Roman nose, small eyes, and oversized mouth, smudges of dirt decorating his workshirt; Smithback, good humor now fully recovered, showing a copy of his book to Black, who was listening dutifully; Luigi Bonarotti, perched on his gear, smoking a Dunhill, as relaxed as if he were sitting in a café on the Boulevard St. Michel; Roscoe Swire, standing by the horse trailers, murmuring soothing words to the nervous horses. *And what about me?* she thought: a bronze-haired woman in ancient jeans and torn shirt. Not exactly a figure of command. *What have I gotten myself into?* She had another momentary stab of uncertainty.

Aaron Black left Smithback and came over, scowling as he looked around. "This tub is god-awful," he winced.

"What were you expecting?" Aragon asked in a dry, uninflected voice. "The *Ile de France*?"

Bonarotti removed a small flask from his carefully pressed khaki jacket, unscrewed the glass top, and poured two fingers into it. Then he added water from a canteen and swirled the yellowish mixture. He rehung the canteen on a davit bolt and offered the glass around.

"What is that?" Black asked.

"Pernod," came the reply. "Lovely for a hot day."

"I don't drink," said Black.

"I do," Smithback said. "Hand it on over."

Nora glanced back at Willard Hicks, who tapped an imaginary watch on his wrist. She nodded in understanding and slipped the mooring lines from the dock. There was an answering roar from the diesels, and the boat began backing away from the ramp with a hideous scraping sound.

Holroyd glanced around. "What about Dr. Goddard?"

"We can't wait around here any longer," Nora said. She felt a strange sense of relief: maybe she wasn't going to have to deal with this mysterious daughter, after all. Let Sloane Goddard come after them, if she wanted.

The team looked at one another in surprise as the barge began a slow turn, the water boiling out from the stern. Hicks gave a short blast on the airhorn.

"You've got to be kidding!" Black cried. "You aren't really leaving without her?"

Nora looked steadily back at the sweaty, incredulous face. "Oh, yes," she said. "I'm really leaving without her."

14

THREE HOURS LATER, THE *LANDLOCKED Laura* had left the chaos of Wahweap Marina fifty miles behind. The wide prow of the barge cut easily through the turquoise surface of Lake Powell, engines throbbing slightly, the water hissing along the pontoons. Gradually, the powerboats, the shrieking jetskis, the garish houseboats had all dropped away. The expedition had entered into a great mystical world of stone, and a cathedral silence closed around them. Now they were alone on the green expanse of lake, walled in by thousand-foot bluffs and slickrock desert. The sun hung low over the Grand Bench, with Neanderthal Cove appearing on the right, and the distant opening of Last Chance Bay to the left.

Thirty minutes before, Luigi Bonarotti had served a meal of cognac-braised, applewood-smoked quail with grapefruit and wilted arugula leaves. This remarkable accomplishment, achieved somehow on the shabby gas grill, had silenced even Black's undertone of complaints. They had dined around the aluminum table, toasting the meal with a crisp Orvieto. Now the group was arranged around the barge in lethargic contemplation of the meal, awaiting landfall at the trailhead.

Smithback, who had dined very well and consumed an alarming quantity of wine, was sitting with Black. Before dinner, the writer had made some cracks about camp cooking and varmint stew, but the arrival of the meal changed his tone to one approaching veneration.

"Didn't you also write that book on the museum murders in New York City?" Black was asking. Smithback's face broke into an immensely gratified smile.

"And that subway massacre a few years back?"

Smithback reached for an imaginary hat and doffed it with a grandiose flourish.

Black scratched his chin. "Don't get me wrong, I think it's great," he said. "It's just that . . . well, I've always understood that the Institute was a low-profile entity."

"Well, the fact is I'm no longer Bill Smithback, terror of the tabloids," Smithback replied. "I work for the buttoned-down, respectable *New York Times* now, occupying the position formerly held by a certain Bryce Harriman. Poor Bryce. He covered the subway massacre, too. Such a pity that my masterpiece of investigative reportage was his lost opportunity." He turned and grinned at Nora. "You see, I'm a paragon of journalistic respectability that even a place as stuffy as your Institute can't object to."

Nora caught herself as she was about to smile. There was nothing amusing in the journalist's braggadocio, even if it was tempered with a touch of self-deprecation. She looked away with a stab of irritation, wondering again at Goddard's idea of bringing a journalist along. She looked toward Holroyd, who was sitting on the metal floor of the barge, elbows on his knees, reading what to Nora's mind was a real book: a battered paperback copy of *Coronado and the City of Gold*. As she watched him, Holroyd looked up and smiled.

Aragon was standing at the bowrail, and Roscoe Swire was again by the horses, wad of tobacco fingered into his cheek, jotting in a battered journal and occasionally murmuring to the animals. Bonarotti was quietly smoking a postprandial cigarette, one leg thrown over the other, head tilted back, enjoying the air. Nora was surprised and grateful for the cook's efforts on this first day of the journey. *Nothing like a good meal to bring people together,* she thought, replaying in her mind the lively meal, the friendly arguments about the origins of the Clovis hunters, and the proper way to excavate a cave sequence. Even Black had relaxed and told an exceedingly foul joke involving a proctologist, a giant sequoia, and tree-ring dating. Only Aragon had remained silent—not aloof, exactly; just remote.

She glanced over at him, standing motionless at the rail, gazing out into the fading light, his eyes hard. Three months on the Gallegos Divide, excavating the burned jacal site, had taught her that the human dynamic in an expedition of this sort was of crucial importance, and she didn't like his resolute silence. Something was not right with him. Casually, she strolled forward until she was standing at the rail beside him. He looked over, then nodded politely.

"Quite a dinner," she said.

"Astonishing," said Aragon, folding his brown hands over the railing. "Signore Bonarotti is to be complimented. What do you suppose is in that curio box of his?"

He was referring to an antique wooden chuckbox with innumerable tiny compartments the cook kept locked and under jealous guard.

"No idea," Nora said.

"I can't imagine how he managed it."

"You watch. It'll be salt pork and hardtack tomorrow."

They laughed together, an easy laugh, and once again Aragon gazed forward, toward the lake and its vast ramparts of stone.

"You've been here before?" Nora asked.

Something flitted across the hollow eyes: the shadow of a strong emotion, quickly concealed. "In a way."

"It's a beautiful lake," Nora went on, uncertain how to engage the man in conversation.

There was a silence. At last, Aragon turned toward her again. "Forgive me if I don't agree."

Nora looked at him more closely.

"Back in the early sixties I was an assistant on an expedition that tried to document sites here in Glen Canyon, before it was drowned by Lake Powell."

Suddenly, Nora understood. "Were there many?"

"We were able to document perhaps thirty-five, and partially excavate twelve, before the water engulfed them. But the estimate of total sites ran to about six thousand. I think my interest in ZST dates from that event. I remember shoveling out—*shoveling* out— a kiva, water lapping just three feet below. That was no way to treat a sacred site, but we had no choice. The water was about to destroy it."

"What's a kiva?" Smithback asked as he strolled over, his new cowboy boots creaking on the rubber deck. "And who were the Anasazi, anyway?"

"A kiva is the circular, sunken structure that was the center of Anasazi religious activity and secret ceremonies," Nora said. "It was usually entered through a hole in the roof. And the Anasazi were the Native Americans who peopled this region a thousand years ago. They built cities, shrines, irrigation systems, signaling stations. And then, around A.D. 1150, their civilization suddenly vanished."

There was a silence. Black joined the group. "Were these sites you worked on important?" he asked, working a toothpick between two molars.

Aragon looked up. "Are there any unimportant sites?"

"Of course," Black sniffed. "Some sites have more to say than others. A few poor outcast Anasazi, scrabbling out a living in a cave for ten years, don't leave us as much information as, say, a thousand people living in a cliff dwelling for two centuries."

Aragon looked coolly at Black. "There's enough information in a single Anasazi pot to occupy a researcher for his entire career. Perhaps it's not a matter of unimportant sites, but unimportant archaeologists."

Black's face darkened.

"What sites did you work on?" Nora asked quickly.

Aragon nodded toward an open reach of water to starboard. "About a mile over there, maybe four hundred feet down, is the Music Temple."

"The Music Temple?" Smithback echoed.

"A great hollow in the canyon wall, where the winds and the waters of the Colorado River combined to make haunting, unearthly sounds. John Wesley Powell discovered and named it. We excavated the floor and found a rare Archaic site, along with many others in the vicinity." He pointed in another direction. "And over there was a site called the Wishing Well, a Pueblo III cliff dwelling of eight rooms, built around an unusually deep kiva. A small site, trivial, of no *importance*." He glanced pointedly at Black. "In that site, the Anasazi had buried with loving care two small girls, wrapped in woven textiles, with necklaces of flowers and seashells. But by then there was no time left. We couldn't save the burials; the water was already rising. Now the water has dissolved the burials, the adobe masonry that held the stones of the city in place, destroyed all the delicate artifacts."

Black snorted and shook his head. "Hand me a tissue, somebody."

The boat moved past the Grand Bench. Nora could see the dark prow of the Kaiparowits Plateau rising far behind it, wild, inaccessible, tinged dusky rose by the setting sun. As if in response, the boat began to turn, heading for a narrow opening in the sandstone walls: the foot of Serpentine Canyon.

Once the boat was inside the narrow confines of the canyon, the water turned a deeper green. The sheer walls plunged straight down, so perfectly reflected it was hard to tell where stone stopped and water began. The captain had told Nora that almost nobody came up into that canyon: there were no camping sites or beaches, and the walls were so high and sheer that hiking was impossible.

Holroyd stretched. "I've been reading about Quivira," he said, indicating the book. "It's an amazing story. Listen to this:

The Cicuye Indians brought forward a slave to show the General, who they had captured in a distant land. The General questioned the slave through interpreters. The slave told him about a distant city, called Quivira. It is a holy city, he said, where the rain priests live, who guard the records of their history from the beginning of time. He said it was a city of great wealth. Common table service was of the purest smoothed gold, and the pitchers, dishes and bowls were also of gold, refined, polished and decorated. He said they despised all other materials."

"Aaah," Smithback said, rubbing his hands with an exaggerated air. "I like that: *they despised all other materials.* Gold. Such a pleasant word, don't you think?"

"There isn't a shred of evidence of any Anasazi Indians having gold," Nora said.

"Dinner plates made of gold?" Smithback said. "Excuse me, Madame Chairman, but that sounds pretty specific to me."

"Then prepare to be disappointed," said Nora. "The Indians were only telling Coronado what they knew he wanted to hear in order to keep him moving on."

"But listen," Holroyd said, "it goes on: 'The slave warned the General not to approach the city. The Rain and Sun Priests of Xochitl guard the city, he said, and call down the God of the Dust Devil on those who approach without their leave, and thereby destroy them.'"

"D-d-d-destroy them?" Smithback leered.

Nora shrugged. "Typical in these old reports. A hard kernel of truth at the center, embellished to increase dramatic effect."

Hicks stepped out of the cabin, his stringy form framed in the battered pilothouse light. "Sonar's giving me shoaling water here," he said. "The canyon bottom's coming up. We'll probably be hitting the end of the lake 'round another bend or two."

Now everyone came to the front rail, peering eagerly into the gloom. A searchlight snapped on above the pilothouse, illuminating the water ahead of them. It had changed color again to a dirty chocolate. The barge nosed its way past battered tree limbs, around dark curtains of stone that rose hundreds of feet.

They passed another sharp bend and dismay suddenly dragged at Nora's heart. Blocking the far end of the canyon was a huge mass of floating debris: scarred tree trunks, branches, and stinking mats of rotting pine needles. Some of the tree trunks were five feet in diameter, horribly gouged and ripped as if by supernatural force. Beyond the tangle, Nora could make out the end of the lake: a wedge of sand at the mouth of a creek, deep crimson in the gloom.

Hicks threw the engine into neutral and came out of the pilothouse, puffing silently and staring down the beam of the searchlight.

"Where did all those huge trees come from?" Nora asked. "I haven't seen a tree since we left Page."

"Flash floods," said Hicks, chewing on his corncob. "All that stuff gets washed down from the mountains, hundreds of miles sometimes. When the wall of water hits the lake, it just dumps everything here." He shook his head. "Never seen such a snarl."

"Can you get through it?"

"Nope," said Hicks. "Tear my propellers right up."

Shit. "How deep is the water?"

"Sonar says eight feet, with holes and channels down to fifteen." He gave her a curious look. "Might be a good time to think about turning around," he murmured.

Nora glanced at his placid face. "Now why would we want to do that?"

Hicks shrugged. "It ain't no business of mine, but I wouldn't head into that backcountry for all the money in the world."

"Thanks for the advice," Nora said. "You have a life raft, right?"

"Yup, inflatable. You sure can't load horses into it."

The expedition had gathered around, listening. Nora

heard Black mutter something about knowing horses were a bad idea.

"We'll swim the horses in," Nora said. "Then we'll bring the gear on the raft."

"Now, hold on—" began Swire.

Nora turned to him. "All we need is a good horse to lead and the others will follow. Roscoe, I'll bet you've got a good swimmer in that bunch."

"Sure, Mestizo, but—"

"Good. You swim him in yourself, and we'll push the others in afterward. They can swim through one of those gaps between the logs."

Swire stared at the blockage before them, a crazy dark tangle in the ghostly illumination of the searchlight. "Those gaps are pretty small. A horse could get snagged on brush, or maybe gut himself on an underwater limb."

"Do you have another idea?"

Swire looked out over the water. "Nope," he said. "Guess I don't."

Hicks opened a large deck locker and, with the help of Holroyd, pulled a heavy, shapeless rubber mass out of its depths. Swire led a large horse out of one of the trailers, then threw a saddle over his back. Nora noticed he did not put on a halter or bridle. Aragon and Bonarotti began to move the gear toward the raft, readying it for transport. Black was standing near the trailers, watching the proceedings with a doubtful expression. Swire handed him a quirt.

"What's this for?" Black asked, holding it at arm's length.

"I'm going to swim this horse in to shore first," Swire replied. "Nora will lead the rest out one by one. Your job is to make them jump into the water after me."

"Oh, really? And just how do I do that?"

"You quirt 'em."

"Quirt them?"

"Whip their asses. Don't let them stop to think."

"That's insane. I'll be kicked."

"None of these horses are kickers, but be ready to dodge

anyway. And make a sound like this." Swire made a loud, unpleasant kissing sound with his lips.

"Maybe flowers and a box of chocolates would be easier," Smithback cracked.

"I don't know anything about horses," Black protested.

" 'Course you don't. But it don't take a professional waddy to whack a horse's ass."

"Won't it hurt the horses?"

"It'll sting some," Swire replied. "But we don't got all night to sweet-talk 'em."

Black continued to stare at the quirt with a frown. Watching him, Nora wasn't sure what the scientist was more upset by: quirting the horses or being ordered about by a cowboy.

Swire vaulted into the saddle. "Keep 'em coming one at a time, but let the water clear so they ain't jumping on each other's backs."

He turned and shoved the spurs to his horse. The animal obeyed instantly and leaped into the water, momentarily disappearing and then surfacing again, blowing hard, nose up to the air. Expertly dismounting in midair, Swire had landed beside the horse, hand on the saddlehorn. Now he began urging the animal forward in a low voice.

The rest of the horses pranced restlessly in the trailers, snorting through dilated nostrils and rolling their eyes with apprehension.

"Let's go," Nora said, easing the second horse forward. It stepped toward the edge of the barge, then balked. "Quirt him!" she cried to Black. To her relief, Black stepped forward with a determined look and smacked the horse across the rump. The horse paused, then leaped, landing with another roar of water and struggling after Swire's horse.

Smithback was watching the proceedings with amusement. "Nicely done!" he cried. "Come on, Aaron, don't tell me that's the first time you've handled a whip. I'm sure I've seen you hanging around the West Village leather bars."

"Smithback, go help Holroyd with the raft," Nora snapped.

"Yassuh." Smithback turned away.

One at a time, they coaxed the rest of the horses into the water until they formed a ragged, struggling line, nose to tail, threading their way through a gap in the tangle of trees and heading for the beach. Nora locked down the trailers, then turned to watch Swire clamber out of the water at the far end, bedraggled and dripping in the yellow glow of the searchlight. Securing his horse, he waded back into the water with yips and shouts, herding the rest onto dry land. Soon he had gathered them into a disconsolate mass and pushed them upcanyon, clearing the landing site.

Nora watched a moment longer, then turned to Black. "That was very well done, Aaron."

The geochronologist blushed with pride.

Nora looked at the rest of the group. "Let's get this gear offloaded. Captain, many thanks for your help. We'll make sure the raft is well hidden while we're upcanyon. See you in a couple of weeks."

"Lest I see you first," Hicks replied dryly as he disappeared into the pilothouse.

Around eleven, in the intense silence of the desert night, Nora took a last tour of the somnolent camp, then threw her bedroll some distance from the others, carefully sculpting the sand underneath for her hips and shoulders. To minimize the panicky, last-minute adjustments that always seemed to accompany packtrips, she had seen to it that the gear was already weighed and stowed in the panniers, ready for loading in the morning. The horses were hobbled some distance away, contentedly chewing the last of their alfalfa. The rest of the group was either asleep in their tents or quickly nodding off in their sleeping bags by the dying light of the fire. And the *Landlocked Laura* was well on her way back to the marina. The expedition had begun in earnest.

She eased into the bedroll, breathing easily. So far, so good. Black was a pain in the ass, but his expertise outweighed his querulous personality. Smithback was an annoying surprise, but with that strong back and arms he'd make a good digger, and she'd make sure he was well occupied with the shovel, whether he liked it or not. Before going to bed, he had insisted on pressing a copy of his book into her hands; she'd dumped it unceremoniously into a duffel.

On the other hand, Peter Holroyd was proving to be a real trouper. She'd caught him giving her several furtive glances during the ride up Lake Powell, and Nora wondered if he wasn't a little bit infatuated. Perhaps she'd inadvertently played on that in persuading him to steal the data from JPL. She felt a momentary twinge of guilt. But then again, she'd kept her promise. He was on the expedition. *The boy's probably mistaking gratitude for puppy love,* she thought, moving on. Bonarotti was one of those unflappable people who never seemed put out by anything, as well as being a fabulous camp cook. And Aragon would probably open up once they got away from his hated Lake Powell.

She stretched out comfortably. It was shaping up to be a good group. Best of all, there was no Sloane Goddard to deal with. Among Black, Aragon, and herself, there was more than enough expertise to go around. Dr. Goddard had nothing but his own daughter's tardiness to blame.

Starlight glowed faintly from the distant bluffs and turrets of Navajo sandstone. A chill had crept into the air: in the high desert, night came on fast and sure. She heard a low murmuring, the drifting smell of Bonarotti's cigarette. Into the silence the faint calls of the canyon wrens echoed back and forth, tinkling like bells, mingling with the faint lapping of water on the shoreline just below the camp. Already they were many miles from the nearest outpost of humanity. And the distant, hidden canyon they were headed to was much farther still.

At the thought of Quivira, Nora felt the weight of responsibility return again. There was a potential for failure here, too, she knew: a tremendous potential. They might not find the city. The expedition might break up over personality conflicts. Worst of all, her father's Quivira might turn out to be some ordinary five-room cliff dwelling. That was what worried her the most. Goddard might forgive her for leaving without his daughter. But despite all the fine words, he and the Institute would not forgive her if she returned with a superb site report on a tiny Pueblo III cliff dwelling. And God only knew what kind of withering article Smithback might write if he felt his precious time had been wasted.

There was the distant yipping of a coyote, and she wrapped the bedroll more tightly around her. Unbidden, her thoughts returned to Santa Fe, to that night in the deserted ranch house. She'd been very careful to keep the maps and radar images under her control at all times. She'd impressed everyone with the need for discretion, citing pothunters and looters as her concern. And then into the midst of her careful plans blundered Smithback. . . .

Still, she knew it was unlikely that Smithback's comments would filter back to Santa Fe, and beyond the mention of her name nothing he'd said was specific enough to give away the purpose of the expedition. And most likely, the bizarre figures who had attacked her had given up by now. Where she was going, it would take a determined, even desperate person to follow, someone who knew the craft of desert travel far better than even Swire did. Certainly no boats had followed them up the lake. The fear and annoyance subsided, and in their absence came sleep, and dreams of dusty ruins, and nodding columns of sunlight cutting through the murk of an ancient cave, and two dead children draped in flowers.

15

TERESA GONZALES SAT UP SUDDENLY, LIS-
tening in the dark. Teddy Bear, her giant Rhodesian Ridge-
back, who generally slept outside in the summer, was whining
at the back door. Ridgebacks had been bred to hunt and kill
lions in Africa. He was a very gentle dog, but he was also extremely protective. She had never heard him whine before.
He was just back from the vet's, where he'd been languishing
for two weeks, recovering from a nasty infection; maybe the
poor thing was still traumatized.

She got out of bed and went through the dark house to the
door. The dog came slinking in, whimpering, its tail clamped
between its legs.

"Teddy," she whispered, "what's wrong? You all right?"

The dog licked her hand and retreated across the kitchen,
sliding his huge bulk under the kitchen table. Teresa looked
out the kitchen door, down into the sea of darkness toward
the old Las Cabrillas ranch house. There were no lights in the
draw, and without a moon Teresa couldn't see the outlines of
the abandoned house. Something out there had scared him
half to death. She listened, and thought she heard a faint
sound of breaking glass and the distant howl of an animal.
Definitely too low-pitched and hoarse to be a coyote, but it
didn't sound like any dog Teresa had heard, either. It

sounded like a wolf, if you got right down to it. But Teddy would never have retreated like that from a lone wolf, or even a cougar. Perhaps it was a whole pack of wolves.

The muttered low howl was answered by another, a little closer. The dog whined again, louder, and pressed itself back into the darkness under the table. There was a dribbling sound, and Teresa saw he was urinating in his fright.

She paused, hand on the doorframe. Until two years ago, there had been no wolves in New Mexico. Then the Game and Fish Department introduced some into the Pecos Wilderness. *Guess a few have wandered down from the mountains,* she thought.

Teresa went back to her room, peeled off her nightgown, slid on her jeans, shirt, and boots, then walked across the room and opened the gun locker. The weapons gleamed dully against the darkness. She reached for her current favorite, a Winchester Defender, with its 18½-inch barrel and extended magazine tube. It was a good, light gun, billed as a defensive weapon with unparalleled stopping power. Just another way of saying it was very good at killing people. Or wolves, for that matter.

She slid in a magazine: eight Federal ammo casings of 12-gauge double-ought lead buck. This wasn't the first time since the attack on Nora that she'd heard sounds from the Kelly ranch. And once, driving back from Santa Fe, she'd seen a low, dark shape skulking around the old mailbox rack. Had to be wolves; nothing else made sense. They'd confronted Nora in the farmhouse that night. Must have rattled her so badly she thought she heard them speak. Teresa shook her head. Not like Nora to wig out like that.

Wolves that didn't fear humans could be dangerous, and Teresa didn't want to meet up with them without a gun. Better to deal with the problem directly. If Game and Fish wanted to make a stink, let them. She had a ranch to run.

She tucked the shotgun under her arm, shoved a flashlight into her back pocket, and crept back to the kitchen door, careful not to turn on any lights. She heard Teddy whining and snuffling as she left, but he made no move to follow her.

She stepped onto the back porch and eased the door shut behind her. There was a faint creaking of floorboards as she moved down the steps. Then she angled toward the well-house and the trail that began just beyond. Teresa was a large, heavy-boned woman, but she had the natural stealthy movements of a feline. At the wellhouse she inhaled deeply, steadied the gun, then eased down the trail in the inky blackness. She had descended the trail countless times to play with Nora when they were children, and her feet remembered the way.

Soon she was on the flat. The Kelly ranch house stood across the draw, just on the side of the rise, its low roof outlined against the night. In the faintest starlight, she could see the front door was open.

She waited for what seemed a long time, listening, but there was only the susurrus of wind in the piñon trees. The shotgun felt cold and reassuring in her hands.

She sampled the breeze: she was downwind of the house, which meant the wolves couldn't scent her. There was a strange odor in the air that reminded her of morning glories, but nothing else. Perhaps the animals had heard her and run off. Or perhaps they were still in the house.

She snapped off the safety and gripped the flashlight tight against the Winchester's barrel. Then she moved toward the front of the house. The building was striped in wavy starlight, looking strangely like a drowned, abandoned temple. She could use the light to freeze any animal that came into view, giving her a stationary target.

And then Teresa heard something, at the edge of audibility, that was not a wolf. She stopped to listen. It was a low, monotonous chanting drone, a hoarse, guttural cadence, dry and faint as parched leaves.

It came from inside the house.

Teresa licked her dry lips and took a deep breath. She stepped onto the front porch and waited for a minute, then two. As quietly as she could, she took two more steps forward, covered the inside of the house with her gun, and switched on the flashlight.

The house was as she remembered it from the previous week: a hurricane of ruin, dust, and old decay. The smell of flowers was stronger here. Quickly, she probed the corners and doorways with the light, seeing nothing. Through a broken rectangle of window, the night wind gently swelled the stained curtains. The chanting was louder now, and it seemed to be coming from upstairs.

She crept to the bottom of the stairs, switching off the light. These were obviously not animals. Perhaps Nora had been right after all: she'd been attacked by men wearing masks, rapists perhaps. She remembered how uncharacteristically frightened Teddy Bear had been. Perhaps it would be better for her to creep quietly home and telephone the cops.

But no—by the time the cops arrived, with their flashing lights and clomping boots, these bastards would have slipped away into the shadows. And Teresa would be left with the nagging worry about when they might show up again. Perhaps they'd try her house next time. Or perhaps they'd catch her out away from home, when she was unarmed . . .

Her grip tightened on the shotgun. The time to act was now, while she could. Her father had taught her how to hunt; she was an expert stalker. She had a weapon that she knew how to use. And she had the advantage of surprise. With infinite caution, she began to ascend the stairs. She moved instinctively, shifting her weight from foot to foot with extreme deliberation.

She paused again at the top of the stairs. The starlight filtering through the windows below was too faint here to make out anything but the vaguest of shapes, but her ears told her that the sound was coming from Nora's old room. She took two steps, then paused to take several breaths, check her control. Whoever it was, she was taking no chances.

She braced herself, gun in both hands, the flashlight firm against the barrel. Then with one smooth, swift motion she stepped forward, kicked the door fully open, swivelled the gun into position, and snapped on the flashlight.

It took a moment for her brain to register what her eyes saw. Two figures, covered head to toe in heavy, dank pelts, crouched in the center of the room. Their red eyes turned toward the light, unblinking, feral. Between them rested a human skull, its top missing. Inside the skull was a small collection of objects—a doll's head, some hair, a girl's barrette—*Nora's old things,* Teresa realized, frozen with horror.

Suddenly one of the forms leaped up, moving faster than she thought possible. It passed out of the beam of her flashlight as she jerked the trigger. The shotgun bucked in her hands and the deafening roar seemed to shake the house itself.

She blinked, straining to see through the dust and smoke. There was nothing but a ragged, smoking hole in the bedroom wall. Both figures had now vanished.

She pumped another round into the chamber and pivoted, covering the room with the yellow pool of light. Her breath rasped in and out as the noise fell away and the dust settled back into the gloom. People didn't move like that. Here, by herself, behind the flashlight, she felt suddenly, terribly vulnerable. She had a momentary impulse to turn off the light, find shelter in the darkness. But she sensed that darkness alone would not protect her from these creatures.

Teresa had grown up a brave girl, big and strong for her age. She'd had no older brothers to keep her in line, and she had been able to beat up anybody in her class, boy or girl. Now—standing in the darkened doorway, breathing hard, eyes alert to any movement—Teresa felt an unfamiliar sense of panic threaten to envelope her.

She tore her gaze from the dark emptiness of the room, pivoted again, and scanned the hallway. The house was utterly silent except for her breathing. Other darkened bedroom doors, black on black, opened to the wrecked hall.

She had to get downstairs, she realized. There, she could switch off the light, let the starlight aid her. She glanced toward the stairs, imprinting their location in her mind. Then she switched off the light and darted forward.

A black shape lunged diagonally out from a far bedroom. With an involuntary cry, Teresa turned and jerked the trigger. Eyes blinded by the muzzle flare, she stumbled backward and half rolled, half fell down the stairs, shotgun clattering away into the darkness. She scrambled to her knees at the bottom step, a sharp pain spiking through one ankle.

At the top of the stairs a large shape crouched, staring silently down at her. Teresa whirled, searching in the faint starlight for her weapon. But instead of the shotgun, her gaze fell upon the second shape, framed in the kitchen doorway, coming toward her with a slow confidence that was somehow terrible.

Teresa stared at the figure for a moment, paralyzed with terror. Then she turned and limped toward the door, scattering glass, a low whimper escaping her throat.

16

THE NEXT MORNING, NORA AWAKENED TO A marvelous smell. She stretched luxuriously, still wrapped within a wonderful, receding dream. Then, hearing the clatter of tins and the murmur of conversation, she opened her eyes and jumped out of her bedroll. It was six thirty, and the camp had already gathered around a pot of coffee hanging over an open fire. Only Swire and Black were missing. Bonarotti was busy at the grill, the delicious aroma wafting from his sizzling fry pan.

She quickly stowed her gear and washed up, embarrassed at oversleeping on the first morning. Up the canyon she caught a glimpse of Swire, brushing down the horses and checking their feet.

"Madame Chairman!" Smithback called out good-humoredly. "Come on over and have a sip of this ebony nectar. I swear it's even better than the espresso at Café Reggio."

Nora joined the group and gratefully accepted a tin cup from Holroyd. As she sipped, Black emerged from a tent, looking frowsy and bedraggled. Wordlessly, he stumbled over and helped himself to coffee, then squatted on a nearby rock, hunched over his tin.

"It's cold," he muttered. "I barely slept a wink. Normally,

on the digs I investigate, they at least have a couple of RVs parked nearby." He looked around at the surrounding cliffs.

"Oh, you slept fine," Smithback said. "I've never heard such a cacophony of snores." He turned to Nora. "How about if we institute co-op camping for the rest of the trip? I've heard all about the 'tent-creeping' that goes on around expeditions like this." He cackled salaciously. "Remember, happiness is a double mummy bag."

"If you want to sleep with the opposite sex, I'll have Swire put you out with the mares," Nora replied.

Black barked a laugh.

"Very funny." Coffee in hand, Smithback settled on a fallen log, next to Black. "Aragon tells me that you're an expert on artifact dating. But what did he mean when he said you were a Dumpster diver?"

"Oh, he said that, did he?" Black gave the older man an angry glare.

Aragon waved his hand. "It's a technical term."

"I'm a stratigrapher," Black said. "Often, midden heaps provide the best information at a site."

"Midden heaps?"

"Trash piles," said Black, his lips compressing. "Ancient garbage dumps. Usually the most interesting part of a ruin."

"Coprolite expert, too," said Aragon, nodding toward Black.

"Coprolite?" Smithback thought for a moment. "Isn't that fossilized shit, or something?"

"Yes, yes," Black said with irritation. "But we work with anything to do with dating. Human hair, pollen, charcoal, bone, seeds, you name it. Feces just happens to be especially informative. It shows what people were eating, what kind of parasites they had—"

"Feces," said Smithback. "I'm getting the picture."

"Dr. Black is the country's leading geochronologist," Nora said quickly.

But Smithback was shaking his head. "And what a business

117

to be in," he chortled. "Coprolites. Oh, God. There must be a lot of openings in your field."

Before Black could answer, Bonarotti announced breakfast was ready. He was dressed, as the day before, in a neatly ironed jacket and pressed khaki trousers. Nora, grateful for the interruption, wondered how he could have kept so prim while everyone else was already verging into grubbiness. The wonderful aroma stanched further curiosity, and she quickly fell in line behind the rest. Bonarotti slid a generous slice of perfectly cooked omelette onto her plate. She took a seat and dug in hungrily. Perhaps it was the desert air, but she'd never tasted eggs half as delicious.

"Heaven," Smithback mumbled, mouth full.

"It has a slightly unusual flavor, almost musky," Holroyd said, looking at the forkful in front of him. "I've never tasted anything like it before."

"Jimson weed?" Swire asked, only half jokingly.

"I don't taste anything," Black said.

"No, I know what you mean," Smithback said. "It's vaguely familiar." He took another bite, then set his fork down with a clatter. "I know. At Il Mondo Vecchio on Fifty-third Street. I had a veal dish with this same flavor." He looked up. "Black truffles?"

Bonarotti's normally impassive eyes lit up at this, and he stared at Smithback with new respect. "Not quite," he replied. The cook turned to his curio box, opened one of the countless drawers, and pulled out a dusky-colored lump, about the size of a tennis ball. It was flat along one side where it had been scraped by a knife.

"Angels and ministers of grace defend us," Smithback breathed. "A white truffle. In the middle of the desert."

"Tuber magantum pico," Bonarotti said, placing it carefully back in the drawer.

Smithback shook his head slowly. "You're looking at about a thousand dollars worth of fungus right there. If we don't find that huge stash of Indian gold, we can always raid the Cabinet of Doctor Bonarotti."

"You are welcome to try, my friend," Bonarotti said impassively, pulling open his jacket and patting a monstrous revolver snugged into a holster around his waist.

There was a nervous laugh all around.

As Nora returned to her breakfast, she thought she heard a noise: distant but growing louder. Looking around, she noticed the others heard it, too. The sound echoed around the canyon walls and she realized it was a plane. As she searched the empty blue sky, the noise increased dramatically and a float plane cleared the sandstone canyon rim, early morning sun glinting off its aluminum skin and bulbous pontoons. From upcanyon, the horses eyed it nervously.

"That guy's awfully low," said Holroyd, staring upward.

"He ain't just low," Swire said. "He's landing."

They watched as the plane dipped, its wings waggling an avitational hello. It straightened its line, then touched down, sending up two fins of water in a flurry of spray. The engines revved as the plane coasted toward the tangle of logs. Nora nodded to Holroyd to take the raft out to meet them. Inside the cockpit, she could see the pilot and copilot, checking gauges, making notes on a hanging clipboard. At last the pilot climbed out, waved, and swung down onto one of the pontoons.

Nora heard Smithback whistle softly beside her as the pilot took off a pair of goggles and a leather helmet, giving her short, straight black hair beneath a shake. "Fly me," he said.

"Stow it," she snapped.

The pilot was Sloane Goddard.

Holroyd had reached the side of the plane by now, and Goddard began swinging duffels into the raft from the cargo area behind the plane's seats. Then she slammed the hatch shut, slid down into the raft, and gave the copilot a sign. As Holroyd rowed back through the tangle of debris, the plane turned and began to taxi down the canyon, where it revved its engines and began its takeoff. Nora's eyes moved from the vanishing plane back to the rapidly approaching figure.

Sloane Goddard was sitting in the rear of the raft, talking to Holroyd. She wore a long aviator's leather jacket, jeans, and narrow boots. Her hair was done in a classic short pageboy, almost decadent in its anachronism, that reminded Nora of a Fitzgerald-era flapper from a 1920s fashion magazine. The almond-shaped, brilliant amber eyes and sensuous mouth with its faint, sardonic curve lent an exotic touch to her features. She looked almost Nora's age, perhaps in her mid- to late twenties. Nora realized, quite consciously, that she was looking at one of the most beautiful women she had ever seen.

As the raft ground to a halt on the shore, Sloane leaped nimbly out and came walking briskly into camp. This wasn't the skinny sorority girl Nora had imagined. The woman approaching her had a voluptuous figure, yet whose movements hinted at quick, lithe strength. Her skin was tan and glowed with health, and she brushed back her hair with a gesture that was both innocent and seductive.

Still grinning, the woman walked over to Nora, slipped off her glove, and extended her hand. The skin was soft, the grip was cool and strong.

"Nora Kelly, I presume?" she said, eyes twinkling.

"Yes," Nora exhaled. "And you must be Sloane Goddard. The belated Sloane Goddard."

The grin widened. "Sorry about the drama. I'll tell you about it later. Right now, I'd like to meet the rest of your team."

Nora's alarm at this easy tone of command abated at the words *your team*. "Sure thing," she said. "You've met Peter Holroyd." She indicated the image specialist, who was now bringing up the last of the woman's gear, then turned toward Aragon. "And this is—"

"I'm Aaron Black," Black said out of turn, approaching the woman with an extended hand, his belly sucked in, his back straight.

Sloane's grin widened. "Of course you are. The famous geochronologist. Famous *and* feared. I remember your paper demolishing the Chingadera Cave dating at the last SAA meeting. I felt sorry for that poor archaeologist, Leblanc. I don't think he's been able to hold his head up since."

At this reference to the destruction of another scientist's reputation, Black swelled with visible pleasure.

Sloane turned. "And you must be Enrique Aragon."

Aragon nodded, face still inscrutable.

"I've heard my father speak very highly of your work. Think we'll find many human remains in the city?"

"Unknown," came the reply. "The burial grounds for Chaco Canyon have never been found, despite a century of searching. On the other hand, Mummy Cave yielded hundreds of burials. Either way, I will be analyzing the faunal remains."

"Excellent," Goddard nodded.

Nora looked around, intending to complete the introductions and get underway as quickly as possible. To her surprise, Roscoe Swire had abruptly shuffled off and was busying himself with the horses.

"Roscoe Swire, right?" Sloane called out, following Nora's eyes. "My father's told me all about you, but I don't think we've ever met."

"No reason we should have," came the gruff answer. "I'm just a cowboy trying to keep a bunch of greenhorns from breaking their necks out here in slickrock country."

Sloane let out a husky laugh. "Well, I heard that you've never fallen off a horse."

"Any cowboy tells you that is a liar," said Swire. "My butt and the ground are tolerably well acquainted, thank you."

Sloane's eyes twinkled. "Actually, my father said he could tell you were a real cowboy, because when you showed up for the interview you had real horseshit on your boots."

Swire finally grinned, fishing a gingersnap out of his shirt. "Well, now," he said, "I'll accept that compliment."

Nora waved toward the writer. "And this is Bill Smithback."

Smithback swept an exaggerated bow, cowlick jiggling frantically atop the brown mop of hair.

"The journalist," said Sloane, and Nora thought she heard a brief note of disapproval in Sloane's voice before the dazzling smile returned full-proof. "My father mentioned he'd be contacting you." Before Smithback could reply, Sloane had turned toward Bonarotti. "And thank God you're along, Luigi."

The cook nodded in return, saying nothing.

"How about breakfast?" she asked.

He turned to the grill.

"I'm ravenous," Sloane added, accepting a steaming plate.

"You've met Luigi before?" Nora asked, sitting down beside Sloane.

"Yes, last year, when I was climbing the Cassin Ridge on Denali. He was operating the base camp kitchen for our group. While everybody else on the mountain was eating gorp and logan bread, we dined on duck and venison. I told my father he had to get Luigi for this expedition. He's very, very good."

"I'm very, very expensive," Bonarotti replied.

Sloane tucked into the omelette with gusto. The others had instinctively drawn round again, and Nora wasn't surprised: the younger Goddard was not only beautiful but—sitting there in the wilderness in her leather jacket and faded jeans—she radiated charisma, ironic good humor, and the kind of easy self-confidence that came with money and good breeding. Nora felt a mixture of relief and envy. She wondered what kind of impact this new development would have on her position as leader. *Best to get things established right away,* she thought.

"So," she began. "Care to explain the dramatic entrance?"

Sloane looked at her with her lazy smile. "Sorry about that," she said, putting aside the empty plate and leaning back, coat thrown open to expose a checked cotton shirt. "I was delayed back at Princeton by a failing student. I've never failed anybody, and I didn't want to start now. I worked with him until it became too late to mess with commercial airlines."

"You had us worried back there at the marina."

Sloane sat up. "You didn't get my message?"

"No."

"I left it with somebody named Briggs. Said he'd pass it along."

"Must have slipped his mind," said Nora.

Sloane's grin widened. "It's a busy place. Well, you did the right thing, leaving without me."

Swire brought the horses back down the canyon from their grazing ground, and Nora went over to help with the saddling. To her surprise, Sloane followed behind and joined in, deftly saddling two horses to Swire's three. They tied the horses to some brush as Swire started on the pack animals, throwing on the pads and sawbuck packsaddles, hooking on the panniers, carefully balancing the more awkward equipment, throwing a manty over each load and tying it down. As soon as each horse was packed they passed it to Sloane, who brought it upcanyon. Bonarotti was packing the last of the cooking gear, while Smithback was stretched out comfortably nearby, debating with the cook whether béarnaise or bordelaise was the more noble sauce for medallions of beef.

At last, Nora stood back from the final horse, breathing hard, and looked at her watch. It was just past eleven: still enough time for a decent ride, but short enough to help break in the greenhorns. She glanced at Swire. "Want to give them their first lesson?"

"Now's as good a time as any," he said, hitching up his pants and looking at the group. "Who here knows anything about riding?"

Black began to raise his hand.

"I do," said Smithback instantly.

Swire ranged his eyes across Smithback, his mustache drooping skeptically. "That right?" he said, spitting a stream of tobacco.

"Well, I *did,* anyway," the writer returned. "It's like riding a bike; it'll come back fast."

Nora thought she saw Swire grin beneath his droopy mustache. "Now the first thing is the introductions."

There was a puzzled moment while Swire gazed around the group. "These two horses are mine, the buckskin and the sorrel. Mestizo and Sweetgrass. Since Mr. Smithback here's an *experienced* rider, I'm gonna give him Hurricane Deck to ride and Beetlebum to pack."

There was a sudden guffaw from Black, with an uncomfortable silence from Smithback.

"Any special significance to the names?" Smithback asked with exaggerated nonchalance.

"Nothing in particular," said Swire. "Just a few habits they have, is all. You got a problem with those two fine horses?"

"Oh, no, no way," said Smithback a little weakly, eyeing the big shaggy gray horse and its strawberry roan companion.

"They've only killed a few greenhorns, and they were all New Yorkers. We don't have any New Yorkers here, do we?"

"Certainly not," Smithback said, pulling on the brim of his hat.

"Now for Dr. Black here, I've got Locoweed and Hoosegow. For Nora, I've got my best mare, Fiddlehead. Crow Bait will be your pack horse. Don't let the name fool you: he may be an ugly, coon-footed, ewe-necked, mule-hipped cayuse, but he'll pack two hundred pounds from here to the gates of hell, no problem."

"Let's hope he doesn't have to go that far," Nora replied.

Swire parceled out the horses according to ability and temperament, and soon everyone was holding a pair of horses by the halters and reins. Nora lofted herself into the saddle, Goddard and Aragon following her example. Nora could see from Sloane's lightly balanced seat that she was an expert horsewoman. The rest stood around, looking nervous.

Swire turned to the group. "Well," he said, "what's taking you? Git on up!"

There was some grunting and nervous hopping, but soon everyone was sitting in the saddle, some slouched, some ramrod straight. Aragon was moving his horse around, backing him up, turning him on the forehand, another clearly experienced rider.

"Just don't make me unlearn any bad habits," Smithback said, sitting on Hurricane Deck. "I like to steer with the saddlehorn."

Swire ignored this. "Lesson number one. Hold the reins in

your left hand, and the pack-horse lead rope in your right. It's simple."

"Yeah," said Smithback, "like driving two cars at once."

Holroyd, sitting awkwardly on his horse, let out a nervous bray of laughter, then fell silent abruptly, glancing at Nora.

"How are you doing, Peter?" Nora asked him.

"I prefer motorcycles," he said, shifting uncomfortably.

Swire walked over first to Holroyd, then Black, correcting their postures and grips. "Don't let the lead rope get wedged under your horse's tail," he said to Black, who was letting his rope droop dangerously. "Or you might find your horse with a sudden bellyful of bedsprings."

"Yes, yes, of course," Black said, hastily drawing in the slack.

"Nora plans to ride point," Swire said. "That's up front, for you dudes. I'll ride drag. And Dr. Goddard over there, she'll ride swing." He leaned over and looked at Sloane. "Where'd you learn to ride?"

"Here and there," Sloane smiled.

"Well, I guess you've done a bit of here-ing and there-ing."

"Remind me how to steer," Black said, clutching the reins.

"First, give your horse some slack. Now move your reins back and forth, like this. The horse gets his cue when he feels one rein or the other touch his neck." He looked around. "Any questions?"

There were none. The air had grown sullen in the late morning heat, and the air smelled of sego lilies and cedar.

"Well, then, let's jingle our spurs."

Nora put heels to her horse and rode forward, Holroyd and the rest falling into place behind her.

"You've taken a reading?" she asked Holroyd.

He nodded and smiled at her, patting the laptop computer that peeped, wildly out of place, from one of his weathered saddlebags. Nora took a final look at her map. Then she nudged her horse forward and they headed into the sandstone wilderness.

17

THEY MOVED UP SERPENTINE CANYON SINGLE file, crossing and recrossing the little creek that flowed in its bottom. On both sides of the canyon, windblown sand had piled up against the stone cliffs in drifts, covered with a scattering of grass and desert flowers. Here and there they passed juniper trees, stunted and coiled into fantastic shapes. Elsewhere, blocks of sandstone had come loose from the canyon walls and spilled across its bottom, creating piles of rubble the horses had to pick through with care. Canyon wrens flitted about in the shadows, and swallows darted out from beneath overhanging lips of sandstone, their mud nests like warts on the underside of the rock. A few white clouds drifted past the canyon rims, a quarter mile above their heads. The group followed silently behind Nora, lost in this strange new world.

Nora inhaled deeply. The gentle rocking motion of Fiddlehead felt familiar and comforting. She glanced at the animal. She was a twelve-year-old sorrel, clearly an experienced dude horse, wise and melancholy. As they proceeded, she proved herself sure-footed in the rocks, putting her nose down and picking her way with the utmost attention to self-preservation. While she was far from handsome, she was strong and sensible. Except for Hurricane Deck, Sloane's horse Compañero, and Swire's own two mounts, the horses were similar to

Nora's: not very pretty, but solid ranch stock. She approved of Swire's judgment; her experience growing up had given her a low opinion of expensive, overbred horses who looked great in the show ring but couldn't wait to kill themselves in the mountains. She remembered her father buying and selling horses with his usual flair and bluster, turning away pampered animals, saying *We don't want any of those country-club horses around here, do we, Nora?*

She twisted in the saddle to look back at the other riders trailing behind her, pack horses in tow. While some of the riders, notably Black and Holroyd, looked lumpy and unbalanced, the rest looked competent, particularly Sloane Goddard, who moved up and down the line with ease, checking cinches and giving suggestions.

And Smithback was a surprise. Hurricane Deck was clearly a spirited horse, and there were a few tense moments at first while Smithback's oaths and imprecations filled the air. But Smithback knew enough to show the horse who was boss, and he was now riding confidently. *He may be full of himself,* she thought, *but he looks pretty good on a horse.*

"Where'd you learn to ride?" she called back.

"I spent a couple of years at a prep school in Arizona," the writer answered. "I was a sickly, whining brat of a kid, and my parents thought it would make a man of me. I arrived late the first term, and all the horses were taken except this one big old guy named Turpin. He'd chewed on barbed wire at some point and torn his tongue, and it was always hanging out, this long pink disgusting thing. So nobody wanted him. But Turpin was the fastest horse at the school. We'd race down the dry creekbeds or bush-bend through the desert, and Turpin always won." He shook his head at the memory, chuckling.

Suddenly, the smile on his face was replaced with a look of shock. "What the hell?" He spun around. Following his gaze, Nora saw Smithback's pack horse, Beetlebum, dart back. A rope of saliva was dripping off Smithback's leg.

"That damn horse just tried to bite me!" Smithback

roared, full of indignation. The pack horse looked back, his face a picture of surprised innocence.

"That old Beetlebum," said Swire, shaking his head affectionately. "He's sure got a sense of humor."

Smithback wiped his leg. "So I see."

After another half hour of uneventful riding Nora brought the group to a halt. From an aluminum tube tied to her saddle, she removed the U.S.G.S. topo onto which Holroyd had superimposed the radar data. She examined it for a moment, then motioned him over.

"Time for a GPS reading," she said. She knew that six miles up Serpentine Canyon they had to branch off into a smaller canyon, marked HARD TWIST on the map. The trick would be identifying which of the endless parade of side canyons they were passing was Hard Twist. Down on the canyon bottom, every bend looked the same.

Holroyd dug into his saddlebag and pulled out the GPS unit, a laptop into which he had downloaded all the navigation and waypoint data. While Nora waited, he booted the computer, then began to tap at the keyboard. After a few minutes he grimaced, then shook his head.

"I was afraid of that," he said.

Nora frowned. "Don't tell me it isn't powerful enough."

Holroyd laughed crookedly. "Powerful? It uses a twenty-four-channel GPS reader with an infrared remote. It can plot positions, geocode locations automatically, leave breadcrumb trails, everything."

"Then what's the problem? Broken already?"

"Not broken, just unable to get a fix. It has to locate at least three geostationary satellites simultaneously to get a reading. With these high canyon walls, it can't even pick up one. See?"

He turned the laptop toward Nora, and she nudged her horse closer. A high-resolution overhead map of the Kaiparowits canyon system filled the screen. Atop lay smaller windows containing magnified charts of Lake Powell, real-time compasses, and data. In one window, she could see a series of messages:

NMEA MODE ENABLED
ACQUIRING SATELLITES . . .
SATELLITES ACQUIRED SO FAR: 0
3-D FIX UNAVAILABLE
LAT/LONG: N/A
ELEVATION: N/A
EPHEMERIS DATA UNAVAILABLE
RELOCATE UNIT AND REINITIALIZE

"See this?" Holroyd pointed to a small window on the screen in which various red dots orbited in circular tracks. "Those are the available satellites. Green means good reception, yellow means poor reception, and red means no reception. They're all red."

"Are we lost already?" called Black from behind, a note somewhere between apprehension and satisfaction in his voice. Nora ignored him.

"If you want a reading," Holroyd said to Nora, "you'll have to go up top."

Nora glanced at the soaring red walls, streaked with desert varnish, and looked back at Holroyd. "You first."

Holroyd grinned, powered down the laptop, and returned it to his saddlebag. "This is a great unit when it works. But I guess way out here, even technology has its limits."

"Want me to climb up and take the reading?" Sloane asked, riding forward with an easy smile.

Nora looked at her curiously.

"I brought some gear," Sloane said, lifting the top of a saddlebag and displaying a gear sling loaded with carabiners, friends, nuts, and pitons. She gave the rock walls a calculating look. "I could make it in three pitches, maybe two. Doesn't look too bad, I could probably free climb my way up."

"Let's save that for when we really need it," Nora said.

"I'd rather not take the time right now. Let's do things the old-fashioned way instead. Dead reckoning."

"It's your gig," Sloane said good-humoredly.

"Dead reckoning," Smithback murmured. "Never did like the sound of that."

"We may not have satellites," Nora said. "But we've got maps." Spreading Holroyd's map across her saddlehorn, she stared at it closely, estimating their approximate speed and travel time. She marked a dot at their probable position, the date and time beside it.

"Done a lot of this before?" Holroyd asked at her side.

Nora nodded. "All archaeologists have to be good at reading maps. It's hell finding some of the remoter ruins. And what makes it harder is this." She pointed to a note in the corner of the map that read WARNING: DATA NOT FIELD-CHECKED. "Most of these maps are created from stereogrammatic images taken from the air. Sometimes what you see from a plane is a lot different from what you see on foot. As you can see, your radar image—which is absolutely accurate—doesn't always correspond to what's printed on the map."

"Reassuring," she heard Black mutter.

Replacing the map, Nora nudged her horse forward and they continued up the canyon. The walls broadened and the stream diminished, in some places even disappearing for a while, leaving only a damp stretch of sand to mark its underground course. Each time they passed a narrow side canyon, Nora would stop and mark it on the map. Sloane rode up beside her, and for a while they rode together.

"Airplane pilot," Nora said, "expert horsewoman, archaeologist, rock climber—is there anything you don't do?"

Sloane shifted slightly in her seat. "I don't do windows," she said with a laugh. Then her face became more serious. "I guess the credit—or the blame—goes to my father. He's a man with exacting standards."

"He's quite a remarkable man," Nora replied, hearing a slightly acerbic tone creeping into Sloane's voice.

Sloane glanced back at her. "Yes."

They rounded another bend and the canyon suddenly widened. A cluster of cottonwoods grew against the reddish walls, late afternoon sunlight slanting through their leaves. Nora glanced at her watch: just after four. She noted with satisfaction a broad sandy bench where they could camp, high enough to be beyond the reach of any unexpected flash flood. And along the banks of the creek were abundant new grass for the horses. True to its name, Hard Twist canyon veered off to the left, making such a sharp turn that it gave the illusion of dead-ending in a wall of stone. It looked ugly—choked with rocks, dry and hot. So far the trip had been an easy ride, but Nora knew that could not last.

She turned her horse and waited while the others straggled up. "We'll camp here," she called out.

The group gave a ragged cheer. Swire helped Black off his horse, and the scientist limped around a bit, shaking out his legs and complaining. Holroyd dismounted by himself, only to fall immediately to the ground. Nora helped him to a tree he could lean against until he got his legs back.

"I don't like the look of that canyon," Sloane said, coming over to Nora. "What if I scout up a ways?"

Nora looked at the younger Goddard. Her dark pageboy had been tousled by the wind, but the disarray only enhanced her beauty, and the golden desert light made her amber eyes as pale as a cat's. During the day Nora had noticed several of the company, particularly Black, clandestinely admiring Sloane, whose tight cotton shirt, unbuttoned at the top and slightly damp with perspiration, left little to the imagination.

Nora nodded. "Good idea. I'll take care of things here in the meantime."

After assigning the camp chores, Nora helped Swire unpack and unsaddle the horses. They lined up the panniers, saddles, and gear on the sand, taking care to keep the high-tech equipment, in its waterproof drysacks, separate from the rest. Out of the corner of her eye, Nora noticed Bonarotti, armed with brush hook, digging trowel, buck knife, and his oversized pistol, marching off upcanyon on some mysterious errand, khakis still miraculously pressed and clean.

As soon as the horses were unpacked, Swire remounted Mestizo. During the ride, he had talked and sung to the horses constantly, making up verses to fit the small events of the day, and he sang another as Nora watched him drive the sweaty remuda toward the creek:

O my poor young gelding
Do you see yonder mare?
Such a lovely young filly
One cannot compare.
Too bad your equipment
Is in disrepair.

Once in the grass, he hobbled several of the lead horses and tied cowbells around their necks, then unsaddled Mestizo and staked him on a thirty-foot rope. At last, he placed himself on top of a rock, rolled a smoke, pulled out a greasy little notebook, and watched the horses settle down to their evening graze.

Nora turned back, surveying the camp with satisfaction. The heat of the day had abated, and a cool breeze rose up from the purling stream. Doves called back and forth across the canyon, and the faint smell of juniper smoke drifted past. Crickets trilled in the gathering twilight. Nora sat down on a tumbled rock, knowing that she should be using the last of the light to write in her journal, but savoring the moment instead. Black sat by the juniperwood fire, massaging his knees, while the others, the work of setting up camp done, were gathering around, waiting for a pot of coffee to boil.

There was the sound of footsteps crunching on sand and Bonarotti came swinging back down the canyon, a sack thrown over his back. He dropped the sack on the cook tarp spread out by the fire. He slapped a grill on the fire, oiled a large skillet, tossed in some minced garlic from his cabinet, and followed this with rice in a separate pot of water. Out of the sack tumbled some hideous, unidentifiable roots and bulbs, bundles of herbs, and several ears of prickly pear cactus. As he worked, Sloane came back into camp from her reconnaissance, clearly tired but still smiling, and sidled over to watch the final preparations. Working the knives with terrifying swiftness, Bonarotti diced up the roots and threw them into the pot, along with the bulb and a bundle of plants. Then he singed the cactus ears on the grill, skinned and julienned them, and threw them into the sizzling garlic. He gave the concoction a final stir, combined it with the rice, and removed it from the fire.

"Risotto with prickly pear, sego lily, wild potato, bolitas, and romano cheese," he announced impassively.

There was a silence.

"What are you waiting for?" Sloane cried. "Line up and *mangia bene!*"

They jumped up, grabbing plates from the kitchen tarp. The cook loaded down each plate, sprinkling chopped herbs on top. They settled back on logs by the fire.

"Is this safe to eat?" Black asked, only half jokingly.

Sloane laughed. "It may be more dangerous for you, Doctor, if you do *not* eat it." And she rolled her eyes melodramatically toward Bonarotti's revolver.

Black gave a nervous laugh and tasted it. Then he took a second bite. "Why, this is quite good," he said, filling his mouth.

"Angels and ministers of grace defend us," intoned Smithback.

"Damn tasty chuck," mumbled Swire.

Nora took a bite, and found her mouth filled with the creamy taste of arborio rice mingled with the delicate flavors of mushroom, cheese, savory herbs, and some indefinable tangy flavor that could only be the prickly pear.

Bonarotti accepted the praise with his usual lack of emotion. The canyon fell into silence while the serious business of eating began.

*　　　*　　　*

Later, as the expedition made ready for bed, Nora walked off to check on the horses. She found Swire in his usual position, notebook open.

"How is everything?" she asked.

"Mighty fine" came the answer, and then she heard a rustle as Swire removed a gingersnap from his breast pocket and inserted it into his face. There was a crunching sound. "Want one?"

Nora shook her head and sat down beside him. "What kind of a notebook are you keeping?" she asked.

Swire flicked some crumbs off his mustache. "Just some poems, is all. Cowboy doggerel. It's a sideline of mine."

"Really? May I see?"

Swire hesitated. "Well," he said, "they're supposed to be spoken, not read. But here, help yourself."

Nora thumbed through the battered journal, peering closely in the mixture of firelight and starlight. There were bits and snatches of poems, usually no more than ten or twelve lines, with titles like "Workin up a Quit," "Ford F-350," "Durango Saturday Night." Then, toward the back of the journal, she found poems of a completely different nature: longer, more serious. There was even a poem that appeared to be in Latin. She turned back to one called "Hurricane Deck."

"Is this about Smithback's horse?"

Swire nodded. "We go way back, that horse and me."

He came tearing down the draw one stormy winter's night,
A brush-tailed mustang, full of piss and fight.
I saddled up a chaser and laid a rope around his neck,
Corralled him and christened him Hurricane Deck.

Hurricane Deck, Hurricane Deck, hard on the eye and the
  saddle,
You whomper-jawed, hay-bellied, cold-backed old spraddle,
Only a blind mare could love your snip-nosed face,
Oh, but I tell you, Hurricane Deck could race.

I trained him for heeling, took him on the road,
At Amarillo and Santa Fe we won a load,
He served me well, from Salinas to Solitude,
But Hurricane's been retired to loading up dudes.

"I need to work on the last stanza," said Swire. "It don't sound right. Ends kind of sudden."

"Did you really catch him wild?" Nora asked.

"Sure did. One summer when I was running a pack string at the T-Cross up in Dubois, Wyoming, I heard talk about this buckskin mustang that nobody could catch. He was an outlaw, never branded, always broke for the mountains when he saw riders. Then that night I saw him. Lightning spooked him, sent him right past the bunkhouse. I chased that son of a bitch for three days."

"Three days?"

"I kept cutting him off from the mountains, circling him back around past the ranch. Each time I picked up a fresh mount. I wore out six horses afore I got a rope on him. He's some horse. The son of a bitch can jump a barbwire fence and I've seen him walk, just as nice as you please, across a cattle guard."

Nora handed back the journal. "I think these are excellent."

"Aw, horsehocky," Swire said, but he looked pleased.

"Where'd you learn the Latin?"

"From my father," came the answer. "He was a minister, always after me to read this and study that. Got it into his head that if I knew Latin, I wouldn't raise so much hell. It was the Third Satire of Horace that finally made me light out of there."

He fell silent, stroking his mustache, looking down toward the cook. "He's a damn fine beanmaster, but he's an odd son of a bitch, ain't he?"

Nora followed his gaze to the tall, heavyset figure of Bonarotti. Postprandial ablutions completed, the cook was now preparing himself for bed. Nora watched as, with finicky

care, Bonarotti inflated an air mattress, applied nocturnal facial creams, and readied what appeared to be a hairnet and a
facial mask.

"What's he doing now?" Swire muttered, as Bonarotti
began working his fingers into his ears.

"The croaking of the frogs disturbs his rest," Sloane Goddard said, emerging from the darkness and taking a seat beside them. She laughed her low, husky laugh, eyes reflecting
the distant firelight. "So he brought along earplugs. And he's
got a little silk pillow that would turn my great aunt green
with envy."

"Odd son of a bitch," Swire repeated.

"Maybe," Sloane said, turning toward the wrangler and
eyeing him up and down, one eyebrow raised. "But he's no
wimp. I've seen him on Denali in a blizzard with the temperature at sixty below. Nothing fazes him. It's as if he has no
feelings at all."

Nora watched the cook slip gingerly into his tent and snug
down the zipper. Then she turned back to Sloane. "So tell me
about your recon. How is it upcanyon?"

"Not so good. A lot of dense willow and salt cedar brush,
with plenty of loose rock."

"How far did you go?"

"A mile and a half, maybe."

"Can the horses make it?" Swire asked.

"Yes. But we're going to need brush hooks and axes. And
there isn't much water." Sloane glanced down at the remnants of the group, lounging around the fire drinking coffee.
"Some of them are going to be unpleasantly surprised."

"How much water?"

"A pothole here and there. Less as you go up. And that's
not all." Sloane reached into a pocket and pulled out a map
and a penlight. "I've been studying the topo. Your father
found Quivira somewhere upcanyon, right?"

Nora frowned, unaware that Sloane had brought along
maps of her own. "That's about right."

"And we're here." Sloane moved the penlight. "Look what's between us and Quivira."

She moved the penlight to a spot on the map where the elevation lines came together in an angry black mass: a ridge, high, difficult, and dangerous.

"I know all about that ridge," Nora said, aware of how defensive she must sound. "My father called it the Devil's Backbone. But I don't see any reason to get everyone worried prematurely."

Sloane snapped off the light and refolded the map. "What makes you think our horses can make it?"

"My father found a way to get his horses over that ridge. If he could do it, we can."

Sloane looked back at her in the starlight; a long, penetrating look, the amused expression never leaving her face. Then she simply nodded.

18

THE NEXT MORNING, AFTER A BREAKFAST only a little less miraculous than its predecessor, Nora assembled the group beside the packed horses.

"It's going to be a tough day," she said. "We're probably going to be doing a lot of walking."

"Walking sounds good to me," Holroyd said. "I'm sore in places I didn't know I had." There was an assenting murmur.

"Can I have a different pack horse?" Smithback asked, leaning against a rock.

Swire ejected a stream of tobacco juice. "Got a problem?"

"Yeah. A horse-sized problem. Beetlebum over there keeps trying to bite me."

The horse tossed its head in a mighty nod, then nickered evilly.

"Likes the taste of ham, I guess," said Swire.

"That's Mr. Prosciutto to you, pal."

"He's just kidding around. If he really wanted to bite, you'd know it. Like I said, he's got a sense of humor, just like you." Swire glanced at Nora.

Despite herself, Nora found the writer's discomfiture covertly satisfying. "Roscoe's right, I'd rather not make any changes unless we have to. Let's give it another day." She climbed into the saddle, then gave the signal to mount up.

"Sloane and I will go first and pick out a trail. Roscoe will bring up the rear."

They moved forward into the dry streambed, the horses pushing through the dense brush. Hard Twist Canyon was hot and close, with none of the charm of the previous day's ride. One side of the canyon lay in deep purple shadow, while the other was etched in sunlight, a contrast almost painful to the eyes. Salt cedars and willows arched over their heads, creating a hot tunnel in which ugly, oversized horseflies droned.

The brush grew thicker, and Nora and Sloane dismounted to hack a path. It was hot, miserable work. Making things worse, they found only a few stagnant potholes of water that did not keep up with the horses' thirst. The riders seemed to bear up well enough, except for Black's sarcastic protest when told they would have to ration water for a while. Nora wondered how Black would react when they reached the Devil's Backbone, somewhere in the wasteland ahead of them. His personality was beginning to seem a high price to pay for his expertise.

At last they came across a large muddy pool, hidden on the far side of a rockslide. The horses crowded forward. In the excitement, Holroyd dropped the lead rope of Charlie Taylor, his pack horse, who eagerly bounded forward into the muddy pool.

Swire turned at the sound. "Wait!" he called, but it was too late.

There was a sudden, terrifying pause as the horse realized it was bogging down in quicksand. Then, in an explosion of flexing muscle, the animal tried to back out, legs churning, spraying thick mud, whinnying in shrill fear. After a few moments it flopped back into the muck, sides shuddering in panic.

Without hesitating, Swire jumped down into the muck beside the horse, drew his knife, and with two deft strokes cut through the diamond hitch. As Nora watched, two hundred pounds worth of provisions slid off the horse's back into the mud. Swire grabbed the lead rope and pulled the horse's head to the side, simultaneously quirting him on the rump. With a great sucking noise the horse struggled free. Swire labored out of the mud himself, dragging the pack behind him. Resheathing his knife, he collected the shaking animal's lead rope and wordlessly handed it to Holroyd.

"Sorry," said the young man sheepishly, throwing a deeply embarrassed glance at Nora.

Swire stuffed a plug of tobacco into his already full cheek. "No problem. Coulda happened to anyone."

Both Swire and the pack were liberally covered in vile-smelling muck. "Maybe this is a good time to stop for lunch," Nora said.

After a quick meal, with the horses watered and the canteens full of purified water, they set out again. The growing heat had baked the canyon into a kind of oppressive somnolence, and all was quiet save for the clatter of horses' hooves and the occasional muttered imprecations from Smithback to his pack horse.

"Goddammit, Elmer," he finally cried, "get your hairy lips off me!"

"He likes you," Swire said. "And his name's Beetlebum."

"Soon as we get back to civilization, it's going to be Elmer," Smithback said. "I'm going to personally escort this nag to the nearest glue factory."

"Now don't go hurtin' his feelings," Swire drawled, punctuating the sentence with a spit of tobacco juice.

Their route branched again into an unnamed canyon. Here, the walls were narrower and well scoured by flash floods, but there was less brush and the riding grew a little easier. At one broad bend, where the canyon temporarily widened, Nora reined in her horse and waited for Sloane to catch up. Looking around idly, she suddenly tensed, pointing toward a cutbank on the inside of the bend where flash floods had sliced through the old streambed.

"See that?" she asked, indicating a long thin swale of stained soil beside what looked like a linear arrangement of stones.

"Charcoal," Sloane nodded as she rode up.

They dismounted and examined the layer. Her breath coming fast with excitement, Nora picked up some tiny fragments of charcoal with a pair of tweezers and placed them in a test tube. "Just like the Great North Road to Chaco," she murmured.

Then she straightened up and looked at Sloane. "I think we've finally found it. The road my father was following."

Sloane smiled. "Never doubted it."

They moved on. Now, wherever the canyon took a sharp bend and the old floor was exposed as a bench high above the stream, they could see charcoal-stained ground and, infrequently, lines of stones. Time and again, Nora found herself picturing her father: riding along this same trail, seeing these same sights. It gave her a feeling of connection she hadn't felt since he died.

Around three o'clock they stopped to rest the horses, taking refuge under an overhang.

"Hey, look," Holroyd said, pointing to a large green plant growing out of the sand, covered with huge, funnel-shaped white flowers. "*Datura meteloides*. Its roots are saturated with atropine—the same poison in belladonna."

"Don't let Bonarotti see it," Smithback said.

"Some Indian tribes eat the roots to induce visions," said Nora.

"Along with permanent brain damage," replied Holroyd.

As they sat with their backs to the rock, eating handfuls of dried fruits and nuts, Sloane retrieved her binoculars and began scanning a series of alcoves in a blind canyon opposite them.

After a minute she turned to Nora. "I thought so. There's a small cliff dwelling up there. First one I've seen since we started out."

Taking the binoculars, Nora peered at the small ruin, perched high on the cliff face. It was set into a shallow alcove, oriented to the south in the Anasazi way, ensuring shade in the summer and warmth in the winter. She could see a low retaining wall along the bottom of the alcove, with what looked like several rooms built in the rear and a circular granary to one side.

"Let me see," Holroyd said. He gazed at the ruin, motionless. "Incredible," he breathed at last.

"There's thousands of little ruins like that in the Utah canyon country," Nora said.

"How did they live?" Holroyd asked, still peering up with the binoculars.

"They probably farmed the canyon bottom—corn, squash, and beans. They hunted and gathered plants. I'd guess it housed a single extended family."

"I can't believe they raised kids up there," Holroyd said. "You have to be pretty brave to live in a cliff face like that."

"Or nervous," said Nora. "There's a lot of controversy over why the Anasazi suddenly abandoned their pueblos on the flats and retreated into those inaccessible cliff dwellings. Some say it was for defense."

"Looks like a no-brainer to me," Smithback said, grabbing the binoculars from Holroyd. "Who'd live up there if they didn't have to? No elevators, and Pizza Hut sure as hell doesn't deliver."

Nora looked at him. "What makes it strange is that there's no overt evidence of warfare or invasion. All we really know is that the Anasazi suddenly retreated to these cliff sites, stayed there for a while, and then abandoned the Four Corners area entirely. Some archaeologists think it was caused by a total social breakdown."

Sloane had been scanning the cliffs with a shaded hand. Now she took the binoculars from Smithback and examined the rock more carefully. "I think I can see a way up," she said. "If you climb that talus slope, there's a hand-and-toe trail pecked up the slickrock which goes all the way to the ledge. From there you can edge over." She lowered the binoculars and looked at Nora, amber eyes lit up with mild excitement. "Do we have time to try it?"

Nora glanced at her watch. They were already hopelessly

behind schedule—one more hour wouldn't matter, and they did have an obligation to survey as many ruins as they could. Besides, it might revive some flagging spirits. She gazed up at the little ruin, feeling her own curiosity aroused. There was always the chance her father had explored this ruin, maybe even left his scrawled initials on a rockface to record his presence. "All right," she said, reaching for her camera. "It doesn't look technical."

"I'd like to go, too," said Holroyd excitedly. "I did some rock climbing in college."

Nora looked at the flushed, eager face. *Why not?*

"I'm sure Mr. Swire would be happy to give the horses an extra rest." Nora looked at the group. "Anybody else want to come?"

Black gave a short laugh. "No thanks," he said. "I value my life."

Aragon glanced up from his notebook and shook his head. Bonarotti had gone off to gather mushrooms. Smithback pushed away from the rock wall and stretched luxuriously. "Guess I'd better tag along with you, Madame Chairman," he said. "It wouldn't do to have you find an Anasazi Rosetta stone while I was loafing around down here."

They crossed the stream, scrambled over boulders and up the talus slope, loose rocks clattering behind them. The sandstone ahead sloped upward at a forty-five-degree angle, notched with a series of eroded dimples set into the rock.

"That's the hand-and-toe trail." Nora pointed. "The Anasazi pounded them out with quartzite hammerstones."

"I'll go first," said Sloane. To Nora's surprise she shot nimbly upward, limbs tawny in the sunlight, hands and feet finding the holds with the instinctive assurance of a veteran rock climber. "Come on up!" she said a minute later, kneeling on the ledge above their heads. Holroyd followed. Then Nora watched Smithback creep cautiously up the slickrock face, gangly limbs clutching at the narrow holds, his face covered with sweat. Something about him made her smile. She waited until he had safely completed the climb, then brought up the rear herself.

In a few moments they were all sitting on the ledge, catching their breath. Nora looked at the camp spread out below their feet, the horses grazing along an apron of sand, the humans looking like splotches of color resting against the red cliffs.

Sloane rose. "Ready?"

"Go for it," said Nora.

They crept along the narrow ledge. It was about two feet wide, but the bottom was canted slightly and scattered with fragments of sandstone, which rattled off into space as they inched along. After a short distance the ledge broadened out, curved around a corner, and the ruin came into view.

Nora made a quick visual inspection. The alcove was perhaps fifty feet long, ten feet high at its highest point, and about fifteen feet deep. A low masonry retaining wall had been built at the lip of the alcove and filled with rubble, leveling the surface. Behind were four small roomblocks of flat stones mortared with mud; one with a keyhole door, the rest with tiny windows. The builders had used the natural sandstone roof of the alcove as their ceiling.

Nora turned to Holroyd and Smithback. "I think Sloane and I should make an initial survey. You wouldn't mind waiting here for a few minutes?"

"Only if you promise not to find anything," Smithback replied.

Nora unbuckled the hood of her camera and walked gingerly along the facade, photographing the exterior of the dwelling. Although Sloane's expertise with the large 4x5 Graflex made her the expedition's official photographer, Nora liked to keep her own record of all the sites she studied.

She stopped to peer more closely at the plastered wall. Here, she could see the actual handprints of the person who had smeared the adobe. Raising her camera again, she took a careful closeup, then another when she noticed a clear set of fingerprints. It was not unusual to find prints preserved in

Anasazi plaster and corrugated pottery, but she always liked to document them when she could. They helped serve as a reminder that archaeology was the study, ultimately, of people, not artifacts—something she felt many of her colleagues seemed to forget.

There was the usual littering of potsherds on the ground—mostly Pueblo III Mesa Verde whiteware and some late Tusayan-style corrugated grayware. A.D. *1240,* Nora thought without surprise.

Sloane, who had been sketching a quick plan of the ruin, now removed a pair of tweezers and some Ziploc bags from her rucksack. Labeling the bags with a marker, she moved carefully forward, picking up a sampling of potsherds and some scattered corncobs with the tweezers. She placed them in the bags, then marked their positions in her sketchbook. She worked quickly and deftly, and Nora watched with growing surprise. Sloane seemed to know exactly what to do. In fact, she worked as if she had been on many professional surveys before.

Reaching into her bag again, Sloane pulled out a small, battery-powered chrome instrument and moved to a viga that projected from one of the roomblocks. There was a small whining sound, and Nora realized she was taking a core from the roofbeam for tree-ring dating. By studying the growth pattern of the rings, a specialist in dendrochronology such as Black could tell the exact year the tree was cut. As the whining ended abruptly and silence returned, Nora felt a sudden annoyance at this mechanized disturbance of the site—or, perhaps, with the fact that Sloane had done it so blithely, without her permission. She instinctively moved forward.

Looking over, Sloane read her face in an instant. "This all right?" she asked, raising her dark eyebrows inquiringly.

"Next time, let's discuss something like this first."

"Sorry," Sloane said, in a tone even more annoying for its apparent lack of sincerity. "I just thought it might be useful—"

"It *will* be useful," Nora said, trying to moderate her voice. "That's not the point."

Sloane glanced at her more closely, a cool, appraising glance that bordered on insolence. Then the lazy grin returned. "I promise," she said.

Nora turned and moved to the doorway. She realized her irritation was partly based on a vague, irrational threat she felt to her leadership. She hadn't realized Sloane was so experienced in fieldwork, spoiling Nora's earlier assumption that she would be leading Goddard's daughter through the basics. She immediately felt sorry for showing her feelings; she had to admit that the pencil-thin core probably contained the most useful piece of information they would take from the ancient ruin.

She shined a penlight inside the first roomblock and found the interior relatively well preserved. The walls were plastered, still showing traces of painted decoration. She angled the beam toward the floor, covered with sand and dust that had blown in over the centuries. In one corner she could see the edge of a metate—a grinding stone—protruding from the dirt, beside a broken mano.

Opening her flash, she took another sequence of pictures in the room and the one beyond, which was exceptionally dusty and—very unusually—seemed at one time to have been painted with thick, heavy black paint. Or perhaps it was from cooking. Moving through a low doorway, she advanced into the third room. It, too, was empty, save for a hearth with several firedogs still propping up a *comal*, or polished cooking stone. The sandstone ceiling was blackened with crusted smoke, and she could still smell the faint odor of charcoal. A series of holes in the plaster wall might have been the anchor for a loom.

Moving back through the rooms, Nora leaned out into the sudden warmth of the sun and beckoned the waiting Holroyd and Smithback. They followed her into the roomblock, stooping through the low doorways.

"This is incredible," Holroyd said in a reverential whisper. "I've never seen anything like it. I still can't believe people lived up here."

"Neither can I," said Smithback. "No cable."

"There's nothing like the feeling of one of these ancient ruins," Nora replied. "Even an unremarkable one like this."

"Unremarkable to you, maybe," Holroyd said.

Nora looked at him. "You've never been in an Anasazi ruin before?"

Holroyd shook his head as they stepped into the second room. "Only Mesa Verde, as a kid. But I've read all the books. Wetherill, Bandelier, you name it. As an adult, I never had the time or money to travel."

"We'll call it Pete's Ruin, then."

Holroyd flushed deeply. "Really?"

"Sure," said Nora, with a grin. "We're the Institute: we can name it anything we want."

Holroyd looked at her a long moment, eyes gleaming. Then he took her hand and pressed it briefly between his. Nora smiled and gently withdrew her hand. *Maybe that wasn't such a good idea,* she thought.

Sloane came from the back of the ruin, shouldering her rucksack.

"Find anything?" Nora asked, taking a swig from her canteen and offering it around. She knew that most rock art was found behind cliff dwellings.

Sloane nodded. "A dozen or so pictographs. Including three reversed spirals."

Nora looked up in surprise to meet the woman's glance.

Holroyd caught the look. "What?" he asked.

Nora sighed. "It's just that, in Anasazi iconography, the counterclockwise direction is usually associated with negative supernatural forces. Clockwise or 'sunwise' was considered to be the direction of travel of the sun across the sky. Counterclockwise was therefore considered a perversion of nature, a reversal of the normal balance."

"A perversion of nature?" Smithback asked with sudden interest.

"Yes. In some Indian cultures today, the reversed spiral is still associated with witchcraft and sorcery."

"And I found this," Sloane said, lifting one hand. In it she held a small, broken, human skull.

Nora turned, uncomprehending at first, and Sloane's grin widened lazily.

"Where did you find that?" Nora asked sharply.

Sloane's smile did not falter. "Back there, next to the granary."

"And you just picked it up?"

"Why not?" Sloane asked, her eyes narrowing. The slight movement reminded Nora of a cat when threatened.

"For one thing," Nora snapped, "we don't disturb human remains unless it's absolutely critical for our research. And you've touched it, which means we can't do bone collagen DNA on it. Worst of all, you didn't even photograph it *in situ*."

"All I did was pick it up," Sloane said, her voice suddenly low.

"I thought I made it clear we were to discuss these things first."

There was a tense silence. Then Nora heard a scratching sound behind her and she glanced at Smithback. "What the hell are you doing?" she demanded. The journalist had his notebook out and was scribbling away.

"Taking notes," he said defensively, pulling the notebook toward his chest.

"You're writing down our discussion?" Nora cried.

"Hey, why not?" Smithback said. "I mean, the human drama's as much a part of this expedition as—"

Holroyd advanced and snatched the notebook away. "This was a private conversation," he said, ripping out the page and handing the notebook back.

"That's censorship," Smithback protested.

Suddenly Nora heard a low, throaty purr that swelled into a mellifluous laugh. She turned to see Sloane still holding up the skull, looking at the three of them, amusement glittering in her amber eyes.

Nora took a breath and ignored the laugh. *Don't lose your*

cool. "Now that it's been disturbed," she said in a quiet voice, "we'll bring it back for Aragon to analyze. Being a ZST type, he may object, but the deed's been done. Sloane, I don't want you ever doing any invasive procedures without my express permission. Is that understood?"

"Understood," said Sloane, looking suddenly contrite as she handed the skull to Nora. "I wasn't thinking. The excitement of the moment, I guess."

Nora slipped the skull into a sample bag and tucked it in her pack. It seemed to her there had been something challenging in the way Sloane had come forward holding the skull, and Nora momentarily wondered if it hadn't been a deliberate provocation. After all, it was clear that Sloane was well versed in the protocol of fieldwork. But then she told herself she was being paranoid. Nora remembered infelicitously seizing a gorgeous Folsom point she once uncovered at a dig, pulling it out of the stratum, and then seeing the horrified looks of everyone around her.

"What's a ZST?" the unrepentant Smithback asked. "Some kind of birth control?"

Nora shook her head. "It stands for Zero Site Trauma. The idea that an archaeological site should never be physically disturbed. People like Aragon believe any intrusion, no matter how careful or subtle, destroys it for future archaeologists who might come along with more sophisticated tools. They tend to work with artifacts that have already been excavated by others."

"ZST groupies consider traditional archaeologists to be artifact whores, digging for relics instead of reconstructing cultures," Sloane added.

"If Aragon feels that way, why did he come along?" Holroyd asked.

"He's not a total purist. I suppose that on a project as potentially important as this, he's willing to put his personal feelings aside to some extent. I think he feels that if anyone is going to touch Quivira, it should be him." Nora looked around. "What do you make of these walls?" she asked

Sloane. "It's not soot, it's some kind of thick dried substance, like paint. But I've never seen an Anasazi room painted black before."

"Beats me," Sloane replied. She removed a small glass tube and a dentist's pick from her pack. Then she glanced with a quick smile at Nora. "May I take a sample?" she paused. "Madame Chairman?"

It's not funny when Smithback calls me that, Nora thought. *And it's even less funny coming from you.* But she nodded wordlessly, watching as Sloane expertly flaked a few pieces into the glass test tube and stoppered it.

The sun was now low in the sky, painting long contrasting stripes along the ancient walls. "Let's get back," Nora said. As they turned to walk out on the ledge, Nora glanced back at the reverse spirals on the wall behind the ruin. She shivered briefly in spite of the heat.

19

THEY WERE FORCED TO MAKE A DRY CAMP that night. The horses were thirsty and off their feed, and by sundown the expedition had made serious inroads into their own supplies of water. Aragon received the skull with the wordless disapproval that Nora had expected. They turned in early, saddle sore and weary, and slept hard.

Shortly after starting out the following morning, they arrived at a triple intersection of narrow canyons. Despite careful examination, Nora and Sloane could find no more traces of the ancient road here; it was either buried or had washed away. The GPS laptop was still not functioning, and Holroyd's map was of little help: at this point of the journey, the underlying topographical elevations on the map were ludicrously off. The radar data became a confusing maze of color.

Nor could Nora find any sign that her father had ever come this way. In the tradition of Frank Wetherill and the other early explorers, Nora knew her father sometimes marked his trail by scratching his initials and a date into the rock. Yet, to her mounting anxiety, she had yet to see any graffiti by him or anyone else, save the occasional petroglyphs of the long-vanished Anasazi.

For the rest of the day, the group toiled up through a warren of fractured canyons, moving deeper into a surreal world that seemed more a landscape of dream than anything of the earth. The mute stone halls spoke of eons of fury: uplift and erosion, floods, earthquakes, and the endless scouring of the wind. At every turn, Nora realized her dead reckoning grew more difficult and prone to error. Each fall of the horses' hooves took them farther from civilization, from the comfortable and the known, deeper into an alien landscape of mystery. Cliff dwellings became more numerous, tucked slyly into the canyon walls, remote and inaccessible. Nora had the irrational feeling, as she stopped for the tenth time to pore over the map, that they were intruding onto forbidden ground.

By evening they were so exhausted that dinner was a cold, silent, impromptu affair. The lack of water had compelled Nora to institute severe rationing. Bonarotti, forced to cook with no water and dirty dishes, grew sullen.

After dinner, the group gravitated apathetically toward the campfire. Swire joined them after giving the horses a final check.

He sat down beside Nora and spat. "Come morning, these horses won't have had decent water for thirty-six hours. Don't know how much longer they can last."

"Frankly, I couldn't give a damn about the horses," Black said from across the fire. "I'm wondering when *we're* going to die of thirst."

Swire turned to him, his face flickering in the light. "Maybe you don't realize it, but if the horses die, we die. It ain't any more complicated than that."

Nora glanced in Black's direction. In the firelight his face was haggard, a look of incipient panic in his eyes.

"Is everything all right, Aaron?" she asked.

"You said we were going to reach Quivira tomorrow," he said huskily.

"That was only an estimate. It's taking longer than I anticipated."

"Bullshit." Black sniffed. "I've been watching you all afternoon, struggling with those maps and trying to get that useless GPS unit to work. I think we're lost."

"No," Nora replied. "I don't believe we're lost."

Black leaned back, his voice growing louder. "Is that supposed to be encouraging? And where's this road? We saw it yesterday. Maybe. But now it's vanished."

Nora had seen this kind of reaction to the wilderness before. It was never pleasant. "All I can say is we'll get there, probably tomorrow, certainly by the next day."

"Probably!" he repeated derisively, slapping his hands on his knees. *"Probably!"*

In the flickering light, Nora looked around at the rest of the group. Everyone was filthy from the lack of water and badly scratched from heavy brush. Only Sloane, sifting sand thoughtfully through her fingers, and Aragon, wearing his usual distant expression, appeared unconcerned. Holroyd was staring into the campfire, for once without a book at his side. Smithback's hair was wilder than ever, his bony knees covered with dirt. Earlier in the afternoon he had complained, eloquently and at great length, about how if God had meant man to ride a horse he would have put a Barcalounger on the animal's back. Even the fact that the apathetic Beetlebum had stopped trying to bite him had been little comfort.

It was a desperate-looking group, and it was hard to believe that the change had taken place in less than forty-eight hours of difficult travel. *Jesus,* Nora thought, *if they look like that, what must I look like?*

"I understand how concerned you all are," she said slowly. "I'm doing the best I can. If any of you have any constructive ideas, I'd like to hear them."

"The answer is to keep going," said Aragon with a quiet vehemence. "And to stop complaining. Twentieth-century humans are unused to any real physical challenge. The people who lived in these canyons dealt with this kind of thirst and heat every day, without complaint." He cast his dark, sardonic eyes around the group.

"Oh, *now* I feel better," said Black. "And here I thought I was suffering from thirst."

Aragon turned his dark eyes on Black. "You are suffering more from an undifferentiated personality disorder than from thirst, Dr. Black."

Black turned to look at him, speechless with rage. Then he stood up on trembling limbs and made his way silently toward his tent.

Nora watched him walk away. *What was happening here?* What seemed so simple on paper—the Anasazi road, the descriptions in her father's letter—had grown hopelessly complicated on the ground. It would only get worse: tomorrow afternoon, if her navigation was correct, they would hit the Devil's Backbone, the massive hogback ridge that separated their canyon system from the even more remote and isolated system in which Quivira was hidden. On the map, it looked impassable. Yet her father had ridden over it. He must have. *Why didn't he leave any signs behind?* But as she asked the question, she realized the answer: he wanted to keep the location of Quivira a secret known only to himself. For the first time, she understood the vagueness in his letter had been deliberate.

The group began to break up, leaving Smithback restlessly dozing and Aragon gazing thoughtfully into the fire. Nora felt movement nearby, then Sloane sat down beside her.

"This campsite isn't all bad," she said. "Look what I just uncovered."

Nora glanced down in the direction Sloane indicated. There, lying half-buried in sand, was a perfect arrowhead, pressure-flaked out of a snow-white agate flecked with pinpoints of red.

Nora picked it up with great care, examining it closely in the light of the fire. "Amazing, isn't it, how much they loved beauty? They always chose the loveliest materials for their stone tools. That's Lobo Mesa agate, from an outcrop in New Mexico about three hundred miles southeast of here. Think of how far they were willing to trade to get the really nice stuff."

She handed it to Sloane, who was looking at her curiously. "That's quite a nice piece of identification," she said with real admiration. She took the point and carefully laid it back in the dust. "Maybe it should lie here, after all."

Aragon smiled. "It is always more fulfilling," he said, "to leave something in its natural place than to lock it in a museum basement." All three fell silent, staring into the dying flames.

"I'm glad you spoke up like that," Nora said at last to Aragon.

"Perhaps I should have done it long before." There was a pause. "What do you plan to do about him?"

"Black?" Nora thought. "Nothing, for the moment."

Aragon nodded. "I've known him for a long while, and he's always been full of himself. With good reason—there's no better geochronologist in the country. But this is a side I hadn't seen before. I think it's fear. Some people fall apart psychologically when removed from civilization, from telephones, hospitals, cars, electric power."

"I was thinking the same thing," Nora said. "If that's the case, once we've made camp and set up communications with the outside world, he'll calm down."

"I think so. But then again, he might not."

There was another silence.

"So?" Sloane prompted at last.

"So what?"

"Are we lost?" she asked gently.

Nora sighed. "I don't know. Guess we'll find out tomorrow."

Aragon grunted. "If this is indeed an Anasazi road, it's unlike any other I've encountered. It's as if the Anasazi wanted to eradicate any trace of its existence." He shook his head. "I sense a darkness, a malignancy, about this road."

Nora looked at him. "Why do you say that?"

Silently, the Mexican reached into the pack and removed

the test tube containing the flakes of black paint, cradling it in his palm. "I performed a PBT with luminol on one of these samples," he said quietly. "It came up positive."

"I've never heard of that test," Nora said.

"It's a simple test used by forensic anthropologists. And police. It identifies the presence of human blood." He gazed at her, his dark eyes in shadow. "That wasn't paint you saw. It was human blood. But not just blood: layers upon layers upon layers of crusted, dried blood."

"My God," Nora said. The passage from the Coronado report came back to her unbidden: *"Quivira* in their language means 'The House of the Bloody Cliff.' " Perhaps "bloody cliff" was not merely symbolic, after all . . .

Aragon removed a small padded bag and carefully pulled out the small skull they had discovered at Pete's Ruin. He handed it to Nora. "After I discovered that, I decided to take a closer look at the skull you found. I reassembled the pieces in my tent last night. It belongs to a young girl, maybe nine or ten years old. Definitely Anasazi: you can see how the back of the skull was flattened by a hard cradleboard when the child was a baby." He turned it over carefully in his hands. "At first, I thought she had died an accidental death, perhaps hit by a falling stone. But when I looked more closely, I noticed these." He pointed to a series of grooves on the back of the skull, near the center. "These were made with a flint knife."

"No," Sloane whispered.

"Oh, yes. This little girl was scalped."

20

SKIP KELLY SAUNTERED DOWN A SHADED walkway of the Institute's manicured campus, rubbing bleary eyes. It was a breathtaking summer morning, warm and dry and full of promise. The sun threw a silken illumination over building and lawn, and a warbler was sitting in a lilac bush, pouring out its heart in rapturous song.

"Shut the hell up," Skip growled. The bird complied.

Ahead of him lay a long, low Pueblo Revival structure, clothed in the same subdued earth tones as the rest of the Institute's campus. A small wooden sign was set into the ground before it, ARTIFACTUAL ASSEMBLAGES spelled out in sans serif bronze letters. Skip opened the door and walked inside.

The door closed behind him with a squeal of metal, and he winced. *Christ, what a headache.* His mouth was parched and tasted of mildew and old socks, and he dug a piece of chewing gum out of his pocket. *Oh, man. Better switch to beer.* It was the same thing he thought every morning.

He looked around, grateful for the dim illumination. He was in a small antechamber, bare of furnishings save for two display cases and an uncomfortable-looking wooden bench. Doors led off in all directions, most of them unmarked.

Another squeal of metal on frame, and one of the far doors

opened. A woman stepped out and approached him. Skip looked at her without interest. Mid-thirties, tall, short dark hair, round oversized glasses, and a corduroy skirt.

The woman extended her hand. "You must be Skip Kelly. I'm Sonya Rowling, senior lab technician."

"Nice outfit," he replied, shaking the proffered hand. *Dressed up for the* Brady Bunch *reunion,* he thought. *Nora, I'll get you for this.*

If the woman heard the compliment, she gave no sign. "We expected you an hour ago."

"Sorry about that," Skip mumbled in reply. "Overslept."

"Follow me." The woman turned on her heel and walked back through the doorway. Skip followed her down a passage and around a corner into a large room. Unlike the antechamber, the space was filled with equipment: long metal tables, covered with tools, plastic trays, and printouts; desks piled high with books and three-ring binders. The walls were hidden by row upon row of metal drawers, all closed. In the corner nearest the door, a young man was standing in front of a keyboard, talking animatedly on the phone.

"As you can see, this is where the real work gets done," the woman said. She waved at a relatively empty desk. "Have a seat and we'll get you started."

Gingerly, Skip eased himself down beside Sonya Rowling. "God, am I hung," he muttered.

Rowling turned her owlish eyes toward his. "I beg your pardon?"

"Hung. Hung over, I mean," Skip added hastily.

"I see. Perhaps that explains your lateness. I'm sure it won't happen again." Something in Rowling's gaze made Skip sit up a little straighter.

"Your sister says you have a natural talent for labwork. That's what I intend to find out in the next couple of weeks. We'll start you off slowly, see what you can do. Have you had much field experience?"

"Nothing formal."

"Good. Then you won't have any bad habits to unlearn."

When Skip raised his eyebrows, she explained. "The public thinks fieldwork is the be-all and end-all of archaeology. But the truth is for every hour spent at the field, five are spent in the lab. And that's where most of the important discoveries are made."

She reached over and pulled a long metal tray with a hinged top toward them. Lifting the lid, Rowling reached inside and carefully removed four oversized Baggies. Each had the words PONDEROSA DRAW scribbled hastily across the top in black marker. Skip could see that many more sealed Baggies lay in the dim recesses of the tray.

"What's all this?" Skip asked.

"Ponderosa Draw was a remarkable site in northeastern Arizona," Rowling replied. "Note I say *was*, not *is*. For reasons we don't fully understand, potsherds of many different styles were found there, scattered in apparent confusion. Perhaps the place was some kind of trading center. In any case, the owner of the land was an amateur archaeologist with more enthusiasm than sense. Over three summers in the early twenties he dug the whole site and collected every last sherd he could find. Scoured the site clean, above and below the surface." She gestured at the bags. "Only problem was, he tossed all his finds together in a single pile, paying no attention to location, strata, anything. The entire provenance of the site was lost. The sherds were eventually given to the Museum of Indian Antiquities, but were never examined. We inherited them when we acquired the museum's collection three years ago."

Skip stared at the bags, frowning. "I thought I was going to work on Nora's Rio Puerco stuff."

Rowling pursed her lips. "The Rio Puerco dig was a model of archaeological discipline. Material was carefully gathered and recorded with a minimum of on-site intrusion. We stand to learn a great deal from your sister's finds. Whereas this . . ." She gestured at the bags, letting the sentence drop.

"I get the picture," Skip said, his scowl deepening. "This

site is broken already. There's nothing I can do to make it worse. And you're going to make me cut my teeth on it."

Rowling's pursed lips curved into what might have been the shadow of a smile. "You catch on fast, Mr. Kelly."

Skip stared at the bags for a long moment. "So I guess these are just the tip of the iceberg."

"Another good guess. There are twenty-five more bags in storage."

Shit. "And what do I have to do, exactly?"

"It's very straightforward. Since we know nothing at all about where these potsherds were found, or their position relative to each other, all we can do is sort them by style and type and do a statistical analysis on the results."

Skip licked his lips. This was going to be worse than he ever imagined. "Could I get a cup of coffee before we start?"

"Nope. No food or drink allowed in the lab. Tomorrow, come early and help yourself to coffee in the staff lounge. And that reminds me." She pointed a thumb at the nearest wastebasket.

"What?"

"Your gum. In there, please."

"Can't I just stick it under the desk?"

Rowling shook her head, unamused. Skip leaned over and spat out his gum.

Rowling passed over a box of disposable gloves. "Now put these on." She tugged on a pair herself, then placed one of the artifact bags between them and unsealed it carefully. Skip peered inside, curious despite himself. The sherds came in a variety of patterns and colors. Some were badly weathered, others still quite fresh. A few were corrugated and blackened with cooking smoke. Many were too small to clearly determine what kind of designs had been painted on them, but some were large enough to make out motifs: wavy lines, series of diamonds, parallel zig-zags. Skip remembered collecting similar sherds with his father. Back when he was a kid, it had been okay to do that. Not anymore.

The lab technician removed a sherd from the bag. "This is

Cortez black-on-white." She laid it gingerly on the table and her fingers moved back into the bag and withdrew another sherd. "And this is Kayenta black-on-white. Take a careful note of the differences."

She put the sherds into two clear plastic containers, then drew another sherd from the bag. "What's this?"

Skip scrutinized it. "It looks like the first one you drew out. Cortez."

"Correct." Rowling put the sherd into the first plastic bin, then drew out another sherd. "And this one?"

"It's the other. Kayenta."

"Very good." Rowling placed the sherd into the other bin, then drew out a fifth sample from the bag. "And how about this?" There was a slightly sardonic expression on Rowling's face, a faint challenge. It looked almost like the second sherd, but not quite. Skip opened his mouth to say Kayenta, then closed it again. He stared, reaching deep into his memory.

"Chuska Wide Banded?" he asked.

There was a sudden pause, and for a moment Rowling's face lost its assurance. "How in the world—?"

"My father liked potsherds," said Skip, a little diffidently.

"That's going to help us a lot," she said, her voice warming. "Maybe Nora was right. Anyway, you'll find all sorts of good things in here: Cibola ware, St. John's Polychrome, Mogollon Brownware, McElmo. But see for yourself." She reached across the table and pulled over a laminated sheet. "This shows you samples of the two dozen or so styles you're likely to find from the Ponderosa Draw site. Separate them by style, and put any questionable sherds to one side. I'll come back and check on your progress in an hour or so."

Skip watched her leave, then sighed deeply and turned his attention to the overstuffed Baggie. At first, the work seemed both boring and confusing, and the heap of questionable sherds began to pile up. But then, almost imperceptibly, he grew more sure in his identification: it was instinctive, almost, the way the shape, condition, even composition of the sherds could speak as loudly as the design itself. Memories of long afternoons spent with his father, pacing over some ruin in the middle of nowhere, came back with a bittersweet tang. And then, back at the house, poring over monographs, sorting and gluing the sherds onto pieces of cardboard. He wondered what had become of all their painstaking collections.

The lab was quiet except for the occasional keytaps of the young technician in the far corner. Skip started when he felt a hand on his shoulder.

"So?" Rowling asked him. "How's it going?"

"Has it been an hour?" Skip asked. He sat up and looked at his watch. The headache was gone.

"Just about." She peered into the bins. "Good heavens, you've worked your way through two bags already."

"Does that make me teacher's pet?" Skip asked, massaging his neck. In the distance, he heard a rap at the laboratory door.

"Let me look over your work first, see how many mistakes you've made," Rowling replied.

Abruptly, a high, tremulous voice rang out on the far side of the room: "Skip Kelly? Is there a Skip Kelly here?"

Skip glanced up. It was the young technician, looking very nervous. And easing past him, Skip could see the source of his nervousness: a large man in a blue uniform. The man walked partway toward Skip, the gun, baton, and handcuffs on his belt clinking slightly, then stopped. He hooked his hands in his belt with a slight smile. The room had fallen silent.

"Skip Kelly?" he asked in a low, calm baritone.

"Yes," said Skip, going cold, his mind racing through a dozen possibilities, all of them unpleasant. *That asshole neighbor must have complained. Or maybe it's that woman with the dachshund. Christ, I only ran over its back leg, and—*

"Could I speak with you outside, please?"

In the solemn darkness of the anteroom, the man flipped open an ID wallet and aimed it in Skip's direction. "I'm Lieutenant Detective Al Martinez, Santa Fe Police Department."

Skip nodded.

"You're a hard man to reach," Martinez said in a voice that

managed to be both friendly and neutral at the same time. "I wonder if I could have a bit of your time."

"My time?" Skip managed to say. "Why?"

"We'll get to that at the station, Mr. Kelly, if you don't mind."

"The station," Skip repeated. "When?"

"Let's see," said Martinez, glancing first at the floor, then at the ceiling, then back at Skip. "Right about now would be nice."

Skip swallowed. Then he nodded toward the open laboratory door. "I'm at work right now. Can't it wait until later?"

There was a brief pause. "No, Mr. Kelly," the policeman replied. "Come to think of it, I don't believe it can."

21

SKIP FOLLOWED THE POLICEMAN OUT OF THE building to a waiting car. The detective was enormous, with a neck like a redwood stump; yet his movements were light, even gentle. Martinez stopped at the passenger side and, to Skip's surprise, held the door open for him. As the car pulled away, Skip glanced in the rearview mirror. He could see a pair of white faces framed by the open door of the Artifactual Assemblages building, watching motionlessly, dwindling at last to invisibility.

"My first day on the job," Skip said. "Great impression."

They pulled through the gates of the compound and began to accelerate. Martinez slipped a stick of gum out of his breast pocket and offered it to Skip.

"No thanks."

The detective folded the stick into his own mouth and began to chew, muscles in his jaw and neck working slowly. The irregular form of the La Fonda Hotel loomed on his right. Then they passed the plaza and the Palace of the Governors, Indians selling jewelry under the portal, the sunlight glinting off the polished silver and turquoise.

"Am I going to need a lawyer?" Skip asked.

Martinez chewed his gum diligently. "I don't think so," he said, " 'Course, you're welcome to one if you want."

The car moved past the library and pulled around behind

the old police building. Several Dumpsters sat in front, filled with broken pieces of drywall.

"Renovating," Martinez explained as they entered a lobby draped in plastic. The lieutenant stopped at a desk and took a folder offered by a uniformed woman. He led Skip along a hallway smelling of paint, down a flight of stairs. Opening a scratched door, he ushered Skip in. Beyond lay a bare room, devoid of furniture except for three wooden chairs, a desk, and a dark mirror.

Skip had never been in such a place before, but he'd seen enough television to instantly recognize its purpose. "This looks like some kind of interrogation room," he said.

"It is." Martinez took a seat with a protest of wood. He laid the folder on the table and offered Skip a chair. Then he pointed to the ceiling. Skip glanced up to see a lens, pointed almost insolently at him. "We're going to videotape you. Okay?"

"Do I have a choice?"

"Yes. If you say no, the interview will be over, and you'll be free to go."

"Great," said Skip, starting to get up.

"Of course, then we'd have to subpoena you, and you'd spend money on that lawyer. Right now, you're not a suspect. So why don't you just relax and answer a few questions? If at any time you want a lawyer or want to terminate the interview, you can. How does that sound?"

"Did you say *suspect*?" Skip asked.

"Yes." Martinez looked at him with uninformative black eyes. Skip realized the man was waiting for an answer.

"Okay," he said, sighing mightily. "Roll 'em."

Martinez nodded to someone behind the one-way glass, then turned back to Skip. "Please state your name, address, and birthdate." They rapidly went through the preliminaries. Then Martinez asked:

"Are you the owner of an abandoned ranch house beyond Fox Run, address Rural Route Sixteen, Box Twelve, Santa Fe, New Mexico?"

"Yes. My sister and I own it together."

"And your sister is Nora Waterford Kelly?"

"That's right."

"And what are the whereabouts of your sister at the moment?"

"She's on an archaeological expedition to Utah."

Martinez nodded. "When did she leave?"

"Three days ago. She won't be back for a couple of weeks, at least." Once again, Skip began to stand. "Does this have to do with her?"

Martinez make a suppressing motion with one palm. "Your parents are both deceased, correct?"

Skip nodded.

"And you are currently employed at the Santa Fe Archaeological Institute."

"I was until you showed up."

Martinez smiled. "And how long have you been employed by the Institute?"

"I told you in the car. This was my first day."

Martinez nodded again, more slowly this time. "And prior to today, where were you employed?"

"I've been job hunting."

"I see. And when were you last employed?"

"Never. Not since I graduated from college last year, anyway."

"Do you know a Teresa Gonzales?"

Skip licked his lips. "Yeah. I know Teresa. She was our neighbor out at the ranch."

"When did you last see Teresa?"

"God, I don't know. Ten months ago, maybe eleven. Shortly after I graduated."

"How about your sister? When did she last see Ms. Gonzales?"

Skip shifted in his chair. "Let's see. A couple of days ago, I think. She helped Nora out at the ranch."

"You mean Nora, your sister?" Martinez asked. "Helped her how?"

Skip hesitated. "She was attacked," he said slowly.

Martinez's neck muscles stopped working for a moment. "Care to tell me about it?"

"Teresa used to call my sister when she heard noises at the old place. Vandals, kids, that kind of stuff. Lately there's been a lot of messing around over there; she's called my sister several times. Nora went over about a week ago. Said she was attacked. Teresa heard the racket, came over with a shotgun, scared them off."

"Did she say anything more? A description of the attackers?"

"Nora said . . ." Skip thought for a moment. "Nora said it was two people. Two people, dressed up as animals." He decided not to mention the letter. Whatever was going on here didn't need any more complications.

"Why didn't she come to us?" Martinez asked at last.

"Can't say for sure. Going to the police really isn't her style. She always wants to do everything for herself. I think she was concerned it might delay her expedition."

Martinez seemed to ponder something. "Mr. Kelly," he began again. "Can you account for your whereabouts over the last forty-eight hours?"

Skip stopped short. Then he sat back, took a deep breath. "Except for showing up at the Institute this morning, I was at my apartment all weekend."

Martinez consulted a piece of paper. "2113 Calle de Sebastian, number two-B?"

"Yes."

"And did you see anybody during that time?"

Skip swallowed. "Larry, at Eldorado Liquors, saw me Saturday afternoon. My sister phoned me late Saturday night."

"Anybody else?"

"Well, my neighbor called me three or four times."

"Your neighbor?"

"Yeah. Reg Freiburg, in the apartment next door. Doesn't like loud music."

Martinez sat back, running his fingers through his close-cropped black hair. He stayed silent for what seemed like a long time. At last he sat forward. "Mr. Kelly, Teresa Gonzales was found dead last night at your ranch house."

Suddenly, Skip's body felt strangely heavy. "Teresa?"

Martinez nodded. "Every Sunday afternoon, she gets a delivery of feed for the farm animals. Last Sunday, she didn't answer the door. The man noticed the animals hadn't been fed, and that her dog was locked in the house. When she still didn't answer the next morning, he got worried and called us."

"Oh, my God." Skip shook his head. "Teresa. I can't believe it."

The lieutenant shifted in his chair, eyes on Skip. "When we went out there, we found her bed unmade, clothes set out. The dog was terrified. It looked like something had gotten her up in the middle of the night. But there was no sign of her on the property, so we decided to visit the neighboring ranches. Your place was our first stop." He took a slow breath. "We saw movement inside. Turned out to be dogs, fighting over something." He stopped, pursed his lips.

But Skip barely heard this. He was thinking of Teresa, trying to remember the last time he'd seen her. He and Nora had gone out to the house to pick up a few things to decorate her apartment. Teresa had been outside in her yard, seen them, and waved her enthusiastic wave. He could see her still, jogging down the path to their house, brown careless hair flapping and dancing in the breeze.

Then his eyes fell upon the single folder lying in the center of the desk. GONZALES, T. was written along one side. The glossy edge of a black-and-white picture peeked from beneath one corner of the folder. Automatically, he reached out for it.

"I wouldn't," Martinez said. But he made no move to stop him. Skip lifted the edge, exposing the photograph; then froze in horror.

Teresa was lying on her back, one leg across the other, left hand thrown up as if to catch an errant football. At least, Skip thought it was Teresa, because he recognized the room as their old kitchen: his mother's ancient stove stood in the top right-hand corner of the picture.

Teresa herself was less recognizable. Her mouth was open, but the cheeks were missing. Through gaps in the ruined flesh, teeth fillings gleamed hollowly in the light of the camera's flash. Even in the black-and-white photograph, Skip saw that the skin was an unnatural mottled shade. Several parts of Teresa were missing: fingers, a breast, the meaty part of a thigh. Small black marks and ragged lines dotted her body: evidence of unhurried sampling by animals approaching satiation. Where Teresa's throat had once been was now just emptiness, a ruined cage of bone and gristle, surrounded by ragged flesh. Congealed blood ran away in a horrific river toward a long hole in the scarred floorboards. Pattering away from the river of blood were countless small marks Skip realized were paw prints.

"Dogs," Martinez said, gently removing Skip's hand and closing the folder.

Skip's mouth worked soundlessly for a moment. "I'm sorry?" he croaked.

"Stray dogs had been working on her body for a day or so."

"Was she killed by dogs?"

"We thought so at first. Her throat had been torn out with a large bite and there were claw and bite marks over the body. But the coroner's initial examination found definitive evidence that it was a homicide."

Skip looked at him. "What kind of evidence?"

Martinez rose with an easy affability that seemed incongruous with his words. "An unusual kind of mutilation to the fingers and toes, among other things. We'll know a lot more when the autopsy is completed this afternoon. Meantime, please do three things for me. Keep this to yourself. Don't go near the farmhouse. And most important of all: stay where we can find you."

He ushered Skip out of the room and down the hall without another word.

22

AT BREAKFAST THE NEXT MORNING, THE expedition was uncharacteristically silent. Nora felt a mood of doubt. All too clearly, Black's comments from the night before had made their mark.

They proceeded northwest, up a harsh, brutal canyon destitute of vegetation. Even at the early hour, heat was rising from the split rocks, making them look airy and insubstantial. The unwatered horses were irritable and difficult to control.

As they continued, the canyon system grew increasingly complex, branching and rebranching into a twisted maze. It continued to be impossible to get a GPS reading from the canyon floor, and the cliffs were so sheer that Sloane could not have climbed to the top to take a reading without putting herself in danger. Nora found she was spending as much time consulting the map as traveling. Several times they were forced to backtrack out of a blind canyon; other times, the expedition had to wait while Nora and Sloane scouted ahead to find a route. Black was uncharacteristically silent, his face sick with a combination of fear and anger.

Nora struggled with her own doubts. Had her father really gone this far? Had they taken a wrong turn somewhere? A few swales and scatterings of charcoal were visible here and there, but so faint and infrequent as to be background noise;

they could easily be the result of wildfires. There was a new thought now she barely dared to consider: what if her father had been delirious when he wrote the letter? It seemed impossible for anyone to have successfully navigated this labyrinth.

At other times, she thought about the broken skull and dried blood, and what it could possibly mean. In her mind, Pete's Ruin had changed from an unremarkable set of roomblocks to a dark, unnerving little mystery.

By midmorning, the canyon had ended in a sudden puzzle of hoodoo rocks. They squeezed through an opening and topped out in a broken valley, peppered with scrub junipers. As she went over the rise, Nora glanced to the right. She could see the Kaiparowits Plateau as a high, dark line against the horizon.

Then she faced forward, and the vista she saw both horrified and elated her.

On the far side of the valley, raked by the morning sun, rose what could only be the Devil's Backbone: the hogback ridge she had been anticipating and dreading since they first set out. It was a giant, irregular fin of sandstone at least a thousand feet high and many miles long, pocked with vesicles and windblown holes, riven with vertical fractures and slots. The top was notched like a dinosaur's back. It was hideous in its beauty.

Nora led the group over to the shade of a large rock, where they dismounted. She stepped aside with Swire.

"Let's see if we can scout a trail up it first," Nora said. "It looks pretty tough."

For a moment, Swire didn't answer. "From here, I wouldn't exactly call it tough," he said. "I'd call it impossible."

"My father made it over with his two horses."

"So you said." Swire spat a thin stream of tobacco juice. "Then again, this ain't the only ridge around here."

"It's a fault-block cuesta," said Black, who had been listening. "It outcrops for at least a hundred miles. Your father's so-called ridge could be anywhere along there."

"This is the right one," Nora said a little more slowly, trying to keep the tone of doubt out of her voice.

Swire shook his head and began to roll a smoke. "I'll tell you one thing. I want to see the trail with my own eyes before I take any horses up it."

"Fair enough," Nora replied. "Let's go find it. Sloane, keep an eye on things until we get back."

"Sure thing," came the contralto drawl.

The two hiked north along the base of the ridge, looking for a notch or break in the smooth rock that might signal the beginnings of a trail. After half a mile, they came across some shallow caves. Nora noticed that several had ancient smudges of black smoke on their ceilings.

"Anasazi lived here," she said.

"Pretty miserable little caves."

"These were probably temporary dwellings," Nora replied. "Perhaps they farmed these canyon bottoms."

"Must've been farming cholla," Swire muttered laconically.

As they continued northward, the dry creek split into several tributaries, separated by jumbled piles of stone and small outcrops. It was a weird landscape, unfinished, as if God had simply given up trying to impose order on the unruly rocks.

Suddenly, Nora parted some salt cedars and stopped dead. Swire came up, breathing hard.

"Look at this," she breathed.

A series of petroglyphs had been pecked through the desert varnish that streaked the cliff face, exposing lighter rock underneath. Nora knelt, examining the drawings more closely. They were complex and beautiful: a mountain lion; a curious pattern of dots with a small foot; a star inside the moon inside the sun; and a detailed image of Kokopelli, the humpbacked flute player, believed to be the god of fertility. As usual, Kokopelli sported an enormous erection. The panel ended with another complicated grid of dots overlain by a huge spiral, which Nora noted was also reversed, like the ones Sloane had seen at Pete's Ruin.

Swire grunted. "Wish I had his problem," he said, nodding at Kokopelli.

"No you don't," Nora replied. "One Pueblo Indian story claims it was fifty feet long."

They pushed a little farther through the cedars and stumbled on a well-hidden ravine: a crevasse filled with loose rock that slanted diagonally across the sandstone monolith. It was steep and narrow, and it rose up the dizzying face and disappeared. The trail had a raised lip of rock along its outer edge that had the uncanny effect of causing most of it to disappear into the smooth sandstone from only several paces off.

"I've never seen anything so well hidden," Nora said. "This has to be our trail."

"Hope not."

She started up the narrow crevasse, Swire behind her, scrambling over the rocks that filled its bottom. About halfway up it ended in a badly eroded path cut diagonally into the naked sandstone. It was less than three feet wide, one side a sheer face of rock, the other dropping off into terrifying blue space. As Nora stepped near the edge, some pebbles dislodged by her foot rolled down the rock and off the edge, sailing down; Nora listened but could not hear their eventual landing. She knelt. "This is definitely an ancient trail," she said, as she examined eroded cut marks made by prehistoric quartzite tools.

"It sure wasn't built for horses," Swire said.

"The Anasazi didn't have horses."

"We do," came the curt reply.

They moved carefully forward. In places, the cut path had peeled away from the sloping cliff face, forcing them to take a harrowing step across vacant space. At one of these places Nora glanced down and saw a tumble of rocks more than five hundred feet beneath her. She felt a surge of vertigo and hastily stepped across.

The grade gradually lessened, and in twenty minutes they were at the top. A dead juniper, its branches scorched by lightning, marked the point where the trail topped the ridge.

The ridge itself was narrow, perhaps twenty feet across, and in another moment Nora had walked to the far edge.

She looked down the other side into a deep, lush riddle of canyons and washes that merged into an open valley. The trail, much gentler here, switchbacked down into the gloom below them.

For a moment, she could not speak. Slowly, the sun was invading the hidden recesses as it rose toward noon, penetrating the deep holes, chasing the darkness from the purple rocks.

"It's so *green*," she finally said. "All those cottonwoods, and grass for the horses. Look, there's a stream!" At this, she felt the muscles in her throat constrict voluntarily. She'd almost forgotten her thirst in the excitement.

Swire didn't reply.

From their vantage point, Nora took in the lay of the landscape ahead. The Devil's Backbone ran diagonally to the northeast, disappearing around the Kaiparowits Plateau. A vast complex of canyons started on the flanks of the Kaiparowits wilderness and spread out through the slickrock country, eventually coalescing into the valley that swept down in front of them. A peaceful stream flowed down its center, belying the great scarred plain to either side that told of innumerable flash floods. Scattered across the floodplain were boulders, some as large as houses, which had clearly been swept down from the higher reaches of the watershed. Beyond, the valley stepped up through several benchlands, eventually ending in sheer redrock cliffs, pinnacles, and towers. It looked to Nora as if the valley concentrated the entire watershed of the Kaiparowits Plateau in one hideous floodplain.

At the far end of the green valley, at the point where it joined the sheer cliffs, the stream passed through a canebreak, then disappeared into a narrow canyon, riven through a sandstone plateau. Such narrow canyons—known as slot canyons—were common among these southwestern wastes but practically unheard of elsewhere. They were thin alleys, sometimes only a few feet across, caused by the action of water against sandstone over countless years. Despite their narrowness, they were often several hundred feet deep, and could go on for miles before widening into more conventional canyons.

Nora peered at the entrance to this one: a dark slit, slicing into the far end of the great plateau. It was perhaps ten feet wide at the entrance. *That,* Nora thought with a rising feeling of excitement, *must be the slot canyon my father mentioned.* She pulled out her binoculars and looked slowly around. She could make out many south-facing alcoves among the cliffs across the valley, ideal for Anasazi dwellings, but as she scanned them with the glasses she could see nothing. They were all empty. She examined the sheer cliffs leading up to the top of the plateau, but if there was a way over and into the hidden canyon beyond, it was well hidden.

Dropping the binoculars, she turned and looked around the windswept top of the ridge. An overlook like this was a perfect place for her father to have carved his initials and a date: the calling card of remote travelers since time immemorial. Yet there was nothing. Still, from the top of the ridge it seemed likely that Holroyd would finally get his GPS reading.

Swire had settled his back against the rock and was rolling a smoke. He placed it in his mouth, struck a match.

"I ain't bringing my horses up that trail," he said.

Nora looked at him quickly. "But it's the only way up."

"I know it," Swire said, drawing smoke into his lungs.

"So what are you suggesting? That we turn around? Give up?"

Swire nodded. "Yep," he said. There was a brief pause. "And it ain't a suggestion."

In an instant, Nora's elation fell away. She took a deep breath. "Roscoe, this isn't an impossible trail. We'll unload and carry everything up by hand. Then we'll guide the horses, unroped, giving them their heads. It might take the rest of the day, but it can be done."

Roscoe shook his head. "We'll kill horses on that trail, no matter what we do."

Nora knelt beside him. "You've *got* to do this, Roscoe. Everything depends on it. The Institute will replace any horse that gets hurt."

From the expression on his face, she saw she had said the wrong thing. "You know enough about horses to know you're talking through your hat," he replied. "I ain't saying they *can't* do it. I'm saying the risk is too high." A truculent note had crept into his voice. "No man in his right mind would bring horses up that trail. And if you want my opinion, I don't think we're on *any* damn trail, Anasazi or otherwise. Neither does anyone else."

Nora looked at him. "So you all think I'm lost?"

Swire nodded, pulled on his cigarette. "All except Holroyd. But that boy would follow you into a live volcano."

Nora felt her face flush. "Think what you want," she said, pointing toward the sandstone plateau. "But that slot canyon out there is the one my father found. It *has* to be. And there's no other way in. That means he brought two horses up this trail."

"I doubt it."

Nora rounded on him. "When you signed on to this trip, you knew the danger. You *can't* back out now. It can be done, and we're going to do it, with you or without you."

"Nope," he said again.

"Then you're a coward," Nora cried angrily.

Swire's eyes widened quickly, then narrowed. He stared at Nora for a long, silent moment. "I ain't likely to forget you said that," he said at last in a low, even tone.

The breeze blew across the fin of rock, and a pair of ravens rode up the air currents, then dipped back down into space. Nora slumped against the rock, resting her forehead in her hands. She didn't know what to do in the face of Swire's flat refusal. They couldn't go on without him, and the horses were technically his. She closed her eyes against a growing sense of failure, terrible and final. And then she realized something.

"If you want to turn around," she said quietly, glancing over at Swire, "you'd better get going. The last water I remember was a two-day ride back."

Swire's face showed a sudden, curious blankness. Then he swore softly, as he realized the water the horses so desperately needed was in the green valley that lay ahead, below their feet.

He shook his head slowly, and spat. Finally, he eyed Nora. "Looks like you get your wish," he said. And something in the way he looked at her made Nora shrink back.

By the time they returned to camp, it was noon. A palpable air of anxiety hung over the group, and the thirsty horses, tied in the shade, were prancing and slinging their heads.

"You didn't happen to pass a Starbucks, did you?" Smithback asked with forced joviality. "I could really use an iced latte."

Swire brushed his way past them and stalked off to where the horses were hobbled.

"What's with him?" Smithback asked.

"We've got a tough stretch of trail ahead," Nora said.

"How tough?" Black blurted out. Once again, Nora could see naked fear on his face.

"Very tough." She looked around at the dirty faces. The fact that several of them were looking to her for guidance and reassurance gave her another twinge of self-doubt. She took a deep breath.

"The good news is, there's water on the far side of the ridge. The bad news is that we're going to have to carry the gear up by hand. Then Roscoe and I will bring the horses."

Black groaned.

"Take no more than thirty pounds at a time," Nora went on. "Don't try to rush things. It's a rough trail, even on foot. We're going to have to make a couple of trips each."

Black looked like he was about to say something, then stopped. Sloane stood abruptly, walked over to the line of gear, and hefted a pannier onto her shoulder. Holroyd followed, walking a little unsteadily, then Aragon and Smithback. At last, Black raised himself from the rocks, passed a shaky hand over his eyes, and followed them.

Almost three hours later, Nora stood at the top of the Devil's Backbone with the others, breathing heavily and sharing the last of the water. The gear had been brought up over the course of three arduous trips, and was now neatly lined up to one side. Black was a wreck: sitting on a rock, soaked with sweat, his hands shaking; the rest were almost as exhausted. The sun had moved westward and was now shining directly into the long grove of cottonwoods far below them, turning the stream into a twisted thread of silver. The sight seemed inexpressibly lush and beautiful after the barren wastes behind them. Nora ached with thirst.

She turned to look back down the hogback ridge up which they had come. The hard part, bringing the horses up, was still before her. *My God,* she thought. *Sixteen of them* . . . The ache in her limbs fell away, replaced by a small sickness that began to grow in the pit of her stomach.

"Let me help with the horses," Sloane said.

Nora opened her mouth to answer, but Swire interrupted. "No!" he barked. "The fewer there are of us on that ridge, the fewer are gonna get hurt."

Leaving Sloane in charge, Nora hiked back down the trail. Swire, his face dark, brought the animals around, bare except for their halters. Only his own horse, which would lead, had a rope clipped to the halter.

"We're gonna drive them up the trail, single file," he said harshly. "I'll guide Mestizo, you bring up the rear with Fiddlehead. Keep your head up. If a horse falls, get the hell out of the way."

Nora nodded.

"Once we get to the upper trail, you can't stop. Not for anything. Give a horse time to think on that ridge, and he'll panic and try to turn around. So keep them moving, *no matter what*. Got that?"

"Loud and clear," she said.

They started up the trail, careful to keep the horses well apart. At one point the animals hesitated, as if by general consensus; but with some prodding Swire got Mestizo moving again and the rest instinctively followed, noses down, picking their way among the rocks. The air was punctuated with the clatter of hooves, the occasional scrabble among the rocks as an animal missed its footing. As they began to gain altitude, the horses grew more fearful; they lathered up and started blowing hard, showing the whites of their eyes.

Halfway up the ridge, the rubble-filled crevasse ended and the much more dangerous slickrock trail began. Nora craned her neck upward. The worst part of the journey stretched ahead, just a cut in the sloping sandstone, eroded by time into the merest whisper of a path. In the places where it had peeled away, the horses would have to step over blue space. She stared at the series of wicked switchbacks, trying to suppress the anxiety that welled up deep within her.

Swire paused and looked back at her, his eyes cold. *We can turn back now,* his expression seemed to say. *Beyond this point, we won't have that option.*

Nora gazed back at the bandy-legged wrangler, his shoulders barely higher than the horse's withers. He looked as frightened as she felt.

The moment passed. Without a word, Swire turned and began leading Mestizo forward. The animal took a few hesitant steps and balked. The wrangler coaxed a few more steps, then the horse balked again, whinnying in fear. His shoe skidded slightly, then bit once again into the sandstone.

Speaking in low tones and flicking the end of his lasso well behind the horse, Swire got Mestizo moving again. The others followed, their trail experience and strong herd attachment keeping them going. They worked their way upward at a painful pace, the only sounds now the thump and scrape of iron-shod toes digging into canted slickrock, the occasional blow of fear. Swire began singing a low, mournful, soothing song, words indistinct, his voice quavering slightly.

They arrived at the first switchback. Slowly, Swire guided Mestizo around the curve, then continued up the rockface and past a deep crack until he was directly above Nora's head. Once, Sweetgrass skidded on the slickrock and scrabbled at the edge, and for a moment Nora thought she would go over. Then she recovered, eyes wide, flanks trembling.

After agonizing minutes they arrived at the second switchback: a wickedly sharp turn over a narrow section of trail. Reaching the far side, Mestizo suddenly balked once again. The second horse, Beetlebum, stopped as well, then began to back up. Watching from below, Nora saw the animal place one hind foot over the edge of the trail and out into space. She froze. The horse's hindquarters dropped and the foot kicked out twice, looking for a purchase that wasn't there. As she watched, the horse's balance shifted inexorably backward; the animal dropped over the edge, rolled once, and then hurtled down toward her, letting out a strange, high-pitched scream. Nora watched, paralyzed. Time seemed to slow as the horse tumbled, limbs kicking in a terrifying ballet. She felt its shadow cross her face, and then it struck Fiddlehead, directly in front of her, with a massive smack. Fiddlehead vanished as both animals hurtled off the edge of the ridge into the void. There was a moment of horrible, listening silence, followed by double muffled thumps and the sharp crackle of falling rocks far below. The sounds seemed to echo forever in the dry valley, reverberating from ever more distant walls.

"Close up and keep moving!" came the harsh, strained command from above. Forcing herself into action, Nora urged the new rearward horse forward—Smithback's horse, Hurricane Deck. But he wouldn't move; a clonus of horror trembled along the animal's flanks. Then, in a galvanic instant, he reared up, whirling around toward her. Nora instinctively grabbed his halter. With a frenzied clawing of steel on rock, Hurricane scrabbled at the edge of the trail, wide eyes staring at her. Realizing her mistake, she released the halter, but her timing was slow and already the falling horse had pulled her off balance. She had a brief glimpse of yawning blue space. Then she landed on her side, her legs rolling over the edge of the cliff, hands scrabbling to grip the smooth sandstone. She heard, as if from a great distance, Swire shouting, and then from below the soggy, bursting sound of a wet bag as Hurricane Deck hit bottom.

She clawed at the rock, fingernails fighting for purchase as she dangled in the abyss. She could feel the updrafts of wind tickling her legs. In desperation, she clutched the stone tighter, her nails tearing and splitting as she continued to slide backward down the tipped surface of stone. Then her right hand brushed against a projecting rill; no more than a quarter inch high, but enough to get a handhold. She strained, feeling her strength draining away. *Now or never,* she thought, and she gave a great heave, swinging herself up sideways. It was just enough to get one foot back onto the trail. With a second heave she managed to roll her body up and over. She lay on her back, heart hammering a frantic cadence. Ahead and above came a whinny of fear, and the clatter of hooves on stone.

"Get the hell up! Keep moving!" she heard faintly from above. She rose shakily to her feet and started forward, as if in a dream, driving the remnant of the remuda up the trail.

She did not remember the rest of the journey. The next clear memory was of lying facedown, hugging the warm, dusty rock of the ridge summit; then a pair of hands were gently turning her over; and Aragon's calm, steady face stared down into her own. Beside him were Smithback and Holroyd, gazing at her with intense concern. Holroyd's face in particular was a mask of agonizing worry.

Aragon helped Nora to a nearby rock. "The horses—" Nora began.

"There was no other way," Aragon interrupted quietly, taking her hands. "You're hurt."

Nora looked down. Her hands were covered with blood from her ruined fingernails. Aragon opened his medical kit.

"When you swung out over that cliff," he said, "I thought you were done for." He dabbed at the fingertips, removing a few pieces of grit and fingernail with tweezers. He worked swiftly, expertly, smearing on topical antibiotic and placing butterfly bandages over the ends of her fingertips. "Wear your gloves for a few days," he said. "You'll be uncomfortable for a while, but the injuries are superficial."

Nora glanced at the group. They were looking back at her, motionless, shocked to silence by what had happened. "Where's Roscoe?" she managed to ask.

"Back down the trail," Sloane replied.

Nora dropped her head into her hands. And then, as if in answer, three well-spaced gunshots sounded below, echoing crazily among the canyons before dying away into distant thunder.

"God," Nora groaned. Fiddlehead, her own horse. Beetle-bum, Smithback's nemesis. Hurricane Deck. Gone. She could still see the wide pleading eyes of Hurricane; the teeth, so strangely long and narrow, exposed in a final grin of terror.

Ten minutes later Swire appeared, breathing heavily. He passed Nora and went toward the horses, redividing and repacking the loads in silence. Holroyd came over to her and gently took her hand. "I got a decent reading," he whispered.

Nora glanced up at him, hardly caring.

"We're right smack on the trail," he said, smiling.

Nora could only shake her head.

Compared to the nightmarish ascent, the trail down into the valley beyond the hogback ridge offered few difficulties. The horses, smelling water, charged ahead. Tired as they were, the group began to jog, and Nora found the events of the last hours temporarily receding in her devouring thirst. They splashed into the water upstream from the horses and Nora fell to her stomach, burying her face in the water. It was the most exquisite sensation she had ever felt, and she drank deeply, pausing only to gasp for air, until a sudden spasm of nausea contracted her stomach. She backed away, retiring to a spot beneath the rustling cottonwoods, breathing hard and feeling the sting of evaporation on her wet clothes. Gradually the waves of nausea passed. She saw Black bent double in the trees, vomiting up water, joined shortly by Holroyd. Smithback was kneeling in the stream, oblivious, bathing his head with cupped hands. Sloane staggered over, sopping wet, and knelt beside Nora.

"Swire needs our help with the horses," she said.

They went downstream and helped Swire drag the horses out of the water, to prevent any possibility of fatal overdrinking. As they worked, Swire refused to meet Nora's eyes.

After a rest, the group remounted and continued downstream into the new world of the valley. The water ran over a cobbled bed, filling the air with tranquil noise. The sounds of life rose about them: trilling cicadas, humming dragonflies, even the occasional eructation of a frog. As Nora's thirst abated, the sickening horror of the accident returned with fresh force. She was riding a new horse now, Arbuckles, and every jarring movement seemed a reproachful memory of Fiddlehead. She thought of Swire's poem to Hurricane Deck, almost a love ballad to the horse. She wondered how she was ever going to work things out with him.

They traveled down the valley, which narrowed as it approached the broad sandstone plateau, rising in front of them now less than a mile away. Nora glanced up at the cliffs as they passed, noting again the odd lack of ruins. This was an ideal valley for prehistoric settlement, and yet there was nothing. If, after all that had happened, this turned to be the wrong canyon system—she shut the thought from her mind.

The stream made another bend. The naked plateau loomed ever closer, the stream at last disappearing into the narrow slot canyon carved into its side. According to the radar map, the canyon should open, about a mile farther along, into the small valley that—she hoped—contained Quivira. But the slot canyon itself that lay between them and the inner valley was clearly too narrow for horses.

As they road up to the massive sandstone wall, Nora noticed a large rock beside the stream with some markings on its flanks. As she dismounted and came nearer, she could see a small panel of petroglyphs, similar to those they had found at the base of the ridge: a series of dots and a small foot, along with another star and a sun. She couldn't help but notice that there was a large reversed spiral carved on top of the other images.

The rest came up beside her. She noticed Aragon gazing at the glyphs, an intent expression on his face.

"What do you think?" she asked.

"I've seen other examples of dot patterns like these along the ancient approaches to Hopi," he said at last. "I believe they give distance and direction information."

"Sure," Black scoffed. "And the freeway interchanges and the location of the nearest Howard Johnson's, I'll bet. Everyone knows Anasazi petroglyphs are indecipherable."

Aragon ignored this. "The footlike glyph indicates walking, and the dots indicate distance. Based on other sites I've seen, each dot represents a walking distance of about sixteen minutes, or three quarters of a mile."

"And the antelope?" Nora asked. "What does that symbolize?"

Aragon glanced at her. "An antelope," he said.

"So this isn't a kind of writing?"

Aragon looked back at the rock. "Not in the sense we're used to. It's not phonetic, syllabic, or ideographic. My own view is that it's an entirely different way of using symbols. But that doesn't mean it's not writing."

"On the other side of the ridge," Nora said, "I saw a star inside the moon, inside the sun. I'd never seen anything like it before."

"Yes. The sun is the symbol for the supreme deity, the moon the symbol for the future, and the star a symbol of truth. I took the whole thing to be an indicator that an oracle, a kind of Anasazi Delphi, lay ahead."

"You mean Quivira?" Nora asked.

Aragon nodded.

"And what does this spiral mean?" asked Holroyd.

Aragon hesitated a moment. "That spiral was added later. It's reversed, of course." His voice trailed off. "In the context of the other things we've seen, I'd call it a warning, or omen, laid on top of these earlier symbols. A notice to travelers not to proceed, an indication of evil."

There was a sudden silence.

"Lions and tigers and bears, oh my," murmured Smithback.

"Obviously, there's still a lot we don't know," Aragon said, the slightest trace of defensiveness in his voice. "Perhaps you, Mr. Smithback, with your no doubt profound knowledge of Anasazi witches and their modern-day descendants, the skinwalkers, can enlighten us further."

The writer rolled his tongue around his cheek and raised his eyebrows, but said nothing.

As they moved away, Holroyd gave a shout. He had walked around to the side of the rock nearest the entrance to the slot canyon. Now he pointed to a much fresher inscription, scraped into the rock with a penknife. As Nora stared at it, she felt her cheeks begin to burn. Still staring, she knelt beside the stone, fingers slowly tracing the narrow grooves that spelled out P.K. 1983.

23

As Nora touched her father's initials on the rock, something inside her seemed to give way. A knot of tension, tightened over the harrowing days, loosened abruptly, and she leaned against the smooth surface of the rock, feeling an intense, overwhelming flood of relief. Her father *had* been here. They had been following his trail all along. She realized dimly that the group was crowding around, congratulating her.

Slowly she rose to her feet. She gathered the expedition under a small grove of gambel oaks, near the point where the stream plunged into the slot canyon. Everyone seemed to be in high spirits except Swire, who silently moved off with the horses to a nearby patch of grass. Bonarotti was busy cleaning the dirty cookware in the stream

"We're almost there," she said. "According to our maps, this is the slot canyon we've been searching for. We should find the hidden canyon of Quivira at the far end."

"Is it safe?" Black asked. "Looks pretty narrow to me."

"I've kept my eyes on the canyon walls," Sloane said. "There haven't been any obvious trails that would lead up and over to the next valley. If we're going on, this is the only way through."

"It's getting late," Nora said. "The real question is, shall we unpack the horses and carry everything in now? Or shall we camp now and go in tomorrow?"

Black answered first. "I'd prefer not to carry any more equipment today, thank you, especially through *that*." He gestured past the canebrake toward the narrow slot, which looked more like a fissure in the rock than a canyon.

Smithback sat back, fanning himself with a branch of oak leaves. "As long as you're asking, I'd just as soon sit here with my feet in the stream and see what victuals Signore Bonarotti brings out of his magic box."

The rest seemed to agree. Then Nora turned toward Sloane. In the woman's eyes, she immediately saw the same eagerness that was kindling within her.

Sloane grinned her slow grin and nodded. "Feel up to it?" she asked.

Nora looked at the entrance to the slot canyon—barely more than a dark seam in the rock—and nodded. Then she turned once again toward the group.

"Sloane and I are going to reconnoiter," she said, glancing at her watch. "We might not be able to get in and back before darkness, so it may turn out to be an overnight trip. Any objections?"

There were none. While the camp settled down to its routine, Nora loaded a sleeping bag and water pump into a backpack. Sloane did the same, adding a length of rope and some climbing equipment to hers. Bonarotti wordlessly pressed small, heavy packets of food into each of their hands.

Shouldering their packs, they waved goodbye and hiked down the stream. Past the grove of oaks, the rivulet burbled across a pebbled bed and entered the canebrake outside the mouth of the slot canyon. Much of the cane had been torn and shredded into a dense tangle, and there were several battered tree trunks and boulders lying about.

They pushed ahead into the cane, which rustled and crackled at their passage. Deerflies and no-see-ums danced and droned in the thick air. Nora led, waving them away with an impatient hand.

"Nora," she heard Sloane say softly behind her, "look carefully to your right. Look, but don't move."

Nora followed Sloane's glance toward a piece of cane perhaps eighteen inches away. A small gray rattlesnake was coiled tightly around it at about shoulder height.

"I hate to tell you, Nora, but you just elbowed this poor snake aside." It was meant to sound lighthearted, but Sloane's voice carried a small tremor.

Nora stared in horrified fascination. She could see the cane still swaying slightly from her passage. "Christ," she whispered, her throat dry and constricted.

"Probably the only reason he didn't strike was because it would have caused him to fall," added Sloane. "*Sistrurus toxidius,* the pigmy gray rattler. Second most poisonous rattlesnake in North America."

Nora continued to stare at the snake, almost perfectly camouflaged by its surroundings. "I feel a little sick," she said.

"Let me walk first."

In no mood to argue, Nora stood by while Sloane went on ahead, gingerly picking her way through the broken cane, pausing every few steps to scrutinize her path.

She stopped suddenly. "There's another one," she pointed. The snake, disturbed, was swiftly gliding down a stalk ahead of them. It gave a sudden, chilling buzz before it disappeared into a tangle of brush.

"Too bad Bonarotti isn't here," said Sloane, moving ahead carefully. "He'd probably make a cassoulet out of them." As she spoke, there was another buzz directly beneath her feet. She leapt backward with a shout, then gave the snake a wide berth.

A few more harrowing moments brought them to the far side of the canebrake. Here the mouth of the canyon opened before them, two scooped and polished stone walls about ten feet apart, with a bottom of smooth sand barely covered by slowly moving water.

"Jesus," Nora said. "I've never seen so many rattlers in one place in my life."

"Probably washed down by a flood," said Sloane. "Now they're wet, cold, and pissed."

They continued down the creek into the slot canyon, splashing in the shallow water. The narrow walls quickly pressed in around them, leaving Nora with the uncomfortable feeling that she was along the bottom of a long, slender container. Eons of floods had sculpted the walls of the canyon into glossy hollows, ribs, pockets, and tubes. There were only occasional glimpses of sky, and they proceeded in a reddish half-light that filtered down from far above. With the high narrow walls of the slot canyon crowding out the sun, the air at its base felt surprisingly chilly. In places where water had scooped out a larger hollow, they encountered pools of loose quicksand. The best way to get past them, Nora found, was to start crawling through on her hands and knees and, when the quicksand at last gave way, to lie on her stomach and breaststroke, keeping her legs rigid and unmoving behind her. The pack, oddly enough, buoyed her, acting as a kind of float on her back.

"It's going to be a wet night," Sloane said, emerging from one of the pools.

As the canyon descended, the light grew dimmer. At one point, a huge cottonwood trunk, horribly scarred and mauled, had somehow become jammed in the canyon walls about twenty feet above their heads. Nearby, there was a narrow hollow in the rockface, above a small, stepped ledge.

"Must've been some storm that put that tree up there," Sloane murmured, glancing upward at the trunk. "I'd sure hate to be caught in a flash flood in one of these canyons."

"I've heard the first thing you feel is a rising wind," Nora replied. "Then you hear a sound, echoing and distorted. Someone once told me it sounded almost like distant voices or applause. At that point, you get your butt out as fast as possible. If you're still in the canyon by the time you hear the roar of water, it's too late. You're dead meat."

Sloane broke out into her low, sultry laugh. "Thanks a lot," she said. "Now you'll have me climbing the walls every time I feel a breeze."

As they walked on, the canyon narrowed still further and sloped downward in a series of pools, each filled with chocolate-colored water. Sometimes the water was only an inch deep, covering shivery quicksand; other times, it was over their heads. Each pool was connected to the next by a pitched slot so narrow they had to squeeze through it sideways, holding their packs. Above their heads, large boulders had jammed between the canyon walls, creating an eerie brown twilight.

After half an hour's struggle, they came to a pourover above an especially long, narrow pool. Beyond, Nora could make out a faint glow. Taking the lead, she eased down into the pool and swam across toward a small boulder, wedged between the walls about six feet above the ground. A thick curtain of weeds and roots trailed from it, through which came a sheen of sunlight.

Nora crawled under the boulder and paused at the shaggy curtain, wringing the water from her wet hair. "It's like the entrance to something magical," Sloane said as she approached. "But what?"

Nora glanced at her for a moment. Then, placing her arms together, she pushed through the dense tangle.

Although not strong, the light of the late afternoon sun beyond seemed dazzling after their journey through the cramped, twisting canyon. As her eyes adjusted, Nora could see a small valley open up below them. The stream tumbled down a defile and spread out into a sandy creek along the valley floor. There was a narrow floodplain, covered with pounded boulders, repeatedly raked by flash floods. Cottonwoods lined the banks of the floodplain, their massive trunks scarred and hung with old flood debris. The creek had cut down through a layer of rock in the center of the valley, creating benchlands on either side that were also dotted with cottonwoods, scrub oak, rabbitbrush, and wildflowers.

The valley had an intimate feeling: it was only about four

hundred yards long by two hundred yards wide, a jeweled pocket in the red sandstone. The mellow sunlight fell upon a riot of color: blooming Apache plumes, Indian paintbrush, scarlet gilia. Puffy cumulus clouds, tinged with the afternoon light, drifted across the narrow patch of sky above the clifftops.

After the long dark crawl through the slot canyon, arriving at this beautiful valley was like stumbling upon a lost world. Everything about it—its intimate size, its high surrounding walls, its incredible remoteness, the tremendous difficulties involved in attaining it—filled Nora with the sensation of discovering a hidden paradise. As she looked around, enraptured, a breeze began to come up. As the trees rustled, cotton fell from their catkins and drifted in the lazy air like brilliant motes of trapped light.

After a moment Nora glanced over at Sloane. The woman had a look of intense, suppressed excitement on her face; the amber eyes seemed to blaze as they darted about, scanning first the canyon floor, then its walls.

Light as a cat, Sloane moved silently down the shallow stream to the canyon floor. Nora lagged behind for a moment. Mingled with her awe of the beauty was a fresh certainty: this was the valley her father had discovered. And with this certainty came another thought, awful in its suddenness. Was the place terrible as well as beautiful? Would she find her father's remains somewhere down there on the canyon floor, or hidden among the ledges above?

But as quickly as it had come, the feeling dissipated. Somebody had found and mailed his letter. That in itself was a mystery, which gnawed at her constantly. But at least it meant that, wherever her father's bones lay, they probably lay somewhere else, closer to civilization. Still, it was several moments before she followed Sloane to the flat sandy benchland, girded with rocks, well above the level of the stream. A small grove of cottonwoods provided shade.

"How's this for a campsite?" Sloane asked, dropping her pack.

"Couldn't be more perfect," Nora replied. She unshouldered her own pack, pulled out her soggy sleeping bag, shook it out, and draped it over a bush.

Then her eyes turned ineluctably back toward the towering cliffs that surrounded them on four sides. Pulling the waterproof binoculars from her pack, she began scanning the rock faces. The sandstone cliffs rose in steplike fashion from the canyon floor: sheer pitches, interrupted by benchlands of softer strata that had eroded back to form flat areas. Near the far end of the valley, a large rockfall had dropped a pitched tangle of house-sized boulders that lay in a precarious jumble against the cliff face. But the rockfall led up to nothing; and there was no sign in the valley of a trail, a ruin, anything.

She shook off the sudden cold feeling in her gut, reminding herself that if the ruined city was obvious, it would have been found. Any caves or alcoves formed in those benches above could not be seen from below. It was precisely the kind of spot favored by the Anasazi.

Her father, however, *had* seen a clear hand-and-toe trail. Her eyes again swept the lower rock faces, searching for the telltale signs of a trail. She saw nothing but smooth faces of red sandstone.

Nora glanced around for Sloane. The woman had already abandoned her scrutiny of the walls and was walking along the base of the cliffs, peering intently at the ground. *Looking for potsherds or flint chips,* Nora thought approvingly: always a good way to locate a hidden ruin above. Every fifty feet, Sloane would stop and squint up the cliff faces at an oblique angle, looking for the telltale shallow notches that would signify a trail.

Nora shoved her binoculars into her damp jeans and walked along the cutbanks and rock shelves above the stream, examining the soil profile for any cultural evidence. She knew they should be using the last of the light to build a fire and prepare dinner. But, like Sloane, she felt compelled to keep searching.

It was the work of ten minutes to reach the opposite side

of the valley. Here, the stream disappeared into another slot canyon, much narrower even than the one they had crawled through. Narrow stone benches crawled up the red walls on either side, and from the gorge below came the sound of falling water. Carefully, she crept up to its edge. Water fell from the valley in a long stream. A plume of mist rose from where it struck the rocks below, filling the end of the canyon with a watery veil she could barely see through. A small microclimate had developed, and the rocks were thickly covered with moss and ferns. She knew from the maps, though, that the stream ran on through a series of descending waterfalls and pools, each separated by twenty or thirty feet of overhanging rock. It would be impossible to descend without a highly technical climb, and in any case at its bottom the slot seemed too narrow to admit a human being. But there would be no point even in trying: as the maps indicated, the stream ran in this impassable fashion for sixteen miles, until it spilled off the North Rim of Marble Gorge and dropped a thousand feet to the Colorado River. Anyone caught in a flash flood and pushed into this canyon would emerge at the Colorado just so much ground beef.

She moved on, pausing at the large rockfall. It was cool in the shadow of the cliffs, and she shivered slightly. The rockfall, with its dark holes and hidden spaces between the huge boulders, looked like a lair of ghosts. It appeared too unstable to climb. And, in any case, the cliff face behind it was sheer and unmarked by toeholds.

She worked her way back up the other side of the creek and encountered Sloane, who had finished her own survey. The almond eyes had lost some of their brilliance.

"Any luck?" Nora asked.

Sloane shook her head. "I'm having trouble believing there was a city here. I haven't found *anything.*"

For once, the trademark smile was missing, and she seemed agitated, almost angry. *This city is as important to her as it is to me,* Nora thought.

"The Anasazi never built a road to nowhere," Nora replied. "There's *got* to be something here."

"Perhaps," Sloane said slowly, peering again at the cliff faces surrounding them. "But if I hadn't seen those radar images and the hogback ridge, I'd have a hard time believing we've been following any sort of road at all the last two days."

The sun had now dipped low enough to bring creeping shadows across the valley floor. "Look, Sloane," Nora said. "We haven't even begun to examine this valley. We'll spend tomorrow morning making a careful survey. And if we still don't find anything, we'll bring the proton magnetometer in and scan for structures beneath the sand."

Sloane was still looking intently up at the cliffs, as if demanding they give up their secrets. Then she looked at Nora, and gave a slow smile. "Maybe you're right," she said. "Let's get a fire going and see if we can dry out these bags."

After she had scooped out a shallow firepit and built a ring of stones, Nora sat by the fire and changed the damp bandages on her fingers. The sleeping bags began to steam slightly in the heat.

"What do you suppose Bonarotti put in those care packages?" Sloane asked as she piled more logs on the fire.

"Let's find out." Nora retrieved a pot from her daypack, then grabbed the small packet Bonarotti had thrust into her hand. She unwrapped it curiously. Inside were two Ziploc bags, still dry, one containing what looked like tiny pasta and the other a mix of herbs. ADD TO BOILING WATER AND COOK SEVEN MINUTES was written on the first bag in black Magic Marker; REMOVE FROM HEAT, DRAIN, ADD THIS MIXTURE was written on the second.

Ten minutes later, they pulled the simmering mixture from the fire, drained off the water, and added the second packet. Instantly, a wonderful aroma rose from the pot.

"Couscous with savory herbs," Sloane whispered. "Isn't Bonarotti a prince?"

From the couscous, they moved on to Sloane's dish— lentils with sun-dried vegetables in a curried beef broth—

then cleared away the dishes. Nora shook her bag out and laid it in the soft sand, close to the fire. Then, stripping off most of her wet clothes, she climbed in and lay back, breathing the clean air of the canyon, gazing at the dome of stars overhead. Despite the words of encouragement she'd given Sloane—despite the remarkable meal—Nora couldn't entirely escape a private fear of her own.

"So what'll we find tomorrow, Nora?" Sloane's husky voice, surprisingly close in the near darkness, echoed her own thoughts.

Nora sat up on one shoulder and glanced over. Sloane was sitting cross-legged on her sleeping bag, combing her hair. Her jeans were drying on a nearby limb, and an oversized shirt spilled across her bare knees. The flickering light threw her wide cheekbones into sharp relief, giving her beautiful face a mysterious, exotic look.

"I don't know," Nora replied. "What do you think we'll find?"

"Quivira," came the reply, almost whispered.

"You didn't seem so sure an hour ago."

Sloane shrugged. "Oh, it'll be here," she said. "My father is never wrong."

The woman's face wore its trademark lazy smile, but something in her voice told Nora it wasn't entirely a joke.

"So tell me about *your* father," Sloane went on.

Nora took a long breath. "Well, the truth is, from the outside he was a traditional Irish screwup. He drank too much. He always had schemes and plans. He hated real work. But you know what?" She looked up at Sloane. "He was the best father anyone could have had. He loved us. He told us he loved us ten times a day. It was the first thing he said to us in the morning and the last thing at night. He was the kindest person I ever knew. He took us on almost all of his adventures. We went everywhere with him, looking for lost ruins, digging for treasure, scouring old battlegrounds with metal detectors. Nowadays, the archaeologist in me is horrified at what we used to do. We packed horses into the Superstition

Mountains trying to find the Lost Dutchman Mine, we spent a summer in the Gila Wilderness looking for the Adams diggings—that sort of thing. I'm amazed we survived. My mother couldn't stand it, and she eventually took steps to divorce him. As a way to win her back, he went off to discover Quivira. And we never heard from him again—until this old letter arrived. But he's the reason I became an archaeologist."

"You think he could still be alive?"

"No," said Nora. "That's out of the question. He would never have abandoned us like that."

She breathed the fragrant night air as silence settled into the canyon. "You have a pretty remarkable father yourself," she went on at last.

A thin trace of light suddenly lanced across the dark sky. "Shooting star," was Sloane's reply. She was silent for a moment. "You said the same thing, back on the trail. I suppose it's true. He is a remarkable father. And he expects me to be an even more remarkable daughter."

"How so?"

Sloane continued to stare at the sky. "I guess you could say he's one of those fathers who holds his child to an almost impossible standard. I was always made to perform, to measure up. I was only allowed to bring home friends who could carry on an intellectual discussion at the dinner table. But nothing I did was ever good enough, and even now he doesn't trust me to succeed."

She shook her head. "I still remember when I was in seventh grade, my piano teacher made all us students attend a recital. I'd worked up this really difficult Bach three-part invention, and I was very proud of myself. But the teacher had this other student, Ursula Rein, who was a true prodigy. She's teaching at Juilliard now. Anyway, she played right before me, and did this Chopin waltz at about twice normal speed." Her face hardened. "When my father heard that, he made me get up and leave with him. I was so angry, so embarrassed. I'd practiced for so long, and I thought he'd be proud of me. . . . Oh, he made up some excuse, said his stomach was bothering him or something. But I knew the real reason was he couldn't stand for me to come in second." She laughed. "I'm still amazed he wanted me on this expedition."

Nora could hear the bitter undertone in the laugh. "It doesn't seem to have hurt you," she replied.

"Because I don't let it hurt me," she said, looking at Nora with a defiant flip of her hair.

Nora realized Sloane might have taken the comment the wrong way. "No, that's not what I meant. I meant, you're—"

"And you know what?" Sloane interrupted, as if she hadn't heard. "I don't ever remember *my* father telling me he loved me."

She looked away. Nora, unsure how to answer, decided to change the subject. "I've been curious. You've got the money, looks, and talent to be anything. So why are you an archaeologist?"

Sloane turned back to her, the grin returning. "Why? Are archaeologists supposed to be poor, ugly, and dumb?"

"Of course not."

Sloane gave a low laugh. "It's the family business, isn't it? The Rothschilds are bankers, the Kennedys are politicians, the Goddards are archaeologists. I'm his only child. He raised me to be an archaeologist and I wasn't strong enough to deny him."

The father again, Nora thought. She looked into Sloane's face. "Don't you like archaeology?"

"I *love* it," came the reply, a brief note of passion sounding in the rich contralto. "I never stop thinking about the precious things and the secrets that lie hidden beneath the soil. They're waiting to teach us something, if only we're smart enough to find them. But I'll never be a good enough archaeologist to satisfy *him*." She paused a moment, then spoke more briskly. "It's funny, Nora, but if I find Quivira, you know who's going to be remembered? You know who's going to go down in the history books like Wetherill and Earl Morris? Not me. Him." She punctuated this with a short, harsh laugh. "Isn't that ironic?"

Nora could not find an answer to this.

Sloane uncrossed her legs and lay down atop her sleeping bag. She sighed, teased her hair back with one finger. "Seeing anyone?"

Nora paused to consider this abrupt change of subject. "Not really," she replied. "And you? Are you dating someone?"

"Not anybody I wouldn't drop in a second if the right person came along." Sloane was silent for a moment, as if thinking about something. "So what do you think of the men in this group of ours? You know, as *men*."

Nora hesitated again, not feeling entirely comfortable talking like this about people she was leading. But the steamy warmth of the sleeping bag, and the brightness of the stars, somehow conspiratorial in their proximity, relaxed her defenses. "I hadn't really thought about them as, you know, potential dating material."

Sloane gave a low laugh. "Well, I have. I'd pegged you for Smithback."

Nora sat up. "Smithback?" she cried. "He's insufferable."

"He's in a position to do a lot for your career if this all works out. Funny, too, if you like your humor dry as a martini. He's led a pretty interesting life these last couple of years. Did you ever read that book of his, about the New York museum murders?"

"He gave me a copy. I haven't really looked at it."

"It's a hell of a read. And the guy's not bad looking, either, in a citified sort of way."

Nora shook her head. "He's about as full of himself as they come."

"Maybe. But I think part of that is just facade. The guy can take it as well as dish it out." She paused. "And something about that mouth tells me he's a great kisser."

"If you find out, let me know." Nora glanced at Sloane. "Got your eyes on anybody?"

By way of answering, Sloane fanned herself absently. "Black," she said at last.

It took a moment for Nora to digest this. "What?" she asked.

"If I had to choose somebody, I'd choose Black."

Nora shook her head. "I don't get it."

"Oh, I know he can be obnoxious. He's terrified of being away from civilization. But you wait. When we find Quivira, he'll come into his own. It's easy to forget out here in the middle of nowhere that he's one of the most prominent archaeologists in the country. With good reason. Talk about someone who could do a lot for a career." She laughed. "And look at that big-boned frame of his. I'll bet he's hung like a fire hydrant."

And with that she stood up, letting the shirt slide off her arms and fall away to the ground. "Now look what you've done," she said. "I'm going down to the stream to cool off."

Nora leaned back. As if at a distance, she heard Sloane down at the stream, splashing softly. In a few moments she returned, her sleek body glistening in the moonlight. She slid noiselessly into her sleeping bag. "Sweet dreams, Nora Kelly," she murmured.

Then she turned away, and within moments, Nora could hear her breathing, regular and serene. But Nora lay still, eyes open to the stars, for a long time.

24

Nora awoke with a start. She had slept so deeply, so heavily, that for a moment she did not know where she was. She sat up in panic. Dawn light was just bloodying the rimrock above her head. A throbbing at the ends of her bandaged fingers quickly brought back the memories of the previous day: the terrible struggle on the hogback ridge; the discovery of the slot canyon and this hidden valley beyond; the lack of any signs of a ruin. She looked around. The sleeping bag beside her was empty.

She rose, sore muscles protesting, and stirred the ashes of the fire. Cutting some dry grass and folding it into a packet, she shoved it in the coals. A thread of smoke came up, then the grass burst into flame. She quickly added sticks. Rummaging in her pack, she filled a tiny two-cup espresso pot with grounds and water, put it on the fire, then went down to the creek to wash. When she returned, the pot was hissing. She poured herself a cup just as Sloane walked up. The perpetual smile was gone.

"Have some coffee," Nora said.

Sloane took the proffered cup and sat down beside her. They sipped in silence as the sun crept down the canyon walls.

"There's nothing here, Nora," Sloane said at last. "I just

spent the last hour going over this place inch by inch. Your pal Holroyd can scan this ground with the magnetometer, but I've never seen a ruin under the sand or in a cliff that didn't leave *some* trace on the surface. I haven't found one potsherd or flint chip."

Nora set down her coffee. "I don't believe it."

Sloane shrugged. "Take a look for yourself."

"I will."

Nora walked to the base of the cliffs and began making a clockwise circuit of the valley. She could see the welter of footprints where Sloane had scoured the ground for artifacts. Nora, instead, took out her binoculars and systematically searched the cliffs, setbacks, and rimrock above her. Every twenty steps she stopped and searched again. The morning invasion of light into the valley continued, each minute creating fresh angles and shadows on the rock. At each pause she forced her eyes across the same rock faces, from different angles, straining to recognize something—a toehold, a shaped building block, a faded petroglyph, *anything* that indicated human occupation. After completing the circuit, she then crossed the valley from north to south and from east to west, heedlessly wading through the stream again and again, peering up at the walls, trying to get every possible view of the towering cliffs above.

Ninety minutes later she came back into camp, wet and tired. She sat down beside Sloane, saying nothing. Sloane was also silent, her head bowed, staring into the sand, idly tracing a circle with a stick.

Nora said nothing. She thought about her father, and all the terrible things her mother had said about him over the years. Was it possible that she could have been right all this time? *Was* he untrustworthy and unreliable—just a fantasist, after all?

They remained beside the dying fire, wordlessly, for perhaps ten minutes, perhaps twenty, as the full weight of the colossal defeat settled upon them.

"What are we going to tell the others?" Nora said at last.

Sloane tossed her short hair back with a shake of her head. "We'll do it by the book," she said. "We can't turn around now without going through the formalities. Like you said last night, we'll bring in the equipment, do an archaeological survey of the valley. And then we'll go home. You to your office. And me . . ." She paused. "To my father."

Nora glanced over at Sloane. A haunted look came into her amber eyes as she spoke. The woman looked back at Nora. As she did so, her expression softened.

"But here I am, moping like a selfish schoolgirl," she said, the old smile returning. "When you're the one who really needs consoling. I can't tell you how sorry I am, Nora. You know how much we all believed in your dream."

Nora looked up at the dark encircling cliffs, the smooth sandstone faces that showed no trace of a trail. There had been no other ruins in the entire canyon system, and this was no exception. "I just can't believe it," she said. "I can't believe I dragged you all out here, wasted your father's money, risked lives, killed horses, for nothing."

Sloane took one of Nora's hands and gave it a reassuring squeeze. Then she stood up.

"Come on," she said. "The others are waiting for us."

Nora stowed the cooking gear and sleeping bag into her pack, then shouldered it wearily. Her mouth felt painfully dry. The thought of the days to come—going through the motions, working without hope—was almost too much to bear. She looked up yet again at the rock, picking out the same landmarks she had seen yesterday. The morning light was coming in at a different angle, raking along the lower cliffs. Her eyes instinctively scoured the rock face, but it remained clear and barren. She raised her eyes higher.

And then she saw something: a single, shallow notch in the rock, forty feet above the ground. The light now lay at a perfect raking angle. It could be natural; in fact, it probably *was* natural. But she found herself digging into her pack anyway for her binoculars. She focused and looked again. There it was: a tiny depression, seemingly floating in space a foot or so below a narrow ledge. Magnified, it looked a little less natural. But where was the rest of the trail?

Angling her binoculars down, she saw the answer: below the lone notch, a section of the cliff face had recently peeled off: the desert varnish—that layer of oxidation built up on sandstone over centuries—was a lighter, fresher color. At the base of the cliffs was the proof—a small heap of broken rubble. Her heart began to pound. She turned and found Sloane staring at her curiously.

She handed over the binoculars. "Look at that."

Sloane examined the indicated spot. Suddenly, her body tensed.

"It's a *moqui* step," she said breathlessly. "The top of a trail. The rest must have fallen away. Jesus, look at that pile of rubble at the bottom. How could I be so stupid? There I was, so busy looking for sherds that I never thought . . ."

"That little landslide must have happened since my father saw the trail," Nora said. But Sloane was already digging into her pack, pulling out a rope shot through with black fibers.

"What are you doing?" she asked.

"No problem," came the response. "It's a friction climb."

"You're going up there?"

"Damn right I'm going up there." She worked frantically, pulling out her equipment, kicking off her hiking boots and tugging on climbing shoes.

"What about me?" Nora asked.

Sloane glanced up at her. "You?"

"There's no way in hell you're going up there without me."

Sloane stood up, began coiling the rope. "Done any climbing?"

"Some. Mostly one-pitch scrambles and boulder problems."

"What about your hands?"

"They're fine," Nora insisted. "I'll wear my gloves."

Sloane hesitated for a moment. "I didn't bring a lot of gear along, so you're going to have to belay me without a harness."

"No problem."

"Then let's do it," said Sloane, with a sudden radiant grin.

In a moment they were at the base of the cliff. Sloane tied on with a figure eight, then helped Nora set up the ground stance and showed her how to use the belay device. Nora braced the rope around her body as Sloane dusted her hands, then turned to address the sheer face. "Climbing," she called out in a clear voice.

As Nora watched, Sloane moved up the rock with care and precision, instinctively finding tiny holds in the cliff face. As she climbed, her small loop of friends, cams, and carabiners dangled in the still air. Nora played out the rope sparingly. Fifteen feet up, Sloane paused to select a nut, insert it into a crack, and pull down sharply, testing for tightness. Satisfied, she attached a quickdraw to the wire and clipped the climbing rope into it. She continued up the face, placing a nut here, a friend there. At one point she called out "Rock!" and Nora dodged a shower of chips. Another minute and Sloane had reached the single toe hold, then gained the ledge above it. She set up the anchor and tied in, yelling "Off belay!" Then, leaning out onto her anchors, she called down to Nora, "On belay!"

There was a brief silence. Then she cried out again. "I can see a route!" The sound echoed crazily around the valley. "It goes up another two hundred feet and disappears over the edge of the first bench. Nora, the city much be recessed in an alcove just above!"

"I'm coming up!" Nora shouted.

"Take it slow," came the voice from above. "Follow my chalk marks for the best holds. Don't jam straight in, use the insides of your feet. The handholds are small."

"Got it," Nora said, freeing the rope from the belay device. "Off belay!"

She began working her way up the cliff face, painfully aware that her climb had none of the grace or assurance of Sloane's. Within minutes, the muscles of her arms and calves were twitching spasmodically from the strain of clinging to the thin holds. Despite the gloves, the ends of her fingers were exquisitely painful. She was aware that Sloane was keeping the rope tighter than normal, but she was grateful for the added lift.

As she approached the single ancient step, she felt her right foot lose its purchase on the rock. Her bandaged hands could not compensate, and she began to slip. "Watch me!" she cried. Immediately, the rope tightened. "Lean away from the rock!" she heard Sloane call. "I'll haul you up!"

Taking short, choppy breaths, Nora half climbed and was half pulled the last few feet onto the ledge. She climbed shakily to her feet, massaging her fingers. From this vantage point she could see that the canyon wall sloped back at a terrifying angle. But at least it wasn't vertical, and as it continued the angle lessened. Sloane was right: though invisible from the ground, from up here the trail was unmistakable.

"You okay?" Sloane asked. Nora nodded, and her companion began a second pitch up the rock, rope trailing from her harness. With the hand-and-toe trail still in place it was a simple pitch. After another fifty feet, she anchored herself and in a few minutes Nora was beside her, breathless from the exertion. The recessed benchland above them loomed closer, its hidden secrets now a single pitch away.

Another ten minutes of climbing, and the trail leveled off considerably. "Let's solo the rest," Sloane said, the excitement clear in her voice.

Nora knew that, technically, they should keep to the safety of the ropes. But she was as eager to reach the bench as Sloane was. On an unspoken signal, they untied from the ropes and began moving quickly up the trail. It was the work of a minute to climb the last remaining stretch of rock.

The bench was about fifteen feet wide, sloping gently, covered with grass and prickly pear cactus. They stood motionless, staring ahead.

There was nothing: no city, no alcove, just the naked shelf of rock that ended in another cliff face twenty feet away, which rose vertically for at least five hundred feet.

"Oh, shit," Sloane groaned. Her shoulders slumped.

In disbelief, Nora scanned the entire bench again. There was nothing. Her eyes began to sting, and she turned away.

And then she glanced across the canyon for the first time.

There, on the opposite cliff face, a huge alcove arched across the length of the canyon, poised halfway between ground and sky. The morning sun shone in at a perfect angle, shooting a wedge of pale light into the recesses below the huge arch. Tucked inside was a ruined city. Four great towers rose from the corners of the city, and between them lay a complicated arrangement of roomblocks and circular kivas, dotted with black windows and doorways. The morning sun gilded the walls and towers into a dream-city: insubstantial, airy, ready to evaporate into the desert air.

It was the most perfect Anasazi city Nora had ever seen; more beautiful than Cliff Palace, as large as Pueblo Bonito.

Sloane looked at Nora. And then she, too, slowly turned to look across the canyon. Her face went deathly pale.

Nora closed her eyes, squeezed them shut, then opened them again. The city was still there. She gazed slowly across the vista, drinking it in. Wedged into the middle of the city, she could make out the circular outline of a Great Kiva: the largest she had ever seen, still roofed. An intact Great Kiva . . . nothing like it had ever been found.

She could see how the alcove itself was set back from the bench, making it invisible from below. The great sandstone cliff above billowed out in a huge convex curve that leaned at least fifty feet beyond the bottom of the alcove. It was this fortuitous artifact of geology and erosion that allowed the city to be hidden, not only from above and below, but also from the opposite canyon rim. She had a fleeting, desperate thought: *I hope my father saw this.*

Suddenly her knees grew weak and she dropped slowly to the ground. Seated, she continued to stare across the valley. There was a rustling sound, and Sloane knelt down beside her.

"Nora," came the voice, the slightest trace of irony leavening the reverence, "I think we've found Quivira."

25

"SHOULD WE?" SLOANE MURMURED TO NORA.

There was a long pause. Nora's eyes followed the bench land as it curved around the canyon. In places where the bench became a narrow ledge of slickrock, she could see that a shallow groove had actually been worn into the sandstone by countless prehistoric feet. One part of her registered all this quite dispassionately; another part was far away, still in shock, unable to comprehend the magnitude of the discovery.

The dispassionate part told her that they should go back for the others, bring in the equipment, begin a formal survey.

"What the hell," she replied. "Let's go."

She rose shakily to her feet, Sloane following. A quick, dreamlike walk brought them around the far end of the canyon to the edge of the great alcove. Here Nora paused. They were now looking on the ruin from the far side, at an acute angle. The morning sun only penetrated the facade of the city; the rest faded back into darkness under the heavy brow of rock, a ghostly ruin melting into purple shadow. Quivira had a gracefulness, a sense of balance, that belied its massive stone construction. It was as if the city had been planned and built as a unit, rather than growing by accretion, as most other large Anasazi cliff dwellings had. There were still traces of gypsum whitewash on the outer walls, and the

Great Kiva showed traces of what had once been a blue disk painted on its side.

The four towers were paired, two on each side of the alcove, with the main city lying between and the circular Great Kiva at the very center. Each tower rose about fifty feet. The front two were freestanding; the rear two were actually mortared to the natural stone roof of the alcove.

The ruin was in beautiful condition, but on closer view it was far from perfect. Nora could see several ugly fractures snaking up the sides of the four towers. In one place, the masonry had peeled off part of an upper story, revealing a dark interior. In the terraced city between the towers, several of the third-story rooms had collapsed. Others appeared to have burned. But overall the city was remarkably well preserved, its huge walls built of stone courses mortared with adobe. Wooden ladders stood against some of the walls. Hundreds of rooms were still intact and roofed—a complicated arrangement of roomblocks and smaller circular kivas, dotted with black windows and doorways—the Great Kiva that dominated the center seemed almost untouched. It was a city made to last forever.

Nora's eyes wandered into the dark recesses of the alcove. Behind the towers, terraced roomblocks, and plazas lay a narrow passageway that ran between the back of the city and a long row of squat granaries. The passageway was low and dim. Behind the granaries appeared to lie a second, even more constricted alleyway—no more than a sunken crawlspace, really—cloaked in darkness. This was unusual: in fact, Nora had never seen anything like it. In most Anasazi cities, the granaries were built directly into the back wall of the cave.

Although the archaeologist in her registered these observations, Nora was aware that her hands were shaking and her heart was thudding at a breakneck pace.

"Is this real?" she heard Sloane mutter hoarsely.

As they slowly approached the city, a remarkable series of pictographs became visible on the cliff face beside them. They had been laid down in several layers, figures painted over figures, a palimpsest of Anasazi imagery in red, yellow, black, and white. There were handprints, spirals, shamanistic figures with huge shoulders and power lines radiating from their heads; antelope, deer, snakes, and a bear, along with geometric designs of unknown meaning.

"Look up," Sloane said.

Nora followed her glance. There, twenty feet above their heads, were rows upon rows of negative handprints: paint sprayed over a hand held against the rock, a great crowd waving goodbye. Above that, on the domed roof itself, the Anasazi had painted a complicated pattern of crosses and dots of various sizes. Something about it was vaguely familiar.

Then it hit her. "My God, it's an Anasazi planetarium."

"Yes. That's the constellation Orion. And there's Cassiopeia, I think. It's just like the Planetarium at Canyon de Chelly, only more elaborate by far."

Instinctively, Nora raised her camera. Then she dropped it again. There would be time, plenty of time, later. Now she just wanted to simply experience it. She took a step forward, then hesitated and glanced at her companion.

"I know what you mean," Sloane said. "I feel the same way. It's as if we don't belong here."

"We don't," Nora heard herself say.

Sloane looked at her a moment. Then she turned and began to move toward the ruin. Nora followed slowly.

As they walked into the cool darkness, their shadows merged with the shadows of the stone. A group of swallows burst out of a cluster of mud nests above their heads, wheeling out into the sunlight, dipping and crying with displeasure at the intrusion.

They walked toward a broad plaza area in front of the towers, their feet sinking into soft sand. Glancing down, Nora saw there was almost no cultural debris on the surface: many inches of fine, windblown dust had covered everything.

At the front of the first tower, Nora stopped and laid her hand on the cool masonry. The tower had been built straight and sure, with a slight inward slope. There were no doors in its face; entry must have been gained from the back. A few notches far up its flank looked like arrow ports. Peering into one of the cracks in the bottom of the tower, she saw the masonry was at least ten feet thick. The towers were obviously for defense.

Sloane walked around the tower's front, Nora following in her wake. It was odd, she thought, how they were instinctively staying together. There was something unsettling about the place, something she couldn't immediately put into words. Perhaps it was the defensive nature of the site: the massive walls, the lack of ground-floor doors. There were even piles of round rocks stacked on some of the frontline roofs, clearly intended as weapons to be dropped on the heads of any invaders. Or maybe it was the absolute silence of the city, the powdery smell of the dust, the faint odor of corruption that unnerved her.

She glanced at Sloane. The woman had recovered her composure and was scratching in her sketchbook. Her calm presence was reassuring.

She turned back to the tower. On the back side, at the second-story level, she could now see a small keyhole doorway, partly collapsed. It was accessible from a flat roof, against which leaned a pole ladder, perfectly preserved. She moved to the ladder and carefully climbed to the roof. Closing her sketchbook, Sloane followed. A moment later, they ducked beneath the doorway and were staring up into the gloom of the tower.

As she had expected, there was no staircase inside. Instead, running up the center, was a series of notched poles, resting on shelves. Stones projected from the inner walls, providing footholds. Nora had seen this type of arrangement before, at a ruin in New Mexico called Shaft House. In order to ascend the tower, one had to climb spraddle-legged, one foot using the notches in the poles, and the other foot using the stones fastened into the wall. It was a deliberately precarious and exposed method of climbing, keeping all four of the climber's limbs occupied. From above, defenders could knock off climbing invaders with rocks or arrows. At the very top of the tower, the last pole ladder went through a small hole into a tiny room beneath the roof: the last redoubt in case of attack.

Nora looked at the huge cracks in the walls, and at the pole ladders, flimsy and brittle with dry rot. Even when first built, it would have been a terrifying climb; now, it was unthinkable. She nodded to Sloane, and they ducked back through the door and climbed down to the stepped-back facade of the city itself. Any exploration of the towers would have to wait.

Walking away from the tower, Nora approached the foot of the nearest roomblock. Over the centuries, windblown sand had drifted up against the front of the houses. In places, the drifts were so high a person could climb to the flat roofs that led to the upper stories, and from there into the second-floor houses themselves. Beyond the roomblocks, she could see the circular form of the Great Kiva and the stylized blue disk incised into its facade, a white band at its top.

Sloane drifted over silently, glancing first at Nora, then the sandpile. Again, Nora realized that protocol dictated they return for the others, establish a formal pattern of discovery. But she also realized that nobody, not even Richard Wetherill, had found an Anasazi city like this one. The urge to explore was too strong to resist.

They scrambled up the sandpile to the first-story roofs. Ahead of them lay a row of darkened, keyhole doorways. As Nora glanced around, she saw, arrayed along the edge of the roof, partly buried in sand, eight gorgeous St. John's Polychrome pots in perfect condition. Three of them still had their sandstone lids.

The women paused at the nearest doorway, once again feeling the strange hesitation. "Let's go inside," Sloane said at last.

Nora ducked through the doorway. Gradually, as her eyes adjusted to the dim light, she could see the room was not empty. On the far side was a firepit with a stone comal. Beside it were two corrugated cooking pots, blackened with smoke. One had broken open, spilling tiny Anasazi corncobs across the floor. Packrats had built a nest in one corner, a junk heap of sticks and cactus husks thickly laid with dung. The acrid scent of their urine permeated the room. As Nora stepped forward, she saw, hanging on a peg near the door, a pair of sandals made from woven yucca fibers.

Sloane switched on her flashlight and played its beam toward a dark doorway that beckoned on the far wall. Stepping through, Nora saw that the second room had a complicated painted design running like a border around the plastered walls. "It's a snake," she said. "A stylized rattlesnake."

"Unbelievable." Sloane ran the beam along the design. "As if it was painted yesterday." The light came to rest in a niche on one wall. "Look, Nora, there's something there."

Nora stepped over. It was bundle of buckskin, about the size of a fist, tightly rolled and tied.

"It's a medicine bundle," she whispered. "A mountain soil bundle, from the look of it."

Sloane stared at her. "Do you know of anyone finding an intact Anasazi medicine bundle?" she asked.

"No," said Nora. "I think this is the first."

They stood in the room for a few moments, breathing in the ancient air. Then Nora found her eyes drawn to a third doorway. It was smaller than the others, and appeared to lead to a storage room.

"You first," Sloane said.

Nora dropped to her hands and knees, crawled through the low doorway, and stood inside a stuffy space. Sloane followed. The yellow pool of light moved about, stabbing through a veil of dust raised by their entry. Gradually, objects and color emerged from the dimness, and Nora's mind began to make sense of the chaos.

Against the back wall, a row of extraordinary pots was arrayed: smooth, polished, painted with fantastical geometric designs. Sticking out of the mouth of one pot was a bundle of prayer sticks, carved, feathered, and painted, gleaming with color even in the dull light. Beside them was a long stone palette shaped like a huge leaf, on which had been placed a dozen fetishes of different animals fashioned from semi-precious stones, each with an arrowhead tied to its back with a string of sinew. Next sat a bowl filled with perfect, tiny bird points, all flaked out of the blackest obsidian. Nearby was a stone banco, on which a number of artifacts had been carefully arranged. As Nora's eyes roamed the dimness with growing disbelief, she could see a rotten buckskin bag from which spilled a collection of mirage stones, some cradle-boards, and several exquisite bags woven from apocynum fiber and filled with red ochre.

The silence, here in the bowels of the ruined city, was absolute. *There's more in this one room*, Nora thought, *than the greatest museums have in their entire collections.*

She followed the beam of light as it revealed ever more remarkable objects. The skull of a grizzly bear, decorated with blue and red stripes of paint, bundles of sweetgrass stuffed into its eye sockets. The rattles of a rattlesnake tied to the end of a painted stick, human scalp attached. A large sheet of mica, cut into the outline of a hideously grinning skull, its teeth inlaid with blood-red carnelians. A quartz crystal carved in the shape of a corn beetle. A delicately woven basket, its outside feathered with hundreds of tiny, iridescent hummingbird breasts.

Instinctively, she sought out Sloane's face in the dim light. Sloane looked back, amber eyes wild. The composure that had returned so quickly was gone again.

"This must have been the storage room for the family who occupied these roomblocks," Sloane finally said, voice trembling. "Just one family. There could be dozens of other rooms like this in this city. Maybe hundreds."

"I believe it," Nora replied. "But what I can't believe is the wealth. Even in Anasazi days, this would represent an inconceivable fortune."

The dust raised by their entry drifted in layers through the cool, heavy air, scattering the yellow light. Nora took a deep breath, and then another, trying to clear her mind.

"Nora," Sloane murmured at last. "Do you realize what we've found?"

Nora tore her eyes away from the clutter of dim objects. "I'm working on it," she said.

"We've just made one of the greatest archaeological discoveries of all time."

Nora swallowed, opened her mouth to reply. But no sound would come, and in the end she simply nodded.

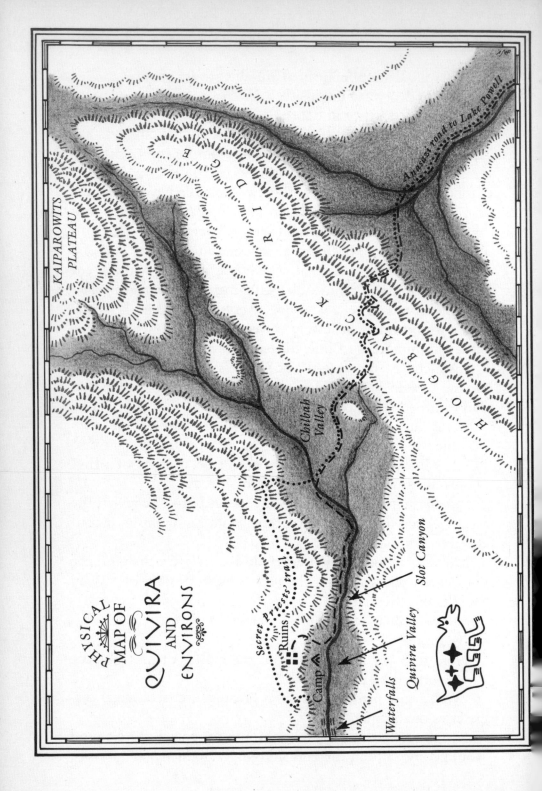

26

TWELVE HOURS LATER, THE CITY OF QUIVIRA lay in shadow, the late afternoon sun blazing its last on the valley cliffs opposite the ruin. Nora rested on the ancient retaining wall below what they'd come to call the Planetarium, feeling as drained as she had ever felt in her life. She could hear the excited voices of the rest of the expedition ringing out of the city, distorted and magnified by the vast pregnant hollow of rock in which Quivira stood. She glanced down at the rope ladder and pulley system, rigged by Sloane to provide quick access to the ruin. Far below, in the grove of cottonwood trees where they had made their camp, she could see the smoke of Bonarotti's campfire and the gray rectangular smudge that was his folding serving table. The cook had promised them medallions of wild javelina with coffee barbecue sauce and—amazingly—two bottles of Château Pétrus in celebration. It had been, she thought, the longest—and greatest—day of her life: *"that day of days,"* as Howard Carter had described it when he first entered King Tutankhamen's tomb. And they had yet to enter the Great Kiva. That, she had decreed, would be delayed until they had made a rough survey and recovered some sense of their perspective.

From time to time, during the course of the day, Nora had found herself searching among the sandy ruins for footprints, inscriptions, excavations—anything that would prove her father actually reached the city. But the rational part of her knew that the constant currents of wind and animal tracks would have long ago erased any marks of his passing. And it could well be that he, like Nora herself, had been so overwhelmed by the majesty of the city as to feel any modern inscription to be a sacrilege.

The group emerged from the ruin, Sloane bringing up the rear. Swire and Smithback came toward Nora and the rope ladder. Swire simply slumped down, flushed beneath his leathery tan, but Smithback remained behind, talking animatedly. "Unbelievable," he was saying, his voice loud and grating in the ruin's stillness. "Oh, God, what a find. This is going to make the discovery of King Tut's tomb look like a . . ." He stopped, temporarily speechless. Nora felt inexplicably annoyed that his thoughts would coincide with her own. "You know, I did some work in the New York Museum of Natural History," he began again, "and their collection couldn't *begin* to hold a candle to this place. There's more stuff here than in *all* the museums in the world, for chrissakes. When my agent hears about this, she's going to get such a—"

Nora's sudden glare silenced the writer.

"Sorry, Madame Chairman." Smithback settled back, looking only momentarily put out. He whipped out a small spiral-bound notebook from a back pocket and began jotting notes.

Aragon, Holroyd, and Black joined them along the wall, followed by Sloane. "This is the discovery of the century," Black boomed. "What a cap to a career."

Holroyd sat down by the retaining wall, slowly and unsteadily, like an old man. Nora could see his face was dirty and streaked, as if he had wept at the sight.

"How are you doing, Peter?" she asked quietly.

He looked at her with a weak smile. "Ask me tomorrow."

Nora turned to Aragon, glancing curiously at his face, wondering if the magnitude of the discovery would break his usual dour reserve. What she saw was a face covered with a sheen of sweat, and a pair of eyes that had grown as dark and glittery as the obsidian the city was full of.

He looked back at Nora. And then—for the first time since she'd met him at the fire circle—he smiled, widely and genuinely, white teeth huge in the brown face. "It's fantastic," he said as he took her hand and pressed it. "Almost beyond belief. We all have a lot to thank you for. Perhaps myself more than the rest." There was a curious force in his low, vibrant voice. "Over the years I'd come to believe, as much as I believed anything, that the secrets of the Anasazi would never be ours. But this city holds the key. I know it. And I feel fortunate to be part of it." He removed his knapsack, placed it on the ground, and sat down next to her.

"There's something I must tell you," he said. "Perhaps now isn't the right time, but it will only become more difficult the longer we are here."

She looked at him. "Yes?"

"You know my belief in Zero Site Trauma. I'm not as zealous as some, but I still feel it would be a terrible crime to disturb this city, to remove its essence and squirrel it away in museum storage rooms."

Black snorted. "Don't tell me you're a sucker for that bullshit. Zero Site Trauma is a passing fad of political correctness. The real crime would be to leave this place unexplored. Think of all we can learn."

Aragon looked at him steadily. "We can learn everything we need to know without looting the city."

"Since when is a disciplined archaeological excavation called looting?" Sloane asked mildly.

"Today's archaeology is tomorrow's plundering," Aragon replied. "Look what Schliemann did to the site of Troy a hundred years ago, in the name of science. He practically bulldozed the place, destroyed it for future generations. And that, for its day, was a disciplined excavation."

"Well, you can tiptoe around all you want, taking pictures and touching nothing," said Black, raising his voice. "But I for one can't wait to tuck into that midden." He turned toward

Smithback. "To the uneducated mind, all these treasures are amazing—but nothing tells you what you want to know like a trash mound. You'd do well to remember that for your book."

Nora looked from one member of the group to the other. She'd expected this discussion, although not quite so soon. "There's no way," she said slowly, "that we can really begin to excavate this city, even if we wanted to. All we can hope to do in the next few weeks is to survey and inventory."

Black began to protest, and she raised her hand. "If we are to properly date and analyze the city, it's necessary to be a little invasive. That's Black's job, and he'll confine any site disturbance to test trenching in the trash mound. No part of the city itself will be excavated, and no artifacts will be shifted or removed, unless absolutely necessary, and with my express permission."

"Site disturbance," Black echoed sarcastically, but he sat back with a satisfied air.

"We'll have to bring back a few type specimens for further analysis at the Institute," she went on. "But we will only bring back inferior artifacts that are duplicated elsewhere in the city. Long-term, the Institute will have to decide what to do with the site. But I promise you, Enrique, that I'll recommend they leave Quivira untouched and intact." She glanced pointedly at Sloane, who had been listening intently. "Do you agree?"

After a brief pause, Sloane nodded.

Aragon glanced from one to the other. "Under the circumstances, that will have to be acceptable." Then he smiled again, suddenly, and stood up. A hush fell on the group.

"Nora," he said, "you have the congratulations of all of us."

Nora felt a sudden flush of pleasure as she listened to the chorus of clapping punctuated by a long loud whistle from Black. Then Smithback too was on his feet, hoisting a canteen.

"And I'd like to propose a toast to Padraic Kelly. If it weren't for him, we'd never be here."

This sudden reference to her father, coming from a source as unexpected as Smithback, brought a sudden welling of emotion that closed Nora's throat. Her father had never been far from her thoughts all day. But in the end, she had seen no trace of him, and she felt grateful for Smithback's remembrance.

"Thank you," she said. Smithback took a drink and passed the canteen.

The group fell silent. Light was draining fast from the valley, and it was time they made their way down the rope ladder to supper. And yet everyone seemed reluctant to leave the magical place.

"What I can't figure out is why the hell they left all that stuff *behind*," Smithback said. "It's like walking away from Fort Knox."

"A lot of Anasazi sites show a similar abandonment," Nora replied. "These people were on foot, they had no beasts of burden. It made more sense to leave your goods behind and make fresh ones when you arrived at your new home. When the Anasazi moved, they usually only carried their most sacred items and turquoise."

"But it looks like even the turquoise was left behind here. I mean, the place is full of it."

"True," Nora said after a moment. "This was not a typical abandonment. It's like they left *everything*. That's part of what makes this site unique."

"The sheer wealth of the city, and the many ceremonial artifacts, makes me think it must have been a religious center that overshadowed even Chaco," said Aragon. "A city of priests."

"A city of priests?" Black repeated skeptically. "Why would a city of priests be located way out here, at the very edge of the Anasazi realm? What I found more interesting was the amazingly defensive nature of the place. Even the site itself, hidden so perfectly in this isolated canyon—it's damn near impregnable. You'd almost think these people were paranoid."

"I'd be paranoid if I had the kind of wealth they had," Sloane murmured.

"If they were impregnable, then why did they abandon the city?" Holroyd asked.

"They probably overfarmed the valley below," Black

replied with a shrug. "Simple soil exhaustion. The Anasazi didn't know the art of fertilization."

Nora shook her head. "There's no way, given its size, that the farmland in the valley could support the city to begin with. There must be a hundred granaries back there. They *had* to have been importing tons of food from someplace else. But all this begs the question: why put such a huge city here in the first place? In the middle of nowhere, at the end of a circuitous road, at the end of a narrow slot canyon? During the rainy season, that canyon would have been impassable half the time."

"As I said," Aragon replied. "A city of priests, at the end of a difficult ritual journey. Nothing else makes sense."

"Of course," Black said scornfully. "When in doubt, blame it on religion. Besides, the Anasazi were egalitarian. They didn't believe in a social hierarchy. The idea of them having a priestly city, or a ruling class, is absurd."

There was another silence.

"What really intrigues me," Smithback said, notebook once again in hand, "is the idea of gold and silver."

There he goes again, Nora thought. "Like I told you on the barge," she said a little more loudly than she intended, "the Anasazi had no precious metals."

"Just a minute," Smithback said, folding his notebook and shoving it into his pants. "What about the Coronado reports Holroyd was reading aloud? All that talk of plates and jugs of gold. You mean that was just bullshit?"

Nora laughed. "Not to put too fine a point on it, yes. The Indians were just telling the Spanish what they wanted to hear. The idea was to tell the Spanish that the gold was somewhere else, far away, to get rid of them as quickly as possible."

"Perhaps something was lost in translation," said Aragon, with a smile.

"Come on," Smithback said. "Quivira wasn't made up by the Indians. So why should the gold be?"

Holroyd cleared his throat a little tentatively. "According to that book I was reading, Coronado had gold samples with him. When he tested the Indians by showing them samples of gold, copper, silver, and tin, the Indians *identified* the precious metals from the base. They knew what they were."

Smithback folded his arms. "See?"

Nora rolled her eyes. One of the foundations of southwestern archaeology was that the Anasazi had no metals. It almost wasn't worth arguing the point.

Black suddenly spoke up. "All over the Southwest," he said, "Anasazi graves have been found containing parrot and macaw feathers imported from the Aztec empires and their Toltec predecessors. They've also found New Mexico turquoise in Aztec burials. And we know that the Anasazi traded extensively with the Toltecs and Aztecs—slaves, obsidian, agate, salt, and pottery."

"What are you getting at?" Nora asked.

"Simply that with all this trade going on, it's not entirely unreasonable to think the Anasazi obtained gold."

Nora opened her mouth, then shut it again, surprised at hearing this from Black. Holroyd, Swire, and even Sloane were listening intently.

"If they did have gold," Nora began, trying to keep patient, "then, in the tens of thousands of Anasazi sites excavated over the last hundred and fifty years, we'd have found some. But not one excavation has ever turned up even the tiniest speck of gold. The bottom line is, if the Anasazi had gold, then where is it all?"

"Maybe right here," said Smithback quietly.

Nora stared at him. Then she began to laugh. "Bill, put a cold compress on that fevered imagination of yours. I just saw a dozen rooms full of incredible stuff today, but not a single glimmer of gold. If we do find gold in Quivira, I'll eat that ridiculous hat of yours. Okay? Now let's get down and see what miracle Chef Bonarotti has prepared for dinner."

27

NORA GAZED ANXIOUSLY UP AT THE FIG-
ure rapelling down the rock wall four hundred feet above her
head, a brightly colored bug against the sandstone. Beside
Nora, Black and Holroyd gaped upward, motionless. Nearby,
Smithback stood, notebook at the ready, as if waiting for
some disaster to happen. A sharp clang rang out as Sloane
drove an angle into the deep red rock with her wall hammer.
As Nora watched, Sloane affixed the next portion of the rope
ladder to the cliff face, then slid easily another ten feet down
the rockface to drive in the next piece of gear.

In order for the weather receiver and communications gear
to operate, it was necessary to place them atop the rim of the
canyon, far above Quivira. Two hours earlier, Nora and
Sloane had determined the best place to set up the gear, bas-
ing their estimates on a combination of the easiest climb and
lowest clifftop. The site turned out to be just beyond the far
end of the city, overlooking the valley floor by the entrance to
the slot canyon through which they had entered.

Easiest climb, perhaps, but still frightful. Nora's eyes had
traveled up the wall, stopping at the last pitch. It was obviously the most difficult, a beetling brow of rock that hung
out into space. But Sloane had just smiled. "Grade 1, 5.10,
A-two," she'd murmured, visually rating the difficulty of the

climb. "Look at that secure crack system, goes almost all the way to the top. No problem." And, in a spectacular feat of bravura climbing, she proved herself correct. An hour later, as they waited nervously below, slings and a haul bag tumbled down from above, indicating that Sloane had reached the top and was ready to hoist up the radio gear.

And now Sloane was making her way back down to the bench that held Quivira, placing the ladder as she went. Another ten minutes, and she dropped nimbly into the group to a round of applause.

"That was fantastic," Nora said.

Sloane shrugged and smiled, obviously pleased. "Another ten feet and we'd have run out of ladder. Is everybody ready?"

Holroyd looked up, swallowing. "I guess so."

"I have important work to do," Black said. "Can someone remind me again why I have to risk life and limb on this little climbing expedition?"

"You won't risk anything," Sloane laughed in her deep contralto. "Those placements of mine are bombproof."

"And it's your misfortune," Nora said, "that you've been on a lot of digs and know how to use the radio equipment. We need a backup for Holroyd."

"Yeah, but why me?" Black grumbled. "Why not Aragon? He's got more field experience than all of us put together."

"He's also got twenty years on the rest of us," Nora replied. "You're much better suited to a physical challenge like this." The buttering-up seemed to have its intended effect: Black pulled in his chest and looked sternly up the cliff.

"Let's get started, then." Sloane turned briefly toward Smithback. "You coming?"

Smithback looked speculatively upward. "I'd better not," he said. "Somebody has to stay behind to catch the ones that fall."

Sloane raised one eyebrow, with a look that said she'd thought as much. "All right. Aaron, why don't you lead, and

I'll follow. Peter, you come third, and Nora, please bring up the rear."

Nora noticed that Sloane had staggered the inexperienced climbers with the more experienced ones. "Why do I have to go first?" Black asked.

"Believe me, it's easier when nobody's ahead of you. Less chance of eating a boot that way."

Black looked unconvinced, but grasped the base of the rope ladder and began hoisting himself up.

"It's just like climbing the ladder to Quivira, only longer," Sloane said. "Keep your body hugged to the rock, and your feet apart. Take a rest at each bench. The longest pitch is the last one, maybe two hundred feet."

But Black, scrabbling at the second step, sudden lost his footing. Sloane moved with the swiftness of a cat as Black came lurching downward. She half caught, half tackled him, and they ended up sprawled in a soft drift of sand at the base of the cliff, Black atop Sloane. They lay still, and Nora came running over. She could see that Sloane was shaking and making a choking sound; but as she bent down in a panic she realized the woman was laughing hysterically. Black seemed frozen in either fear or surprise. His face was buried between Sloane's breasts.

"Death, where is thy sting?" Smithback intoned.

Sloane continued to gasp with laughter. "Aaron, you're supposed to be climbing up, not down!" She made no move to push Black away, and after a few moments the scientist sat up, hair askew. He backed away, looking from Sloane to the rope ladder and back to Sloane again.

Sloane sat up, still giggling, and dusted herself off. "You're letting yourself get psyched out," she said. "It's just a ladder. But if it's falling you're afraid of, I've got a wall harness you can use instead." She stood up and walked over to her equipment duffel. "It's for emergencies, really, but you can use it to get familiar with the climb." She pulled out a small harness constructed of nylon webbing and fastened it around Black.

"You are just going to jumar your way up the rope. That way, you can't fall."

Black, strangely quiet, simply looked at Sloane and nodded. This time, with the mental security of the harness and Sloane's encouragement, he got the hang of using the jumar and was soon moving confidently up the cliff. Sloane followed, then Holroyd reached hold of the lowest rung.

Nora had noticed that, in the sudden scramble, Sloane hadn't bothered to check on the image specialist's state of mind. "You up to this, Peter?" she asked.

Holroyd looked at her and smiled bashfully. "Hey, it's just a ladder, like she said. Anyway, I'm going to have to climb this thing once a day. I'd better get used to it."

He took a deep breath, then began to climb. Nora followed carefully. She tested one or two of Sloane's placements and found them to be as tight and secure as the woman had said. She'd learned from experience it was best not to look down on a long climb, and she kept her eyes on the three figures ranged up the face above her. There were long minutes of almost vertical climbing. They caught their breaths at each ledge. The final pitch ended with a brief, frightening moment of hanging backward as she worked around the protruding rimrock. For an instant, Nora was reminded of the Devil's Backbone: the scrabbling at the slickrock, the frightened screaming of the horses as they hurtled to their deaths below her feet. Then she took another determined step upward, hoisted herself onto the top of the cliff, and collapsed, gasping, to her knees. Nearby sat Holroyd, sides heaving, head resting on crossed arms. Beside him was Black, trembling with exhaustion and stress.

Sloane, alone, seemed unaffected by the climb. She began moving the small array of equipment a safe distance from the edge of the cliff: Holroyd's satellite positioning unit, now sporting a long UHF whip antenna; the microwave horn; the solar panel and deep-cycle battery; rack-mounted receivers and transmitters. Beside them, winking in the morning light, the satellite dish was still enmeshed in nylon netting from the trip up the cliff face. Nearby was the weather-receiving unit.

Holroyd struggled to his feet and moved toward the equipment, followed reluctantly by Black. "Let me get this stuff set up and calibrated," Holroyd said. "It shouldn't take long."

Nora glanced at her watch with satisfaction. It was quarter to eleven, fifteen minutes before the appointed hour for their daily transmission to the Institute. As Holroyd initialized the radio unit and aligned the dish, Nora looked around at the surrounding vista. It was breathtaking: a landscape of red, yellow, and sepia clifftops, unfolding for countless miles under brilliant sunlight, covered with sparse piñon-juniper scrub. Far to the southwest, she could make out the sinuous gorge through which ran the Colorado River. To the east stood the brooding rim of the Devil's Backbone, running off and behind the Kaiparowits Plateau. The purple prow of the Kaiparowits thrust above the land, like a great stone battle-ship ploughing through the wilderness, its flanks stripped to the bone by erosion, riven by steep canyons and ravines. The landscape ran on endlessly in all directions, an uninhabited wilderness of stone covering many thousands of square miles.

To improve reception, Holroyd climbed into one of the stunted juniper trees nearby and screwed the twenty-four-hour weather receiver into the highest part of the trunk. He then wrapped the unit's wire antenna around a long branch. As he adjusted the receiver's gain, Nora could hear the monotonous voice of the forecaster reading out the day's report for Page, Arizona.

Black, having watched Holroyd set up the equipment, was now standing well away from the rim, looking pleased with himself, the smugness somewhat diluted by the harness that still clung to his haunches. Sloane, meanwhile, stood perilously close to the edge. "It's amazing, Nora," she called out. "But looking down from here, you'd never know there was an alcove, let alone a ruin. It's uncanny."

Nora joined her at the edge. The ruin, set far back, was no

longer visible, and the brow of rock below their summit shut out any hint that a cave lay underneath. Seven hundred feet below, the valley lay nestled between walls of stone like a green gem in a red setting. The stream ran down the center of the valley, and Nora could see more clearly the tortuous boulder-strewn path of the frequent floodwaters, a hundred yards wide, that ripped through the center of the valley. She could see the camp, blue and yellow tents scattered among the cottonwoods well above the floodplain, and a wisp of smoke curling up from Bonarotti's fire. It was a good, safe camp.

As eleven o'clock neared, Holroyd shut off the weather receiver and returned to the radio unit. Nora heard a bark of static, the whistle of frequency overload. "Got it," Holroyd said, tugging on a pair of headphones. "Let's see who's out there." He began murmuring into the microphone, almost toylike in its diminutive size. Then he straightened up abruptly. "You won't believe it, but I've got Dr. Goddard himself," he said. "Let me patch this through to the speaker."

Abruptly, Sloane moved away from the edge and busied herself coiling rope. Nora watched her a moment, then turned her glance to the microphone, feeling the excitement of the discovery kindling once again inside her. She wondered how the elder Goddard would react to the news of their success.

"Dr. Kelly?" came the distant voice, crackling and small. "Nora? Is that you?"

"Dr. Goddard," said Nora. "We're here. We made it."

"Thank God." There was another crackle of static. "I've been here at eleven every morning. Another day, and we would have sent out a rescue party."

"The canyon walls were too high, we couldn't transmit en route. And it took us a few more days than we anticipated."

"That's just what I told Blakewood." There was a brief silence. "What's the news?" Goddard's excitement and apprehension was palpable even through the wash of static.

Nora paused. She hadn't quite prepared herself for what to say. "We found the city, Dr. Goddard."

There was a sound that might have been a gasp or an electronic artifact. "You found Quivira? Is that what I just heard?"

Nora paused, wondering just where to begin. "Yes. It's a large city, six hundred rooms at least."

"Damn this static. I didn't catch that. How many rooms?"

"Six hundred."

There was a faint sound of wheezing or coughing, Nora couldn't tell which. "Good lord. What kind of condition is the ruin?"

"It's in beautiful condition."

"Is it intact? Unlooted?"

"Yes. Nothing's been touched."

"Wonderful, wonderful."

Nora's excitement grew stronger. "Dr. Goddard, that's not the most important thing."

"Yes?"

"The city is unlike any other. It's absolutely filled with priceless, *priceless* artifacts. The Quivirans took nothing with them. There are hundreds of rooms filled with extraordinary artifacts, most of them perfectly preserved."

The voice took on a new tone. "What do you mean, extraordinary artifacts? Pots?"

"That and much more. The city was amazingly wealthy, unlike any other Anasazi site. Textiles, carvings, turquoise jewelry, painted buffalo hides, stone idols, fetishes, prayer sticks, palettes. There are even some very early Kachina Cult masks. All in a remarkable state of preservation."

Nora fell silent. She could hear another brief cough. "Nora, what can I say? To hear all this . . . Is my daughter there?"

"Yes." Nora handed the microphone to Sloane.

"Sloane?" came the voice from Santa Fe.

"Yes, Father."

"Is all this really true?"

"Yes, Father, it is, and it's no exaggeration. It's the greatest archaeological discovery since Simpson found Chaco Canyon."

"That's a pretty tall statement, Sloane."

Sloane did not answer.

"What are the plans for the survey?"

"We've decided that everything should be left *in situ*, undisturbed, except for test trenching in the trash mound. There's enough here for a year's worth of surveying and cataloguing, without moving anything. Day after tomorrow we plan to enter the Great Kiva."

"Sloane, listen to me: be very, very careful. The entire academic world is going to be judging your every move after the fact, second-guessing you, picking apart everything you did. What you do in the next days will later be analyzed to death by the self-appointed experts. And because of the magnitude of the discovery, there will be jealousy and ill will. Many of your colleagues will not wish you well. They will all think they could have done it better. Do you understand what I'm saying?"

"Yes," said Sloane, returning the mike. Nora thought she detected a momentary edge of irritation, even anger, in the woman's voice.

"So what you do has to be *perfect*. That goes for everyone else. Nora, too."

"We understand," said Nora.

"The greatest discovery since Chaco," Goddard echoed. Again, there was a long period of static, punctuated by electronic pops and hisses.

"Are you there?" Nora finally asked.

"Very much so," came Goddard's voice, with a little laugh, "although I have to admit an urge to pinch myself to make sure. Nora, I can't emphasize how much you are to be commended. And that goes for your father."

"Thank you, Dr. Goddard. And thanks for your faith in me."

"Good lady. We'll expect your transmission tomorrow

morning, at the same time. Perhaps then you can provide some more concrete details about the city."

"Yes. Goodbye, Dr. Goddard."

She handed the mike back to Holroyd, who powered-down the transmitter and began securing a lightweight tarp over the electronics. Nora turned to find Sloane gathering her climbing gear, a dark look on her face.

"Everything all right?" Nora asked.

Sloane slung a coiled rope over her shoulder. "I'm fine. It's just that he never trusts me to do anything right. Even from eight hundred miles away, he thinks he can do it better."

She began to walk away, but Nora put a restraining hand on her arm. "Don't be too hard on him. That caution was as much to me as it was to you. He trusts you, Sloane. And so do I."

Sloane looked at her for a moment. Then the darkness passed and she broke into her lazy smile.

"Thanks, Nora," she said.

28

SKIP STOPPED AT THE TOP OF THE RISE, THE sudden dust cloud rolling over the car and drifting off into the hot afternoon sky. It was a parched June day, the kind that only occurred before the onset of the summer rains. A single cumulus cloud struggled pathetically over the Jemez Mountains.

For a moment he decided the best thing would be to simply turn around and go back into town. He'd sat up in bed the night before with a sudden inspiration. Thurber was still missing, and Skip still felt responsible, in some formless way, for the disappearance. So, to make up, he'd take Teresa's dog, Teddy Bear, under his wing. After all, Teresa had been killed in their home. And who better to take care of her dog than her old neighbor and friend, Nora?

But what seemed like such a good idea last night didn't seem so great now. Martinez had made it clear that the investigation was still active and that he wasn't to go to the house. Well, he wasn't *going* to the house: he was going to Teresa's place. Still, Skip knew he could get in a lot of trouble just for being here.

He put the old car into gear, eased off the brakes, and coasted down the hill. He drove past their old ranch house and up the rise to Teresa's place. The long, low structure was dark and silent, the livestock all taken away. *This was stupid,*

Skip thought. Whoever took the animals probably took Teddy Bear, as well. Still, he'd come all this way.

Leaving the car running and the door open, he got out, walked around to the front, and called out. There was no answering bark.

He walked up to the front of the house. The old screen door, taped in countless places with black electrical tape, was shut tight. His hand raised automatically to knock, then he stopped himself.

"Teddy Bear!" he called out, turning.

Silence.

He found himself looking down in the direction of Las Cabrillas. Maybe the dog had wandered down toward their old house. He started forward for the old path, then stopped. His hand slid down to his belt and rested briefly on the handle of his father's old .357. It was big and clumsy, it fired like a cannon, but it stopped whatever it hit. He'd only fired it once, damn near fracturing his wrists and making his ears ring for two days. Reassured, he continued down the dirt path, then circled around to the back of the ranch house. "Yo, Teddy, you old mutt!" he called in a softer voice.

He stepped up onto the portal, through the doorless frame and into the house. The kitchen was a whirlwind of ruin, the floor torn apart, holes like ragged eye sockets staring at him from every wall. At the far end of the room, he could see a yellow band of crime-scene tape barring entry into the living room. Several small lines of small, purplish-black pawprints ran from the living room to the kitchen door. Avoiding the prints, he stepped gingerly forward.

The smell assailed him first, followed almost instantly by the roar of flies. He took an instinctive step backward, gagging. Then, with a deep breath, he moved cautiously up to the tape and peered into the living room.

A huge pool of blood had congealed in the center of the room, punctuated here and there by the blacker holes of missing floorboards. Involuntarily, Skip gasped with revulsion. *Jesus, I didn't know a human body held that much blood.*

It seemed to spread in twisted, eccentric rivulets almost to the far walls. At its periphery, countless little pawprints could be seen. He could make out blowfly maggots wriggling in the places where the blood had pooled deeper.

Skip swayed slightly, and he reached for the doorframe to steady himself. The flies, disturbed, rose in an angry curtain. A camera tripod stood folded in one corner, SANTA FE P.D. stenciled in white along one leg.

"Oh, no, no," Skip murmured. "Teresa, I'm so sorry."

He stared hard at the room for a minute, then two. Then he turned and walked on wooden legs back through the kitchen.

Outside, the air seemed almost cool after the dark oppressive heat of the house. Skip stood on the portal, breathing slowly, looking around. He cupped his hands. "Teddy Bear!" he called out one last time.

He knew he should leave. Some cop, maybe even Martinez, could come by at any time. But he remained another minute, looking out over the backyard of his childhood. Although what had happened to Teresa remained a mystery, the house itself felt somehow tired and empty to him. It was almost as if whatever evil might have lurked here had dissipated. Or, perhaps, gone elsewhere.

Teddy Bear had clearly been taken away with the livestock. With a sigh, he stepped down into the dirt and walked back up the hill toward his car. It was an old '71 Plymouth Fury, his mother's, faded olive green and pocked with rust; yet it was one of his most treasured possessions. The front grille, with its heavy chrome fangs, listed slightly to the left, giving it a shambling, menacing appearance. There were just enough dents here and there around the body to let other drivers know that one more wouldn't make any difference.

There, sitting in the driver's seat, was Teddy Bear. His monstrous tongue hung out in the heat and was dripping saliva all over the seat, but he looked fine.

"Teddy Bear, you old rascal!" cried Skip.

The dog whined, slobbering over his hand.

"Move over, for chrissakes. I'm the one with a driver's license." He shoved the hundred-pound dog into the passenger seat and got behind the wheel.

Placing the gun in the glove compartment, Skip put the car in gear and maneuvered back onto the dirt road. He realized that he felt better than he had all day; somehow, despite the grimness and tragedy of the scene, it was a relief to put this particular pilgrimage behind him. Mentally, he began sorting out his evening. First he'd have to load up on dog food; it would bust his slim budget, but what the hell. Then he'd swing by the Noodle Emporium for some curried Singapore mei fun, and study the book on Anasazi pottery styles that Sonya Rowling had given him two days before. It was a fascinating text, and he'd found himself staying up late, underlining passages, scribbling notes in the margin. He'd even forgotten to crack open the new bottle of mescal that stood on his living room table.

The car rattled over the cattle guard and Skip lurched onto the main road, pointing the Fury toward town and gunning the engine, eager to put the ranch house far behind. The dog hung his head out the window, the low whining now replaced by an eager snuffling and slobbering. Strings of saliva curled away into the breeze.

Skip descended the hill toward Fox Run, fitting pot pieces together in his mind, as the desert dirt road fell away and macadam and manicured golf links took its place. Some half a mile ahead, at the base of the long downhill, the road curved sharply before passing the clubhouse. As a boy, Skip had ridden his father's dirt bike right through where the clubhouse now stood. *That was ten years ago*, he mused. There hadn't been a house within three miles. Now it was home to seventy-two holes of golf and six hundred condominiums.

The big car had picked up speed and the curve was coming up fast. Mentally returning to his potsherds, Skip put his foot on the brake.

And felt it sink, without resistance, to the metal floorboards.

Instantly he sat forward, adrenaline burning through his

limbs. He pressed the pedal again, then stamped on it. Nothing. He looked ahead through wide eyes. Just a quarter mile ahead now, the road veered to the left, avoiding a huge ledge of basalt that thrust out of the desert. With horrible clarity, Skip could see a metal plaque screwed into the ledge.

FOX RUN COUNTRY CLUB
CAUTION: GOLFERS CROSSING

He glanced at the speedometer: sixty-two. He'd never make the turn; he'd wipe out, turn over. He could throw it into reverse, or even park, but that might pitch the car out of control and wrap him around the ledge.

In desperation, he jammed on the emergency brake. There was a sudden lunge and a high squealing sound, and the smell of burning steel filled the car. The dog sprawled forward, yelping in surprise. Dimly, he was aware of a party of white-haired golfers on a nearby green, swiveling their necks and staring, open-mouthed, as he flew by. Somebody jumped out of a golf cart and began to sprint toward the clubhouse.

The wheel bucked in Skip's hands and he realized he was losing control. The basalt ledge yawned ahead, no more than a few seconds away. He turned the car sharply to the left. It twisted beneath him, turning wide, then swinging around in one complete revolution, then another. Skip was shouting now but he couldn't hear himself over the squealing of the tires. In a dense pall of burning rubber, the car sheered off the road, still spinning, the tires catching first gravel, then grass. There was a tremendous lurch and the car came to a violent stop. A thick wash of cream-colored sand settled on the dashboard and hood.

Skip sat motionless, fingers glued to the dead wheel. The squeal of tires was replaced by the tick of cooling metal. Dimly, he was aware that he had landed in a bunker, canted sharply to one side. Black, foul-smelling, slobbering lips and tongue hovered before his eyes as Teddy Bear frantically licked at his face.

The sounds of pattering feet, quick worried conversation,

then a rap on the windshield. "Sonny?" came the concerned voice. "Hey, son, you okay?"

If Skip heard, he gave no sign. Instead, he removed his trembling hands from the wheel, grasped the two ends of the seat belt, and slowly fastened them around his waist.

29

THE REST OF THE FIRST FULL DAY OF WORK AT Quivira went exceptionally well. The core members of the expedition set to their tasks with a professionalism that both impressed and heartened Nora. Black, in particular, had settled down and was quickly confirming his reputation as a top-notch field-worker. With remarkable speed, Holroyd had assembled a wireless paging network, designed around a central transmitter, to allow the members of the group to communicate with each other from anywhere within the site. The fascination and allure of Quivira worked a special magic on professional and amateur alike. Around the campfire that evening, again and again, conversation would spontaneously cease; and, as if with a single mind, all eyes would be irresistibly drawn up the dark walls of the canyon, in the direction of the invisible hollow where the city was concealed.

As the following morning drew to a close, early summer heat had settled in the canyon below; but halfway up the cliff face, beneath the shadow of the rock, the city itself remained cool. Holroyd had ascended the ladder, checked in with the Institute, and descended without incident, returning to his task of scanning the roomblocks with the proton magnetometer. Once that was done, he would use a handheld remote for the GPS system to survey the major points of the site.

Nora sat on the retaining wall at the front of the city, near the rope ladder leading down to the valley floor. Bonarotti had sent up their sack lunches using the pulley system, and Nora opened hers with anticipation. Inside was a wedge of Port du Salut cheese, four generous slices of prosciutto di Parma, and a marvelously thick and dense hunk of bread that Bonarotti had baked in his Dutch oven that morning after breakfast. She ate with little ceremony, washing the meal down with a swig from her canteen, and then rose to her feet. As leader, she was putting together the data for a field specimen catalogue, and it was time to check on the progress of the others.

She walked beneath the shadows of the ancient adobe walls to the far end of the ruin's front plaza. Here, near the foot of the Planetarium, Black and Smithback were working in the city's great midden heap: a dusty, oversized mound of dirt, broken animal bones, charcoal, and potsherds. As she approached, she could see Smithback's head pop up from a cut at the far end, face dirty, cowlick bobbing with displeasure. She smiled despite herself at the sight. Though she'd never give him the pleasure of knowing it, she'd begun dipping in to the book he had given her. And, she had to admit, it was a fascinating, frightening story, despite the near-miraculous way Smithback had of taking part in almost every important or heroic event he described.

Black's voice came echoing off the cave wall. "Bill, haven't you finished grid F-one yet?"

"Why don't you F one yourself," Smithback muttered in return.

Black came around the mound in high spirits, carrying a trowel in one hand and a whiskbroom in the other. "Nora," he said, with a smile, "this will interest you. I don't believe there's been a clearer cultural sequence since Kidder excavated the mound at Pecos. And that's just from the control pit we dug yesterday; now we're completing the first baulks of the test trench."

"The man says 'we.'" Smithback leaned on his shovel, and held out a trembling hand to Nora. "For the love of Jaysus, can ye not spare a wee drop for a poor dying sinner?"

Nora handed him her canteen, and he drank deeply. "That man is a sadist," he said, wiping his mouth. "I'd have been better off building the pyramids. I want a transfer."

"When you signed on, you knew you were going to be a digger," Nora said, retrieving the canteen. "What better way to get your hands dirty, literally and figuratively? Besides, I'll bet it isn't the first time you've done some muckraking."

"Et tu, Brute?" Smithback sighed.

"Come and see what we've done," said Black, guiding Nora to a small, precise cut in the side of the mound.

"This is the control pit?" Nora asked.

"Yes," Black nodded. "Beautiful soil profile, don't you think?"

"Perfection," Nora replied. She'd never seen such neat work or such potentially rich results. She could see where the two men had cut through the midden, exposing dozens of thin layers of brown, gray, and black soil, revealing how the trash mound had grown over time. The stratified layers had each been labeled with tiny, numbered flags, and even smaller flags marked spots where artifacts had been removed. On the ground beside the cut were dozens of Baggies and glass tubes, carefully aligned, each with its own artifact, seed, bone, or lump of charcoal. Nearby, Nora could see that Black had set up a portable water flotation lab and stereozoom microscope for separating pollen, small seeds, and human hair from the detritus. Next to it was a small paper chromatography setup for analyzing solubles. It was a highly professional job, executed with remarkable assurance and speed.

"It's a textbook sequence," said Black. "At the top is Pueblo III, where we see corrugated and some red ware. Under that is Pueblo II. The sequence begins abruptly at about A.D. 950."

"The same time the Anasazi started building Chaco Canyon," Nora said.

"Correct. Below this layer"—he pointed to a layer of light brown dirt—"is sterile soil."

"Meaning the city was built all at once," Nora said.

"Exactly. And take a look at this." Black opened a Ziploc bag and gently slid three potsherds onto a nearby piece of felt. They glinted dully in the noon sun.

Nora drew in her breath sharply. "Black-on-yellow micaceous," she murmured. "How beautiful."

Black raised an eyebrow. "The rarest of the rare. So you've seen the type before?"

"Once, on my Rio Puerco dig. It was very weathered, of course; nobody's ever found an intact pot." It was a testament to the richness of the site that Black had found three such sherds in just one day's digging.

"I'd never actually seen a piece before," Black said. "It's amazing stuff. Has anybody ever dated it?"

"No. Only two dozen sherds have ever been found, and they've all been too isolated. Maybe you'll find enough here for the job."

"Maybe," Black replied, returning the fragments to the plastic bag with rubber-tipped tweezers. "Now look at this." He squatted beside the soil profile and pointed his trowel tip at a series of alternating dark and light bands. Each was littered with distinct layers of broken pottery. "There was definitely a seasonal occupation of the site. For most of the year, there were not many people in residence, I'd guess fifty or less. And then there was a large influx every summer; obviously a seasonal pilgrimage, but on a far vaster scale than at Chaco. You can tell by the volume of broken pots and hearth ashes."

A seasonal pilgrimage, Nora thought. *Sounds like Aragon's ritual journey to a city of priests.* She decided not to antagonize Black by saying this aloud. "How can you tell it was summertime?" she asked instead.

"Pollen counts," Black sniffed. "But there's more. As I

said, we've only started the test trench. But already it's clear that the trash mound was segregated."

Nora stared at him curiously. "Segregated?"

"Yes. In the back part of the mound there are fragments of beautiful painted pottery and the bones of animals used for food. Turkeys, deer, elk, bear. There are a lot of beads, whole arrowheads, even chipped pots. But in the front we find only the crudest, ugliest corrugated pottery. And the food we found in the front of the mound was clearly different."

"What kinds of foods?"

"Mostly rats," said Black. "Squirrels, snakes, a coyote or two. The flotation lab has brought up a lot of crushed insect carapaces and parts as well. Cockroaches, grasshoppers, crickets. I did a brief microscopic examination, and most of them seem to have been lightly toasted."

"They were eating insects?" Nora asked incredulously.

"Without a doubt."

"I prefer my bugs *al dente*," said Smithback, with an unpleasant smacking of his lips.

Nora looked at Black. "What's your interpretation of this?"

"Well, there's never been anything like it in Anasazi sites. But in other sites, this kind of thing points directly to slavery. The masters and slaves ate different things and dumped their trash in different places."

"Aaron, there isn't a shred of evidence that the Anasazi had slaves."

Black looked back at her. "There is now. Either slavery, or we're looking at a deeply stratified society: a priestly class that lived in high luxury, and an underclass living in abject poverty, with no middle class in between."

Nora glanced around the city, quiet in the noonday sun. The discovery seemed to violate all that they knew about the Anasazi. "Let's keep an open mind until all the evidence is in," she said at last.

"Naturally. We're also collecting carbonized seeds for C-fourteen dating and human hair for DNA analysis."

"Seeds," Nora repeated. "By the way, did you know that

most of those granaries in the rear of the city are still bulging with corn and beans?"

Black straightened up. "No I didn't."

"Sloane told me earlier this morning. That suggests the site was abandoned in the fall, at harvest time. And that it was abandoned very quickly."

"Sloane," Black repeated casually. "She came by here a little earlier. Where is she now, anyway?"

Nora, who'd been looking away, looked back. "Somewhere in the central roomblocks, I think. She's beginning the preliminary survey, with the help of Peter and his magnetometer. I'll be checking in with her later. But now I'm off to see what Aragon is up to."

Black seemed to be thinking about something. Then he turned and laid a hand on Smithback's shoulder. "Care to finish up F-one, my muckraking friend?"

"Slavery still exists," Smithback muttered.

She raised her radio to her lips. "Enrique, this is Nora. Do you read?"

"Loud and clear," came the answer after a moment of silence.

"Where are you?"

"In the crawlspace behind the granaries."

"What are you doing back there?"

There was a short silence. "Better see for yourself. Come in from the west side."

Nora walked around the back of the midden heap and past the first great tower. *Typical cautious Aragon,* she thought; why couldn't the man simply come out and say what was up?

Just beyond the tower she picked up the small passageway that ran behind the granaries toward the back of the cave. It was dark and cool here behind the ruin, and the air smelled of sandstone and smoke. The passageway doglegged through a gap in the granaries, and there she came to a sunken passage—Aragon's Crawlspace—at the very rear of the city. Once again, the Crawlspace was a feature unique to Quivira. As Nora moved forward, the ceiling of the passageway became so low that she had to drop to her hands and knees. There was a long moment of close, oppressive darkness, then ahead she could see the glow from Aragon's lantern.

She rose to her feet inside a cramped space. Before her sat Aragon. Nora drew in her breath: beyond him lay a sea of human bones, their knobby surfaces thrown into sharp relief by the light. To her surprise, Aragon was holding a bone in one hand, examining it with jeweler's loup and coordinated calipers. Beside him lay the tools for excavating human remains from surrounding matrix, barely necessary here: bamboo splints, wooden dowels, horsehair brushes. The place was silent save for the hiss of the lantern.

Aragon looked up as she approached, his face an unreadable mask.

"What is all this?" Nora asked. "Some kind of catacomb?"

Aragon did not reply for some time. Then he carefully placed the bone back on the heap beside him. "I don't know," he said in a flat tone. "It's the largest ossuary I've ever encountered. I've heard of such things in Old World megalithic sites, but never in North America. And never, ever, on this kind of scale."

Nora glanced from him to the bones. There were many complete skeletons lying on the top of the pile, but beneath them appeared to be a thick scattering of disarticulated bones, most of them broken, including countless crushed skulls. Punched into the stone walls at the back of the cave were dozens of holes, a few rotten timbers still jutting out of them.

"I've never seen anything like this either," Nora said in a low voice.

"It's like no burial practice, or cultural behavior, I've seen before," Aragon said. "There are so many skeletons, so loosely thrown about, even a horizontal section is unnecessary." He gestured at the closest skeletons. "It's clearly a multiple interment of sorts: a series of primary burials, overlaying a vast number of secondary burials. These skeletons on top, the complete ones, weren't even 'buried' in the archaeological sense of the word. The bodies seem to have been dragged in here and hastily thrown on top of a deep layer of preexisting bones."

"Are there any signs of violence on the bones?"

"Not on the whole skeletons on top."

"And the bones underneath?"

There was a short pause. "I'm still analyzing them," Aragon replied.

Nora looked around, feeling an unpleasant gnawing in the pit of her stomach. She was far from squeamish, but the charnel-house nature of the place made her uncomfortable. "What could it mean?" she asked.

Aragon glanced up at her. "A large number of simultaneous burials usually means a single cause," he said. "Famine, disease, war . . ." He paused. "Or sacrifice."

At that moment her radio crackled. "Nora, this is Sloane. Are you there?"

Nora pulled her radio from her side. "I'm with Aragon. What is it?"

"There's something you need to see. Both of you." Through the microphone, the quiver of suppressed excitement in Sloane's voice was clear. "Meet me at the central plaza."

A few minutes later, Sloane was leading them through a complicated series of second-story roomblocks at the far end of the ruin. "We were doing a routine survey," she was saying, "and then Peter found a large cavity in one of the floors with the proton magnetometer." They stepped beneath a doorway and entered a large room, only dimly lit by the portable lantern. Unlike most of the other rooms she had seen at the ruin, this one was strangely empty. Holroyd stood in a far corner, tinkering with the magnetometer: a flat box rolling on sliding wheels, the long handle projecting from its side ending in an LCD screen.

But Nora wasn't looking at Holroyd. She was gazing into the center of the room, where a section of floor had been removed, exposing a slab-lined cyst. The enormous flat stone that had covered it lay tipped up carefully against one wall.

"Who opened this grave?" she heard Aragon ask sharply.

Nora stepped forward, anger at this breach of authority flooding through her. Then she looked down and stopped short.

Within the cyst was a double burial. But it was no ordinary Anasazi burial, graced perhaps with a few pots and a turquoise pendant. The two completely disarticulated skeletons lay in the center of the grave, the broken bones of each arranged in a circular pattern in its own large painted bowl, surmounted by their broken skulls. Over each bowl had been draped cotton mantles, which had rotted down to the warp. Enough shreds remained, however, to see that they had once been extraordinarily fine, a pattern of grinning skulls and grimacing faces. The scalps of both individuals had been laid in the grave on top of their skulls. One had long white hair, beautifully braided and decorated with incised turquoise ornaments. The other had brown hair, also braided, with two huge dishes of polished abalone fixed to the ends of each braid. In both skulls, the front teeth had been drilled and inlaid with red carnelian.

Nora stared in astonishment. The bodies were surrounded by an unheard-of wealth of grave goods: pots filled with salt, turquoise, quartz crystals, fetishes, and ground pigments. There were also two small bowls, carved of quartz, filled to the brim with some kind of fine reddish powder—more red ochre, perhaps. Nora's eyes moved over the cyst, picking out bundles of arrows, buffalo robes, soft buckskins, mummified parrots and macaws, elaborate prayer sticks. The entire burial was covered with a thick layer of yellow dust.

"I examined that dust under the stereozoom," said Sloane. "It's pollen, from at least fifteen different species of flowers."

Nora stared at her in disbelief. "Why pollen?"

"The entire cyst was once filled with hundreds of pounds of flowers."

Nora shook her head in disbelief. "The Anasazi never

buried their dead like that. And I've never seen inlaid teeth like that before."

Suddenly, Aragon knelt by the grave. At first, Nora had the odd notion he was going to pray. But then he bent down, shining a flashlight over the bones, scrutinizing them from a very close distance. As he probed the two pots of bones with his light, Nora noticed that many of the bones had been broken, and some showed signs of charring at their ends. Then Nora heard a sharp intake of breath, and Aragon quickly straightened up. His expression had suddenly changed.

"I would like permission to temporarily remove several bones for examination," he said, his voice coldly formal.

More than anything else, this request, coming from Aragon, capped Nora's mystification. "After we photograph and document everything, of course," she heard herself say.

"Naturally. And I'd like to take a sample of that reddish powder."

He departed wordlessly, but Nora continued to stand at the edge of the cyst, staring down into the dark hole in the floor. Sloane began setting up the 4x5 camera at the edge of the gravesite, while Holroyd powered down the magnetometer. Then he came over to Nora.

"Incredible, isn't it?" he murmured in her ear.

But Nora paid no attention to this, or to the excited undercurrent of Sloane's voice in the background. She was thinking of Aragon, and the sudden look that had come over his face. She felt it too: there was something odd, even *wrong*, about the burial. In some ways, she thought, it wasn't like a burial at all. True, some Pueblo IV cultures cremated their dead, and others dug up and reburied their dead in pots. But this: the bones broken and burned; the thick flower dust; the grave goods ranged so carefully.

"I wonder what Black will make of this burial," came Sloane's voice, intruding on her reverie.

I don't think this is a burial at all, Nora thought to herself. *I think it's an offering.*

*   *   *

As they stepped out onto the first-floor roof, its farthest edges tipped in noontime sun, Nora gently laid a hand on Sloane's arm.

"I thought we had an agreement," she said.

Sloane turned to look at her. "What are you talking about?"

"You shouldn't have opened that grave without consulting me first. That was a major violation of the ground rules for this dig."

The amber color of Sloane's eyes seemed to deepen as she listened to Nora. "And you don't think opening the burial was a good idea?" she replied, her voice suddenly low, an almost feline susurrus.

"No, I don't. We have a whole city to survey and catalog, and burials are particularly sensitive. But like I told you at Pete's Ruin, that's not the point. This isn't how a professional archaeologist should work, simply digging up what interests her."

"You're saying I'm not a professional?" Sloane asked.

Nora took a deep breath. "You're not as experienced as I thought you were."

"I *had* to open that cyst," said Sloane abruptly.

"Why?" asked Nora, failing to keep the sarcasm from her voice. "Were you looking for something?"

Sloane started to answer, then stopped short. She moved closer, so close that Nora could feel the heat and anger radiating from her. "You, Nora Kelly, are a control freak. You're just like my father. You've been breathing down my neck, hoping for mistakes, ever since I first flew in. I did nothing wrong in opening that burial. The magnetometer showed a cavity and all I did was lift the stone. I touched *nothing*. It was no more invasive than walking through a doorway."

Nora struggled to maintain her composure. "If you can't abide by the rules," she said as evenly as she could, "I'll place you under Aragon, where you can learn respect for the integrity of an archaeological site. And obedience to the expedition director."

"Director?" Sloane sneered. "By all rights, *I* should be the expedition director. Don't forget who's paying for all this."

"I haven't forgotten," Nora said, voice steady despite the heat of her anger. "Just one more example of your father not trusting you, isn't it?"

For a moment, Sloane stood before her speechlessly, limbs taut, face dark under the deep tan. Then, wordlessly, she pivoted on her heel. Nora watched her descend the ladder and walk deliberately away, erect and proud, her dark hair burned violet by the sun.

30

THE GROUP ASSEMBLED IN THE EARLY MORN-
ing silence at the base of the rope ladder leading to the city.
Even Swire and Bonarotti were on hand. The swallows, now
acclimated to the human intrusion, no longer raised their
usual clamor of indignation. An unusually subdued Bill Smithback was fumbling with a cassette recorder. Beside him stood
Aragon, face gray and thoughtful. Despite his preoccupation
with the bone-filled crawlspace, he had left his work to join
them. This, more than anything, underscored the importance
of what they were about to undertake.

A rough preliminary survey of the city had been completed, and Holroyd had downloaded the location coordi-
nates and field elevations established by his GPS equipment
into a geographic information systems database. It was time
to enter the Great Kiva, the central religious structure of the
city. For much of the previous night, Nora had lain awake,
wondering about what they might find. In the end, her imagination had failed her. The Great Kiva was equivalent to the
cathedral of a medieval city: the center of its religious activity,
the repository of the most sacred items, the locus of social
life.

Black was resting on a rock, drumming his fingers with ill-
disguised anticipation. And chatting with him, oversized

plant in his hand, was Peter Holroyd, loyal and uncompli- cated. The only person missing was Sloane, whom Nora had scarcely seen since the previous day's confrontation.

As if sensing her glance, Holroyd looked her way. Then he stood and approached her, shaking the plant he was holding. "Have a look at this, Nora," he said.

She took the plant: an oversized, bushy explosion of green stalks, with a tapered root at one end and a creamy flower at the other.

"What is it?" she asked.

"Oh, about five to ten in a Federal prison." Holroyd laughed.

She threw him an uncomprehending gaze.

"It's datura," he explained. "That root's loaded with a highly potent hallucinogen."

"Hallucinogen?"

"The alkaloid is concentrated in the upper sections of the root," Aragon interjected. "Among Yaqui shamans, fortitude is measured by just how far up the root you can ingest." He glanced at Holroyd. "But certainly you've noticed that's not the only illegal plant in this valley."

Holroyd nodded. "Not only datura, but psilocybin, mescal cactus . . . the place is a veritable smorgasbord of psyche- delics."

"The curious thing," Aragon said, "is that those three plants you mention—which seem to run riot here—are some- times taken by shamans and medicine men. In combination, they can induce a wild frenzy. It's like an overdose of PCP: you could get shot at close range and never feel it."

"Those priests knew what they were doing, settling here," Smithback cackled.

"The flower's pretty, at least," Nora said.

"Looks like a morning glory, doesn't it?" Holroyd asked. "That's another funny thing. There's an enzyme in the datura root that the body can't metabolize. Instead, it gets exuded in the sweat. And I've heard that's exactly what people who take it smell like. Morning glories."

Unconsciously, Nora leaned forward, bringing the flower to her nose. It was large and white, almost sexual in its ripeness. She inhaled the delicate scent deeply.

Then she froze, fingers turning cold. In a moment, her mind was back in the upstairs hallway of her parents' abandoned ranch house, hearing the crunch of glass underfoot, smelling the scent of crushed flowers on the still night air . . .

She heard a clatter, and turned to see Sloane approaching, burdened by a portable acetylene lantern, a chalk information board, and the 4x5 camera. Sloane caught her eye. Immediately, the woman put down the equipment and came over. She slid a graceful arm around Nora's waist.

"Sorry," she whispered in Nora's ear. "You were right. As usual."

Nora nodded, pulling herself back to the present. "Let's not talk about it."

Sloane drew away slightly. "I guess it's obvious. I have a problem with authority. Something else I have to thank my father for. It won't happen again."

"Thank you," Nora said, dropping the plant. "And I shouldn't have made that crack about your father. It was unkind."

Then she turned to the group, doing her best to push thoughts of Holroyd's plant out of her mind. "Okay, here's the protocol. Sloane and I will enter the kiva first, to make an initial analysis and do the photography. The rest of you will follow. Agreed?"

Black frowned, but there was nodding and murmuring from the rest of the group.

"Good. Then let's get started."

One at a time, they ascended the rope ladder. Moving through the central plaza, they climbed a nearby sandpile and walked across the first setback of roofs. Mounting an Anasazi ladder placed against the second story—still in perfect condition, lashed with sinew—they topped out on the second story setback. The entrance to the Great Kiva lay at the back, its vast circular bulk in purple shadow. Another ladder had been placed against its wall, and in a moment Nora and Sloane stood on the roof. It was covered with a thick layer of adobe and felt immensely solid beneath Nora's feet. As with all kivas, it was entered from a hole in the roof. Protruding from the opening were the two ends of a ladder, leading down into the interior. As she stared at the ladder, Nora felt her mouth go dry.

She moved slowly toward it, stopping just before the opening. "Let's light the lantern," she said.

There was the hiss of gas, and with a pop of ignition the lantern sprang to life. As they knelt by the opening, Sloane directed the brilliant white light down into the gloom.

The ladder descended about fifteen feet, ending in an anchor groove cut into the sandstone floor. Sloane angled the beam around, but from their vantage point nothing but bare floor was visible: the kiva was sixty feet in diameter, and the walls were beyond reach.

"You can go first," Nora said.

Sloane looked at her. "Me?"

Nora smiled.

Quickly, Sloane climbed down the first five rungs, then held up her hand for the lamp. Climbing down a few more rungs, she stopped to direct the light around the walls. Nora could not see what Sloane was looking at, but she could see the expression on the young woman's face. The kiva, she knew then, was not empty.

Sloane rapidly descended to the bottom, and after a last deep breath Nora followed. A moment later she stepped off the ladder, her eyes following the lamp's broad illumination.

The circular wall of the kiva was covered with a brilliantly colored mural. The images were highly stylized, and Nora had to examine them for a moment before she realized what they represented. Ranged around the top were four huge thunderbirds, their outstretched wings almost covering the entire upper part of the kiva wall. Jagged lightning shot from the birds' eyes and beaks. Below, clouds drifted across a field of brilliant turquoise, dropping dotted curtains of white rain.

Running through the clouds was a rainbow god, his long body encircling almost the entire circumference of the kiva, his head and hands outstretched and meeting at the north. Toward the bottom of the mural was the landscape of the earth itself. Nora noticed the four sacred mountains, placed at each of the cardinal directions. It was the cosmography that still ran through most present-day southwestern Native American religions: the black mountain in the north, the yellow mountain in the west, the white mountain in the east, and the blue mountain in the south. The mural was executed in the finest detail, and the colors, so long buried in darkness, seemed as fresh as if they had been painted the day before.

Nora dropped her eyes. Below the mural, ranging around the circumference of the kiva, was a stone banco. On the banco lay a huge number of gleaming objects, appearing and disappearing as the lantern beam moved slowly over them. As she stared, Nora realized, with a kind of remote surprise, that they were all skulls. There were dozens, if not hundreds of them: human, bear, buffalo, wolf, deer, mountain lion, jaguar—each completely covered with an inlay of polished turquoise. But it was the eyes that struck Nora most of all. In each eye socket lay a carved globe of rose quartz crystal, inlaid with carnelian, that refracted, magnified, and threw back the beam of the lamp, causing the eyes to gleam hideously pink in the murk. It was a grinning crowd of the dead, a host of lidless ghouls, ranged around them, their eyes glowing maniacally, as if caught in the headlights of a car.

Aside from the skulls, Nora saw, the room was completely bare. There was the usual *sipapu*, the hole to the underworld, in the exact center of the kiva, and two firepits on either side. To the east, she noticed the standard spirit opening, a narrow keyhole channel running up and out of the kiva. But the mural and the skulls were, like almost everything else in Quivira, unique.

Nora glanced at Sloane, who had already turned away from the sights and was arranging the camera's three flash units.

"I'm going to invite the others in," said Nora. "There's

253

very little they can disturb in here if they stay away from the walls."

Sloane nodded curtly. As she busied herself with the exposure meter, Nora thought she saw a kind of disappointment on the woman's face. Then the first bank of flashes went off, illuminating the entire grinning company for a ghastly moment.

The others filed down the ladder in silent astonishment and gathered at the bottom. Nora found herself drawn to a curious design of two large circles at the northern end of the mural. One circle enclosed an incised disk of blue and white, showing miniature clouds and rain, done in the usual Anasazi geometric style: a miniature version of the huge circle painted on the kiva's exterior. The second circle was painted yellow and white, and it enclosed an incised disk of the sun, surrounded by rays of light. As the beam of the lantern moved across it, the image glittered like a disk of gold. As Nora examined it closely, she could see that the effect had been created using crushed flakes of mica mixed with the pigment.

Sloane had repositioned the camera, and she now gestured for Nora to move out of the way of her shot. As Sloane bent over the ground glass screen of her camera, Nora heard a sharp intake of breath. Sloane abruptly straightened up, walked over to the small image of the sun, and began examining it intently.

"What is it?" Nora asked.

Sloane turned away and her face broke into a broad lazy smile. "Nothing in particular. Curious design. I hadn't noticed it before." She went back to the camera, finished photographing the design, and moved on.

"This is obviously a moiety," said Black, approaching. He pointed at the two circles, his large, craggy face backlit by the lamp.

"A moiety?"

"Yes. Many Anasazi societies—as well as other societies— were organized into moieties. They were divided into halves. Summer and winter societies, male and female, earth and sky." He pointed to the two circles. "This blue disk matches the one outside this kiva. That would imply that this city was divided into rain and sun societies. The first circle represents the Rain Kiva, and the second the Sun Kiva."

"Interesting," said Nora, surprised.

"Of course. We must be standing in the Rain Kiva itself."

There was another blinding leap of light as Sloane took a third exposure.

"So?" said Smithback, who had been listening. "Go ahead and drop the other shoe."

"What do you mean?" Black replied.

"If this is the Rain Kiva, then where's the Sun Kiva?"

There was a silence, interrupted only by the soft sound of another flash. Finally Black cleared his throat. "That's actually a very good question."

"It must be at some other site, if it exists at all," Nora said. "There's only one Great Kiva here at Quivira."

"No doubt you're right," Aragon murmured. "Still, the longer I am here, I, too, have this feeling of something . . . something that, for whatever reason, we're not seeing."

Nora turned to him. "I don't understand."

The older man returned the glance, his eyes looking hollow and dark in the lantern light. "Don't you get the sense that there's a piece of the puzzle still missing? All the riches, all the bones, all this massive construction . . . there has to be some reason for it all." He shook his head. "I thought the answer would be in this kiva. But now, I am not so sure. I dislike making value judgments, but I feel there was an overarching purpose to all this. A *sinister* purpose."

But Black was still considering Smithback's question. "You know, Bill," he said, "your question raises another one."

"And what's that?" Smithback asked.

Black smiled, and Nora saw something in his face, a kind of glittering intensity that she had not seen before. "Turquoise was the stone the Anasazi used in the rain ceremony. This was true at Chaco Canyon, and it is obviously true here. There must be hundreds of pounds of turquoise in this room. That's quite a lot for a culture in which even a single bead had great value."

Smithback nodded. Nora looked from one to the other, wondering where Black was headed.

"So I ask you: if turquoise was the material used in the rain ceremony, what material was used in the sun ceremony?" He pointed to the image of the Sun Kiva, its mica disk glittering in the reflected light. Both Bonarotti and Swire had come over, and were listening intently. "What does this look like to you?"

Smithback gave a low whistle. "Gold?" he ventured.

Black merely smiled.

"Come on," Nora said impatiently, "let's not start on that business again. This is the only Great Kiva in the city. And the thought of a Sun Kiva, or *any* kiva, being filled with gold is ridiculous. I'm surprised to hear this kind of wild speculation from you, of all people."

"Is it wild speculation?" Black asked. "First," he said, ticking the points off on his fingers, "we have legends of gold among the Indians. Then we have Coronado's and Fray Marcos's reports of gold, among others. And now we have this pictograph, which is a pretty remarkable imitation of gold. As Enrique will confirm, the dental modifications to these skulls are pure Aztec, and we know *they* had tons of gold. So I'm beginning to wonder if there isn't some reality behind the legends."

"Find me this Sun Kiva full of Aztec gold," said Nora wearily. "Then I'll revise my opinion. But until then, stifle the treasure talk, okay?"

Black grinned. "Is that a challenge?"

"It's more like a plea for sanity."

There was a laugh behind her, husky and *sotto voce*. Nora glanced over to see Sloane, looking from her to Black and back again, her amber eyes twinkling with some private amusement of her own.

31

NORA SLEPT POORLY AND AWOKE EARLY, the memory of ugly dreams receding quickly into forgetfulness. The gibbous moon was setting and the valley was heavy with moonshadows, the night just yielding to color. She sat up, immediately wide awake, and heard the distant plash of water in the creek. She glanced around. Swire was already up and gone on his wearisome daily slog through the slot canyon to check on the horses. The rest of the camp slumbered in the predawn darkness. For the second night in a row, the light had remained on in Aragon's tent; now, in the early dawn, it was dark and silent.

She dressed quickly in the shivery cold. Shoving her flashlight into her back pocket, she walked over to the kitchen area, unbanked the coals, and tossed some twigs on to start the fire. Reaching for the blue-flecked enamel coffeepot that always stood at the ready, she filled it with water and placed it on the grill.

As she did so, she saw a form emerge from the darkness of a distant grove of cottonwoods: Sloane. Nora momentarily wondered why she had not slept in her tent. *Probably likes to sleep under the stars, like me*, she thought.

"Sleep well?" Sloane asked, tossing her bedroll into her tent and taking a seat beside Nora.

"Not especially," Nora said, gazing into the fire. "You?"

"I did all right." Sloane followed her gaze to the fire. "I can see why the ancients worshiped fire," she went on smoothly. "It's mesmerizing, never the same. And it sure beats watching TV. No ads." She grinned at Nora. She seemed in high spirits, a stark contrast to Nora's own subdued mood.

Nora smiled a little wanly, and unzipped her jacket to let in the heat of the fire. The coffeepot began to stir and shake on the grill as the water boiled. Heaving herself to her feet, Nora removed it from the fire, threw in a fistful of grounds, and stirred the pot with her knife.

"Bonarotti would die if he saw you making that cowboy coffee," Sloane said. "He'd brain you with his espresso pot."

"Waiting for him to get up and make coffee in the morning is like waiting for Godot," Nora said. While they were on the trail, the cook had always been the first one up. But now that they were encamped at Quivira and working a more routine schedule, Bonarotti had steadfastly refused to leave his tent in the morning until the sun could be seen striking the clifftops.

She put the pot back on the fire for a moment and stirred the grounds down. Then she poured them each a cup. Steam came off the surface of the coffee, filling her nose with the strong bitter scent. She inhaled it gratefully.

"Bet I can guess what you're thinking about," Sloane said.

"Probably," Nora replied. They sipped their coffee a while in silence.

"It's just so unexpected," Nora found herself saying, as if they'd been conversing all the while. "We find this place, this enchanted and marvelous place. Filled with more artifacts, more information, than we could ever hope for. Suddenly it seems as if we'll get all the answers, after all." She shook her head. "But all we get is riddles, strange unsettling riddles. That kiva filled with skulls is a perfect example. Why skulls? What does it mean? What could the ceremony have possibly been?"

Sloane put down her coffee and looked searchingly at Nora. "But don't you see," she said in a low voice, "we *are* getting the answers. It's just that they aren't the ones we expected. Scientific discovery is always like that."

"I hope you're right," Nora replied. "I've discovered things before. And they never felt like this. Something in my gut just doesn't feel right. And it hasn't felt right since I first laid eyes on Aragon's Crawlspace, littered with those countless bones, thrown about like so much trash."

She fell silent as dark shapes bundled out of the dark. Smithback and Holroyd came over and joined them at the fire. Black soon appeared out of the twilight and hunkered down beside them. The dark branches of the cottonwoods were just beginning to separate themselves from the night.

"It's as cold as a Lenin's balls around here in the mornings," Smithback said. "And on top of that, my valet neglected to polish my boots, although I specifically left them outside my door."

"It's so *hard* to find good help these days," said Black, in a whiny imitation of Smithback's voice, and poured himself a cup. He held it to his nose. "What a barbarous way to make coffee," he said, setting the cup down. "And when are we going to eat? Why can't that Italian fellow get himself out of bed a little earlier? What kind of camp cook is this who won't get up until the crack of noon?"

"He's the only cook I know who can make *pommes Anna* as well as the best chefs of Paris, but with a twentieth of the equipment," said Smithback. "Anyway, forget breakfast. Only savages and children eat breakfast."

They sat around the fire, all but Sloane grumpy in the predawn air, nursing their coffee and speaking little. Nora wondered if the discoveries in the city and the Great Kiva were casting a pall over them, as well. Gradually the rising sun poured more color into the landscape, transforming it from gray to rich reds, yellows, purples, and greens.

Smithback saw Nora's eyes traveling around the cliffs, and he said, "Paint by the numbers, right?"

"What a poetic thought," said Nora.

"Hey, poetic thinking is my business." Smithback chuckled and fished some grounds out of his coffee with a spoon, flicking them into the bushes behind him.

Nora heard the whisper of footfalls on sand and looked up to see Aragon, bundled against the chill. He sat down and wordlessly poured himself a cup of coffee. He drank it off with extreme rapidity and refilled the cup, hands unsteady.

"Burning the midnight oil again, Enrique?" Nora asked.

It was as if Aragon hadn't heard. He continued drinking his coffee and staring into the fire. At last, he turned his dark eyes to Nora. "Yes, I was up quite late. I hope I did not disturb anyone."

"No, not at all," Nora replied quickly.

"Still working on those bones of yours, I suppose?" asked Black.

Aragon took a final swig of his coffee and refilled the cup a third time. "Yes."

"So much for ZST. Find anything?"

There was a long pause. "Yes," Aragon repeated.

There was something in his tone that silenced the company.

"Share with us, brother," intoned the oblivious Smithback.

Aragon set his cup down and began slowly, deliberately, almost as if he had prepared his words ahead of time. "As I told Nora when I first discovered it, the placement of the bones in the Crawlspace is exceedingly odd." There was a pause while he carefully removed from his coat a small plastic container. He placed it on the ground and gently unbuckled the lid. Inside were three fragmentary bones and a portion of a cranium.

"Lying sprawled on top are perhaps fifty or sixty articulated skeletons," he continued. "Some still have the remains of clothing, rich jewelry, and personal adornment. They were well-fed, healthy individuals, most in the prime of their lives. They all seemed to have died at the same time, yet there is no sign of violence on the bones."

"So what's the explanation?" Nora asked.

"It seems to me that whatever happened, it happened so suddenly that there wasn't time to give the bodies a proper burial," Aragon replied. "My analysis turned up no clear disease process, but many viral and biological diseases leave no osteological traces. Apparently, the bodies were simply dragged, intact, into the back and thrown on top of a huge existing pile of bones." His expression changed. "Those bones underneath tell a very different story. They are the broken, disarticulated remains of hundreds, even thousands, of individuals, accumulated over years. Unlike the skeletons on top, these bones come from individuals who clearly died of violence. Extreme violence."

He passed his dark eyes around the group. Nora felt her unease grow.

"The bones from the bottom layer display several unusual characteristics," Aragon said, wiping his face with a soiled bandanna. He pointed with a pair of rubber-tipped forceps at a broken bone in the tray. "The first is that many of the long bones have been broken, perimortem, in a special way, like this bone here."

"Perimortem?" asked Smithback.

"Yes. Broken not before death, and not long afterward, but about the time of death."

"What do you mean, broken in a special way?" Black asked.

"It's the same way the Anasazi broke deer and elk bones. In order to extract the marrow." He pointed. "And here, in the cancellous tissue of the humerus, they actually reamed out the center of the bone to get at the marrow inside."

"Wait," said Smithback. "Hold on. You mean to extract the marrow for—?"

"Let me finish. Second, there are small marks on the bone. I have examined these marks under the microscope and they are consistent with the marks made by stone tools when a carcass is dismembered. Butchered and defleshed, if you will. Third, I found dozens of fractured skulls among the litter of bones, mostly of children. There were cut marks on the calvaria that are made only by scalping: just like the skull we found at Pete's Ruin. Furthermore, the children's skulls in particular showed 'anvil abrasions.' When I reexamined the Pete's Ruin skull, I found anvil abrasions on it, as well. I also found that many of the skulls had been drilled, and a circular piece of bone removed."

"What are anvil abrasions?" Nora asked.

"A very specific kind of parallel scratch mark, made when the head is laid on a flat rock and another rock is brought down on it to break open the brainpan. You normally see it on animal skulls whose brains have been extracted for food."

From the corner of her eye, Nora saw that Smithback was furiously taking notes.

"There's more," Aragon said. "Many of the bones show this." He picked up a smaller bone with the forceps and turned it to the light. "Take a look at the broken ends with this loup."

Nora examined it under magnification. "I can't see anything unusual, except maybe for this faint sheen on the broken ends, as if they used the bone for scraping hides."

"Not scraping hides. That sheen has been called 'pot polish.'"

"Pot polish?" Nora whispered, the coil of fear growing tighter within her.

"It only occurs to bones that have been boiled and stirred in a rough ceramic pot for a long time, turned around and around." And then he added, unnecessarily: "It's how you make soup."

Aragon reached again for the coffee pot and found it empty.

"Are you saying they were cooking and *eating* people?" Holroyd asked.

"Of course that's what he's saying," Black snapped. "But I've found no evidence of human bones in the trash mound. Though it was filled with animal bones that had clearly been consumed for food."

Aragon did not respond.

Nora looked away from him, turning her gaze out over the canyon. The sun was rising above the rimrock, gilding the clifftops while leaving the valley below in Magritte-like shadow. But the beautiful canyon now filled her with apprehension.

"There's something else I should mention," Aragon said in a low voice.

Nora looked back. "More?"

Aragon nodded to Sloane. "I don't believe the tomb you found was a burial at all."

"It seemed like an offering," Nora heard herself say.

"Yes," said Aragon. "But even more than that, it was a *sacrifice*. From the marks on the skeletons, it seems the two individuals had been dismembered—butchered—and the cuts boiled or roasted. The cooked meats were probably arranged in those two bowls you found. There were bits of a brown, dusty substance lying with the bones: no doubt those were the mummified pieces of meat that had retracted and fallen off the bone."

"How revolting," Smithback said, writing eagerly.

"The individuals were also scalped, and their brains extracted and made into a kind of—how does one say it?—a compote, a *mousse*, spiced with chiles. I found the . . . the substance placed inside each of the skulls."

As if on a macabre cue, the cook emerged from his tent, fastidiously zipped up the flap, then approached the fire.

Black shifted restlessly. "Enrique, you're the last person I would have suspected of jumping to sensational conclusions. There are dozens of ways bones could be scratched and polished other than cannibalism."

"It is you who use the term 'cannibalism,'" Aragon said. "I'll keep my conclusions to myself for the moment. I am merely reporting what I've seen."

"Everything you've *said* has hinted at that conclusion," Black bellowed. "This is irresponsible. The Anasazi were a peaceful, agrarian people. There's never been any evidence of cannibalism."

"That's not true," Sloane said in a low voice, leaning suddenly forward. "Several archaeologists have theorized about cannibalistic practices among ancient Native Americans. And not only among the Anasazi. For example, how do you explain Awatovi?"

"Awatovi?" Black repeated. "The Hopi village destroyed in 1700?"

Sloane nodded. "After the villagers of Awatovi were converted to Christianity by the Spanish, the surrounding Indian towns massacred them. Their bones were found thirty years ago, and they bear the same kind of marks Aragon found here."

"They may have been facing a period of starvation," said Nora. "There are plenty of examples of starvation cannibalism in our own culture. And anyway, this is far from Awatovi, and these people are not related to the Hopi. If this was cannibalism, it was ritualized cannibalism on a grand scale. Institutionalized, almost. A lot like—" She stopped and glanced at Aragon.

"A lot like the Aztecs," he said, finishing the sentence. "Dr. Black, you said Anasazi cannibalism is impossible. But not *Aztec* cannibalism. Cannibalism not for food, but as a tool of social control and terror."

"What's your point?" Black said. "This is America, not Mexico. We're digging an Anasazi site."

"An Anasazi site with a ruling class? An Anasazi site protected by a god with a name like Xochitl? An Anasazi site that features royal burial chambers, filled with flowers? An Anasazi site that may or may not display signs of ritual cannibalism?" Aragon shook his head. "I also did a number of forensic tests on skulls from both the upper and lower set of bones in the Crawlspace. Differences in cranial features, variations in incisor shoveling, point to the two groups of skeletons as being from *entirely* different populations. Anasazi slaves beneath, Aztec rulers above. *All* the evidence I've found at Quivira demonstrates one thing: a group of Aztecs, or rather their Toltec predecessors, invaded the Anasazi civilization around A.D. 950 and established themselves here as a priestly nobility. Perhaps they were even responsible for the great building projects at Chaco and elsewhere."

"I've never heard anything so ridiculous," Black said. "There's never been any sign of Aztec influence on the Anasazi, let alone enslavement. It goes against a hundred years of scholarship."

"Wait," Nora said. "Let's not be too hasty to dismiss it. Nobody's ever found a city like this before. And that theory would explain a lot of things. The city's strange location, for one thing. The annual pilgrimages you discovered."

"And the concentration of wealth," Sloane added, in a low, thoughtful voice. "Maybe *trade* with the Aztecs has been the wrong word all along. These were foreign invaders, establishing an oligarchy, maintaining power through religious ritual and sacrificial cannibalism."

As Smithback began to ask a question, Nora heard a distant shout. In unison, the group turned toward the sound. Roscoe Swire was running down the canyon, bashing and stomping crazily through the brush as he approached camp.

He came to a frantic stop before them, still dripping wet from the slot canyon, breathing raggedly. Nora stared at him in horror. Bloody water dripped from his hair, and his shirt was stained pink.

"What is it?" she asked sharply.

"Our horses," Swire said, gasping for air. "They've been gutted."

32

NORA RAISED HER HANDS TO SILENCE THE immediate explosion of talk. "Roscoe," she said, "I want you to tell us exactly what happened."

Swire sat down near the fire, still heaving from his scramble through the slot canyon, oblivious to a nasty gash on his arm that was bleeding freely. "I got up around three this morning, just as usual. Reached the horses about four. The cavvy had drifted over to the northern end of the valley—looking for grass, I figured—but when I reached them, I found they were all lathered up." He stopped a moment. "I thought maybe a mountain lion had been after them. A couple were missing. Then I saw them . . . what was left of them, anyway. Hoosegow and Crow Bait, gutted like . . ." His face darkened. "When I catch the sons-a-bitches that did this, I'll—"

"What makes you think humans did it?" Aragon asked.

Swire shook his head. "It was done all scientific. They slit open the bellies, pulled out the guts, and—" He faltered.

"And?"

"Sort of made them into a display."

"What?" Nora asked sharply.

"They unwound the guts and laid them out in a spiral. There were sticks with feathers, shoved into the eyes." He paused. "Other stuff, too."

"Any tracks?"

"No footprints that I could see. Must've all been done from the backs of horses."

At the mention of the spirals, the feathers shoved into the eyes, Nora had gone cold. "Come on," she heard Smithback say. "Nobody could do all that from the back of a horse."

"There ain't no other explanation," Swire snapped. "I told you, I saw no footprints. But . . ." He paused again. "Yesterday evening, when I was about to leave the horses for the night, I thought I saw a rider atop the hogback ridge. Man on a horse, just standing there, looking down at me."

"Why didn't you mention this before?" Nora asked.

"I thought it was my imagination, a trick of the setting sun. Can't say I expected to see another horse atop that goddamned ridge. Who'd be way the hell out here?"

Who indeed? Nora thought, desperation rising within her. Over the past several days, she'd grown certain she had left the strange apparitions from the ranch house far behind. Now that certainty was fading. Perhaps they'd been followed, after all. But who could have had the skill, or the desperate resolve, to track them across such a harsh and barren landscape?

"That's dry sandy country," Swire was saying, the dark uncertain look replaced with a new resolve. "They can't hide a track in it forever. I just came in here to tell you I'm going after them." He stood up abruptly and went into his tent.

In the ensuing silence, Nora could hear the rattle of metal, the sound of bullets being pushed into chambers. A moment later he reemerged, rifle slung behind his back, revolver buckled around his waist.

"Wait a minute, Roscoe," Nora said.

"Don't try to stop me," Swire said.

"You can't just rush off," she replied sharply. "Let's talk about this."

"Talking to you only causes trouble."

Bonarotti walked wordlessly to his cabinet and began loading a small sack with food.

"Roscoe," Sloane said, "Nora's absolutely right. You can't just head off like—"

"You shut your mouth. I'm not going to have a bunch of goddamn women telling me what to do with my own horses."

"Well, how about a goddamn man, then," said Black. "This is foolhardy. You could get hurt, or worse."

"I'm done with discussion," Swire said, accepting the small sack from Bonarotti, tying it into his slicker, and throwing it over his shoulder.

As Nora watched him, her fear and disappointment at this new development suddenly turned to anger: anger at whatever was bent on disturbing a dig that had begun so successfully; anger at Swire for behaving so truculently. "Swire, *stand down*!" she bellowed.

There was a breathless hush in the little valley. Swire, momentarily taken aback, turned to face her.

"Now look," Nora went on, aware that her heart was hammering in her rib cage and that her tone was uneven, "we have to think this through. You can't just run off without a plan and go kill someone."

"I've got a plan," came the answer. "And there's nothing to think about. I'm gonna find the bastard that—"

"Agreed," Nora said, cutting off Swire's words. "But you're not the person to do it."

"What?" Swire's expression turned to one of scornful disbelief. "And just who else is going to do it for me?"

"I am."

Swire opened his mouth to speak.

"Think for a minute," Nora went on quickly. "He, or they, or whatever, killed two horses. Not for food, not for sport, but to *send a message*. Doesn't that tell you something? What about the rest of the horses? What do you think is going to happen to them while you set out on your lynching party? Those are *your* animals. You're the only person who knows enough to keep them safe until all this is resolved."

Swire pursed his lips and smoothed a finger over his mustache. "Someone else can watch the horses while I'm gone."

"Like who?"

Swire didn't answer for a moment. "You don't know the first thing about tracking," he said.

"As a matter of fact, I do. Anyone who grew up on a ranch knows something about tracking. I've looked for plenty of lost cows in my day. I may not be in your league, but you said it yourself: out here in sandy country, there's no great trick to it." She leaned toward him. "The fact is, if somebody has to go, I'm the only choice. Aaron, Sloane, and Enrique's work is essential here. You're vital to the horses. Luigi's our only cook. Peter isn't an experienced enough rider. And besides, he's necessary for communications."

Swire looked at her appraisingly, but remained silent.

Black turned to Nora. "This is insane. You, alone? You can't go, you're the expedition director."

"That's why I can't ask anybody else to do this." Nora looked around. "I'll only be gone a day, overnight at the most. Meanwhile, you, Sloane, and Aragon can make decisions by majority consent. I'll find out who did this, and why."

"I think we should simply call the police," Black said. "We have a radio."

Aragon burst out in a sudden, uncharacteristic laugh. "Call the police? What police?"

"Why not? We're still in America, aren't we?"

"Are we?" Aragon murmured.

There was a brief pause. Then Smithback spoke up, surprisingly quiet and firm. "It's pretty obvious that she can't go alone. I'm the only person who can be spared from the dig. I'll go with her."

"No," Nora said automatically.

"Why not? The trash mound can spare me for a day. Aaron over here hasn't been getting nearly enough exercise lately. I'm not a bad horseman and, if necessary, I'm not a bad shot, either."

"There's something else to think about," Aragon said. "You said these killings were meant to send a message. Have you thought about the other possibility?"

Nora looked at him. "And what's that?"

"That the killings were done to lure people away from camp, where they could be dealt with individually? Perhaps this man on the ridge showed himself to Swire deliberately."

Nora licked her lips.

"Another reason for me to go," Smithback said.

"Now hold on," came the cold voice of Swire. "Aren't we forgetting about the Devil's Backbone? Three of my horses are already dead, thanks to that goddamn ridge."

Nora turned to him. "I've been thinking about that," she said. "You said you saw a rider atop the ridge the other day. And obviously, people got into the outer valley on horseback last night. There's no other way in save over the ridge. I'll bet they used unshod horses."

"Unshod?" Smithback asked.

Nora nodded. "A horse without shoes would have surer footing on a narrow trail like the Devil's Backbone. Iron on stone is like a skater on ice. But the keratin of a horse's hoof would grip the stone."

Swire was still staring at her. "I'm not letting my horses get their hooves all chewed up out in that bad country."

"We'd tack the shoes back on once we get to the bottom of the ridge. You've got farrier's tools, don't you?"

Swire nodded slowly.

"All I'm going to do," she continued, "is try to find out who did this, and why. We can let the law take care of it when we get back to civilization."

"That's just what I'm afraid of," said Swire.

"Do you want to spend the rest of your life in prison for murder?" Nora asked. "Because that's exactly what will happen if you go out there and shoot somebody."

Swire did not reply. Wordlessly, the cook turned on his heel and entered his tent. A moment later, he emerged with his weapon, a box of bullets, and a leather holster. He handed them to Nora. Strapping the holster around her waist, Nora opened the heavy gun, spun the cylinder, and closed it again. Ripping the top off the box of bullets, she poured its contents into one hand and rapidly shoved them into the bullet loops. Then she dropped the empty box into the fire and turned toward Swire.

"We'll take care of it," she said evenly.

33

SKIP PAUSED AT THE METAL DOOR TO ELMO'S Auto Shoppe, pausing a moment to build up a full head of righteous indignation. The metal, quonset-hut garage lay baking in the heat at the long sad end of Cerrillos Road, an ugly strip of fast-food restaurants, used automobile dealerships, and malls south of town. Beyond Elmo's stretched nothing but bulldozed flat prairie, decorated with billboards, FOR LEASE and WILL BUILD TO SUIT signs—the expanding edge of Santa Fe's uncontrolled growth.

Skip set the expression on his face and pushed through the door, pulling Teddy Bear behind him on a short, thick leather leash. In the farthest bay, perched high atop the hydraulic lift, sat his Fury, tires drooping mournfully. It was a great deal sandier than it had been the day before.

Beneath it stood the proprietor of Elmo's Auto Shoppe, a tall, gangly man in faded dungarees and torn T-shirt. The shirt was liberally stained with oil, and it sported an oversized Rolling Stones tongue, jutting salaciously from dewlap lips. The shirt formed an appropriate reflection of Elmo's own pendulous lips and doleful expression.

"Why'd you have to bring that with you?" Elmo whined, nodding at the dog. "I'm allergic to dog hair."

Skip opened his mouth to deliver his speech and Elmo

raised his clipboard in protest. "Broken rocker assembly," he began quickly, licking a long, grease-sodden finger and folding the pages on his clipboard back as he spoke. "Emergency brake trashed. Hub bent. You're looking at, oh, five, six hundred at least. Plus the tow from the third fairway."

"Like hell I am!" Skip dragged Teddy Bear forward and paced angrily in the shadow of his car, forgetting his carefully crafted speech. "I had this in here for an oil change and tuneup just three weeks ago. Why the hell didn't you tell me the brakes were going?"

Elmo turned his lachrymose face toward Skip. His droopy eyes always looked on the verge of weeping. "I checked that invoice already. There was nothing wrong with the brakes."

"That's bullshit." Skip glanced at the mechanic in disbelief. He so rarely bothered to pay for car servicing that now, having shelled out fifty-seven dollars just a few weeks before, his righteous indignation knew no bounds. "I tell you, I had zero brakes left. *Zero*. I might as well have tried to use a kickstand. I could have been killed. And now you want me to *pay* for the privilege? Yeah, right."

"The brake system was dry as a bone," said Elmo, doggedly, looking at the floor.

"See?" Skip slapped a balled fist against his palm. "That proves it. You should have seen that leak when the car was here before. I'm not going to pay for—"

"But there ain't no leak."

Skip halted in mid-rant. "Huh?"

Elmo shrugged, his eyes rolling toward Skip. "We pressure-tested the brake system. There's no leak, no sprung seal, nothing."

Skip stared at Elmo. "That doesn't make sense."

Elmo shrugged again. "Besides, there would have been signs of a leak. Look at that." He grabbed a basket lamp and pointed it up at the Fury.

"It's the underside of a car. It's sandy and greasy. So what?"

"But none of that's brake fluid. No drips, no spray marks.

Nothing to show any leak at all. Where do you park it regularly?"

"In my driveway, of course—"

"You see a big stain on the ground lately?"

"Nothing I noticed."

Elmo looked down again, nodding sagely, his big ears wagging.

Skip started to retort, then stopped, mouth open. "What are you saying?" he said at last.

"I ain't saying nothing. Your brakes were drained clean." Elmo's rubbery lips twisted into what might have been a smile, and he licked at them with a red tongue. "Got any enemies?"

Skip scoffed. "That's crazy. No, I . . ." He paused a moment thinking. "You mean, somebody could've drained them? Deliberately?"

Elmo nodded again, and inserted a finger into one ear, giving it a few hard twists. "Only problem is the brake fluid cap was rusted shut, so's how it got drained is kind of problematical."

But Skip was still thinking. "No," he repeated at last in a softer voice. "The brakes were working fine one minute, gone the next." He glanced at his watch, irritation once again welling up within him. "I'm late for work. I've got this boss who rips the balls off people who are late. And on top of everything else, you give me this—" He gestured at Elmo's loaner car, an ancient Volkswagen Beetle with a crumpled rear fender and doors of mismatched colors. "I'd rather drive my own, even without brakes."

Elmo worked his shoulders through their perpetual shrug. "It'll be ready by five P.M. Friday."

"And rework that bill while you're reworking the car," Skip replied. "There's no way I'm paying six hundred for somebody else's negligence." With effort, he stuffed Teddy Bear into the Beetle, then lowered himself gingerly into the driver's seat and cranked the engine.

He eased into first and chugged noisily out into traffic,

pointing the car's snout down the strip that eventually would bring him back to town, the Institute, and the waiting Sonya Rowling. He could feel a headache coming on, faint for the moment but getting stronger. It seemed to encircle his temples, like a headband. Despite his bluster, he felt profoundly disturbed, and his heart raced as he worked his way up through the gears. For a minute, he thought of heading back out to Teresa's, checking the ground where he'd parked the car for a puddle of fluid. But even as the thought came to him, he knew he never wanted to see the place again.

Then, on impulse, he pulled the car onto the shoulder and slipped the gearshift into neutral. Something about this didn't seem right, at all. And it wasn't just the bizarre circumstances, either; the moment Elmo had mentioned enemies, a sudden chill had enveloped Skip.

He sat on the shoulder, thinking. Vaguely, very vaguely, he remembered his father, sitting at the dinner table, drinking coffee and telling him a story. For some reason, Skip couldn't remember the story. But he remembered his mother frowning, telling Skip's dad to talk about something else.

Something else . . . there was something else that had happened recently, something that dovetailed with all this in a strange and awful way.

Suddenly, Skip put the Volkswagen into gear and, with a quick glance over his shoulder, urged the car back into traffic. But instead of heading toward the Institute, he peeled off at the next corner and began threading his way through a maze of seedy side streets, urging the old car forward, cursing it, his fingers drumming impatiently on the wheel.

Pulling up at last in front of his apartment, he half ran, half leaped up the flight of stairs, dragging Teddy Bear behind him, fumbling with his keychain and unlocking both locks as quickly as he could.

Inside, the apartment smelled of unwashed socks and ancient half-eaten meals. Jerking the chain of an overhead light, Skip made a beeline to the cinderblock-and-plywood bookshelf that leaned precariously against a far wall. Kneeling in front of the lowest row, his finger traced across the old spines of the books that had been his father's, the faded titles etched faintly in lines of dust.

Then his finger stopped on a thin, battered gray book. "*Skinwalkers, Witches, and Curanderas: Witchcraft and Sorcery Practices of the Southwest,*" Skip softly breathed the title aloud.

The urgent rush that had propelled him back to the apartment was now replaced by hesitation and uncertainty. There was terrible and hideous knowledge in this book, he recalled. More than anything, Skip did not want to have that knowledge confirm the fear that was now growing inside him.

He knelt there, by the old books, for what seemed a long time. Then at last he gripped the volume in both hands, carried it to the orange couch, opened it carefully, and began to read.

34

As they emerged from the gloom of the slot canyon into the cottonwood valley, Nora could tell at a glance something was wrong. Rather than being scattered indolently across the sparse grass, the horses were bunched together by the stream, snorting and tossing their heads. She quickly scanned the valley floor, the stone ramparts, the ragged form of the Devil's Backbone. There was nobody.

Swire snugged the revolver into his belt and led the way to the horses. "You take Compañero," he said to Smithback, reaching for a saddle. "He's too dumb to be scared."

Nora found her own saddle from among the pile, located Arbuckles, and threw it over his back. Then she held the horses still while Swire knelt to remove the shoes. He worked in silence, using a chisel to get underneath the clinched end of each nail and bending it straight, taking great pains not to clip or crack the nailhole. Once all the nails were straight, he pried the shoe from the hoof with a clinch cutter. Nora found herself impressed by his skill: shoeing and unshoeing a horse in the field without an anvil was neither a common nor desirable practice.

At last he stood up, wordlessly handing Nora fresh nails along with the shoes, hammer, and clincher. "Sure you can do this?" he asked. Nora nodded, and the wrangler gestured for Smithback to mount.

"There was a lot of wind in the valley last night," Swire said, cinching the saddle tight and handing the reins to Smithback. "Maybe that's why there ain't no tracks down here in all this loose sand. Might have better luck on top, or down the far side."

Nora secured the saddlebags, tested the saddle's fit, then swung up. "Smithback's going to need a gun," she said.

After a moment, the wrangler silently handed over his pistol, along with a handful of bullets.

"I'd rather have the rifle," the writer said.

Swire shook his head. "If anybody comes over that ridge, I want to have a good bead on him," he replied.

"Just make sure it isn't us," Smithback said as he mounted Compañero.

Nora looked around for a final time, then turned to Swire. "Thanks for the horses." She nosed Arbuckles away from the group.

"Just a minute." Nora turned back to see Swire looking at her evenly.

"Good luck," he said at last.

They rode away from the stream, angling across the uneven land toward the heavy bulk of the ridge ahead, in shadow despite the bright morning sun. Over the thin murmur of the stream and the call of the canyon wrens, Nora could now hear a different sound: a low, steady drone, like the hum of a magneto. Then they topped a small rise and two low forms came into view: the remains of Hoosegow and Crow Bait. A black cloud of flies hung over them.

"Jesus," Smithback muttered.

Arbuckles began to prance and whinny beneath her, and Nora veered left, giving the carcasses a wide berth on the upwind side. Even so, as they passed she caught a brief glimpse of coiled ropes of entrails, bluish-gray and steaming in the sun, webbed in black traceries of flies. Beyond the scene of the massacre, she stopped.

"What are you doing?" Smithback asked.

"I'm going to take a minute to look more closely."

"Mind if I stay here?" Smithback asked in a strained voice.

Dismounting and giving her reins to Smithback, Nora walked back over the rise. The flies, disturbed by her approach, rose in a roaring, angry mass. The high winds had scoured the ground, but here and there she could make out old horse tracks and some fresher coyote prints. Except for the marks of Swire's boots, there were no human footprints. As Swire had said, the entrails had been arranged in a spiral pattern. Brightly colored macaw feathers, shockingly out of place in the arid landscape, protruded from the eye sockets. The carcasses had been stabbed with some painted and feathered twigs.

As she was about to turn away, she noticed something else. A circular patch of skin had been cut from the foreheads of both horses. Examining these more closely, Nora saw that similar patches had been removed symmetrically from a spot on either side of the horse's chests, and from two more spots on either side of their lower bellies. *Why there? What could this possibly mean?*

She shook her head and retreated from the killing ground.

"Who could do such a thing?" Smithback asked as she remounted.

Who indeed? It was the question Nora had been asking herself for the last hour. The answer that seemed most likely was too frightening to contemplate.

Within twenty minutes they had reached the base of the ridge. In another twenty, following the gentle trail up, they crested the top of the Devil's Backbone. Nora brought the horses to a stop and dismounted again, gazing slowly over the vista ahead. The great divide looked out over thousands of miles of slickrock canyons. To the north, she could see the distant blue hump of Barney Top, and to the northeast, the silent sentinel of the Kaiparowits.

And, directly ahead, were the narrow vicious switchbacks

that led down the face of the hogback ridge. Somewhere at the bottom lay Fiddlehead, Hurricane Deck, and Beetlebum.

"Tell me we're not really going down that again," Smithback said.

Nora remained silent. She dismounted and took a few steps from the horses, scouring the patches of sand that lay among the rocks. There were no signs of a horse; but then, the wind at the top of the ridge would have swept them away.

She looked back down the way they had come. Though she'd kept a careful lookout as they climbed, she had seen nothing but old hoofprints. She shivered; she knew very well there was no other way into the valley. And yet, somehow, the mysterious horse killers had left no sign of their passing.

Tearing her eyes away, she looked back around to the steep trail ahead of them, leading down the front of the Devil's Backbone. It seemed to simply disappear over the edge into sheer space. She knew it was always more dangerous to descend than to ascend. The terrifying memory of how she'd scrabbled at the cliff face, feet kicking in dead space, returned with redoubled force. She rubbed her fingertips, now free of bandages but still tingling with the memory.

"I'm going to hike down a ways on foot," Nora murmured. "You wait here."

"Anything to stay off that trail," Smithback said. "I can't imagine a worse way down a cliff than that. Except falling, of course. And at least that's faster."

Nora began to pick her way down the steep trail. The first part, all slickrock, not surprisingly showed no signs of the mysterious rider. But when she reached the rock strewn part of the trail, she stopped: there, in a small patch of sand, was a fresh hoofprint. And it was from an unshod horse.

"Are we going down?" Smithback asked with a distinct lack of enthusiasm as she returned to the top of the ridge.

"Yes," she replied. "Swire wasn't seeing things. Somebody did come up here on horseback."

She took a deep breath, then another. And then she began carefully down the ridge, leading Arbuckles. The horse balked at the lip of the trail, and after some firm coaxing Nora got him to take one step, and then another. Smithback followed, leading Compañero. Nora could hear the horse snorting, the scrape of bare hoof on stone. She kept her eyes firmly fixed on the trail ahead, breathing regularly, trying to keep them from straying over the edge into the infinite space below. Once, instinctively, she looked over: there was the dry valley below, the strange rock formations like tiny piles of pebbles, the stunted junipers mere black dots. Arbuckles's legs were shaking, but he kept his head down, nose to the ground, and they inched their way down. Having been up the trail before, Nora was now aware of the most difficult spots, and worked to guide her horse past them when it was most necessary.

Just before the second switchback, Nora heard Arbuckles's hooves skid, and in a panic she dropped the lead rope, but after a brief scrabble the horse stopped, shaking. Clearly, the unshod hooves had better purchase on the trail. As she bent down to pick up the rope, two crows, riding air currents up the face of the cliff, hovered past them. They were so close, Nora could see their beady eyes swiveling around to look at them. One let fly a loud croak of displeasure as he passed by.

After twenty more heart-stopping minutes, Nora found herself at the bottom of the trail. Turning, she saw Smithback make the last pitch to the bottom. She was so relieved she almost felt like hugging him.

Then the wind shifted, and a terrible stench reached her nostrils: the three dead horses, lying perhaps fifty yards away, draped over some broken boulders.

Whoever had come this way would no doubt have inspected those horses.

Giving Arbuckles's reins to Smithback, she walked in the direction of the dead horses, fighting rising feelings of horror and guilt. The animals lay widely scattered, their bellies burst open, their guts thrown across the rocks. And there, too, were the tracks she was seeking: the tracks of the unshod horse. To her surprise, she saw the tracks had not come up from the south, as their expedition had, but led instead from

281

the north: in the direction of the tiny Indian village of Nankoweap, many days' ride away.

"The trail goes north," she said to Smithback, indicating for him to dismount.

"I'm impressed," the writer replied as he slipped to the ground. "And what else can you tell about the trail? Was it a stallion or a mare? Was it a pinto or a palomino?"

Nora pulled the horseshoes from a saddlebag and knelt beside Arbuckles. "I can tell it was probably an Indian's horse."

"How in the hell can you tell that?"

"Because Indians tend to ride unshod horses. Anglos, on the other hand, shoe their horses from the moment they start them under saddle." She fitted the shoes to Arbuckles's hooves, tapped the nails through, then carefully clinched them down. Swire's horses, their hooves soft from years of wearing horseshoes, could not be left shoeless a moment longer than necessary.

Smithback pulled out the gun Swire had given him, checked it, then replaced it in his jacket. "And was there somebody on that horse?"

"I'm not *that* good a tracker. But I sure don't think Roscoe's the type to be seeing things."

Nora fitted the shoes onto Smithback's horse. Then, leading Arbuckles by the guide rope, she began following the single track, which showed two sets of prints: one going, the other coming. Although the wind had scoured small sections away, the trail was clearly visible as it wound north through the scattered clumps of Mormon tea bushes. For a while, it ran along the base of the hogback ridge, and then it veered away, into a series of parallel defiles hemmed in by low ridges of a black volcanic rock.

"Where'd you learn to track, anyway?" Smithback asked. "I didn't know the Lone Ranger was still on the lecture circuit."

Nora shot him an irritated glance. "Is this for your book?"

Smithback looked back in comical surprise, his long face

drooping. "No. Well, yes, I suppose. Everything is fair game. But mostly I'm just curious."

Nora sighed. "You Easterners think tracking is some kind of art, or maybe some instinctive ethnic skill. But unless you're tracking across rock, buffalo grass, or lava, it's not all that difficult. Just follow the footprints in the sand."

She continued northward, Smithback's voice vexing her concentration. "I can't get over how remote this land is," he was saying. "When I first got here, I couldn't believe how ugly and barren it all was, not at all like the Verde Valley where I went to school. But there's something almost comforting in its spareness, if you think about it. Something clean in the emptiness. Sort of like a Japanese tea room in that way. I've been studying the tea ceremony a lot this last year, ever since—"

"Say, do you think you could hobble that lip?" Nora interrupted in exasperation. "You could talk Jesus out of going to heaven."

There was a long moment of blissful silence. Then Smithback spoke again. "Nora," he asked quietly, "what is it, exactly, you don't like about me?"

Nora stopped at this, turning toward him in surprise. The writer wore a serious expression, one of the few she remembered seeing on his face. He stood, silently, in the shadow of Compañero. The cowboy clothes, which had seemed so ridiculous a week before, had now become a real working outfit, creased and dusty, well suited to his long frame. The pasty complexion was gone, replaced by a ruddy tan that matched his brown hair. She realized, with a small shock, that this was the first time she had heard him call her by name instead of the odious "Madame Chairman." And although she couldn't analyze it—and didn't have the time, even if she felt inclined to do so—a part of her was pleased to think Smithback was concerned about how she felt about him.

Nora opened her mouth to reply: *You mean, other than the fact that you're a brash, smug guy with an ego the size of Texas?* But she stopped and turned away, realizing this wasn't fair to

Smithback. For all his eccentric ways, she had grown fond of the journalist. Now that she knew him better, she realized his ego was tempered by a certain self-deprecation that was charming in its own way. "I didn't mean to snap at you just now," she said. "And I don't dislike you. You almost screwed up everything, that's all."

"I did what?"

Nora decided not to answer. It was too hot, and she was too tired, for this kind of discussion.

They moved on slowly as the sun climbed toward noon. Though the trail was relatively easy to follow, tracking by eye was still exhausting work. The hoofprints took them through a weird country of broken rocks, knobs, and humps of sand-stone. The prints appeared to be following a faint and very old trail. On horseback now, Nora kept them moving as quickly as she could without losing the track. The midday sun beat down relentlessly, burning off the glaring white sand, flattening and draining all the color from the landscape. There was no sign of water anywhere. And then, unexpect-edly, they passed through a lush valley, full of grass-covered sand and prickly pear, sprawling in gorgeous bloom.

"This is like a garden of Eden," Smithback said as they made their way through the brief, verdant patch. "What's it doing here in the middle of the desert?"

"Probably the result of a heavy rainfall," Nora replied. "Rain out here isn't like it is back in the east. It's very local-ized. You can get a huge downpour in one place, and a mile away see ground still parched and dry."

They made their way out of the lush valley and back into the stony desert. "What about lunch?" Smithback asked.

"What about it?"

"Well, it's almost two. I like to dine fashionably late, but my stomach has its limits."

"It's really that late?" Nora looked at her watch in disbe-lief, then stretched in the saddle. "We must have covered fif-teen miles from the base of the ridge." She paused a moment, considering. "Pretty soon we'll be crossing into Indian land. The Nankoweap reservation begins somewhere up ahead."

"So what does that mean? Any chance of a Coke machine?"

"No, the village is still a two-day ride from here, and it doesn't have electricity in any case. What I mean is, we'll be subject to their laws. Any Indians we meet aren't likely to look too kindly on a couple of outsiders blundering in, accusing them of being horse killers. We have to be careful how we do this."

Smithback considered this a moment. "On second thought, maybe I'm not so hungry."

The faint trail seemed to go forever, winding through a senseless tangle of arroyos, hidden valleys, shadowy ravines, and dunefields. Vaguely, Nora guessed that by now they had crossed into Indian country, but there was no fence and, of course, no sign. This was the kind of land that the white men had given to the Indians all over the West, she knew; utterly remote and useless for just about anything.

"So exactly how did I screw things up?" Smithback asked suddenly.

Nora twisted to look at him. "Huh?"

"At the bottom of the ridge, you said that I almost screwed things up for you. I've been thinking about that, and I don't see what I've done that you weren't already doing yourself."

Nora urged Arbuckles forward. "I'm afraid that anything I say, you'll just use in your book."

"I won't, honest."

Nora moved forward without speaking.

"Really, Nora, I mean it. I just want to know what's going on with you."

Again, Nora felt a strange sense of pleasure from his interest. "What do you know about how I discovered Quivira?" she asked, returning her eyes to the trail.

"I know how Holroyd helped you pinpoint the location. It was Dr. Goddard who told me your father was the one who originally discovered it. I'd been meaning to ask you more about that, only . . ." Smithback's voice fell away.

Only you knew I'd snap your head off, Nora thought with a twinge of guilt. "About two weeks ago," she began, "I was attacked in my family's old ranch house by a couple of men. At least, I think they were men, dressed up as animals. They demanded I give them a letter. My neighbor chased them away with her shotgun. At the time, I didn't know what they were talking about. But then I came upon this letter my father had written to my mother, years and years ago. Somebody mailed it, just recently. Who, or why, I don't know, and I can't get that out of my head. Anyway, in the letter, my father said that he'd discovered Quivira. He gave directions— vague, but with Peter's help, enough to get us here. I think those stalkers also wanted to learn the location of Quivira. So they could loot it, strip it of its treasures."

She paused and licked her lips, painfully dry in the sun. "So I tried to keep the expedition a secret. Everything was coming together just right. And then you showed up at the marina, notebook in one hand and megaphone in the other."

"Oh." Even without turning around, she could hear the sheepish note in the writer's voice. "Sorry. I knew the purpose of the expedition was secret, but I didn't realize the expedition *itself* was." He paused. "I didn't give anything away, you know."

Nora sighed. "Maybe not. But you certainly created quite a stir. But let's forget it, okay? I overreacted. I was a little tense myself—for obvious reasons."

They rode quietly for a while. "So what do you think of my story?" Nora asked at last.

"I think I'm sorry I said I wouldn't print it. Do you suppose these guys are really still after you?"

"Why do you think I insisted on taking this little field trip myself? I'm pretty sure that the people who killed our horses, and the ones who attacked me, might be the same. If so, that means they've learned where Quivira is."

Abruptly, the trail left the weird tangle of stone and topped out on a narrow, fingerlike mesa. Breathtaking views surrounded them on all sides, canyons layered against canyons, disappearing into the purple depths. The snowcapped peaks of the Henry Mountains were now visible to the east, blue and inexpressibly lonely in the vast distance. At the far side of the mesa stood some rocks, hiding the landscape beyond from view.

"I didn't realize we were gaining so much altitude," said Smithback, stopping his horse and gazing around.

Just then Nora caught a faint whiff of cedar smoke. She signaled Smithback to dismount quietly.

"Smell that?" she whispered. "We're not far from a campfire. Let's leave our horses here and go ahead on foot."

Tying their mounts to sagebrush, they began walking through the sand. "Wouldn't it be nice if there were a bathtub full of ice and cervezas on the other side?" Smithback said under his breath as they approached the jumble of rocks. Nora dropped to her knees and peered through a gap in the rocks. Smithback did the same, creeping up beside her.

At the naked end of the mesa, under a dead, corkscrewed juniper, was a small fire, smoking faintly. What appeared to be a jackrabbit, skinned and spitted, was propped between two forked sticks nearby. An old army bedroll lay unrolled in the lee of the rock, beside several buckskin bundles. To the left of the little camp the mesa sloped downward, and Nora could see a horse, picketed on a fifty-foot rope, grazing grass.

The view from the point of the mesa was spectacular. The land dropped away in a great sweep of erosion, down into a wrinkled and violent landscape, dry, lifeless, webbed with alkali washes, dissolving into a badlands peppered with great rock megaliths, casting long shadows. Beyond lay the heavily forested Aquarius Plateau, a black irregular line on the horizon. A grasshopper scratched forlornly in the late afternoon heat.

Nora slowly exhaled. It was a barren place, and she knew she ought to feel a little silly, crawling up the ridge, peering melodramatically through the rocks on hands and knees.

Then she thought about the matted, hairy figures in the deserted farmhouse, and about the coils of horse entrails, fly-blown and steaming in the sun.

The unshod tracks they had been following led around the rocks and straight into the camp.

"Looks like nobody's home," whispered Nora. Her voice sounded loud and thin in her ears, and she could feel her skin prickle with fear.

"Yeah, but they couldn't be far. Look at that rabbit. What do we do now?"

"I think we mount up and ride in, nice and easy. And then wait until they or whoever returns."

"Oh, sure. And get shot right out of the saddle."

Nora turned to him. "Got a better idea?"

"Yeah. How about if we head back and see what Bonarotti's got cooking for supper?"

Nora shook her head impatiently. "Then I'll go in there alone, on foot. They're not likely to kill a lone woman."

Smithback considered this. "I wouldn't recommend that. If these are the same guys who attacked you, being a woman didn't stop them before."

"So what do we do?"

Smithback thought for a while. "Maybe we should hide ourselves, and just wait near here for them to return. We could surprise them."

Nora looked at the writer. "Where?"

"Back up in those rocks, behind us. We can look down and over the end of the mesa. We'll see them as they come in."

They returned to their horses, moved them well off the trail, and brushed out their tracks. Then they climbed up behind the camp and waited in a small nook between two large boulders. As they settled in, Nora heard an ominous, rattling buzz. About fifty yards away, in the shadow of a rock, a rattlesnake had reared up in an S-coil, its anvil-shaped head swaying slightly.

"Now you can show me your brilliant marksmanship," said Smithback.

"No," said Nora instantly.

"Why not?"

"That gun's going to make a pretty loud doorbell. Do you really want to alert whoever's out there?"

Smithback suddenly stiffened. "I think it's too late for that," he said.

There, on one of the flanking ridges behind them, Nora saw a lone man silhouetted against the sky, his face in shadow. A gun was hanging off his right hip. How long he had been waiting there, watching them, Nora could not say.

A dog appeared over the ridge behind the man. As it saw them, it broke into a flurry of outraged barking. The man spoke a brief command and it slunk behind his legs.

"Oh, God," Smithback muttered. "Here we are, hiding in the rocks. This isn't going to look too good."

Nora waited in indecision. The weight of her own gun felt heavy on her hips. If this was one of the men who had attacked her, killed the horses . . .

The man stood motionless as the late afternoon deepened.

"You got us into this," Smithback said. "What do we do now?"

"I don't know. Say hello?"

"There's brilliance for you." Smithback raised a tentative hand. After a moment, the man on the ridge made a similar gesture.

Then he stepped down from the ridge and began walking toward them, a curious walk on stiff, long legs, the dog trotting behind him.

And then, in a instant of terrifying speed, Nora saw him stop short, draw his gun, and fire.

35

INSTINCTIVELY, NORA'S HAND DROPPED TO her own weapon as the rattler's head blew apart in a spray of blood and venom. She glanced from the snake to Smithback. The writer's face was ashen, his gun drawn.

The man walked toward them with slow deliberate steps. "Jumpy, ain't you," he said, holstering his gun. "These damned rattlers. I know they keep the mice down, but when I go out to piss at night, I don't want to step on any mouse-hunting coontail."

He was an extraordinary-looking man. His hair was long and white, and plaited in two long braids in the traditional Native American fashion. A bandanna was tied around his head and formed into a bun to one side. His pants, indescribably old but very clean, were at least eight inches too short. Beneath, dusty, sticklike legs plunged sockless into a pair of red high-top sneakers, brand-new and laced up tight. His shirt was beautifully made out of tanned buckskin, decorated with strips of fine beadwork, and a turquoise necklace circled his neck. But it was the face above the necklace that most arrested Nora. There was a gravity and dignity to the face; a gravity that seemed at variance with the glittering, amused liveliness of his black eyes.

"You look a long way from home," the man said in a thin,

reedy voice, with the peculiar kind of clipped yet melodious tone common to many native speakers in the Southwest. "Did you find what you needed in my camp?"

Nora looked into the mercurial eyes. "We didn't disturb your camp," she said. "We're searching for the person that murdered our horses."

The man gazed back steadily, the eyes narrowing slightly. The good humor seemed to vanish. For a moment, Nora wondered if he would raise his gun again, and she felt her right hand flex involuntarily.

Then the tension seemed to ease, and the man took a step forward. "It's a hard thing to lose horses," he said. "I've got some cool water down there in camp, and some roasted jackrabbit and chiles. Why don't you come along?" He paused.

"We'd be happy to," said Nora. They followed him down the rockpile and into camp. He gestured for them to find a seat on the nearby rocks, then he squatted by the fire and turned the jackrabbit. He poked a stick into the ashes and pulled out several tinfoil-wrapped chiles, piling them at the edge of the fire to keep warm. "I heard you folks coming, so I decided to head on up there and check you out from above. Don't get a lot of visitors out here, you know. Pays to be careful."

"Were we that obvious?" Smithback asked.

The man looked at him with cool brown eyes.

"Really," said Smithback. "That obvious, huh?"

The man pulled a canteen out of the sand in the shadow of a rock and passed it to Nora. She accepted the water silently, realizing how thirsty she was. The man stirred the ashes of the fire, freshened it with a few pieces of juniper, then turned the jackrabbit again.

"So you're the folks down in Chilbah Valley," he said, sitting down across from them.

"Chilbah?" Smithback asked.

The man nodded. "The valley over the big ridge back there. I saw you the other day, from the top." He turned to Nora. "And I guess you saw me. And now you're here, because someone killed your horses and you thought it might be me."

291

"We only found one set of tracks," Nora said carefully. "And they led right here."

Instead of answering, the man rose, tested the rabbit with the point of his knife, then sat back down on his heels. "My name is John Beiyoodzin," he said.

Nora paused a moment to consider this reply. "Sorry we didn't introduce ourselves," she replied. "I'm Nora Kelly, and this is Bill Smithback. I'm an archaeologist and Bill is a journalist. We're here on an archaeological survey."

Beiyoodzin nodded. "Do I look like a horse murderer to you?" he asked suddenly.

Nora hesitated. "I guess I don't know what a horse murderer should look like."

The man digested this. Then the glittering eyes softened, a smile appeared on his face, and he shook his head. "Jackrabbit's done," he said, standing and flipping the spit up with an expert hand. He leaned it on a flat rock and expertly carved off two haunches. He placed each on a flat thin piece of sandstone and handed them to Nora and Smithback. Then he unwrapped the chiles, carefully saving the tinfoil. He quickly slipped off the roasted skin of each chile and handed them over. "We're a little short on amenities," he said, skewering his own piece of rabbit with a knife.

The chile was almost indescribably hot, and Nora's eyes watered as she ate, but she felt famished. Beside her, Smithback was attacking his own meal avidly. Beiyoodzin watched them a moment, nodding his approval. They completed the little meal in silence.

Beiyoodzin passed the canteen around and afterward there was an awkward pause.

"Nice view," said Smithback. "What's the rent on this joint?"

Beiyoodzin laughed, tilting his head back. "The rent is in the getting here. Forty miles on horseback over waterless country from my village." Then he looked around, the wind stirring his hair. "At night, you can look out over a thousand square miles and not see a single light."

The sun was beginning to set, and the strange, complicated

bowl of landscape was turning into a pointillist surface of gold, purple, and yellow. Nora glanced in Beiyoodzin's direction. Though he had never actually denied it, somehow she felt certain he was not the one they were searching for.

"Can you help us find out who killed our horses?" she asked him.

Beiyoodzin glanced at her intently. "I don't know," he said at last. "What kind of survey you doing?"

Nora hesitated, uncertain if this was a change of subject or the beginning of some revelation. Even if he hadn't killed the horses himself, perhaps he knew who had. She took a deep breath, confused and tired. "It's kind of confidential," she said. "Would it be all right if I didn't tell you right now?"

"It's in Chilbah Valley?"

"Not exactly," said Nora.

"My village," he said, gesturing northward, "is that way. Nankoweap. It means 'Flowers beside the Water Pools' in our language. I come out here every summer to camp for a week or two. The grass is good, plenty of firewood, and there's a good spring down below."

"You don't get lonely?" Smithback asked.

"No," he said simply.

"Why?"

Beiyoodzin seemed a little taken aback by his directness. He gave Smithback a curiously penetrating look. "I come here," he said slowly, "to become a human being again."

"What about the rest of the year?" Smithback asked.

"I'm sorry," Nora jumped in. "He's a journalist. He always asks too many questions." She knew that in most Native American cultures it was rude to show curiosity and ask direct questions.

Beiyoodzin, however, merely laughed again. "It's all right. I'm just surprised he doesn't have a tape recorder or a camera. Most white people carry them. Anyway, I herd sheep most of the time, and I do ceremonies. Healing ceremonies."

"You're a medicine man?" Smithback asked, unchecked.

"Traditional healer."

"What kind of ceremonies?" Smithback asked.

"I do the Four Mountain ceremony."

"Really?" Smithback asked with obvious interest. "What's it for?"

"It's a three-night ceremony. Chanting, sweats, and herbal remedies. It cures sadness, depression, and hopelessness."

"And does it work?"

Beiyoodzin looked at the journalist. "Sure it works." He seemed to grow evasive in the wake of Smithback's continued interest. "Of course," he went on, "there are always those even our ceremonies can't reach. That's also why I come out here. Because of the failures."

"Some kind of vision quest?" Smithback asked.

Beiyoodzin waved his hand. "If you call coming out here, praying, and even fasting for a while, a vision quest, then I suppose that's what it is. I don't do it for visions, but for spiritual healing. To remind myself that we don't need much to be happy. That's all."

He shifted, looking around. "But you folks need a place to lay your bedrolls."

"Plenty of room out here," said Nora.

"Good," said Beiyoodzin. He leaned back and threw his wizened hands behind his head, resting his back on the rock. They watched as the sun sank below the horizon and darkness came rolling over the landscape. The sky glowed with residual color, a deep strange purple that faded to night. Beiyoodzin rolled a cigarette, lit it, and began puffing furiously, holding it awkwardly between thumb and index finger, as if it were the first time he had smoked.

"I'm sorry to bring this up again," Nora said, "but if you know anything about who might have killed our horses, I'd like to hear it. It's possible our activities might have offended someone."

"Your activities." The man blew a cloud of smoke into the still twilight. "You still haven't told me about those."

Nora thought for a moment. It seemed that information was the price of his assistance. Of course, there was no guarantee he could help them. And yet it was critical they find out who was behind the killings. "What I'm about to say is confidential," she said slowly. "Can I count on your discretion?"

"You mean, am I going to tell anyone? Not if you don't want me to." He flicked the cigarette butt into the fire and began rolling another. "I have many addictions," he said, nodding at the cigarette. "That's another reason I come out here."

Nora looked at him. "We're excavating an Anasazi cliff dwelling."

It was as if Beiyoodzin's movements were suddenly, completely arrested, his hand freezing in the act of twisting the cigarette ends. Then he was in motion again. The pause was brief but striking. He lit the cigarette and sat back again, saying nothing.

"It's a very important city," Nora continued. "It contains priceless, unique artifacts. It would be a huge tragedy if it were looted. We're afraid that these people might want to drive us away so they can plunder the site."

"Plunder the site," he repeated. "And you will remove these artifacts? Take them to a museum?"

"No," said Nora. "For now, we're going to leave everything as is."

Beiyoodzin continued to smoke the cigarette, but his movements had become studied and deliberate, and his eyes were opaque. "We never go into Chilbah Valley," he said slowly.

"Why not?"

Beiyoodzin held the cigarette in front of his face, the smoke trickling between his fingers. He looked at Nora through veiled eyes. "How were the horses killed?" he asked.

"They were sliced open," she replied. "Their guts pulled out and arranged in spirals. Sticks tipped with feathers were shoved into their eyes. And pieces of skin had been cut off."

The effect of this on Beiyoodzin was even more pronounced. He became agitated, quickly dropping the cigarette into the fire and smoothing a hand across his forehead. "Skin cut off? Where?"

"In two places on the breast and lower belly, and on the forehead."

The old man said nothing, but Nora could see his hand was shaking, and it frightened her.

"You shouldn't be in there," he said in a low, urgent voice. "You should get out immediately."

"Why?" Nora asked.

"It's very dangerous." He hesitated a moment. "There are stories among the Nankoweap about that valley, and that other valley . . . the valley *beyond*. You might laugh at me, because most white people don't believe in such things. But what happened to your horses is a kind of witchcraft. It's a terrible evil. What you're doing, digging in that city, is going to kill you if you don't get out, right now. Especially now that . . . they've found you."

"They?" Smithback asked. "Who's 'they'?"

Beiyoodzin's voice dropped. "The spotted-clay witches. The skinwalkers. The wolfskin runners."

In the darkness, Nora's blood went cold.

Beside her, Smithback stirred. "I'm sorry," he spoke up. "You said *witches*?"

There was a faint tone in his voice that the Indian picked up. He gazed at the writer, his face indistinct in the growing darkness. "Do you believe in evil?"

"Of course."

"No normal Nankoweap person would kill a horse: to us, horses are sacred. I don't know what you call your evil people, but we call ours skinwalkers, wolfskin runners. They have many names, and many forms. They are completely outside our society, but they take what is good in our religion and turn it upside down. Whatever you may think, Nankoweap wolfskin runners exist. And they are drawn to Chilbah. Because the city was a place of sorcery, cruelty, witchcraft, sickness, and death."

But Nora barely heard this. *Wolfskin runners.* Her mind fled back to the shadow-knitted ranch house: the dark matted form that had towered over her, the furred thing that had kept pace with her truck along the rutted dirt road.

"I don't doubt what you say," Smithback replied. "Over the last couple of years, I've seen some pretty strange things myself. But where do these skinwalkers come from?"

Beiyoodzin fell silent, arms propped on his knees, dark hands clasped. He rolled another cigarette, then turned his gaze toward the ground and fell motionless. The silence grew as the minutes passed. Nora could hear the faint cropping sounds of the horse grazing in the draw. Then, eyes still fixed on the ground, cigarette held loosely between two fingers, Beiyoodzin spoke again.

"To become a witch, you have to kill someone you love. Someone close, brother or sister, mother or father. You *kill* them, to get the power. Then, when that person is buried, you secretly dig the body up." He lit the cigarette. "Then you turn the life force of that person to evil."

"How?" Smithback whispered.

"When life is created, Wind, *liehei*, the life force, enters the body. Where the Wind enters the body, it leaves a little eddy, like a ripple in water. It leaves these marks on the tips of the fingers, toes, the back of the head. The witch cuts these off the corpse. They dry them, grind them up, make a kind of powder. And they drill out the skull behind and make a disk, for throwing spells. If it is a murdered sister, the witch has sex with the dead body. He uses the fluids to make another powder. It's called *Alchi'bin lehh tsal*. Incest corpse powder."

"Good God," Smithback groaned.

"You go to a remote spot at night. You strip off your clothes. You cover your body with spots of white clay, and wear the jewelry buried with the dead, the silver and turquoise. You place wolfskins or coyoteskins on either side of you. Then you say certain lines of the Night Wind Chant backwards. One of those skins will leap off the ground and stick to you. And then you have the power."

"What is this power?" Nora asked.

Beiyoodzin lit the cigarette. The repeated hoot of an owl echoed mournfully through the endless canyons.

"Our people believe you get the power to move at night, like the wind, but without sound. You can become invisible. You learn powerful spells, spells to witch people from a distance. And with the corpse powder, you can kill. Oh, can you *kill*."

"Kill?" Smithback asked. "*Witch* people? How, exactly?"

"If a skinwalker can get something from their victim's body—spit, hair, a sweaty piece of clothing—they place it in the mouth of a corpse. With that, they can cast a spell on the person. Or on his horse, his sheep, his house, his belongings. They can break his tools, make his machines refuse to operate. They can make his wife fall sick, kill his dogs or children."

He lapsed into silence. The owl hooted again, closer now.

"Witch people from a distance," Smithback repeated. "Move at night, without sound." He grunted, shook his head.

Beiyoodzin glanced at the writer briefly, his eyes luminous in the gathering darkness, then looked away again.

"Let me tell you a story," Beiyoodzin said, after a moment's hesitation. "Something that happened to me many years ago, when I was a boy. It's a story I haven't told for a long, long time."

A hot red ember flashed out of the dark, and Beiyoodzin's face was briefly lit crimson as he drew on the cigarette.

"It was summer," he went on. "I was helping my grandfather bring some sheep up to Escalante. It was a two-day trip, so we brought the horse and wagon. We stopped for the night at a place called Shadow Rock. Built a brush corral for the sheep, turned the horse out to graze, went to sleep. Around midnight, I woke up suddenly. It was pitch black: no moon, no stars. There was no noise. Something was wrong. I called out to my grandfather. Nothing. So I sat up, tossed twigs into the coals. As they flared up I caught a glimpse of him."

Beiyoodzin took a long, careful drag on the cigarette. "He was lying on his back, eyes gone. His fingertips were missing. His mouth had been sewed shut. Something had been done to the back of his head." The red firebrand of the cigarette tip wavered in the dark. "I stood up and threw the rest of the brush onto the fire. In the light I could see our horse maybe twenty feet away. He was lying on the ground, guts mounded beside him. The sheep in the pen were all dead. All this—*all* this—without even the sound of a mouse."

The pinpoint of red vanished as Beiyoodzin ground out the cigarette. "As the fire died back, I saw something else," he continued. "A pair of eyes, red in the flames. Eyes in the darkness, but nothing else. They never blinked, they never moved. But somehow, I *felt* them coming closer. Then I heard a low, puffing sound. Dust hit my face, and my eyes stung. I fell back, too scared even to cry out.

"I don't remember how I made my way home. They put me to bed with a high fever. At last, they put me in a wagon and took me to the hospital in Cedar City. The doctors there said it was typhoid, but my family knew better. One by one, they left my bedside. Except for my grandmother, I didn't see any of my relatives for a couple of days. But by the time they returned to the hospital, the worst of the sickness had passed. To the surprise of the doctors."

There was a brief silence. "I later learned where my relatives had been. They'd returned to Shadow Rock, where we'd camped. They took the village's best tracker with them. A set of huge wolfprints led away from the site. They followed the tracks to a remote camp east of Nankoweap. Inside was . . . well, I guess you would have to call him a man. It was noon, and he was sleeping. My relatives took no chances. They shot him while he slept." He paused. "It took a great many bullets."

"How did they *know*?" Smithback asked.

"Beside the man was a witchcraft medicine kit. There were certain roots, plants, and insects: taboo items, forbidden items, used only by skinwalkers. They found corpse powder. And up in the chimney, they found certain . . . pieces of meat, drying."

"But I don't understand how . . . ?" Smithback's question trailed off into the darkness.

"Who was it?" Nora asked.

Beiyoodzin did not answer directly. But after a moment, he turned. Even in the dark, Nora could feel the intensity of his gaze.

"You said your horses were cut in five places, on the forehead and two places on each side of breast and belly," he said. "Do you know what those five places have in common?"

"No," Smithback said.

"Yes," Nora whispered, her mouth dry with sudden fear. "Those are the five places where the fur of a horse forms a whorl."

The light had completely vanished from the sky, and a huge dome of stars was cast over their heads. Somewhere in the distance, out on the plain, a coyote began yipping and wailing, and was answered by another.

"I shouldn't have told you any of this," Beiyoodzin said. "No good can come to me. But maybe now you know why you must leave this place at once."

Nora took a deep breath. "Mr. Beiyoodzin, thank you for your help. I'd be lying if I told you I wasn't frightened by what you've said. It scares me to death. But I'm running the excavation of a ruin that my father gave up his life to find. I owe it to him to see it through."

This seemed to astonish Beiyoodzin. "Your father died out here?" he asked.

"Yes, but we never found his body." Something about the way he spoke put her on guard. "Do you know something about it?"

"I know nothing." Then the man was abruptly on his feet. His agitation seemed to have increased. "But I'm sorry to hear about it. Please think over what I've said."

"We're not likely to forget it," said Nora.

"Good. Now I think I'll turn in. I've got to get up early. So I'll say goodbye to you right now. You can turn your horses out to graze in the draw. There's plenty of grass down by the stream. Tomorrow, help yourself to breakfast if you like. I won't be around."

"That won't be necessary—" Nora began. But the old man

was already shaking their hands. He turned away and began to busy himself with the bedroll.

"I think we've been given the brushoff," murmured Smithback. They went back to their horses, unsaddled them, and made a small camp of their own on the far side of the pile of rocks.

"What a character," Smithback muttered a little later as he unrolled his bag. The horses had been watered and were now nickering and muttering contentedly, hobbled nearby. "First he spooks us with all that talk about skinwalkers. Then he suddenly announces it's bedtime."

"Yes," Nora replied. "Just when the talk got around to my father." She shook out her own bedroll.

"He never said what tribe he was from."

"I think Nankoweap. That's how the village got its name."

"Some of that witchcraft stuff was pretty vile. Do you believe it?"

"I believe in the power of evil," Nora said after a moment. "But the thought of wolfskin runners, witching people with corpse powder, is tough to swallow. There are millions of dollars worth of artifacts at Quivira. It seems more likely that we're dealing with a couple of people playing at witchcraft to frighten us away."

"Maybe so, but it seems like a pretty elaborate plan. Dressing up in wolfskins, cutting up horses . . ."

They both fell silent, and the cool night air moved over them. Nora rubbed her arms in the sudden chill. She could offer no explanation for what had happened to her at the ranch house, the matted form running alongside her truck. Or the same dark figure, racing away from her kitchen door. Or the disappearance of Thurber.

"Which way is downwind?" Smithback asked suddenly.

Nora looked at him.

"I want to know where to put my boots," he explained. In the dark, Nora thought she could see a crooked smile on the journalist's face.

"Put them at the foot of your bedroll and point them east," she said. "Maybe they'll keep the rattlers away."

She pulled off her own boots with a sigh, lay down, and pulled the bag up around her dusty clothes. A half-moon had begun to rise, veiled by tatters of cloud. A few yards away, she could hear Smithback grunting as he flounced around, making preparations for sleep. In the calm darkness, the thought of skinwalkers and witches fell away under the weight of her weariness.

"It's strange," Smithback said. "But something is definitely rotten in the State of Denmark."

"What, your shoes?"

"Very funny. Our host, I mean. He's hiding something. But I don't think it has to do with the horses."

From far overhead came the sound of a jet. Idly, Nora located its faint, blinking light, crawling across the velvety blackness. As if reading her mind, Smithback spoke: "There's some guy," he said, "sitting up in that plane, guzzling a martini, eating smoked almonds, and doing the *New York Times* crossword puzzle."

Nora laughed quietly. "Speaking of the *Times*, how long have you written for them?"

"About two years now, since my last book was published. I took a leave of absence to come on this trip."

Nora sat up on one elbow. "Why did you come?"

"What?" The question seemed to take the writer by surprise.

"It's a simple enough question. This is a dangerous, dirty, uncomfortable trip. Why did you leave comfortable old Manhattan?"

"And maybe miss out on the greatest discovery since King Tut's tomb?" Smithback turned in his sleeping bag. "Well, I guess it's more than that. After all, I knew there was no guarantee we'd find anything. If you get right down to it, newspaper work can be boring. Even if it's the *New York Times* and everyone genuflects when you enter the room. But you know what? *This* is what it's all about, really; discovering lost cities, listening to tales of murder, lying under the stars with a lovely—" He cleared his voice. "Well, you know what I mean."

"No, I don't," Nora said, surprised at the sudden excitement that flooded through her.

"Lying under the stars with someone like you," he finished. "Sounds kind of lame, doesn't it?"

"As come-ons go, yes it does. But thanks just the same."

She glanced at the lanky form of Smithback, faintly outlined in starlight, his eyes glinting as he looked skyward. "So?" she said after a moment.

"So what?"

"Over the last week, you've had your spine realigned by hard saddles, you've gone without water, been bitten by horses, almost fallen off cliffs, avoided rattlesnakes, quicksand, and skinwalkers. So are you glad you came along?"

His eyes turned toward her, luminous in the starlight. "Yes," he said simply.

Holding his gaze in her own, she reached toward him in the darkness. Finding his hand, she squeezed it briefly.

"I'm glad, too," she replied.

36

BY MIDNIGHT, A HALF-MOON HAD RISEN IN the dark sky, and the gnarled badlands of southern Utah were bathed in pale light. At the foot of Lake Powell, Wahweap Marina dozed, its jetskis and houseboats silent. To the north and west, the labyrinthine system of narrow canyons leading ultimately toward the Devil's Backbone were still.

In the valley of Chilbah, two forms moved slowly up a secret notch. It was less a trail than a fissure in the rock, fiendishly hidden, now worn away to the faintest of lines after centuries of erosion and disuse. It was the Priest's Trail: the back door to Quivira.

Emerging out of the inky blackness of the rocks, the figures topped out on the sandstone plateau in which the valley of Quivira was hidden. Far below, in the long valley behind them, a horse nickered and stamped in agitation. But this evening they had left the horses unharmed, just as they had slipped past the cowboy who guarded them without running a knife across his throat. He sat there still, hand on his gun, the ground around him damp with tobacco juice. Let him sit; his time would come soon enough.

Now, with animal stealth, they scuttled along the wide mesa far above the valley floor. Though the moon laid a dappled byway across the sandstone, the figures avoided the faint light, keeping to the shadows. The heavy animal pelts on their backs draped down over their sides, dragging along the rough rock beneath them. The figures moved on, silent as ghosts.

After an eternity of movement they stopped, as if possessed of a single mind. Ahead, a well of darkness loomed: the tiny valley of Quivira. Far below, at the base of the canyon, the little stream shimmered in the moonlight. From the higher ground away from the stream, a faint glow arose from the dying campfire, and the even fainter smell of woodsmoke reached the figures peering down from the canyon rim.

Their eyes moved from the fire to the dim figures that lay around it.

Several tents ringed the camp, pallid in the dim moonlight. A number of bedrolls lay near the campfire, seemingly flung down at random. With the tents closed and darkened, it was impossible to count the number of the company. They stared long, bodies motionless. Then they eased forward along the brow of rock.

With consummate stealth they moved along the top of the canyon, pausing now and then to look down toward the sleeping expedition. Occasional sounds drifted up from below: the call of an owl, the babble of water, the rustle of leaves in a night breeze. Once, a belt of silver conchas clinked around the midriff of one of the figures; otherwise, they made no noise in the time it took to reach the top of the rope ladder.

Here the figures paused, examining the communications equipment with intense interest. A minute passed, then two, without movement.

Then one of the figures glided to the edge of the cliff face and gazed down the thin ladder. It disappeared back beneath the brow of rimrock. The figure looked out, into the valley. He was almost directly above the camp now, and the glow of the fire, eight hundred feet below, seemed strangely close, an angry nugget of red in the darkness. A low, guttural sound rose out from deep within his frame, at last dying away into a groan that resolved itself into a faint, monotonous chant. Then he turned back toward the equipment.

In ten minutes, their work there was done.

Slinking further along the rimrock, they made their way to the end of the canyon. The ancient secret trail wormed down through a cut in the rimrock, descending toward the narrow canyon at the far side of the Quivira valley. The trail was perfectly concealed against the rock, and terrifyingly precipitous. The faint sounds of the waterfall echoed up below them, the water thrashing and boiling its way on the long trip down to the Colorado River.

In time, the figures reached the sandy bottom. They moved stealthily out of the curtain of mist, past the rockfall, then along the base of the canyon wall, keeping in the deeper darkness of moonshadow. They stopped when they neared the first member of the expedition: a figure beyond the edge of the camp, sleeping beneath the stars, pale face looking deathlike in gray half-light.

Reaching into the matted pelt that lay across his back, one of the figures pulled out a small pouch. It was made of cured human skin, and in the glow of the moon it gave out an otherworldly, translucent sheen. Loosening the leather thong around it, the figure reached inside and, with extreme caution, drew out a disk of bone and an ancient tube of willow wood, polished with use and incised with a long reverse spiral. The disk flashed dully in the moonlight as he turned it over once, then again. Then, placing one end of the tube to his lips, he leaned toward the face of the sleeping figure. There was a sudden breath of wind, and a brief cloud of dust flowered in the moonlight. Then, with the tread of ghosts, the two figures retreated back toward the cliff face, disappearing once again into the woven shadows.

37

COUGHING, PETER HOLROYD WOKE abruptly out of dark dreams. Some stray breeze had chased dirt across his face. Or more likely it was dust from the day's work, he thought blearily, still weeping out of his pores. He wiped his face and sat up.

It had not been the dust alone that awakened him. Earlier, there had been a sound: a strange cry, borne faintly on the wind, as if the earth itself were groaning. He might have thought he'd dreamed the noise, except that nothing remotely like it had ever existed in his imagination. He was aware that his heart was racing.

Gripping the edges of his bedroll, he looked around. The half-moon threw zebra stripes of silvery-blue light across the camp. He glanced from tent to tent, and at the still black lumps of bedrolls. Everything was still.

His eyes stopped at a spot on a small rise, perhaps twenty yards from the campfire. Usually Nora would be at that spot, sleeping. Tonight she was gone—gone with Smithback. Many times during the desert nights Holroyd had found himself looking in her direction. Wondering what it would be like to creep over and talk to her, tell her how much all this meant to him. How much *she* meant to him. And, always, the last thing he wondered was why he just never had the guts to do it.

Holroyd lay back with a sigh. Even if Nora had been around, though, tonight he had no desire to do anything but rest. He was bone-tired; more tired than he remembered ever being in his life. In Nora's absence, Sloane had directed him to clear away a tidal wave of sand and dust that had risen up against the back wall of the ruin, not far from Aragon's Crawlspace. He hadn't understood why he needed to dig that particular spot; there were many sites in the front of the ruin that had yet to be studied. But Sloane had brushed off his questions with a quick explanation about how important pictographs were often found at such sites at the rear of Anasazi cities. He was surprised at how quickly and completely, after Nora left, Sloane assumed command. But Aragon had been working by himself in a remote corner of the city, his face dark and severe; apparently, he'd made yet another disturbing discovery, and he was too preoccupied to pay attention to anything else. As for Black, he seemed to yield up all critical sense in Sloane's presence, automatically agreeing with whatever she said. And so, from morning until dark, Holroyd had wielded a shovel and a rake. And now it seemed to him that, even after a month's worth of baths, he'd never get all the dust out of his hair, nose, and mouth.

He stared up at the night sky. There was a funny taste in his mouth, and his jaw ached. The beginning of a headache was forming around his temples. He didn't know what he'd expected to do on the expedition, but his vague romantic notions of opening rich tombs and deciphering inscriptions seemed a far cry from the endless grunt work he'd been doing. All around lay fantastic ruins of a mysterious civilization, while they were immersed in gridding this and surveying that. *And* moving piles of empty sand. He was sick of digging, he decided. And he didn't like working for Sloane. She was too aware of her perfection and the influence she cast on others, too willing to use her charm to get what she wanted. Ever since the confrontation with Nora at Pete's Ruin, he'd felt on his guard when she was around.

He sighed, closing his eyes against the pressure in his head.

It wasn't like him to be this grouchy. Normally, he only got grumpy when he was coming down with something. Sloane was all right, really; she was just outspoken, used to getting her way, not his type. And it didn't matter if he was digging sand or breaking rocks. The important thing was he was *here*—here at Quivira, at this miraculous, mythical place. Nothing else mattered.

Suddenly, he stiffened, eyes opening wide. *That sound again.*

Pushing the blanket to one side, he rose to his knees as quietly as he could. Whatever he'd heard, it had stopped. No, there it was again: a murmur, a low groan.

But this sound was different from the sound that had awakened him. It was softer, somehow; softer and nearer.

In the pale light, he hunted around for a stick, a penknife, anything that could be used as a weapon. His hand closed around a heavy flashlight. He hefted it, thought of switching it on, then decided against it. He rose to his feet, staggering a moment before gaining his balance. Then, silently, he moved in the direction of the noise. All had grown quiet again, but the sound seemed to have come from beyond the stand of cottonwoods near the stream.

Cautiously picking his way around boxes and shrouded packs, Holroyd moved away from the camp toward the stream. A cloud had passed over the moon, darkening the landscape to an impenetrable murk. He felt hot, uncomfortable, disoriented in the close darkness. The headache had grown worse when he stood up, and it almost seemed as if a film lay in front of his eyes. In a detached way, he made out what looked like a patch of highly poisonous druid's mantle a few feet away. Instead of taking a closer look, he regarded it with uncharacteristic disinterest. He should be resting in his blanket, not wandering around on a fool's errand.

As he was about to turn back, he heard another sound: a moan, the soft slap of skin against skin.

Then the moon was out again. Stealthily, he moved forward, looking carefully to both sides. The sounds were clearer now, more regular. He tightened his grip on the flashlight, grasped the trunk of a cottonwood, and peered through the curtain of moonlit leaves.

The first thing he saw was a tangle of clothes on the ground beyond. For a moment, Holroyd thought somebody had been attacked, and their body dragged off. Then his eyes moved farther.

On the soft sand beyond the cottonwoods lay Black. His shirt was bunched up around his armpits, his bare legs were splayed, knees bent toward the sky. His eyes were squeezed shut. A small groan escaped him. Above, Sloane was straddling Black's hips, her fingers spread wide against his chest, the sweat on her naked back glowing in the moonlight. Holroyd leaned forward with an involuntary movement, staring in shock and fascination. His face flushed, whether in embarrassment or shame at his own naïveté, he could not say. Black grunted in combined effort and pleasure as he sheathed himself within her, thigh muscles straining. Sloane leaned over him, her dark hair falling over her face, her breasts swaying heavily with each thrust. Holroyd's eyes traveled slowly up her body. She was staring at Black's face intently, with a look more of rapt attention than of pleasure. There was something almost predatory in that look. For a moment, he was reminded of a cat, playing with a mouse.

But that image dissolved as Sloane thrust downward to meet Black, again and again and again, riding him with relentless, merciless precision.

38

With a tug on the guide rope, Nora brought Arbuckles to a halt. She stood beside the horse and looked down from the crest of the Devil's Backbone, into the valley the old Indian had called Chilbah. She felt drained, sickened, by the climb back to the top, and Arbuckles was shaking and lathered with stress. But they had made it: his hooves, once again freed of iron, had gripped the gritty sandstone.

The wind was blowing hard across the fin of rock and several ragged afternoon thunderheads were coalescing over the distant mountains to the north, but the valley itself remained a vast bowl of sunlight.

Smithback came to a stop beside her, white, silent. "So this is Chilbah, sinkhole of evil," he said after a moment. His tone was meant to be light, but his voice still held a quiver of stress from the terrifying ascent of the hogback ridge.

Nora did not reply immediately. Instead, she knelt to reshoe the horses, letting a full sense of control return to her limbs. Then she stood, dusted herself off, and reached into a saddlebag for her binoculars. She scanned the bottomlands with them, looking for Swire and the horses. The cottonwoods and swales of grass were a welcome sight after the long, hot ride back from the sheep camp. It was now half past one. She located Swire alongside the creek, sitting on a rock, watching the remuda graze. As she stared, she could see him looking up toward them.

"People are evil," she said at last, lowering the binoculars. "Landscapes are not."

"Maybe so," said Smithback. "But right from the beginning, I've felt there was something strange about the place. Something that gave me the willies."

Nora glanced at the writer. "And I've always thought it was just me," she replied.

They mounted their horses and moved forward, making the descent into the valley in silence. Nosing their horses directly toward the grassy banks of the creek, they remained in their saddles while the animals waded in to drink, the water burbling around their legs. From the corner of her eye, Nora could see Swire trotting up the creekbed toward them, riding bareback, without bridle or reins.

He pulled to a stop on the far side of the creek, looking from Nora to Smithback and back. "So you brought back both horses," he said, looking at Nora with ill-disguised relief. "What about the sons of bitches who killed my horses—you catch them?"

"No," said Nora. "The person you saw at the top of the ridge was an old Indian man camping upcountry."

A look of skepticism crossed Swire's face. "An old Indian man? What the hell was he doing on top of the ridge?"

"He wanted to see who was in the valley," Nora replied. "He said nobody from his village ever goes into this valley."

Swire sat silent a moment, his mouth working a lump of tobacco. "So you followed the wrong tracks," he said at last.

"We followed the only tracks up there. The tracks of the man you saw."

In reply, Swire expertly shot a string of tobacco juice from his lips, forming a little brown crater in the nearby sand.

"Roscoe," Nora went on, careful to keep her tone even, "if you'd met this man, you'd realize he's no horse killer."

Swire's mouth continued working. There was a long,

strained silence as the two stared at each other. Then Swire spat a second time. "Shit," he said. "I ain't saying you're right. But if you are, it means the bastards that killed my horses are still around." Then, without another word, he spun his horse with invisible knee pressure and trotted back down the creek.

Nora watched his receding back. Then she glanced over at the writer. Smithback merely shrugged in return.

As they set off across the valley toward the dark slot canyon, Nora looked up. The northern sky had grown lumpy with thunderheads. She frowned; normally, the summer rains weren't due for another couple of weeks. But with a sky like this, the rains could be upon them as early as that very afternoon.

She urged her horse into a trot toward the slot canyon. *Better get through before the system moves in,* she thought. Soon, they reached the opening. They unsaddled their horses, wrapped and stowed the saddles, then turned the animals loose to find the rest of the herd.

It was the work of a long, wet, weary hour to toil through the slot canyon, the gear dead weight on their backs. At last, Nora parted the hanging weeds and began walking down toward the camp. Smithback fell in step beside her, breathing hard and shaking mud and quicksand from his legs.

Suddenly, Nora stopped short. Something was wrong. The camp was deserted, the fire untended and smoking. Instinctively, she looked up the cliff face toward Quivira. Although the city itself was hidden, she could hear the faint sounds of loud, hurried conversation.

Despite her weariness, she shrugged the pack from her back, jogged toward the base of the rope ladder, and climbed to the city. As she clambered onto the bench, she saw Sloane and Black near the city's central plaza, talking animatedly. On the far side of the plaza sat Bonarotti, legs crossed, watching them.

Sloane saw her approaching and broke away from Black. "Nora," she said. "We've been vandalized."

Exhausted, Nora sank onto the retaining wall. "Tell me about it," she said.

"It must have happened during the night," Sloane went on, taking a seat beside her. "At breakfast, Peter said he wanted to go up and check his equipment before getting to work. I was going to tell him to take the day off, actually—he didn't look that well. But he insisted. Said he'd heard something during the night. Anyway, next thing I know he was calling down from the top of the cliff. So I went up after him." She paused. "Our communications equipment, Nora . . . it's all been smashed to pieces."

Nora looked over at her. Sloane was uncharacteristically unkempt; her eyes were red, her dark hair tousled.

"Everything?" Nora asked.

Sloane nodded. "The transmitter, the paging network—everything but the weather receiver. Guess they didn't think to look up in that tree."

"Did anybody else see or hear anything?"

Black glanced at Sloane, then turned back to Nora. "Nothing," he said.

"I've kept a sharp eye out all day," Sloane said. "I haven't seen anybody, or anything."

"What about Swire?"

"He went out to the horses before we learned about it. I haven't had a chance to ask him."

Nora sighed deeply. "I want to talk to Peter about this. Where is he now?"

"I don't know," Sloane said. "He went down the ladder from the summit before I did. I figured he'd gone back to his tent to lie down. He was pretty upset and . . . well, frankly, he wasn't making much sense. He was sobbing. I guess that equipment really meant a lot to him."

Nora stood up and walked to the rope ladder. "Bill!" she shouted down into the valley.

"Ma'am?" the writer's voice floated up.

"Check the tents. See if you can find Holroyd."

She waited, scanning the tops of the canyon walls. "Nobody home," Smithback called up a few minutes later.

Nora returned to the retaining wall, shivering now. She realized she was still wet from the trip through the canyon. "Then he must be in the ruin somewhere," she said.

"That's possible," Sloane replied. "He said something yesterday about calibrating the magnetometer. Guess we lost track of him in all the confusion."

"What about the horse killers?" Black interrupted.

Nora hesitated a moment. She decided there was no point in alarming everybody with Beiyoodzin and his story of witches. "There was only one set of prints on the ridge, and they led to the camp of an old Indian. He clearly wasn't the killer. Since our equipment was smashed last night, that probably means the horse killers are still around here somewhere."

Black licked his lips. "That's great," he said. "Now we're going to have to post a guard."

Nora looked at her watch. "Let's find Peter. We're going to need his help setting up some kind of emergency transmitter."

"I'll check the roomblock where he stashed the magnetometer." Sloane walked away, Black following in her wake. Bonarotti came over to Nora and drew out a cigarette. Nora opened her mouth to remind him that smoking wasn't allowed in the ruin, but decided she couldn't summon up the energy.

There was a scuffling noise, then Smithback's shaggy head appeared at the top of the rope ladder. "What's up?" he said, coming over to the retaining wall.

"Somebody snuck into the valley last night," Nora replied. "Our communications gear was smashed." She was interrupted by an urgent shout from within the city. Sloane had emerged from one of the roomblocks on the far side of the plaza, waving an arm.

"It's Peter!" her voice echoed across the ghostly city. "Something's wrong! He's sick!"

Immediately Nora was on her feet. "Find Aragon," she

said to Bonarotti. "Have him bring his emergency medical kit." Then she was running across the plaza, Smithback at her side.

They ducked inside a second-story roomblock complex near the site of the burial cyst. As Nora's eyes grew accustomed to the dim light, she could see Sloane on her knees beside Holroyd's prone form. Black was standing well back, a look of horror on his face. Beside Holroyd lay the magnetometer, its case open, components scattered across the floor.

Nora gasped and knelt down. Holroyd's mouth was wide open, his jaw locked solid. His tongue, black and swollen, protruded from puffy, glaucous lips. His eyes were bulging, and a foul graveyard stench washed up from each shallow breath. A slight, thready gasp escaped his lungs.

There was movement in the doorway, then Aragon was beside her. "Hold my light, please," he said calmly, laying two canvas duffels on the floor, opening one of them, and removing a light. "Dr. Goddard, could you please bring the fluorescent lantern? And the rest of you, please step outside."

Nora trained the light on Holroyd, his eyes glassy, pupils narrowed to pinpoints. "Peter, Enrique's here to help you," she murmured, taking his hand in hers. "Everything's going to be fine."

Aragon pressed his hands beneath Holroyd's jaw, probed his chest and abdomen, then pulled a stethoscope and blood pressure cuff from the duffel and began to check his vital signs. As the doctor opened Holroyd's shirt and pressed the stethoscope to his chest, Nora saw to her horror a scattering of dark lesions across the pale skin.

"What is it?" Nora said.

Aragon just shook his head and shouted for Black. "I want the rest of you to get a tarp, ropes, poles, anything we can use for a stretcher—and tell Bonarotti to get some water boiling."

Aragon peered intently back into Holroyd's face, then examined the man's fingertips. "He's cyanotic," he murmured, fishing in one of the duffels and pulling out a slender oxygen tank and a pair of nasal cannula. "I'll set the flow at two liters," he said, handing the tank to Nora and fixing the cannula into Holroyd's nostrils.

There was the sound of feet, then Sloane returned with the lantern. Suddenly, the room was bathed in chill greenish light. Aragon pulled the stethoscope from his ears and looked up.

"We've got to get him down into camp," he said. "This man needs to go to a hospital immediately."

Sloane shook her head. "The communications gear is completely trashed. The only thing still functioning is the weather receiver."

"Can we cobble something together?" Nora asked.

"Only Peter could answer that question," Sloane replied.

"What about the cell phone?" Aragon asked. "How far to the nearest area of coverage?"

"Up around Escalante," said Sloane. "Or back at Wahweap Marina."

"Then get Swire on a horse, give him the phone, and tell him to get going. Tell him to call for a helicopter."

There was silence. "There's no place to land a helicopter," Nora said slowly. "The canyons are too narrow, the updrafts on the clifftops too precarious. I looked into that very thoroughly when I was planning the expedition."

Aragon looked at Peter, then looked back at Nora. "Are you absolutely certain?"

"The closest settlement is three days' ride from here. We can't take him out on horseback?"

Aragon gazed at Peter again, then shook his head. "It would kill him."

Smithback and Black appeared in the doorway, carrying between them a crude stretcher of tarps lashed to two wooden poles. Moving quickly, they set Holroyd's rigid body on the stretcher, restraining him with ropes. Then, carefully, they hoisted him from the ground and carried him out into the central plaza.

Aragon followed them with his kit, despair on his face. As

they came out from beneath the shadow of the overhanging rock and approached the rope ladder, Nora felt a cold drop on her arm, then another. It was beginning to rain.

Suddenly Holroyd gave a strangled cough. His eyes bulged wider still, ringed red with panic, searching aimlessly. His lips trembled, as if he was trying to force speech from a paralyzed jaw. His limbs seemed to stretch, stiffening even further. The ropes restraining him creaked and sighed.

Instantly, Aragon ordered them to ease the stretcher to the ground. He knelt at Holroyd's chest, fumbling in his duffels at the same time. Instruments went clattering to one side as he pulled out an endotrachial tube, attached to a black rubber bag.

Holroyd's jaws worked. "I let you down, Nora," came a strangled whisper.

Immediately, Nora took his hand once again. "Peter, that's not true. If it weren't for you, none of us would have found Quivira. You're the whole reason we're here."

Peter began to struggle with more words, but Nora gently touched his lips. "Save your strength," she whispered.

"I'm going to have to tube him," Aragon said, gently laying Holroyd's head back and snaking the clear plastic down into his lungs. He pressed the ambu bag into Nora's hands. "Squeeze this every five seconds," he said, dropping his ear to Holroyd's chest. He listened, motionless, for a long moment. Another tremor passed through Holroyd's body, and his eyes rolled up. Aragon straightened up and, with violent heaves, began emergency heart massage.

As if in a dream, Nora sat beside Holroyd, filling his lungs, willing him to breathe, as the rain picked up, trickling down her face and arms. There were no sounds except for the patter of the rain, the cracking thumps of Aragon's fists, the sigh of the ambu bag.

Then, it was over. Aragon sat back, agonized face drenched with rain and sweat. He looked briefly up at the sky, unseeing, and let his face sink into his hands. Holroyd was dead.

39

AN HOUR LATER, THE ENTIRE EXPEDITION had gathered around the campfire in silence. Swire joined them, wet from the slot canyon. The rain had ended, but the afternoon sky was smeared with metal-colored clouds. The air carried the mingled scents of ozone and humidity.

Nora glanced at each haggard face in turn. Their expressions betrayed the same emotions she felt: numbness, shock, disbelief. Her own feelings were augmented by an overpowering sense of guilt. She'd approached Holroyd. She'd convinced him to come along. And, in some unconscious way, she realized she had manipulated his feelings for her to further her own goal of finding the city. Her eyes strayed toward the sealed tent that now held his body. *Oh, Peter*, she thought. *Please forgive me.*

Only Bonarotti continued with business as usual, thumping a hard salami down on his serving table and setting loaves of fresh bread beside it. Seeing that nobody was inclined to partake, the cook flung one leg over the other, leaned back, and lit a cigarette.

Nora licked her lips. "Enrique," she began, careful to keep her voice even, "what can you tell us?"

Aragon looked up, his black eyes unreadable. "Not nearly as much as I would like. I didn't expect to be performing any postmortems out here, and my diagnostic tools are limited. I've cultured him up—blood, sputum, urine—and I've stained and sectioned some tissue. I took some exudate from the skin lesions. But so far the results are inconclusive."

"What could have killed him so fast?" Sloane asked.

Aragon turned his dark eyes to her. "That's what makes diagnosis so difficult. In his last minutes, there were signs of cyanosis and acute dyspnea. That would indicate pneumonia, but pneumonia would not present that quickly. Then there was the acute paralysis . . ." He fell silent for a moment. "Without access to a laboratory, I can't do a tap or a gastric wash, let alone an autopsy."

"What I want to know," Black said, "was whether this is infectious. Whether others might have been exposed."

Aragon sighed and stared at the ground. "It's hard to say. But so far, the evidence doesn't point in that direction. Perhaps the crude bloodwork I've done, or the antibody tests, will tell us more. I've got test cultures growing in petri dishes on the off chance it is some infectious agent. I really hate to speculate . . ." His voice trailed off.

"Enrique, I think we need to hear your speculations," Nora said quietly.

"Very well. If you asked me for my initial impression—it happened so fast, I would say it looked more like acute poisoning than disease."

Nora looked at Aragon in sudden horror.

"Poisoning?" Black cried, visibly recoiling. "Who could have wanted to poison Peter?"

"It may not be one of us," said Sloane. "It may have been whoever killed our horses and wrecked our communications gear."

"As I said, it's speculation only." Aragon spread his hands. He looked at Bonarotti. "Did Holroyd eat anything that the others didn't?"

Bonarotti shook his head.

"And the water?"

"It comes from the creek," Bonarotti replied. "I run it through a filter. We've all been drinking it."

Aragon rubbed his face. "I won't have test results for several hours. I suppose we have to assume it might be infectious. As a precaution, we should get the body out of camp as soon as possible."

Silence fell in the canyon. There was a roll of distant thunder from over the Kaiparowits Plateau.

"What are we going to do?" Black asked.

Nora looked at him. "Isn't it obvious? We have to leave here as quickly as possible."

"No!" Sloane burst out.

Nora turned to her in surprise.

"We can't leave Quivira, just like that. It's too important a site. Whoever destroyed our communications gear knows that. It's obvious they're trying to drive us out so they can loot the city. We'd be playing into their hands."

"That's true," said Black.

"A man has just *died*," Nora interrupted. "Possibly of an infectious disease, possibly even by murder. Either way, we have no choice. We've lost all contact with the outside world. The lives of the expedition members are my first responsibility."

"This is the greatest find in modern archaeology," Sloane said, her husky voice now low and urgent. "There's not one of us here who wasn't willing to risk his life to make this discovery. And now that somebody has died, are we going to just roll things up and leave? That would cheapen Peter's sacrifice."

Black, who paled a bit during this speech, still managed to nod his support.

"For you, and me, and the rest of the scientific team, that may be true," Nora said. "But Peter was a civilian."

"He knew the risks," Sloane said. "You *did* explain them, didn't you?" She looked directly at Nora as she spoke. Though she said nothing more, the unspoken comment couldn't have been clearer.

"I know Peter's presence here was partly my doing," Nora replied, fighting to keep her tone even. "That's something I'll have to live with. But it doesn't change anything. The fact is, we still have Roscoe, Luigi, and Bill Smithback with us. Now that we know the dangers, we have no right to jeopardize their safety any further."

"Hear, hear," Smithback murmured.

"I think they should make their own decisions," Sloane said, her eyes dark in the stormy light. "They're not just paid sherpas. They have their own investment in this expedition."

Nora looked from Sloane to Black, and then at the rest of the expedition. They were all looking back at her silently. She realized, with a kind of dull surprise, that she was facing a critical challenge to her leadership. A small voice within her murmured that it wasn't fair: not now, when she should be grieving for Peter Holroyd. She struggled to think rationally. It was possible that she could, as expedition leader, simply order everyone to leave. But there seemed to be a new dynamic among the group now, in the wake of Holroyd's death; an unpredictable urgency of feeling. This was no democracy, nor should it be: yet she felt she would have to roll the dice and play it as one.

"Whatever we do, we do as a group," she said aloud. "We'll take a vote on it."

She turned her eyes toward Smithback.

"I'm with Nora," he said quietly. "The risk is too great."

Nora looked next at Aragon. The doctor returned her gaze briefly, then turned toward Sloane. "There is no question in my mind," he said. "We have to leave."

Nora glanced at Black. He was sweating. "I'm with Sloane," he said in a high, strained voice.

Nora turned to Swire. "Roscoe?"

The wrangler glanced up at the sky. "As far as I'm concerned," he said gruffly, "we should never have entered this goddamned valley in the first place, ruin or no ruin. And now the rains are here, and that slot canyon's our only exit. It's time we got our butts out."

Nora glanced at Bonarotti. The Italian waved his hand vacantly, sending cigarette smoke spiraling through the air. "Whatever," he said. "I will go along with whatever."

Nora returned her gaze to Sloane. "I count four against two, with one abstention. There's nothing more to discuss." Then she softened her tone. "Look, we won't just leave willy-nilly. We'll take the rest of the day to finish up the most pressing work, shut down the dig, and take a series of documentary photographs. We'll pack a small selection of representative artifacts. Then we'll leave first thing tomorrow."

"The rest of the day?" Black said. "To close this site properly will take a hell of a lot longer than that."

"I'm sorry. We'll do the best we can. We'll only pack up the essential gear for the trip out—the rest we'll cache, to save time."

Nobody spoke. Her face an unreadable mask of emotions, Sloane continued to stare at Nora.

"Let's get going," Nora said, turning away wearily. "We've got a lot to do before sunset."

40

SMITHBACK KNELT BY THE TENT AND GINGERLY
lifted the flap, gazing inside with a mixture of pity and revulsion. Aragon had wrapped Peter Holroyd's body in two layers of plastic and then sealed it inside the expedition's largest
drysack, a yellow bag with black stripes. Despite the carefully
sealed coverings, the tent reeked of betadine, alcohol, and
something worse. Smithback leaned away, breathing through
his mouth. "I'm not sure I can do this," he said.

"Let's just get it over with," Swire replied, picking up a
pole and ducking into the tent.

No book advance is worth this, Smithback thought. Reaching into his pocket for his red bandanna, he tied it carefully
over his mouth. Then he tugged a pair of work gloves over
the rubber gloves Aragon had given him, picked up a coil of
rope, and followed Swire into the tent.

Wordlessly, Swire laid the pole alongside the bagged
corpse. Then, as quickly as possible, the two men lashed it to
the pole, winding the rope around and around until it was secure. Swire tied off the ends with half-hitches. Then, grasping each end, they hefted the body out of the tent.

Holroyd had a slight frame, and Smithback raised one end
of the pole onto his shoulder with relative ease. *I'll bet he
weighs one fifty, one sixty, max,* he thought. *That means eighty*

pounds for each of us. Strange how, at times of severe stress, the mind tended to dwell on the most trivial, the most quotidian details. Smithback felt a pang of sympathy for the friendly, unassuming young man. Just three nights before, under Smithback's journalistic probing by the campfire, Holroyd had opened up at last and talked, at unexpected length, about his deep and abiding love for motorcycles. As he'd talked, the shyness had left him, and his limbs had filled with animation. Now those limbs were still. All too still, in fact; Smithback did not like the stiff, unyielding way Holroyd's bagged feet jostled up against his shoulder as they proceeded toward the slot canyon.

He thought back to the discussion about what to do with the body. It had to be placed somewhere secure, away from camp, elements, and predators, until it could be retrieved at a later time. They couldn't bury it in the ground, Nora had said; coyotes would dig it up. They talked about hanging it in a tree, but most of the trees were inaccessible, their lower branches stripped away in flash floods. Anyway, Aragon said it was important to get the body as far from camp as possible. Then Nora remembered the small rock shelter about a quarter of the way through the slot canyon, above the high-water mark and accessible via a stepped ledge. It was a perfect place to store the body. The place was impossible to miss: the shelter was twenty feet off the canyon bottom, just above the trunk of a massive cottonwood that had been wedged between the walls by some earlier flood. The threat of rain had passed—Black had checked the weather report from the canyon rim—and the slot canyon would be safe for the time being. . . .

Smithback brought himself back to the present. There was a reason his mind was wandering. He knew himself well enough to understand what was happening: he was thinking about something, *anything*, to keep his mind off the job at hand. Deep down, for some reason he didn't fully understand, Smithback realized he was profoundly frightened. He'd been in more than his share of life-threatening situations before: struggling against a killer in a vast museum; and later, caught fighting for his life in a warren of tunnels far beneath New York City. And yet here, in the pleasant afternoon light, he felt as threatened as he ever had in his life. There was something about the diffuse, vague nature of the evil in this valley that unsettled him most of all.

Once again, Holroyd's rigid foot pressed sharply into Smithback's shoulder. Ahead, Swire had stopped and was glancing upward toward the mouth of the slot canyon. Smithback followed his gaze into the narrow, scarred opening. Clearing skies, Black had said; Smithback hoped to hell the weather report was right.

Once in the slot, they were able to float the wrapped body, buoyed by the drysack, across the stretches of slack water. At the base of each pourover, however, Holroyd's corpse had to be half pushed, half dragged up to the next pool. After twenty minutes of pushing, wading, swimming, and dragging, the two men stopped to catch their breath. Farther up the winding passage, Smithback could make out the massive cottonwood trunk that marked the location of the rock shelter. He moved a few feet away from the drysack, untied the bandanna from his mouth, shook it out, and stuffed it into his shirt pocket.

"So you think that Indian you saw had nothing to do with killing my horses," Swire said. They were the first words he'd spoken since they left Holroyd's tent.

"Absolutely not," Smithback replied. "Especially since the people who killed your horses must have been the ones who wrecked our communications gear. And we were with the shepherd when that happened."

Swire nodded. "That's what I've been thinking."

Smithback saw that Swire was still staring at him. The brown eyes had long ago lost the humorous squint Smithback remembered from the first days of their ride. In Swire's sunken cheeks, bony face, and tight jaw, Smithback could see a great sorrow. "Holroyd was a good kid," he said simply.

Smithback nodded.

Swire spoke in a low voice. "It's one thing to get in trouble back there"—he jerked his head in the hypothetical direction of civilization—"but it's a whole other deal to run into trouble out here."

Smithback looked from Swire to Holroyd's body, then back to Swire. "That's why Nora's doing the right thing," he said. "Getting us out as quickly as possible."

Swire spat a line of tobacco across a nearby rock. "She's a brave woman, I'll give her that," he said. "Volunteering to track those horse killers on her own . . . that took guts. But guts alone ain't enough. I've seen even the smallest problem end up killing people in a place like this. And you know what? Our problems ain't small."

Smithback didn't answer. His thoughts were still on Nora: her quick tongue, appraising eyes, resourceful pluck—her courage and determination. And he realized, with a sense of astonishment, that he was scared, not so much for himself but for her.

Swire appraised him, eyes glittering. Then he stood up and grabbed the lead end of the pole. Smithback rose, snugged the bandanna once again around his mouth, and scrambled toward the corpse. They climbed the rest of the way to the rock shelter in silence.

41

Aaron Black stood in the dappled shadows of the westernmost tower, surveying his test trenches and portable lab setups with a practiced eye. The soil profiles were perfect, naturally: a textbook model of the latest in stratigraphic analysis. And the labs were, as always, a picture of economy, efficiency, and accuracy.

As he stared, the satisfaction he usually felt when admiring his work was eclipsed by a stab of disappointment. Muttering under his breath, he drew a large tarp over the test trench and staked it down, pinning the sides with rocks. It was a wholly unsatisfactory way to preserve his accomplishments, but at least it was better than backfilling. Here he was, about to run away from the site that, by all rights, should be the crowning glory of his career. God knows what they would find when they returned. If they returned at all.

He shook his head in disgust and pulled a tarp over the second trench. Still, he wasn't entirely sorry to be leaving. His usual assistant, Smithback, was off burying Holroyd, and as Black worked he managed to feel deeply thankful that particular task had not fallen to him. It didn't really matter whether poison or disease had killed the technician. Either one was dangerous. A part of Black hungered for civilization—telephones, fine restaurants, hot showers, and toilets that flushed—a world hundreds of miles away from Quivira. Of course, he'd never admit this to Sloane, who had moved off in stony silence to take the final photographic records of the site.

As his thoughts turned to Sloane, he felt a hot flush begin to spread out from his vitals. Memories of the night before gave way to hopes and fantasies for the night to come. Black had never had much luck with women, and Sloane was a woman, all right; a woman who . . .

Tearing himself from these thoughts with difficulty, he turned to the flotation lab. Unhooking the jug of distilled water from the apparatus, he dumped the water pan over the edge of the cliff. Then, with a sigh, he began unscrewing the equipment, draining the hoses, and packing everything into two metal suitcases filled with custom-cut foam. It was a job he had done many times before, and despite everything he prided himself on his tidiness. Snapping the suitcases closed, he set them aside and began breaking down the paper chromatography setup.

He paused in the act of stacking the unused papers into plastic folders. By rights, they would have all been used over the coming weeks, forming the foundation for half a year of analysis back in his comfortable lab. He stared at them, all the brilliant articles he planned to write for the most prestigious scientific journals going up in smoke inside his head.

Suddenly, a gust of wind caught a pack of the chromatography papers, blowing them toward the back of the cave. He watched as they scattered and disappeared into the darkness.

Black swore out loud. The papers were ruined—contaminated—but he couldn't just leave them. He'd publicly humiliated more than one archaeologist for leaving trash in a ruin.

He finished packing the chromatography setup and buckled the case shut. Then he stood up and walked toward the back of the cave, eyes to the ground. The papers had scattered along the very back of the midden heap; he could see some still blowing about in the random eddies of wind. Muttering again, he walked past the first granary along the rear wall of the ruin, trapping the papers with his foot as he went, picking them up and shoving them into a pocket. Soon he had counted eleven. The papers came twelve in a pack, he knew; where the hell was the last one?

Ahead of him lay the narrow opening to the Crawlspace, and he moved toward it, bending low under the rock roof. It was too dark to see, and he fumbled in his pocket for a penlight. Its feeble gleam struggled to pierce the darkness, illuminating dust, scattered bones, and—about ten yards away—the last paper, caught on a piece of broken skull.

To hell with Aragon and his ZST, Black thought sourly, getting down on his hands and knees and childishly shoving the bones out of his way. Another eddy of wind stirred up the dust inside the Crawlspace, and he sneezed explosively. Kicking the bones aside, he grabbed the final paper and stuffed it in his pocket. As he turned to go, he saw a large pack rat shamble into the beam of his flashlight, disturbed by the clatter of bones. It turned to face him, yellow teeth bared.

Black shied back, sneezed again, and waved his hand. The animal backed up with a chattering protest and a flick of its tail, but it did not flee.

"Yah!" Black cried, picking up a longbone and aiming it at the rat. With a sudden movement, the rat vanished into a small pile of rock, lying against the back wall of the Crawlspace.

Curious, he moved forward. On closer inspection, he could see that the rocks had not fallen from the ceiling of the Crawlspace, as he had assumed; they were of a different material than the sandstone cave. In the bottom of the pile of rocks the pack rat had made his opening, lined with twigs and cactus husks.

Black crawled closer, wrinkling his nose at the strong smell of guano and rat urine. As he played his light into the rathole, he saw that it led to a black space beyond: a large black space.

He examined the rocks again. It looked to his expert eyes that they were not a natural event. Rather, they had been piled there deliberately. A great deal of care had been taken to conceal this opening: Aragon must have passed it at least two dozen times without noticing anything, and Aragon had sharp eyes, even for an archaeologist. But his own eyes, Black mused, were better.

He sat in the darkness, feeling his heartbeat quicken. Something had been deliberately hidden behind the rock pile; painstakingly, cunningly hidden. A burial, most likely, or even a catacomb. Obviously of great archaeological value. He glanced up and down the Crawlspace. He was alone, Aragon busy elsewhere on Holroyd's postmortem analysis. He shone his light into the hole once more, probing farther.

This time, something glinted back at him.

Black withdrew the light, sat up, and remained motionless for a moment. And then he did something he had never done before. He picked up a stray bone and began working loose the small rocks around the rathole. Carefully at first, then with greater and greater urgency, he scrabbled with the rocks, pulling them out. Soon, a small opening in the back of the cave became visible. Thoughts of discomfort, disease, and poison evaporated from his mind, replaced by a new thought: a consuming desire to see what lay on the far side.

Dust began to cake on his sweaty skin; he tied a bandanna over his mouth and nose and continued. The bone fell apart and he continued working with his hands. In five minutes, he had cleared an opening large enough to admit his bulk.

Breathing deeply, he wiped his hands on the seat of his pants and plucked the bandanna from his mouth. Then he put his hands on either side of the opening and pulled himself through.

In a moment he was on the far side. He scrambled to his feet, panting hard. The air was thick, hot, and surprisingly humid. He looked around, his penlight stabbing through skeins of dust.

Almost immediately he saw the glint again—the unmistakable glint of gold—and for a moment his heart stopped. He was in a large black cavern. There, rising in front of him, dominating the cavern, was another Great Kiva. Incised and painted on its side was a huge disk that winked gold in his light. The Great Kiva had once had a door in the side, also blocked with loose stones and half buried in sand. Behind it stood an exquisite Anasazi pueblo, small but perfect, its two-storied roomblocks and ladders sealed in the cave and untouched for more than seven centuries.

He scrambled to his feet and approached the kiva, touching the gold disk with a trembling hand. The effect of gold had been created with a deep yellow pigment—Black guessed it was yellow ochre of iron—mixed with crushed flakes of mica. The whole thing had then been polished, creating a shimmering surface that looked remarkably like gold. It was the same method used to make the image in the Rain Kiva, only this disk was ten feet in diameter.

He knew then that he had found the Sun Kiva.

42

THE DIRTY SKY OF THE AFTERNOON HAD lifted, and the air above the canyon of Quivira was suffused with the last golden light of sunset. Already, the gloom of night was gathering in the bottom of the canyon, in strange juxtaposition to the brilliant narrow strip of sky above. The brief rain had released the scents of the desert: wet sand, the sweet smell of cottonwoods, mingled with the fragrant cedar-wood from Bonarotti's fire.

Nora, struggling to close one of the drysacks, noticed none of the beauty, smelled none of the scents. To her, still numbed by the events of the day, the valley was anything but benign. A few minutes before, Swire and Smithback had returned from their grisly errand, and they now rested by the fire, exhausted, faces blank.

With an effort, she heaved the drysack alongside the growing pile of equipment, then grabbed an empty duffel and began to fill it. Much of the evening would be spent packing the gear, caching some of it, getting the rest ready for the long, wet trip out the slot canyon to the horses. Once they had packed and gotten away from the valley and its divisive influences, she felt sure, they would be able to function as a team once again; at least, long enough to bring the details of their remarkable find back to the Institute.

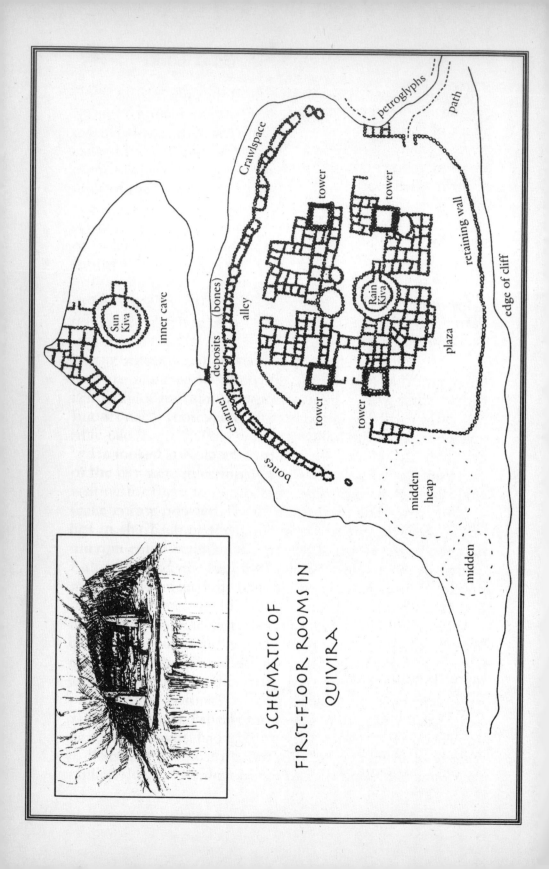

SCHEMATIC OF
FIRST-FLOOR ROOMS IN
QUIVIRA

petroglyphs

Path

Crawlspace

tower

tower

retaining wall

Sun
Kiva

inner cave

(bones)

deposits

alley

channel

Rain
Kiva

edge of cliff

plaza

bones

tower

tower

midden
heap

midden

A harsh, ragged shout from the direction of the rope ladder intruded on her thoughts. She looked up to see the tall figure of Aaron Black come striding through the gloaming, his face gray with dirt, his clothing streaked, hair wild. For a terrifying moment, she was certain he had caught whatever it was that killed Holroyd. But this fear was quickly dispelled by the look of triumph on his face.

"Where's Sloane?" he boomed, looking around animatedly. He cupped his hands around his mouth. "Sloane!" The valley reverberated with his shouts.

"Are you all right?" Nora asked.

As Black turned toward her, Nora could see sweat springing from the mud caked to his brow, running in dun-colored rivulets down his face. "I found it," he said.

"Found what?"

"The Sun Kiva."

Nora straightened up, releasing her hold on the duffel and letting it fall back into the sand. "You found *what?*"

"There was a blocked opening behind the city. Nobody noticed it before. But *I* did. I found it." Black's chest was heaving, and he could barely get out the words. "Behind the Crawlspace is a narrow passageway that leads into another cavern behind the city. And, Nora, there's a whole secret city hidden back there. Right in front is a Great Kiva, a sealed kiva. It's like nothing we've seen before."

"Let me get this straight," Nora said slowly. "You broke through a wall?"

Black nodded, his smile broadening.

Nora felt sudden anger course through her. "I specifically forbade any disturbance like that. My God, Aaron, all you've done is open up a new area to be looted. Have you forgotten we're about to leave?"

"But we *can't* leave now. Not after this discovery."

"We absolutely *are* leaving. First thing in the morning."

Black stood rooted in place, anger and disbelief growing in his face. "You haven't heard what I said. *I found the Sun Kiva.* We can't leave now. The gold will be stolen."

Nora looked more intently at his face. "Gold?" she repeated.

"Christ, Nora, what else do you think is in there? Corn? The evidence is overwhelming. I just found the Anasazi Fort Knox."

As Nora stared at him, in growing consternation and disbelief, she saw Sloane come up through the twilight, oversized camera under one arm.

"Sloane!" Black called out. "I found it!" He rushed over and embraced her. Smiling, she disentangled herself, and looked from him to Nora with a quizzical expression. "What's this?" she asked, carefully setting down the camera.

"Black found a sealed cave behind the city," Nora replied. "He says the Sun Kiva is inside it."

Sloane looked at Black quickly, smile vanishing as comprehension dawned.

"It's there, Sloane," he said. "A Great Kiva, sixty feet in diameter, with a sun disk painted on its side."

A powerful play of emotions ran quickly across Sloane's face. "What kind of disk?"

"A great sun in yellow pigment, mixed with mica and polished. It looks just like gold. I thought it *was* gold when I first saw it."

Sloane suddenly became very pale, then flushed deeply. "Paint mixed with mica?"

"Yes. Crushed biotite mica, which has a golden cast to it. A brilliant imitation of the real thing. Which is exactly the kind of symbolic representation you'd find on the *outside* if they were storing—"

"Take me to it," Sloane said urgently. Black grabbed her hand and they turned away.

"Hold on!" Nora barked.

The two turned to look at her, and with dismay Nora read the passion in their faces. "Just a minute," she continued. "Aaron, you're acting like a pothunter, not a scientist. You should never have broken into the back of the cave. I'm sorry, but we can't have any more disturbance."

Sloane looked at her, saying nothing, but Black's face grew dark. "And *I'm* sorry," he said loudly, "but we're going up there."

Nora looked into Black's eyes, saw there was no point in arguing with him, and turned to Sloane instead. "For good or ill, everything that happens here is going into the final report," she went on urgently. "Sloane, consider how your father will react if he hears we busted willy-nilly into that kiva. If Black is right, this could be the most important discovery yet. Even more reason why we have to proceed carefully."

At the mention of her father, the sudden hunger seemed to leave Sloane's face. She tensed, struggling to regain her composure.

"Nora, come up with us," she said with a quick smile. "All we'll do is look. What harm is there in that?"

"Absolutely," said Black. "I've touched nothing. Nothing has happened here that can't go into a public report."

Nora looked at each of them in turn. Smithback, Swire, and Bonarotti had come over and were listening intently. Only Aragon was missing. She glanced at her watch: almost seven o'clock. She thought about what Black had said: a hidden city, the Sun Kiva. What was it Aragon had said in the Rain Kiva? "There's a piece of the puzzle still missing. I thought it would be in this kiva. But now, I am not so sure." If Aragon were here, no doubt he'd disapprove. But she knew Black's find could mean the key to everything. The fact that it might be looted and destroyed after they were gone filled her with a helpless anger. Because of that, they had an obligation to document the inner cave, at least in photographs. Besides, if she were to keep the group together, she felt she had no choice but to bend just a little. The harm had been done; Black's transgression would be dealt with later, and not by her.

"All right," she said. "We'll make a short visit. Only long enough to take photographs and decide how best to reseal the cave. No more violations of any sort. Am I understood?"

She turned to Sloane. "Bring the four-by-five camera. And Aaron, you get the fluorescent lamp."

Ten minutes later, a small group stood huddled together in the confines of the inner cave. Nora gazed in awe, overwhelmed despite herself by the richness of the site, by the perfect little gem of an Anasazi city hidden behind the mysterious kiva. The greenish glare of the lamp threw magic-lantern patterns on the irregular walls. It was a small pueblo, no more than thirty rooms; no doubt some kind of *sanctum sanctorum* for the priests. For that reason alone, it would be exceedingly interesting to study.

The Sun Kiva itself was unadorned except for the great polished disk, glinting in the harsh light. Thick ribbed dust lay in drifts against its base and along its walls. The kiva had been carefully plastered with adobe, and she saw that the only opening in its side had been blocked with rocks.

"Look at that stonework," said Black. "It's the most fortified kiva I've ever seen."

A pole ladder was leaning against one side of the kiva. "That was leaning against the roomblocks," Black said eagerly, following Nora's glance. "I brought it over and climbed onto the roof. There's no roof opening. It's been totally sealed shut." His voice dropped a notch. "As if it's hiding something."

Sloane broke away from the group and walked up to the sun disk. She stroked it lightly, almost reverently, with her fingers. Then she glanced back at Nora, briskly unpacked her camera kit, and began setting up the first shot.

The group stood silently while Sloane moved about the cavern, shooting the kiva and its associated roomblocks from a variety of angles. Soon she rejoined them, folded up her tripod, and put the camera body back in its case.

Even the loquacious Smithback had remained silent and, most uncharacteristically, taken no notes. There was a palpable tension in the air; a tension quite different, Nora realized, than any she had felt at the site before.

"Done?" she asked. Sloane nodded.

"Before we leave tomorrow morning," Nora went on, careful to keep her voice neutral, "we'll reblock the hole as best we can. There's not much to bring a looter back behind the granaries. If we hide it well, they'll miss it."

"Before we leave?" Black repeated.

Nora looked at him and nodded.

"By God, not until we open this kiva," said Black.

Nora looked at his face, then at Sloane. And then at Swire, and Bonarotti, and Smithback. "We're leaving tomorrow," she said quietly. "And nobody's opening this kiva."

"If we don't do it now," Sloane said, her voice loud, "nothing will be left when we return."

There was a tense silence, broken by Bonarotti. "I would also like to see this kiva full of gold," he said.

Nora waited, taking measured breaths, thinking about what she was going to say and how she was going to say it.

"Sloane," she began quietly. "Aaron. This expedition is facing a crisis. One person has died. There are people out there who killed our horses, and who may try to kill us. To open and document this kiva properly would take days. We don't *have* days." She paused. "I'm the leader of this expedition. It's my choice to make. And we're leaving tomorrow."

A tense silence gathered in the cave.

"I don't accept your so-called *choice*," Sloane said in a low tone. "Here we are, on the verge of the greatest discovery, and what is your answer? Go home. You're just like my father. You have to control everything. Well, this is *my* career, too. This is *my* discovery as much as it is yours. If we leave now, this kiva will be looted. And you'll have thrown away perhaps the greatest discovery in American archaeology." Nora saw that she was shaking in anger. "I've been a threat to you from the beginning. But that's your problem, not mine. And I'm not going to let you do this to my career."

Nora looked hard at Sloane. "You mention your father," she said slowly. "Let me tell you what he said to us, right before we left for Quivira: 'You are representing the Institute.

And what the Institute represents is the very highest standard of archaeological research and ethical conduct.' Sloane, what we do here, what we say here, will be studied, debated, second-guessed by countless people." She softened her tone. "I know how you feel. I want to open this kiva as much as you do. And we *will* be back to do this the right way. I promise you'll get all the credit you deserve. But until that time, I absolutely forbid the opening of this kiva."

"If we leave here now, there will be nothing left when we return," Sloane said, her eyes locked on Nora. "And then *we'll* be the ones doing the second-guessing. Go on and run, if you want. Just leave me a horse and some supplies."

"Is that your final word?" Nora asked quietly.

Sloane merely stared in return.

"Then you leave me no choice but to relieve you of your position on the archaeological team."

Sloane's eyes widened. Then her gaze swivelled to Black.

"I'm not sure you can do that," Black said, a little weakly.

"You're damn right she can do it," Smithback suddenly spoke up. "Last time I checked, Nora was leader of this expedition. You heard what she said. We leave the kiva alone."

"Nora," Black said, a pleading note entering his voice, "I don't think you appreciate the magnitude of this discovery. Just on the other side of that adobe wall is a king's ransom in Aztec gold. I just don't think we can leave it for . . ."

His voice trailed off. Ignoring Black, Nora continued to look hard at Sloane. But Sloane had turned away, her eyes fixed on the large painted disk on the kiva's side, glowing brilliantly in the fluorescent light. Then she gave Nora one last, hateful look and walked to the low passageway. In a moment she was gone. Black stood his ground a little longer, staring from the kiva to Nora and back again. Then, swallowing heavily, he tore himself away and wordlessly made his way out into the Crawlspace.

43

Skip Kelly made his careful way down the far reaches of Tano Road North, doing his best to keep the VW from bottoming out on the dirt road. It was terrible road, all washboard and ruts: the kind of road that was a much-coveted asset in many of Santa Fe's priciest neighborhoods. Every quarter mile or so, he passed another enormous set of wrought-iron gates, flanked by adobe pillars, beyond which a narrow dirt road wound off through piñon trees: portals to unseen estates. Occasionally, he caught glimpses of buildings—a caretaker's cottage, an immaculate set of barns, an enormous house rising from a distant ridgeline—but most of the great estates along Tano Road were so well hidden that one hardly knew they existed.

The road narrowed, the piñons crowding in on either side. Skip slowed even further, eased his foot onto the clutch, elbowed Teddy Bear's huge muzzle out of his face, and once again checked the number scribbled onto a folded sheet of paper, dim in the evening light. Not far now.

He came over the brow of a hill and saw the road peter out a quarter mile ahead, ending in a thicket of chamisa. To the left, a great rock of granite rose out of the earth. Its face had been polished flat, and ESG had been engraved on it in simple, sans-serif letters. Beyond the rock was an old ranch gate.

It looked much more battered than the shiny monstrosities he had just driven past. As he eased the car closer, however, he saw that the shabbiness of the gate belied its immensely strong construction. Beside it was a small keypad and an intercom.

Leaving the engine running, he got out of the car, pushed the single red button beneath the intercom's speaker, and waited. A minute passed, then two. Just as he was preparing to get back into the car, the speaker crackled into life.

"Yes?" came a voice. "Who is it?"

With mild surprise, Skip realized that the voice wasn't that of a housekeeper, chauffeur, or butler. It was the authoritative voice of the owner, Ernest Goddard himself.

He leaned toward the intercom. "It's Skip Kelly," he said.

The speaker was silent.

"I'm Nora Kelly's brother."

There was a brief movement in the vegetation beside the gate, and Skip turned to see a cleverly hidden camera swivel toward him. Then it panned away, toward the Volkswagen. Skip winced inwardly.

"What is it, Skip?" the voice said. It did not sound particularly friendly.

Skip swallowed. "I need to talk to you, sir. It's very important."

"Why now? You're working at the Institute, are you not? Can't it wait until Monday?"

What Skip didn't say was that he had spent the entire day locked in a debate with himself over whether or not to make this trip. Aloud, he said, "No, it can't. At least, I don't think it can."

He waited, painfully conscious of the camera regarding him, wondering what the old man would say next. But the intercom remained silent. Instead, there was the heavy clank of a lock being released, and the old gate began to swing open.

Skip returned to the car, put it in gear, and eased past the fence. The winding driveway threaded its way along a low ridge. After a quarter of a mile, it dipped down, made a sharp turn, then rose again. There, on the next crest, Skip saw a magnificent estate spread along the ridgeline, its adobe facade brocaded a rich evening crimson beneath the Sangre de Cristo Mountains. Despite himself, he stopped the car for a moment, staring through the windshield in admiration. Then he drove slowly up the remainder of the driveway, parking the Beetle between a battered Chevy truck and a Mercedes *Gelaendewagen*.

He got out of the car and closed the door behind him. "Stay," he told Teddy Bear. It was an unnecessary command: even though the windows were rolled all the way down, the dog would never have been able to squeeze his bulk through them.

The entrance to the house was a huge set of eighteenth-century zaguan doors. *Pulled from some hacienda in Mexico, I'll bet*, Skip thought as he approached. Clutching a book under one arm, he searched for a doorbell, found nothing, and knocked.

Almost immediately the door opened, revealing a long hallway, grandly appointed but dimly lit. Beyond it he could see a garden with a stone fountain. In front of him stood Ernest Goddard himself, wearing a suit whose muted colors seemed to match the hallway beyond almost exactly. The long white hair and closely trimmed beard framed a pair of lively but rather displeased blue eyes. He turned without a word and Skip followed his gaunt frame as it retreated down the hall, hearing the click of his own heels on the marble.

Passing several doors, Goddard at last ushered Skip into a large, two-story library, its tall rows of books clad in dark mahogany shelves. A spiral staircase of ornate iron led to a second-story catwalk, and to more books, row upon row. Goddard closed and locked a small door on the far side of the room, then pointed Skip toward an old leather chair beside the limestone fireplace. Taking a seat opposite, Goddard crossed his legs, coughed lightly, and looked enquiringly at Skip.

Now that he was here, Skip realized he had no idea exactly

how to begin. He fidgeted with unaccustomed nervousness. Then, remembering the book beneath his arm, he brought it forward. "Have you heard of this book?" he asked.

"Heard of it?" murmured Goddard, a trace of irritation in his voice. "Who hasn't? It's a classic anthropological study."

Skip paused. Sitting here, in the quiet confines of the library, what he thought he had discovered began to seem faintly ridiculous. He realized the best thing would be to simply relate what had happened.

"A few weeks ago," he said, "my sister was attacked at our old farmhouse out past Buckman Road."

"Oh?" said Goddard, leaning forward.

"She was assaulted by two people. Two people wearing wolfskins, and nothing much else. It was dark, and she didn't get a very good look at them, but she said they were covered with white spots. They wore old Indian jewelry."

"Skinwalkers," Goddard said. "Or, at least, some people playing as skinwalkers."

"Yes," said Skip, relieved to hear no note of scorn in Goddard's voice. "They also broke into Nora's apartment and stole her hairbrush to get samples of her hair."

"Hair." Goddard nodded. "That would fit the skinwalker pattern. They need bodily material from an enemy in order to accomplish their witching."

"That's just what this book says," Skip replied. Briefly, he recounted how it had been his own hair in the brush, and how he had been the one who almost died when his brakes failed so mysteriously.

Goddard listened silently. "What do you suppose they wanted?" he asked when Skip had finished.

Skip licked his lips. "They were looking for the letter Nora found. The one written by my father."

Goddard suddenly tensed, his entire body registering surprise. "Why didn't Nora tell me of this?" The voice that had previously expressed mild interest was now razor-sharp with irritation.

"She didn't want to derail the expedition. She figured she

needed the letter to find the valley, and that if she got out of town fast and quietly, whoever or whatever it was would be left behind."

Goddard sighed.

"But that's not all. A few days ago, our neighbor, Teresa Gonzales, was murdered in the ranch house. Maybe you heard about it."

"I recall reading something about that."

"And did you read that the body was mutilated?"

Goddard shook his head.

Skip slapped *Witches, Skinwalkers, and Curanderas* with the back of his hand. "Mutilated in just the way described in this study. Fingers and toes sliced off, the whorl of hair on the back of the head scalped off. A disk of skull cut out underneath. According to this book, that's where the life force enters the body."

Goddard's blue eyes flashed. "The police must have questioned you about the murder. Did you tell them any of this?"

"No," Skip said, hesitating. "Not exactly. Well, how do you think they'd react to a story about Indian witches?" He put the book aside. "But that's what they were. They wanted that letter. And they were willing to kill for it."

Goddard's look had suddenly gone far away. "Yes," he murmured. "I understand why you've come. They're interested in the ruins of Quivira."

"They vanished just about the time the expedition left, maybe a day or two later. Anyway, I haven't seen or heard any sign of them since. And I've been keeping a close eye on Nora's apartment. I'm worried they may have followed the expedition."

Goddard's drawn face went gray. "Yesterday we lost radio contact."

A feeling of dread suddenly gripped Skip's heart. This had been the one thing he didn't want to hear. "Could it be equipment trouble?"

"I don't think so. The system had redundant backups. And

according to your sister, that imaging technician, Holroyd, could have rigged a transmitter out of tin cans and string."

The older man rose and walked to a small window set among the bookshelves, gazing out toward the mountains, hands in his pockets. A quietness began to gather in the library, punctuated by the steady ticking of an old grandfather clock.

"Dr. Goddard," Skip blurted suddenly, unable to contain himself any longer. "Please. Nora's the only family I've got left."

For a moment, Goddard seemed not to have heard. Then he turned, and in his face Skip could see a sudden, iron resolve.

"Yes," he said, striding to a telephone on a nearby desk. "And the only family I've got left is out there with her."

44

THAT NIGHT, A SOFT BUT STEADY RAIN drummed on the tents of the Quivira expedition, but when morning came the sky was a clear, clean, washed blue, without a cloud in sight. After a long and restless night during which she'd split the guard duty with Smithback, Nora was grateful to step out into the cool morning world. The birds filled the trees with their calls, and the leaves dripped with water that caught and fractured the bright rays of the rising sun.

As she emerged from her tent, her boots sunk into soft wet sand. The creek had risen, she could see, but only slightly—these first rains had been soft enough to soak into the sand without running off. But now the ground was saturated. They had to get out of the canyon before another hard rain, if they didn't want to be trapped by rising water . . . or, God forbid, something worse.

She glanced toward the row of packed equipment, arranged the night before for transport out of the canyon. They were only taking the minimum they needed to get back to Wahweap Marina—food, tents, essential equipment, documentary records. The rest was being cached in an empty room in the city.

Uncharacteristically, Bonarotti was up early, tending the fire, the espresso pot just signaling its completion with a brief roar. He looked up as Nora came over, rubbing the sleep out of her eyes. "Caffé?" he asked. Nora nodded her thanks as he handed her a steaming cup.

"Is there really gold in that kiva?" Bonarotti asked in a quiet voice.

She eased herself down on the log and drank. Then she shook her head. "No, there isn't. The Anasazi didn't have any gold."

"How can you be so sure?"

Nora sighed. "Trust me. In a century and a half of excavations, not one grain of gold has been found."

"But what about Black? What he said?"

Nora shook her head again. *If I don't get them out of there today,* she thought, *I'm never going to get them out.* "All I can tell you is, Black's wrong."

The cook refilled her cup, then turned back to his fire, silent and dissatisfied. As she sipped her coffee, the rest of the camp began to stir. As they approached, one at a time, it was clear to Nora that the tension of the previous day had not gone away. If anything, it had increased. Black took a seat by the fire and hunched over his coffee, his face dark and inflamed. Smithback gave Nora a tired smile, squeezed her shoulder, then retreated to a rock to scratch quietly in his notebook. Aragon looked distant and absorbed. Sloane was the last to appear. When she did, she refused to meet Nora's eyes. A resolute silence gripped the camp. Nobody looked like they had slept.

Nora realized she had to establish a momentum, keep things moving toward departure, not allow anyone time to brood. She finished her cup, swallowed, cleared her throat. "This is how it's going to work," she said. "Enrique, please secure the medical gear we'll need. Luigi will pack up the last of the food. Aaron, I want you to climb to the top of the rim and get a weather report."

"But the sky is blue," protested Black, with a distasteful look at the dangling ladder.

"Right here, it's blue," said Nora. "But the rainy season

has started, and this valley drains off the Kaiparowits. If it's raining there, we could get a flash flood just as sure as if it were raining directly on top of us. Nobody goes through the slot canyon until we get the weather report."

She looked at Sloane, but the woman hardly registered that she had heard.

"If it's clear," Nora continued, "we'll make the final preparations to leave. Aaron, after you get the weather report, I want you to seal the entrance to the Sun Kiva. You broke into it—you leave it just as you found it. Sloane, you and Smithback will take the last of the drysacks up to the caching spot. As soon as Aaron gets the weather report, I'll take a load out through the canyon, then make sure the site is secure."

She looked around. "Is everyone clear on their duties? I want us out of here in two hours."

Everyone nodded but Sloane, who sat with a dark, unresponsive look on her face. Nora wondered what would happen if, at the last minute, she refused to go. Nora felt sure that Black wouldn't stay behind—deep down, he was too much of a coward—but Sloane was another matter. *We'll cross that bridge when we come to it,* Nora thought.

Just as she was rising, a flash of color caught her eye: Swire, emerging from the mouth of the slot canyon and coming down the valley. Something about the way he was moving toward them filled her with dread. *Not more horses, please.*

Swire sprinted across the creek and into camp. "Someone got Holroyd's body," he said, fighting to catch his breath.

"Someone?" Aragon asked sharply. "Are you sure it wasn't animals?"

"Unless an animal can scalp a man, cut off his toes and fingers, and drill out a piece of his skull. He's lying up there in the creek, not far from where we buried him."

The group looked at one another in horror. Nora glanced at Smithback and could tell from his expression that he, too, remembered what Beiyoodzin had said.

"Peter . . ." Nora's voice faltered. She swallowed. "Did you go on to check the horses?" she heard herself ask.

"Horses are fine," said Swire.

"Are they ready to take us out?"

"Yes," he said.

"Then we have no more time to waste," Nora continued, standing up and placing her cup on the serving table. "I'll take that load out through the slot canyon, and pick up Peter's body on the way. We're just going to have to pack it out on one of the horses. I'll need someone to give me a hand."

"I'll help," said Smithback quickly.

Nora nodded her thanks.

"I will go, too," said Aragon. "I would like to examine the corpse."

Nora glanced at him. "There are things here that you need to do—" The sentence went unfinished as she saw the significant look on his face. She turned away. "Very well. We could use a third hand with the body. And listen, all of you: stay in pairs. I don't want anyone going anywhere alone. Sloane, you'd better go with Aaron."

Nobody moved, and she glanced around at the faces. The tension that had drawn her nerves tight as a bowstring—the fear and revulsion she felt at the thought of Peter's body, broken and violated in death—suddenly coalesced into exasperation.

"Damn it!" she cried out. "What the hell are you waiting for? Let's move!"

45

SILENTLY, AARON BLACK FOLLOWED SLOANE toward the rope ladder. Their private discussion the night before had resolved nothing. At the last minute, Sloane would refuse to leave; Black felt certain she would. But when he questioned her, she had been impatient and evasive. Though he would never admit it to her, Black's own intense desire to stay had been slightly tempered by fear: fear of what killed Holroyd, and, worse, of what had attacked their horses and equipment; and now, added to that, fear of what had mutilated Holroyd's body.

Reaching the base of the ladder, Sloane pulled up onto the first rung and began to climb. Black, irritated when she did not wait to see him safely into the harness, pulled the reinforced loops into place around his waist and crotch, tested the ropes, and started up. He hated this climb; harness or no harness, it terrified him to be swaying five hundred feet up on a cliff, hanging on to nothing but a flimsy nylon rope.

But as he mounted the ladder, slowly, one painful rung at a time, the terror began to abate. A phrase began running through his mind; a phrase that had never been far from him since he first discovered the Sun Kiva, stuck in his head like a singsong melody. As he climbed, he recited the entire passage, first silently, then under his breath. "And then, widening the hole a little, I inserted the candle and peered in. As my eyes grew accustomed to the light, details of the room emerged slowly from the mist, strange animals, statues, and gold—everywhere the glint of gold."

Everywhere the glint of gold. It was that final phrase, more than anything else, that kept repeating itself in his mind like a mantra.

He thought back to his childhood; to when he was twelve years old and had first read Howard Carter's account of discovering the tomb of Tutankhamen. He remembered that moment as well as he remembered the passage itself: it was the very moment when he decided to become an archaeologist. Of course, college and graduate school quickly dispelled any notion that he would find another tomb like King Tut's. And he had found rich professional rewards in the mere dirt—very rich rewards indeed. He had never felt the slightest dissatisfaction with his career.

Until now. He climbed hand over hand, moving up the ladder, stopping occasionally to check his harness. Now, dirt seemed a poor substitute for gold. He thought about all the gold that Cortéz had melted down into bars and sent back to Spain; all the splendid works of art turned into bullion, lost to the world. Its twin treasure sat in that kiva.

The fever he had felt as a twelve-year-old, first reading that account, now burned in him again. But again he was torn: there was danger here, he knew. And yet, leaving the valley without seeing the inside of the Sun Kiva seemed almost unimaginable to him.

"Sloane, talk to me," he called. "Are you going to leave the kiva behind, just like that?"

Sloane didn't answer.

He heaved up the ladder, sweating and grunting. Above, he saw Sloane preparing to make the final climb around the terrifying brow of rock below the summit. Here, the sandstone was still streaked with moisture from the rain, and it glowed a blood-drenched crimson.

"Sloane, say something, please," he gasped.

"There's nothing to say," came the clipped response.

Black shook his head. "How could your father have made a mistake like putting her in charge? If it were you, we'd be making history right now."

Sloane's only response was to disappear around the brow of rock. Taking a deep breath, Black followed her up the last pitch. Two minutes later, he struggled up over the rim and threw himself into the sand, exhausted, angry, utterly despondent. He sucked the air deep into his lungs, trying to catch his breath. The air was a lot cooler up here, and a stiff breeze was blowing. The sparse vegetation cover smelled of pine and juniper. He sat up, pulling off the annoying harness. "All this way," he said. "All this work. Just to be cheated out of the greatest discovery at the last minute."

But Sloane didn't answer. He was aware of her presence standing to one side, silent and unmoving. *Everywhere the glint of gold. . . .* Remotely, he was curious why Sloane was just standing there, making no move to get started. With a muttered curse, he stood up and glanced at her.

Sloane's expression was so unfamiliar, so unexpectedly dramatic, that he simply stared. Her face had lost all its color. She remained where she was, unmoving, staring out over the trees, her lips slightly drawn back from her teeth. In a strange trick of the light he saw her amber eyes deepen to mahogany, as if a sudden shadow had been cast upon them. At last, unlocking his eyes from her face, he slowly turned to follow her gaze.

A dark mass rose above and far beyond the ridge, so enormous and fearsome it took Black a moment to comprehend its true nature. Above the lofty prow of the Kaiparowits Plateau rose a thunderhead the likes of which he had never seen. It looked, he thought distantly, more like an atomic explosion than a storm. Its moiled foot ran at least thirty miles along the spine of the plateau, turning the ridge into a zone of dead black; from this base rose the body of the storm, surging and billowing upward to perhaps forty thousand feet. It flattened itself against the tropopause and sheared off into

an anvil-shaped head at least fifty miles across. A heavy, tene-
brous curtain of rain dropped from its base, as opaque as
steel, obscuring all but the very point of the distant plateau in
a veil of water. There was a monstrous play of lightning inside
the great thunderhead, vast flickerings and dartings, omi-
nously silent in the distance. As he watched, mesmerized and
terrified at once, the thunderhead continued to spread, its
dirty tentacles creeping across the blue sky. Even the air on
the canyon rim seemed to grow charged with electricity, the
scent of violence drifting through the piñons as if from a faraway battleground.

Black remained motionless, transfixed by the awful sight,
as Sloane moved slowly, like a sleepwalker, toward the stunted
tree that held the weather receiver. There was a snap of a
switch, then a low wash of static. As the unit locked onto the
preset wavelength, the static gave way to the monotonous,
nasal voice of a weather announcer in Page, Arizona, giving a
litany of details, statistics, and numbers. Then Black heard,
with superhuman clarity, the forecast: "Clear skies and
warmer temperatures for the rest of the day, with less than
five percent chance of precipitation."

Black swivelled his eyes from the thunderhead to the sky
directly above them: bright, flawless blue. He looked down
into the valley of Quivira, peaceful and quiet, the camp awash
in morning sunlight. The dichotomy was so extreme that, for
a moment, he could not comprehend it.

He stared back at Sloane. Her lips, still withdrawn from
her teeth, looked somehow feral. Her whole being was tense
with an internal epiphany. Black waited, suddenly breathless,
as she snapped off the instrument.

"What—?" Black began to ask, but the look on Sloane's
face silenced him.

"You heard Nora's orders. Let's get this disassembled and
down into camp." Sloane's voice was brisk, businesslike, neutral. She swung up into the stunted juniper and in a moment
had unwound the antenna, taken down the receiver, and
packed it in a net bag. She glanced at Black.

"Let's go," she said.

Without another word, she swung the bag over her shoulder and walked to the ladder. In a moment, she had disappeared down into blue space.

Confused, Black slowly buckled on his harness, took hold of the rope ladder, and began to follow her down.

Ten minutes later, he stepped off the rope ladder. His distraction was so complete that he only knew he had reached the bottom when his foot sank into the wet sand. He stood there, irresolutely, and again turned his eyes upward. Overhead, the sky was an immaculate azure from rim to rim. There was no hint of the cataclysm taking place twenty miles away, at the head of their watershed. He removed the harness and walked back toward camp, his steps stiff and wooden. Despite the burden of the receiver, Sloane had scuttled down the cliff face like a spider, and she was in camp already, dropping the equipment beside the last pile of drysacks.

Nora's urgent voice brought Black out of his reverie. "What's the report?" he heard her ask Sloane.

Sloane didn't answer.

"Sloane, we have no time. Will you please give me the weather report?" The exasperation in Nora's voice was unmistakable.

"Clear skies and warmer temperatures for the rest of the day," Sloane said, in a monotone. "Less than a five percent chance of precipitation."

Black watched as the strained look on Nora's face was replaced by a flood of relief. The suspicion and concern vanished from her eyes. "That's great," she said with a smile. "Thanks, you two. I'd like everybody to help take the last of the drysacks up to the caching site. Then, Aaron, you can go ahead and seal up the entrance to the hidden cavern. Roscoe, perhaps you should go with him. Keep a close eye on each other. We'll be back to help you take the last load out in ninety minutes or so."

A strange, utterly foreign sensation began to creep up

Black's spine. With a growing sense of unreality, he came up beside Sloane and watched as Nora gave a shout and a wave to Smithback. They were quickly joined by Aragon. Then the three walked toward the rows of supplies, shouldered their drysacks, and started for the mouth of the slot canyon.

After a moment, Black tore himself away and turned toward Sloane. "What are you doing?" he asked, his voice cracking.

Sloane met his gaze. "What am I doing? I'm not doing anything, Aaron."

"But we saw—" Black began, then faltered.

"What did we see?" Sloane hissed suddenly, rounding on him. "All I did was get the weather report and give it to Nora. Just as she demanded. If *you* saw something, say so now. If not, then shut your mouth about it forever."

Black stared into her eyes: her whole frame was trembling, her lips white with emotion. He glanced upcanyon, in time to see the group of three cross the stream, toil briefly up the scree slope, and disappear into the dark, terrible slit of rock.

Then he looked back at Sloane. As she read his eyes, the tension in her frame ebbed away. And then, slowly, she nodded.

46

JOHN BEIYOODZIN HALTED HIS HORSE AT THE top of the hogback ridge and looked down into the valley of Chilbah. The horse had taken the trail well, but he was still trembling, damp with perspiration. Beiyoodzin waited, murmuring soothing words, giving him time to recover. The late morning sun was glinting off the peaceful thread of water winding through the valley bottom, a ribbon of quicksilver amid the lush greenery. On the high benchlands above, the wind stirred the cottonwoods and copses of oaks. He could smell sage and ozone in the air. There was a sudden stirring of wind that pressed at his back, as if urging him over the side. Beiyoodzin restrained an impulse to look; he knew all too well what loomed up behind him.

The buckskin shook out his mane, and Beiyoodzin patted him soothingly on the neck. He closed his eyes a moment, calming himself, trying to reconcile his mind to the confrontation that lay ahead.

But calm would not come. He felt a sudden surge of anger at himself: he should have told the woman everything when he had the chance. She had been honest with him. And she deserved to know. It had been foolish to tell her only half of the story. Worse, it had been unkind and selfish to lie. And now, as a result of his weakness, he found himself on a journey that he would have given almost anything to avoid. He could hardly bring himself to contemplate the terrible nature of the evil he had to confront. And yet he had no choice but to prepare himself for conflict; perhaps, even, for death.

Beiyoodzin finally saw the situation clearly, and he was not happy with the role he had played. Sixteen years before, a small imbalance, a minor ugliness—*ni zshinitso*—had been injected into the small world of his people. They had ignored it. And as a result the small imbalance had become, as they should have known it would, a great evil. As a healer, he should have guided them to doing what was right. It was precisely because of this old imbalance, this absence of truth, that these people were now down in Chilbah, digging. He shuddered. And it was because of this imbalance that the *eskizzi*, the wolfskin runners, had become active again. And now it had fallen to him to correct the imbalance.

At last, he reluctantly turned around and gazed toward the storm, amazed to see it still growing and swelling, like some vast malignant beast. Here, as if he needed it, was a physical manifestation of the imbalance. It was releasing ever thicker, blacker, denser columns of rain down onto the Kaiparowits Plateau. It was a tremendous rain, a five-hundred-year rain. Beiyoodzin had never seen its equal.

His gaze moved over the distant guttered landscape between the thunderhead and the valley, trying to pick out the flash of moving water; but the canyons were too deep. In his mind's eye he could see the torrential rains falling hard on the slickrock of the Kaiparowits, the drops coalescing into rivulets, the rivulets into streams, the streams into torrents— the torrents into something that no word could adequately describe.

He untied a small bundle from one of his saddle strings— a drilled piece of turquoise and a mirage stone tied up in horsehair around a small buckskin bag, attached to an eagle feather. He opened the bag, pinched out some cornmeal and pollen, and sprinkled it about, saving the last for his horse's poll. He brushed first himself, then his horse's face, with the eagle feather. The horse was prancing now in growing agitation, eyes rolling toward the thunderhead. The leather strings of the saddle slapped restlessly in the growing wind.

Beiyoodzin chanted softly in his language. Then he repacked his medicine kit, dusted the pollen from his fingers. The landscape was now divided sharply between brilliant sunlight and a spreading black stain. A chill, electrically charged wind eddied around him. He would not, of course, attempt to ride into the second valley, the valley of Quivira, through the slot canyon. The flood would be coming through within minutes. That meant he would have to take the secret Priest's Trail over the top: the long, difficult rimrock trail that his grandfather had told him of in broken whispers but that he himself had never seen. He thought back, trying to recall his grandfather's directions precisely. It would be necessary to do so, because of the cleverness with which the trail was hidden: it had been designed to be an optical illusion, its cliff edge cut higher than the edge along the rockface, rendering it practically invisible from more than a few feet away. The trail, he had been told, started up the cliffs some distance from the slot canyon, crossed the wide slickrock plateau, and then descended into the canyon at the far end of the valley of Quivira. It might be very difficult for an old man. Maybe, after all these years, it would be impossible. But he had no choice; the imbalance had to be corrected, the natural symmetry had to be restored.

He started quickly down into the valley.

47

Nora parted the curtain of weeds and glanced upward. The slot canyon snaked ahead of her, the sunshine striated and shadowy in the reddish half-light, the hollows and polished ribs of stone stretching ahead like the throat of some great beast. She eased into the water and breaststroked across the first pool, Smithback following, Aragon bringing up the rear. The water felt cool after the dead, oppressive heat of the valley, and she tried to empty her mind to it, concentrating on the pure physical sensation, refusing for the moment to think of the long trip that lay before them.

They traveled in silence for a while, going from pool to pool, wading along the shallows, the quiet sounds of their passage whispering off the confined spaces of canyon. Nora hefted the drysack from one shoulder to the other. Despite everything, she felt less troubled than she had over the last three days. It had been her great fear that Black and Sloane would descend the ladder with reports of bad weather brewing. It would have been credible, given the recent rains. And she would have had to decide whether they were telling the truth or giving a phony report in order to remain at Quivira. But the report of good weather—though grudgingly given— proved they were resigned to leaving the city. Now all that remained was the grueling multiple portages out through the slot canyon to the horses.

No, that was not quite all; her mind had never been far from Holroyd's remains, waiting for them a quarter mile up the slot canyon. And with those remains came the message that the skinwalkers were close; perhaps watching them right now, waiting to make their next move.

She glanced back toward Aragon: the man had made it clear he wanted to speak to her about something. Aragon looked up, read the question in her eyes, and merely shook his head. "When we reach the body," was his only reply.

Nora swam across another pool, climbed up a pourover, and squeezed sideways through a narrower section. Then the steep walls widened a little around her. In the distance ahead, she could make out the massive cottonwood trunk, suspended like a gigantic spar, wedged across the walls of the canyon. Just above it, in deep shadow, was the narrow ledge that led to the space where Holroyd's body had been laid.

Nora's eyes fell from the ledge, to the jumble of rocks below, to the narrow pool that stretched the eight or ten feet across the canyon's bottom. Her gaze came to rest at a smear of yellow, floating at the near end. It was Holroyd's body bag. Gingerly, she came forward. Now she could see a long, ragged gash in one side of the bag. And there was Holroyd's body, lying on its back half out of the water. He looked strangely plump.

She stopped dead. "Oh, God," came Smithback's voice by her shoulder. Then: "Are we exposing ourselves to some kind of disease, wading about in this water?"

Aragon heaved himself up behind them. "No," he said, "I don't believe we are." But there was no consolation in his face as he spoke these words.

Nora remained still, and Smithback, too, hesitated behind her. Aragon gently pushed past them toward the body. Nora watched as the doctor pulled it onto a narrow stone shelf beside the pool. Reluctantly, she forced herself forward.

Then she stopped again with a sudden gasp.

Holroyd's decomposing body was swollen inside its clothes, a grotesque parody of obesity. His skin, protruding from his shirt sleeves, was a strange, milky bluish-white. The fingers were now just pink-edged stubs, having been cut away at the first joints. His boots lay on the rocks, slashed and torn, and his feet, that same pale white against the chocolate rock, were missing their toes. Nora gazed in mingled disgust, horror, and outrage. Even worse was the back of the head: a large circular whorl of hair been scalped off, and the disk of skull directly beneath drilled out. Brain matter bulged from the hole.

Working swiftly, Aragon donned a pair of plastic gloves, removed a scalpel from his kit, positioned it just below the last rib, and with a short movement opened the body. Reaching inside with a long narrow set of forceps, he twisted his hand sharply, then retracted it. On the end of the scalpel was a small bit of pink flesh that looked to Nora like lung tissue. Aragon dropped it inside a test tube already half filled with a clear liquid. Adding two drops from a separate vial, he stoppered the tube and swirled it around in his hands. Nora watched as the color of the solution turned a light blue.

Aragon nodded to himself, carefully placed the tube inside a styrofoam case, and repacked his instruments. Then, still kneeling, he turned toward Nora. One gloved hand lay, almost protectively, over the corpse's chest.

"Do you know what killed him?" Nora asked.

"Without more precise tools, I can't be a hundred percent sure," Aragon replied slowly. "But one answer does seem to fit. All the crude tests I've been able to run verify it."

There was a moment of silence. Smithback took a seat on a rock a cautious distance from the body.

Aragon glanced at the writer, then back to Nora. "Before I go into that, I need to tell you some things I've discovered about the ruin."

"About the *ruin?*" Smithback asked. "What does that have to do with his death?"

"Everything. I believe the abandonment of Quivira—in-

362

deed, perhaps even the reason for its very existence—is intimately connected with Holroyd's death." He wiped his face with the sleeve of his shirt. "No doubt you've noticed the cracks in the towers, the collapsed third-story rooms of the city."

Nora nodded.

"And you must have noticed the great rockfall at the far end of the canyon. While you were off searching for the horse killers, I talked with Black about this. He told me that the damage to the city was done by a mild earthquake that struck around the same time the city was abandoned. 'The dates are statistically equal,' he said. The landslide, according to Black, also occurred at the same time, no doubt triggered by the earthquake."

"So you think an earthquake killed all those people?" Nora asked.

"No, no. It was just a tremblor. But that rockfall, and the collapse of some buildings, was enough to raise a large cloud of dust in the valley."

"Very interesting," Smithback said. "But what does a seven-century-old dustcloud have to do with Holroyd's death?"

Aragon gave a wan smile. "A great deal, as it turns out. Because the dust within Quivira is riddled with *Coccidioides immitis*. It's a microscopic fungal spore that lives in soil. It's usually associated with very dry, often remote desert areas, so people don't come into contact with it much. Which is a very good thing. It's the cause of a deadly disease known as coccidioidomycosis. Or, as you might know it, valley fever."

Nora frowned. "Valley fever?"

"Wait a minute," Smithback interjected. "Wasn't that the disease that killed a bunch of people in California?"

Aragon nodded. "Valley fever, or San Joaquin fever, named after a town in California. There was an earthquake in the desert near San Joaquin many years ago. That quake triggered a small landslide that raised a cloud of dust, which rolled over the town. Hundreds became ill and twenty died, infected with coccidioidomycosis. Scientists came to call this type of deadly dustcloud a 'tectonic fungal cloud.'" He frowned. "Only the fungus here in Quivira is a far more virulent strain. In concentrated form, it kills in hours or days, not weeks. You see, to get sick you must inhale the spores—either through dust, or through . . . other means. Mere exposure to a sick person is not enough."

He wiped his face again. "At first, Holroyd's symptoms were baffling to me. They did not seem to be from any infectious agent I knew of. Certainly he died too quickly for any of the more likely suspects. And then I remembered that rust-colored powder from the royal burial."

He looked at Nora. "I told you about my discoveries with the bones. But do you recall those two pots, full of reddish dust? You thought they might be a kind of red ochre. I never told you that the dust turned out to be dried, ground-up human flesh and bone."

"Why didn't you tell us?" Nora cried.

"Let's just say you were preoccupied with other things. And I wanted to understand it myself before I dangled yet another mystery in front of you. In any case, while puzzling over Holroyd's death, I remembered that reddish dust. And then I realized exactly what it was. It is a substance known to certain southwestern Indian tribes as 'corpse powder.'"

Nora glanced at Smithback and saw her own horror reflected in his eyes.

"It's used by witches to kill their intended victims," Aragon continued. "Corpse powder is still known among some Indian groups today."

"I know," Nora whispered. She could almost see Bei-yoodzin's drawn face in the starlight, telling them of the wolf-skin runners.

"When I examined this powder under the microscope, I found it absolutely packed with *Coccidioides immitis*. It is, quite literally, corpse powder that really kills."

"And you think Holroyd was murdered with it?"

"Given the huge dose he must have received to die so

quickly, I would say yes. Although his illness was surely made worse by constant exposure to dust. He did quite a lot of digging in the rear of the ruin in the days before his death. The fact is, we've *all* been exposed to it."

"I did my share of digging," Smithback said, his voice a little shaky. "How much longer before we get sick, too?"

"I don't know. A lot depends on the health of our immune systems, and on the degree of exposure. I believe the fungus is much more concentrated in the rear of the city. But regardless, it's vital that we get out of here and get treatment as soon as possible."

"So there's a cure?" Smithback asked.

"Yes. Ketoconazole, or in advanced cases where the fungus has invaded the central nervous system, amphotericin B injected directly into the cerebrospinal fluid. The ironic thing is, ampho is a common antibiotic. I almost brought some along."

"How sure are you about this?" asked Nora.

"As sure I can be without more equipment. I'd need a better microscope to be absolutely sure, because in tissue the spherules are only about fifty microns in diameter. But nothing else explains the onset of symptoms: the cyanosis, dyspnea, the mucopurulent sputum . . . the sudden death. And the simple test I just performed on Peter's lung tissue confirmed the presence of coccidioidin antibodies." He sighed. "It's only in the last day or so that I began putting this together. Late yesterday evening, I spent some time in the ruin, and found other examples of corpse powder stored in pots, as well as various odd types of tools. From this, and from all the trashed bones in the Crawlspace, it became quite clear that the inhabitants of Quivira were actually *manufacturing* corpse powder. As a result, the whole city is contaminated with it. The entire subsoil of the ruin is full of the spores, its density increasing toward the back. That puts the greatest concentration in the Crawlspace, and especially in the cavern of the Sun Kiva that Black discovered."

He paused. "I told you my theory that this city was not

really Anasazi after all. It was Aztecan in origin. These people brought human sacrifice and witchcraft to the Anasazi. It's my belief that they are the marauders, the conquerors, who caused the collapse of Anasazi civilization and the abandonment of the Colorado Plateau. *They* are the mysterious enemies of the Anasazi that archaeologists have sought all these years. These enemies did not kill and exert control through open warfare, which is why we've never found the evidence of violence. Their means of conquest and control were more subtle. Witchcraft and the use of corpse powder. Which leaves little or no trace."

His voice fell. "When I first analyzed that burial cyst Sloane uncovered, I felt it to be a result of cannibalism. The marks on the bones seemed to point to that. In fact, Black's protests to the contrary, it was the obvious deduction to make: Anasazi cannibalism is currently a hot, if controversial, theory. But I no longer think cannibalism is at the bottom of all this. I now believe those marks on the bones tell an even more terrible tale."

He looked at Nora with haunted eyes. "I believe the priests of the city were infecting prisoners or slaves with the disease, waiting for them to die, and then processing their bodies to make corpse powder. The trash from that terrible operation lies in the back of the cave. With the powder, these conquerors could maintain their rule through ritual and terror. But in the end, the fungus turned on them. The mild earthquake that damaged the towers and caused the landslide must have raised a tectonic fungal cloud in the valley here, just like in San Joaquin. Except that here, in the confined space of the canyon, the dustcloud had no place to go. It filled the alcove, enshrouded the city of Quivira. All those skeletons, thrown atop the broken bodies in the back of the cave, were its priestly Aztec victims."

Aragon stopped speaking and looked away from Nora. His face, she thought, had never looked so drawn, so exhausted.

"Now, it's time for me to tell you something," Nora replied slowly. "Modern-day witches may be the ones trying to drive us out of the valley." She briefly told Aragon about the attack in the ranch house and the more recent conversation with Beiyoodzin. "They followed us out here," she concluded. "And now that they've found the site, they're trying to drive us away so they can loot it for themselves."

Aragon thought for a moment, then shook his head. "No," he said. "No, I don't think they're here to loot the city."

"What are you talking about?" Smithback interjected. "Why else would they be trying to drive us away?"

"Oh, I don't dispute they're trying to drive us away. But it's not to loot the city." He glanced once again at Nora. "You've been assuming all along that these skinwalkers were trying to find the city. What if they were actually trying to *protect* it?"

"I don't—" Smithback began.

"Just a minute," Nora broke in. She was thinking quickly.

"How else could they have traced us here so quickly?" Aragon asked. "And, if indeed they killed Holroyd with corpse powder, where else could they have gotten it, except from this place?"

"So they weren't after the letter to learn Quivira's location," Nora murmured. "They wanted to *destroy* the letter. To keep us from coming here."

"Nothing else makes sense to me," Aragon replied. "Once, I believed that Quivira was a city of priests. Now, I believe it was a city of witches."

They sat a moment longer, three figures ranged around the still form of Holroyd. Then a sudden breeze, chill with moisture, stirred the hair on Nora's forehead.

"We'd better get going," she said, rising. "Let's get Peter's body out of the canyon."

Silently, they began rewrapping the body in the ripped dry-sack.

48

As John Beiyoodzin urged his horse down the trail into the valley of Chilbah, his heart quickly sank. From the first switchback, he could make out the expedition's horses; the remuda was watering at the stream. The tiny creek meandered down the center of a great floodplain, torn and guttered, scattered with boulders and tree trunks. He glanced upward anxiously, but the thunderhead was now out of sight, hidden behind the fin of rock.

He knew only too well that this valley was a bottleneck for the vast watershed of the Kaiparowits. The flood, coming down the miles off the Kaiparowits Plateau, would gradually coalesce as the canyons came together in the upper reaches of the Chilbah Valley. It was all uninhabited, from the Kaiparowits to the Colorado River—except for the archaeologists in the valley beyond, which lay directly in the path of the water.

He looked to his right, where the valley broke up into a series of canyons and dry washes. The water coming off the Kaiparowits Plateau would enter the Chilbah Valley through these circuitous, twisting canyons. It would then race through the lower valley in one overwhelming mass. It would be colossal, covering the entire floodplain and probably tearing into the banks. If the horses weren't moved well out of the plain and up into the high benchlands on either side of the valley, they would be swept away. Many of his people's horses had died in flash floods. It was a terrible thing. And if there were people on the floodplain of the valley beyond—or, even worse, in the slot canyon that connected the two valleys . . .

He urged his horse into a plunging lope down the rubbled trail. He just might have time to reach the horses and scare them up to higher ground.

Within five minutes he had reached the bottom, his horse heaving and slick. He let the animal drink at the creek, all the while listening up the valley with a keen ear for the sound he knew only too well: the peculiar vibration that signaled a flash flood.

Out of sight of the thunderhead, the horse was calmer, and he drank deeply. When he had slaked his thirst, Beiyoodzin steered the animal across the floodplain, then urged him up the steep banks. Once up in the rocky benchlands well away from the stream, he kicked the buckskin into a lope, then a hand gallop. As long as they stayed on the high ground, they would be safe.

As he galloped, winding among huge boulders and outcrops of rock, Beiyoodzin's thoughts returned to the people in the second, smaller valley beyond. He wondered if they would hear the flood coming. He knew there was some benchland on either side of the creek, and he hoped the people had known enough to pitch their camp up there. The woman, Nora, had seemed to know a little about the ways of the desert. They could survive if they were smart—and if they heeded the warnings.

Suddenly, he reined his horse to a violent stop. As the flurry of sand subsided around them, Beiyoodzin remained still, listening intently.

It was coming. So far, it was only a vibration in the ground, an unsettling tingle in his bones. But it was unmistakable.

He clicked his tongue and urged the horse forward. At a dead run, the buckskin flashed across the sandy ground, leaping rocks and bushes, dodging cottonwoods, racing toward the grazing horses. Now, he could hear the ugly sound rising up in the valley, even over the noise of his own galloping horse. It was a sound without direction, coming from every-where and nowhere at once, climbing quickly in pitch from the subsonic to a shriek. Along with it came a wind that started as a gentle breeze and quickly gained strength, shiver-ing the leaves of the cottonwoods.

Again in his mind's eye he saw a world out of balance. Six-teen years ago, it had seemed a small, harmless thing indeed. Ignore it, everyone had said. If these were to be the conse-quence of that action, they were terrible consequences indeed.

He reached the edge of the benchland. Below, in the floodplain, he could see the expedition's horses. They had stopped grazing now and were standing alert, their ears pricked up, staring upstream. But it was already too late to save them. To ride down into the floodplain now would be suicide. He shouted and waved his hat; but his voice did not carry above the growing roar, and the herd's attention was elsewhere.

The ground trembled. As the noise continued to intensify, Beiyoodzin became unable to separate the terrified whinnies of his own horse from the scream of the coming water. He looked upstream, into the maw of an even stronger wind that thrashed at the salt cedars and pressed the willows almost hor-izontal to the ground.

Then he saw *it* come around the bend: a vertical wall twenty feet high, moving with the speed of a freight train, driving the howling wind before it.

But it was not a wall of water. Instead, Beiyoodzin beheld a seething rampart of tree trunks, roots, boulders, and boil-ing dirt; a huge churning mass, pushed ahead by the flood at eighty miles an hour. He struggled to control his horse.

The horses below wheeled in hopeless fright and ran. As Beiyoodzin watched—in a mixture of amazement, horror, and fearful reverence—the monstrous wall bore down on them relentlessly. In rapid succession the animals were struck and blown apart, turned inside out like the abrupt blossom-ing of a rose, the ropy eruptions of scarlet, chunks of meat, and shattered legs disappearing into the roiling mass of logs and boulders.

Piled behind the murderous wall of debris came the great engine of its momentum: a tidal wave of chocolate-colored water two hundred yards wide, boiling from benchland to benchland in a flow that for the moment was greater than the Colorado River itself. It blasted a path through the valley, leaping into haystacks of water and standing waves ten feet high. The flood ripped at the edges of the plain like a chainsaw, tearing out hundred-ton chunks of earth and sucking away cottonwood trees. At the same time, Beiyoodzin felt a wave of intense humidity pass over him. The air grew suddenly pregnant with the rich scent of wet earth and lacerated vegetation. Despite his distance, he instinctively backed up his horse as the walls of the benchland began caving in before him.

From still higher ground, he stared down at the humped and gnarled backside of the tidal wave as it thundered down the valley toward the dark slot canyon in the far rock face. As the flood struck the opening of the slot, he felt the brutal crash ripple beneath his feet. An enormous shockwave shuddered backward through the torrent, momentarily stopping the forward motion of the flood, atomizing the water. A vast curtain of brown spume erupted along the rock face, rising several hundred feet up the cliffs with terrifying speed before gradually falling back.

Now the torrent settled into a new pattern. The floodwaters continued to pile up against the slot canyon, forcing their way in, creating an instant lake: a huge, angry maelstrom of water boiling at the canyon's mouth. Man-sized splinters of wood were thrown from the water as the swirling trees were torn apart by the violent pressure.

Another huge piece of benchland caved in before him. Shaking, Beiyoodzin turned his horse from the appalling scene and headed in the direction of the old Priest's Trail: the back door into the valley of Quivira. It had been too late to save the horses. And now he wondered if anyone—including himself—would get out of Chilbah Valley alive.

49

WITH THE HELP OF ARAGON AND SMITH-back, Nora tied off the ripped covering around Holroyd's body bag and lashed it to the pole. Then she stood back, wiping her brow with the back of her hand. Although she knew it had to be done, she was reluctant to begin the awkward, arduous, depressing task of lugging Holroyd's body, along with several drysacks full of gear, out to where the packhorses waited.

She looked up, scanning the canyon ahead. On the far side of the pool and well above her head was the massive cottonwood trunk. Beyond was a steep climb to the next pool; it was going to be hell, she knew, to get across it. The rising wind blew a strand of hair across her face, which she unconsciously tucked back behind her ear. She took a deep breath, knelt, and grasped one end of the pole.

Then she froze. There was another breath of wind on her cheek, stronger this time. Along with it came the sudden, strangely pleasant scent of crushed vegetation.

Fear sent blood surging in her ears. The wind was accelerating with an almost machinelike precision, very different from a natural, intermittent breeze. Even as she paused it became stronger.

"Flash flood," she said.

"Yeah?" The sky overhead was calm and blue; Smithback's tone was curious, not worried. "How can you tell?"

But Nora didn't hear him. Her mind was calculating furiously. They were at least a quarter mile into the slot canyon. There was no way to get out in time. Their only chance was to climb, to get above the level of the flood.

Quickly, she pointed up toward the cavity in the rock where Holroyd's corpse had been stored. "Drop the body," she said urgently, "drop everything. Let's go!"

Smithback began to protest. "We can't just—"

"Move!" Aragon said urgently, releasing the other end of the pole. The body slid into the pool, turning lazily. Nora began thrashing through the water downstream, toward the spot where the ledge angled upward to the small cave.

"Where are you going?" Smithback called, disbelief strong in his voice. "Shouldn't we be heading the other way?"

"No time!" she cried. "Come on, hurry! *Hurry!*"

Beneath the driving wind, Nora could now hear a faint noise: a low-frequency sound, deep and menacing. The calm pools of water in the stream broke into a dancing chop. The hastily abandoned drysacks began to bob and roll wildly.

She floundered across the pool, breath coming in sobs. The wind grew, and grew, and then there was a painful pop in her ears: a drastic change in air pressure. She looked back at Smithback and Aragon, wet and bedraggled, and tried to scream at them to hurry. Her voice was drowned by a vast, distorted roar that washed through the slot canyon, popping her ears a second time.

In its wake came an intense silence. The wind had suddenly dropped.

She hesitated, confused, her ears straining to catch every nuance of sound. From what seemed to be a vast distance, she could make out clatterings and crunchings, strangely distinct despite their remoteness. She whirled toward the ledge again, realizing she was hearing the sound of boulders and logs jamming into the stone slot, ricocheting off the narrow canyon walls on their way toward them. As she ran, a fresh wind rose to a screaming pitch, tearing shreds of water from the surface of the stream. The flood, she knew, would first turn the slot canyon into a wind tunnel.

She thrashed forward. The sound in the canyon grew to a terrible howl, and the ever-rising hurricane of wind tore at their backs. *We're not going to make it,* Nora thought. She glanced back and saw that Aragon had fallen behind. She held out her hands to him, urging him on, screaming words that had no sound over the blast.

Suddenly a boulder came down the canyon from behind them, bounding between the rock walls with thunderous booms, roaring over their heads with horrifying speed. Another, even larger, followed in its wake, propelled ahead of the water by a stochastic amplification of momentum. It hit the jammed cottonwood trunk with a shattering force and continued down-canyon, leaving behind the smell of smoke and crushed stone.

Gasping and coughing, Nora reached the ledge and grasped it with both hands, pulling herself out of the water. She scrambled up the rock, trying to maintain her purchase on the slippery ledge. The air had grown full of pulverized water, which lashed at them mercilessly. She hugged the rockface in an effort to keep the wind from plucking her off.

An advance guard of water blasted through the canyon just below them, and the light above dimmed. Events were happening so quickly—the day had grown so suddenly, completely violent—for a moment it seemed to Nora that she was locked in some terrible dream. She could barely make out Aragon's form below her, struggling up the ledge.

A second tongue of twisting water came racing past below them, almost sucking Aragon from the canyon wall. Pausing in his climb, Smithback reached back, grabbed Aragon's shirt, and hauled him upward. As Nora watched from above, powerless to help, another surge grabbed at Aragon's leg. Over the cry of the flood, she thought she heard the man scream: a strange, hollow, despairing sound.

Smithback lunged for a better hold as Aragon was dragged from the ledge, dangling into space. A passing rock smacked into Aragon, spinning him around; there was a soundless parting of fabric and Smithback fell back against the cliff, a tattered remnant of Aragon's collar in his hand. A furious gust of wind buoyed Aragon above the dancing rocks, whirling him downstream. Caught by another packet of water, his body was slammed into the canyon wall and dragged across it like cheese across a grater. In his wake, gobbets of red lay scraped across dark rock, vanishing quickly, like Aragon himself, into the boiling spume.

Choking back a sob, Nora turned and grabbed the next handhold, hoisted herself up, then reached for the next. *Higher,* she thought. *Higher.* Behind her, Smithback was coming up fast. She scrambled, slid back, regained her footing, then fell again, the wind tearing her from the rock. As she slid away, Smithback's arm wrapped itself around her, and she felt herself pulled up the narrow ledge, closer and closer to the cavity in the rock.

And then, at last, the main body of the flood came: a huge shadow, looming far above them, a wedge of darkness shutting out the last of the light; a foaming spasm of air, water, mud, rock, and brutalized wood, pushing before it a wind of tornadolike intensity. Nora felt Smithback lose his grip briefly, then regain it. As he jammed her into the cavity, forcing himself in after her, there was a sudden fusillade of sound as countless small rocks scoured the walls of the canyon. She felt Smithback go rigid, heard the wet hollow thumps as the rocks glanced off his back.

Then the beast descended, wrapping them inside an endless, black, suffocating roar. The noise went on, and on, and on, the roar and vibration so loud that Nora felt she was losing her sanity. Rolled into a protective ball, she squeezed her arms tighter around herself and prayed for the shaking to stop. Jets of water forced their way into the cavity around her, battering her shoulders, pulling at her limbs as if trying to suck her out of the refuge.

In a remote corner of her mind, it seemed strange that it was taking so long to die. She tried to breathe, but the oxy-

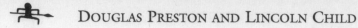

gen seemed to have been sucked out of the air. She felt the iron grip of Smithback's arms relax with a horrifying twitch. She tried to breathe again, hiccupped, choked, tried to scream—and then the world folded in on itself and she lost consciousness.

50

BLACK SAT ON THE RETAINING WALL, BREATHing heavily. The four expedition members remaining in camp had all taken several trips up into Quivira, lugging the unnecessary gear into the empty caching room they had chosen in a remote part of the city. There—with any luck—it would remain hidden, dry and free from animals until they returned.

Until they returned. . . . Black found himself sweating profusely. He licked his lips, staring at the blue sky above the canyon rim. Maybe nothing would happen. Maybe it would happen someplace else.

One at a time, Sloane, Swire, and Bonarotti emerged from the darkness of the city and joined Black at the retaining wall. Bonarotti removed a canteen and wordlessly passed it around. Automatically, Black took a drink, tasting nothing. His eyes roved over what remained of the camp: the tents, already broken down and ready to be carried out; the neat row of drysacks beside them; the small pile of equipment that still had to be lugged up to the cache site . . .

It was then that he heard something. Or perhaps he felt it, he wasn't exactly sure: a strange movement of the air, almost a vibration. His heart began to race, and he looked toward Sloane. She was staring out into the valley. Aware of his gaze, she glanced toward him for a moment, then rose to her feet.

"Did you hear something?" she asked nobody in particular. Handing the canteen back to Bonarotti, she moved toward the edge of the cliff, followed by Swire. A moment later, Black came up behind.

The valley below still looked pastoral: somnolent in the heat, drenched in late morning sunlight. But the vibration, like a deep motor coming to life, seemed to fill the air. The leaves of the cottonwoods began to dance.

Bonarotti came up beside him. "What is it?" he asked, looking around curiously.

Black didn't answer. Two emotions were warring inside him: terror and a breathless, almost nauseating excitement. There was now a rising wind coming from the mouth of the slot canyon: he could make out the saltbushes at its fringe gyrating as if possessed. Then the canyon emitted a long, distorted, booming screech that grew louder, then still louder. *It must be in the canyon now,* thought Black. There was a buzzing sound, but he wasn't sure if it was coming from the valley or inside his head.

He glanced at the company ranged beside him. They were all staring toward the mouth of the slot canyon. On Swire's face, puzzlement gave way first to dawning understanding, then horror.

"Flash flood," said the wrangler. "My God, they're in the canyon . . ." He broke for the ladder.

Black held his breath. He thought he knew what was coming; he felt that he was prepared for anything. And yet he was totally unprepared for the spectacle that followed.

With a basso profundo groan, the slot canyon belched forth a mass of boulders and splintered tree trunks—hundreds of them—which burst from the narrow crevice and came spinning down to earth. Then, with the swelling roar of a beast opening its maw, the slot vomited forth a liquid mass—chocolate-brown water, mingled with ropes of viscous red. It coalesced into a rippling wall that fell in thunder against the scree slope, sending up secondary spouts and smoking plumes. It tore down the floodplain, smoking along the banks, ripping away chunks of the slope and even peeling off pieces of the canyon wall in the extremity of its violence. For a moment Black thought, with horror, that it would actually surmount the steep banks on either side of the plain and take away their camp. But instead it worried, chewed, and ate away at the stone edges of the benchland, its fury contained but made all the more violent. Near the bank of cottonwoods, he could make out Swire, shielding his face with his arms, beaten back toward camp by the fury of the blast.

Black stood at the edge of the cliff, buffeted by the wind, motionless in shock and horror. Beside him, Bonarotti was yelling something, but Black did not hear it. He was staring at the water. He could never have imagined water capable of such fury. He watched as it swept down the center of the valley, tearing at the banks, engulfing entire trees, instantly turning the lovely, sun-dappled landscape into a watery vision of hell. A thousand rainbows sprung up from the spume, glistening in the appalling sunlight.

Then he saw a flash of yellow amid the churning chocolate: Holroyd's body bag. And then, moments later, something else, caught in a standing wave: a human torso, one arm still attached, wearing the shredded remnants of a tan shirt. As Black stared in mingled shock and disgust, the gruesome object erupted off the top of the wave and spun around once, the limp arm flapping in a travesty of a gesture of help. Then it bobbed over in a haze of chocolates and grays and was swallowed in the flood.

Almost unconsciously, he took a step backward, then another and another, until he felt his heel bump against the rock of the retaining wall. He half sat, half collapsed onto it, then turned his back to the valley, unwilling to see any more.

He wondered what it was he had done. Was he a murderer, after all? But no: not even a lie had been told. The weather report had been clear and unequivocal. The storm was twenty miles away; the water could have gone anywhere.

The roar of the flood continued behind him, but Black tried not to hear it. Instead, he raised his eyes to the cool depths of the city that lay spread before him: dark even in the bright morning sun, serene, utterly indifferent to the calamity that was taking place in the valley beyond. Looking at the city, he began to feel a little bit better. He breathed slowly, letting the tightness in his chest ease. His thoughts began trending once again toward the Sun Kiva and the treasure it contained—and especially of the immortality that it represented. Schliemann. Carter. Black.

He started guiltily, then glanced over toward Sloane. She was still standing at the edge of the cliff, staring down into the valley. Her look was veiled, but on her face he read a play of emotions that she could not hide completely: amazement, horror, and—in the glint of the eye and the faintest curl of the lip—triumph.

51

Ricky Briggs listened to the distant sound with irritation. That rhythmic swat meant only one thing: a helicopter, heading this way by the sound of it. He shook his head. Helicopters were supposed to keep out of the marina's airspace, although they rarely did. There were often choppers doing flybys of the lake, or en route to the Colorado River or the Grand Canyon. They annoyed the boaters. And when the boaters got annoyed, they complained to Ricky Briggs. He heaved a sigh and went back to his paperwork.

After a moment, he looked up again. The helicopter sounded different from usual: lower, throatier somehow. And the sound of the engine seemed strangely staggered, as if there were more than one. Over the drone, he could hear a diesel pulling up beside the building, the chatter of onlookers. Idly, he leaned forward to glance out the window. What he saw caused him to jump from his seat.

Two massive helicopters were beating up from the west, coming in low. They sported amphibious hulls, and Coast Guard logos were emblazoned on their sides. They slowed into a hover just beyond the marina's no-wake zone, huge airfoils beating the sky. A large pontoon boat dangled from one of them. Below, the water was being whipped into a frenzy of whitecaps. Houseboats were rolling heavily, and pink-skinned bathers were gathering curiously along the concrete apron.

Briggs grabbed his cellular and ran outside onto the shimmering tarmac, punching up the number for the Page air-control tower as he lumbered along.

Out in the baking heat, an additional surprise awaited him: a huge horse trailer parked at the ramp, same as before, SANTA FE ARCHAEOLOGICAL INSTITUTE stenciled on one side. As he watched, two National Guard trucks pulled in behind it. Ranks of guardsmen scrambled out of the rears, traffic barriers in hand. A murmur came up from the crowd as the pontoon boat was dropped from the helicopter with an enormous splash.

His phone chirruped, and a voice sounded through the tiny speaker. "Page," it said.

"This is Wahweap!" Briggs screamed into the telephone. "What the hell is going on at our marina?"

"Calm yourself, Mr. Briggs," came the unruffled voice of the air-traffic supervisor. "There's a big search-and-rescue being organized. Just learned about it a few minutes ago."

One group of guardsmen was laying down the traffic barriers, while another group had gone down to the ramp to clear a trail, shooing boats away from the marina. "What does that have to do with me?" Briggs shouted.

"It's in the back country, west of Kaiparowits."

"Jesus. What a place to be lost. Who is it?"

"Don't know. Nobody's saying anything."

Must be those dumb-ass archaeologists, Briggs thought. *Only a crazy person would go into that back country.* Another approaching engine added to the din, and he turned to see a semi backing a large, sleek-looking motorboat toward the water. Twin-diesel housings jutted from its stern like machine gun turrets.

"Why the helicopters?" Briggs complained into the phone. "There's such a maze of canyons back there you'd never find anything. Besides, you couldn't land anywhere even if you *did* find something."

"I understand they're just ferrying equipment to the far end of the lake. I told you, this is *big*."

The boat had been set in the water with remarkable speed, and with a roar the semi pulled away, leaving the ramp awash. The boat rumbled to life, turned, and nudged the dock, waiting just long enough for two men to board: one, a young man wearing a José Cuervo T-shirt, the other a thin, gray-haired man in khakis. A monstrous-looking brown dog leaped in behind them. Immediately, the boat took off, roaring through the no-wake zone at full speed, leaving a hundred jetskis bobbing madly in its wake. The huge helicopters dug their noses in the air and turned to follow.

Briggs watched with disbelief as the horse trailer came sliding down the ramp toward the waiting pontoon boat.

"This can't be happening," he murmured.

"Oh, it's happening," came the laconic reply. "I'm sure they'll be calling you, too. Gotta go."

Briggs punched at the phone furiously, but even as he did so it began to ring: a shrill, insistent chirp over the grinding of gears and the calls of the onlookers.

52

Black sank down beside the dead fire, exhausted and soaked through. The belated rain beat its regular cadence upon his shoulders; not as furiously as it had an hour before, but steadily, with large, fat drops. He paid it no heed.

Although the initial surge of the flood had abated, the water continued to roar down the center of the valley, its brown moiling surface like the muscled back of some monstrous beast. Distantly, he watched its wide course, around and over stranded trees, arrowing for the mouth of the smaller slot canyon at the far end of the valley. There, in the confined space, the violence of the water returned, and huge spumes of froth and spray leaped up toward the cloud-heavy sky.

For almost two hours they had hovered at the water's edge. Sloane had made a valiant rescue effort: roving the banks, spanning the flood with rescue ropes, scanning the water ceaselessly for survivors. Black had never seen such a heroic attempt. Or such a believable piece of acting, for that matter. He passed a hand over his eyes as he sat hunched forward. Perhaps it *wasn't* an act; right now, he was too tired to care.

Eventually, all except Sloane had gravitated away from the

water's edge to the camp. The remaining drysacks, scattered by the wind, had been organized; the tents repitched and restaked; the riot of twigs and branches cleared away. Nobody had spoken, but all had lent a hand. It was as if they had to do something, *anything*, constructive; anything was easier to endure than standing uselessly, staring at the rushing water.

Black sat back, took a deep breath, and looked around. Beside him, in neat rows, lay the gear that had been intended for the trip home: still packed and ready to be hauled out, a silent mockery of the portage out the slot canyon that had never happened. Nothing else remained to be done.

Bonarotti, taking his cue from Black, came over and silently began to unpack his kitchen gear. This, more than anything else, seemed to be a mute statement that hope had been lost. Pulling out a small ring burner and a propane shield, he put on a pot of espresso, protecting it from the rain with his body. Soon Swire came over, looking shocked and subdued. Sloane followed after a few minutes, walking silently up from the rushing waters. Bonarotti pressed a cup of coffee into each of their hands, and Black drank his gratefully, gulping it down, feeling the warmth of the coffee trickle into his aching limbs.

Sloane accepted her cup from Bonarotti, turning her amber eyes toward him. Then she looked at Swire, and then—more significantly—at Black, before returning her gaze to the cook. At last, she broke the silence.

"I think we have to accept the fact that nobody survived the flood." Her voice was low and a little unsteady. "There just wasn't time for them to make it through the slot canyon."

She paused. Black listened to the rush of the water, the patter of rain.

"So what do we do now?" Bonarotti asked.

Sloane sighed. "Our communications gear is destroyed, so we can't radio for assistance. Even if a rescue mission is mounted, it would take them at least a week to reach the outer valley, maybe more. And our only way out has been blocked by water. We'll have to wait until it goes down. If the rains continue, that could mean a long time."

Black glanced around at the others. Bonarotti was looking at Sloane, hands protectively cradling his mug of coffee. Swire was staring blankly, still dazed by what had happened.

"We've done everything we can," Sloane went on. "Fortunately, most of our gear survived the flood. That's the good news."

Her voice dropped. "The bad news—the terrible news—is that we've lost four teammates, including our expedition leader. And about that, there's nothing we can do. It's a tragedy I think none of us yet can fully comprehend."

She paused. "Our first duty is to mourn their loss. We will have time, in the days and weeks ahead, to remember them in our thoughts. But let's take a minute now to remember them in our prayers."

She lowered her head. A silence fell, broken only by the sound of water. Black swallowed. Despite the dampness around him, his throat was painfully dry.

After a few minutes, Sloane looked up again. "Our second duty is to remember who we are, and why we came here. We came here to discover a lost city, to survey it and document it. Luigi, a few minutes ago, you asked what we should do now. There's only one answer to that. As long as we're trapped in here, we must carry on."

She paused to take a sip of coffee. "We cannot allow ourselves to become demoralized, to sit around doing nothing, waiting for a rescue that may or may not come. We need to keep ourselves occupied in productive work." She spoke slowly and deliberately, taking time to look around at the small group with each new sentence. "And the most productive work of all is still to come: documenting the Sun Kiva."

At this, the faraway look left Swire's face. He glanced at Sloane in surprise.

"What happened today was a tragedy," Sloane continued, more quickly now. "But it's within our power to keep it from becoming something even worse: a tragic waste. The Sun

Kiva is the most miraculous find of a miraculous expedition. It's the most certain way to ensure that Nora, Peter, Enrique, and Bill are remembered not for their deaths but for their discoveries." She paused. "It's what Nora would have wanted done."

"Is that right?" Swire spoke up suddenly. The surprise and confusion had left his face, replaced with something uglier. "What Nora would have wanted, you say? Tell me, was this before or after she fired you from the expedition?"

Sloane turned to him. "Do you have an objection, Roscoe?" she asked. Her tone was mild, but her eyes glittered.

"I have a *question*," Swire replied. "A question about that weather report of yours."

Black felt his gut seize up in sudden fear. But Sloane simply returned the cowboy's gaze with a cool one of her own. "What about it?" she asked.

"That flash flood came down twenty minutes after you reported clear weather."

Sloane waited, staring at Swire, deliberately letting the uncomfortable tension build. "You of all people know how localized, how unpredictable, the weather is out here," she said at last, more coldly now.

Black could see the faltering certainty in Swire's face.

"There's no way of knowing just where the water came from," Sloane continued. "The storm could have come from anywhere."

Swire seemed to digest this for a moment. Then he said, in a lower tone: "You can see a whole lot of anywhere from the top of that canyon."

Sloane leaned toward him. "Are you calling me a liar, Roscoe?"

There was something so subtly menacing in her silky tone that Black saw Swire draw back. "I ain't calling you nothing. But last I heard, Nora said we wasn't to open up that kiva."

"Last *I* heard, you were the horse wrangler," Sloane said icily. "This is a decision that does not concern you."

Swire looked at her, his jaw working. Then he stood up abruptly, drawing away from the group.

"You say Nora will be remembered if we open this kiva," he spat out. "But that ain't true. It's *you* that'll be remembered. And you damn well know it."

And with that, he walked out of camp and disappeared among the cottonwoods.

53

BLACK PULLED HIMSELF UP THE LAST RUNG of the rope ladder with a grunt and stepped onto the rocky floor of Quivira, slinging the small bag of equipment beside him. Sloane had gone ahead, and was waiting at the city's retaining wall, but on impulse Black turned around once again to survey the valley. It was hard to believe that, barely four hours before, he had stood at this same spot and witnessed the flash flood. Now, afternoon light, fresh and innocent, glowed off the walls of the canyon. The air was cool, and perfumed with moisture from the rain. Birds were chirping. The camp had been cleaned up and supplies moved to high ground. The only signs of the catastrophe were the torrent of rushing water that divided the small valley like a brown scar, and the appalling wreckage of trees and earthen bank that lay along and within it.

He turned away and approached Sloane, who had arrayed her gear along the retaining wall and was giving it a final inspection. He noticed that she had snugged the camp's spare pistol into her belt.

"What's that for?" he asked, pointing at the weapon.

"Remember what happened to Holroyd?" Sloane replied, eyes on the gear. "Or the gutted horses? I don't want any nasty surprises while we're documenting that kiva."

Black paused a moment, thinking. "What about Swire?" he asked.

"What about him?"

Black looked at her. "He didn't seem too enthusiastic about all this."

Sloane shrugged. "He's a hired hand. He has nothing to say that anybody would want to hear. Once our find becomes known, it'll be front-page news across the country for a week, and in the Southwest for a month." She took his hand, gave it a squeeze, smiled. "He'll fall into line."

Bonarotti came into view at the top of the ladder, the over-sized .44 hanging from his side, digging tools slung over his shoulder. Sloane withdrew her hand and turned to retrieve her gear.

"Let's go," she said.

With Bonarotti beside him, Black followed Sloane across the central plaza toward the rear of the dead city. He could feel his heart beating fast in his chest.

"Do you really think there's gold in that kiva?" Bonarotti asked.

Black turned to see the cook looking over at him. For the first time that he could recall, Black saw animation, even strong emotion, in the man's face.

"Yes, I do," he replied. "I can't think of any other conclusion. All the evidence points to it."

"What will we do with it?"

"The gold?" Black asked. "The Institute will decide, of course."

Bonarotti fell silent, and for a moment, Black scrutinized the man's face. It occurred to him that he really had no idea what motivated a man like Bonarotti.

It also occurred to him that, in all his constant dreaming about the kiva, he had never once thought about what might happen to the gold after the kiva was opened. Perhaps it would be put on display at the Institute. Perhaps it would tour the museum circuit, as King Tut's treasure had. In point of fact, it didn't really matter; it was the find itself—the initial moment of discovery—that would make him a household name.

They made their way through the Crawlspace to the narrow passageway, then ducked into the inner sanctum. Sloane set up two portable lamps beside the kiva, aiming them at the rock-filled entrance. Then she stood back to prepare the camera while Black and Bonarotti laid out the tools. As if from a distance, Black noticed that his movements were slow, careful, almost reverent.

And then, in unison, the two men turned toward Sloane. She fixed the oversized camera to a tripod, then returned their glances.

"I don't need to emphasize the importance of what we're about to do," she said. "This kiva is the archaeological find of several lifetimes, and we're going to treat it as such. We'll proceed by the book, documenting every step. Luigi, you dig the sand and dust away from the doorway. Do it very carefully. Aaron, you can remove the rubble and stabilize the doorway. But first, let me take a couple of exposures."

She ducked behind the camera, and the dark cavern was illuminated by a quick series of flashes. Then she stepped away and nodded.

As Bonarotti picked up a shovel, Black turned his attention to the rock pile that covered the kiva's entrance. The rocks had been jammed into place without mortar, and were clearly without archaeological significance; he could remove them by hand, without having to resort to time-consuming excavation techniques. But they were heavy, and the muscles of his arms soon began to grow tired. Although the rock pile itself was curiously free of the dust that had settled so thickly over the rest of the kiva's surface, Black still found breathing difficult: Bonarotti's shoveling quickly raised a choking cloud around the kiva's entrance.

Sloane maintained a supervisory position well back from the kiva, taking an occasional photograph, jotting notes in a journal, recording measurements. Every now and then she would caution Bonarotti against growing too eager. Once she even barked at Black when a stray rock fell against the kiva wall. Almost imperceptibly, she had taken over the role of leader. As he worked, Black realized that perhaps he should be annoyed by this; he had more experience and seniority by far. But he was now too caught up in the excitement to care. *He* had been the one to first speculate on the kiva's existence. *He* had been the one to find it. And his many future publications on the gold of the Anasazi would make that abundantly clear. Besides, he and Sloane were a team now, and—

His thoughts were cut short by a racking cough. He stepped back from the doorway for a moment, wiping his face with his sleeve. The dust had risen to a miasmic thickness, and in the center of it all was Bonarotti, toiling with his shovel. Slanted columns of dust hung in the beams of artificial light. It was a scene worthy of Breughel. Black looked over at Sloane, perched some distance away on a rock, scribbling her observations. She looked up at him and flashed a brief, wry smile.

Taking a few more deep breaths, he waded back in. The upper tier of rocks had been removed, and he began to work on the course below them.

Suddenly he stopped. Behind the rocks, he could now make out a patch of reddish brown.

"Sloane!" he called. "Take a look."

In a moment, she was beside him. She waved away the dust and took several closeups with a handheld camera.

"There's a mud seal behind these rocks," she said. Eagerness elevated her contralto voice to an artificially high pitch. "Clear the rocks away, please. Be careful not to damage the seal in the process."

Now that Black had cleared the top of the doorway, the going was easier. Within minutes, the seal was fully exposed: a large square of clay stamped against what seemed to be a layer of plaster. A reversed spiral had been molded into the seal.

Once again, Sloane came forward to investigate.

"This is odd," she said. "This seal looks fresh. Take a look."

Black examined the seal more carefully. It was definitely fresh—*too fresh*, he thought, to be seven hundred years old. The mortared door, filled with rocks, had worried him from the start: the door just looked too invasive to be part of the original sealed structure. And it was odd that the omnipresent dust had not settled on the rocks massed in front of the door. For a moment, calamitous despair threatened to settle on his shoulders.

"It's impossible that anyone was here before us," Sloane murmured.

Then she looked at Black. "This sealed doorway has been extremely well protected. There are several feet of stones sheltering it from the elements. Right?"

"Right." Black felt the despair vanish instantly, the excitement returning. "That could explain why the seals look so fresh."

Sloane took some more photographs, then stepped back. "Let's keep going."

His breath coming in short, excited gasps, Black redoubled his efforts at clearing the wall of rocks.

54

FAR ABOVE THE FLOOD-RAVAGED CANYON OF Quivira, the domes and hollows of the wide slickrock plateau were warmed by the late afternoon sun. Gnarled juniper trees dotted the strange landscape, and Mormon tea bushes, wild buckwheat, and a sprinkling of purple verbena grew in sandy patches. Small, steep gullies intersected the landscape, winding through the red sandstone, the deeper potholes along their rock beds still shimmering with rainwater. Here and there, hoodoo rocks stood above the land, capped with a darker stratum of stone, like foul dwarfs crouching among the trees. To the east, another, smaller rainstorm was advancing. But here, a thousand feet above the Quiviran plateau, the sky was still pleasantly flecked with shredded bits of cloud, turning from white to yellow in the aging light.

In a hidden gully along the plateau, two pelted, masked figures moved in stealthy silence. Their progress was halting, furtive, as if they were unused or unwilling to move about in daylight. One stopped briefly, crouched, drank from a pothole. Then they moved on again, angling toward a patch of deep shade beside a fin of rock. Here, they stopped.

Reaching into the folds of his fur pelt, one of the skinwalkers removed a buckskin bag. Silver conchas clinked with the movement. The figure produced a human calvarium, filled with dry, shriveled pellets, like gray buttons. The second skinwalker produced another skull bowl and a long, shriveled root in roughly the shape of a twisted human being, laying it on the sand beside the first skull. Both began to chant in low, quavering tones. An obsidian knife flashed as the tips were cut off the dry root.

They worked swiftly and silently. A hand, decorated with white clay strips, caressed the wrinkled pellets. Then the skinwalker cupped one, two, and finally three of the pellets in his palm, pushing them through the mouthhole of his mask in rapid succession. There was a loud swallowing sound. The second figure repeated the action. The chanting grew faster.

A tiny twig fire was built, and wisps of smoke curled around the sheltering rock. The root was cut lengthwise into thin strips, smoked briefly in the fire, and set aside. Feathers were placed in the fire, slowly curling, crackling, and melting. Next, several live iridescent beetles were placed atop the embers, to jitter, die, and parch. They were removed, placed in the second skull bowl, crushed into flakes, and mixed with water from a leather bag.

The bowl was raised toward the north, the chanting even faster now, and the figures drank in turn. The strips of root were placed back on the fire, where they curled and turned black, sending up an ugly stream of yellow smoke. The figures bowed their heads over the fire, breathing heavily, rasping in the smoke. The chanting had now become a frenzied ditty, a low, fast quavering sound like the buzzing of cicadas.

The new storm advanced from the east, drawing a shadow across the landscape. Reaching once again into his matted pelt, the first skinwalker threw handfuls of creamy datura flowers into the fire. They quickly shriveled, releasing billows of smoke into the darkening air. The figures bent over the smoke, inhaling greedily. The air of the plateau was suddenly perfumed with the intensely beautiful scent of morning glories. The pelted backs began to quiver, and the silver conchas clinked violently.

A hand rose once again, sprinkling black pollen in the four

cardinal directions: north, south, east, and finally west. The skull bowl was now empty, all its shriveled contents ingested. One of the figures raised its head to the sky, a heavy stream of mucus running from beneath the buckskin mask, two palsied hands raised. The chanting, angry now, rose in volume and urgency.

And then, quite suddenly, silence fell. The last wisps of smoke drifted across the face of stone. And with terrible swiftness the figures were gone, racing like black shadows across the landscape, disappearing down the end of the Priest's Trail into the gloom of the valley of Quivira.

55

ROSCOE SWIRE SAT ATOP A BROKEN BOULDER, turning a worn headstall around in his hands, poetry notebook lying forgotten on the rock beside him. He was profoundly agitated. Not far away, near the edge of the rushing water, stood a large cottonwood, listing and swaying as the pressure of the passing water tore at its roots. Long, thin loops of flotsam dangled from several of the lower branches.

Swire knew those loops for what they were: the gray, ropy guts of a horse. One of his horses. And because of their well-developed herd attachment, he knew that if one were killed, all must have been killed.

The valley had grown dark, but the sky above was still painfully bright. The place seemed suspended between night and day, caught in that mysterious stasis that occurred only in the deepest canyons of Utah.

Swire glanced toward his notebook, toward the eulogy to Hurricane Deck he'd been trying, unsuccessfully, to write. He thought of Hurricane Deck: his three-day chase, the spirit of that magnificent horse. Arbuckles: dim, friendly, capable. He thought of all the horses he had lost on this trip, each one with its own personality, and of all the little things that had made up his life with them. The quirks, the peculiar habits, the trails they had ridden . . . it was almost more than he could bear.

And then his thoughts turned to Nora. More than once, she had made him very angry. But he had been forced to admire her bravery, the occasional recklessness of her determination. It was a terrible way to die. She would have heard her own death coming, would have known exactly what it meant.

He glanced around the valley, a vista of deepening purples, greens, and golds beneath a bright turquoise sky. It was a beautiful place. And yet it was malevolent in its beauty.

His eyes swivelled up in the direction of the hidden city. To think those three were up there now, opening the kiva as if nothing had happened. They would get the glory. And Nora would get a memorial plaque, nailed onto some wall at the Institute. He spat disgustedly, sighed, and turned to collect his notebook.

Then he stopped and looked around again at the darkened canyon. Except for the rumbling of water and the occasional birdsong, everything was quiet.

But instinct told him he was being watched.

Slowly, he reached over for the notebook. Turning a few pages, he sat back with an air of indifference, pretending to read the scribbled lines.

The feeling did not go away.

Swire's sixth sense had been honed over many hard years of wrangling horses in wild, sometimes hostile country. He had learned to trust his life with it.

His right hand dropped to the holster and rested easily there, confirming the presence of the gun. Then the hand rose again, this time to thoughtfully stroke his mustache. The roar of the water echoed and re-echoed off the canyon walls, magnified and distorted. The edge of another storm cloud was moving into the sky, staining the turquoise an ugly shade of gray.

He casually slipped the notebook into his pocket. Then, just as casually, he slipped the trigger thong out of its catch.

He waited. Nothing.

He rose to his feet, using an extended stretch as an excuse to take another look around. Again, nothing. Yet his instincts were rarely wrong. Perhaps it *was* his imagination. To say he'd had a tough afternoon would be putting it mildly.

Still, he felt a presence. More than that: he felt stalked.

Swire wondered what could be after him. There had been no wolves or mountain lions in the valley before, and none sure as hell had come in today. Perhaps it was human. But who? Nora and the others who had entered the slot canyon were dead. And the rest of them were busy with the kiva. Besides, none of them would want to—

With a flash, he realized who it must be. He was confused, in shock from the day's events, or he would have realized it before. They were the ones who had killed his horses. The bastards who had gutted his animals.

And now they were coming for him.

A surge of anger pushed away his rising apprehension. He couldn't roll back time; he couldn't save his horses, or prevent Nora from entering the canyon. But he could sure as hell do something about *this*.

The rock was not a good place to be. Lightly, he hopped off and strolled out into the open, glancing around, looking for a place from which to defend himself. On the surface the valley looked unchanged; but here, in the open, he could feel the presence more strongly.

His eyes moved toward a small grove of gambel oaks near the far end of the valley. Twelve hours before, the trees had been fifty feet from the water. Now, they were at its edge.

He nodded slowly to himself. From there, the water would be advantageously at his back. And the oaks would hide him from view. They wouldn't know where he was among the trees. But he would have a view out across the benchland. It would give him time for several clear shots.

He began strolling down toward the river, his shoulder blades crawling with the sense of hidden eyes. When he was halfway to the grove, he stopped, spat out his tobacco, and hiked up his pants, in the process loosening the gun in its holster. It was only a .22 magnum long barrel, but it had the advantage of high accuracy in repeated shots. A good gun for the kind of work he had in mind.

He paused in the gathering gloom. This would be his last chance for a good look at the valley before entering the trees, and he wanted to sense which direction his stalkers might come from. By daylight, there were few hiding places in the valley. But as night neared, the number grew: stands of cottonwoods and chamisa, areas in dark shadow. And yet, he saw no unusual movement, nothing out of place.

Once again, he questioned his instincts. They were still screaming: *Run, hide!* A few raindrops began to fall, splattering heavily in the sand. His heart beat faster as his apprehension grew. He was not a man to walk away from a fight. But it was hard, not knowing who you were fighting, or from where they would come, or if in the end they were just your imagination, after all. He tried to remind himself that these were the bastards that had killed his horses. But as his thoughts returned to the horses, he saw them again in his mind's eye: ritually sliced, feathers protruding from the glazed dead eyes, the grayish-blue guts wound in spirals. *What kind of monsters could do that . . .*

He started forward again, quickening his pace toward the copse. Once he almost turned around, heart beating fast, but he checked himself in time: he must not show that he knew they were there.

A few more steps brought him into the stand of the oaks. Moving quickly to the far side, he crouched, then swivelled around, putting his back to the water. It was dark beneath the hanging limbs, and water dripped onto his head and back. The sound of the flood seemed magnified in the close space: it bore down on him confusingly, coming in from all sides. He shook his head to clear it, taking a step backward as he did so. He was at the very edge of the flood now, and the water gurgled through the tree trunks, curling and tugging around his boots. He moved back yet again, slowly, his boots making a light plashing noise.

With a dull, hollow thud of fear, he realized it had been a mistake to retreat to this grove. Darkness was descending so swiftly on the canyon that he could make out little beyond the dense thicket of trees. He waited, shivering slightly, feeling the coldness of the water creep into his boots. His eyes widened as he tried to separate the shapes of the trees from each other, to distinguish them in the damp, dark gloom.

Now he slipped his gun out of the holster, waiting. He took another step back into the swirling water. It surged a little higher, and a distant, detached part of him noted that the flood was coming up again. His anger was no longer a comfort; now all he felt was cold, naked fear. It was too dark to see anything. If only he could hear, he might be able to act: but the sound of the water was like a heavy cloak, depriving him of his most valuable sense. All he had left, in fact, was smell. And even that wasn't working properly: by some trick of his overcharged brain, he felt surrounded by the beautiful, delicate scent of morning glories.

Just then, to his left, he saw a terrible movement of shadow: a violent wrenching of black upon black. Too late, he realized the things had been in the grove all the time, watching and waiting, while he came to *them*. He raised the gun with a cry, but the shot went wild and the weapon tumbled into the flood. As the muzzle flare died away, Swire saw—or thought he saw—the blade of a knife, impossibly black and cold, slicing down through the night.

56

I N THE DEPTHS OF THE HIDDEN CAVERN, Black carefully edged a penknife beneath the uppermost clay seal, his arms shaking with exhaustion and excitement. He turned one hand, trying to apply an even pressure to the seal, but his aching fingers twitched and the seal popped free, along with a piece of the plastered door.

"Easy," Sloane said from her position behind the large camera, some distance away.

Black craned his neck toward the small hole, but it was too small and uneven to make out anything within. From the valley outside the city, there was a faint, muffled crump of distant thunder.

Black coughed into his hand, then again, more violently, finding flecks of mud in the phlegm. He shook it away in disgust and returned to the stone facade. Bonarotti, who had now dug away the piles of sloping dust around the kiva door, joined him in the work.

In another half hour, a second seal came into view. Enough courses of stone had now been removed to expose over three feet of plastered door. Sloane came forward to take a series of photographs. Then she stepped back out of the pall of hanging dust, scribbling in her notebook. Black slid his knife beneath the second seal, pried it carefully away from the underlying plaster, and set it aside. All that now stood between him and the crowning validation of his theory was a thin, featureless wall of plaster and mortar. He reached down for a pick, hefted it in his bruised hands, then swung it toward the wall.

A piece of plaster fell away. Black swung the pick again, then again, enlarging the hole considerably: a dark, ragged rectangle in the glare of the lights. Excitedly, he dropped the pick.

Instantly, Sloane returned to his side. Taking a flashlight from her pocket, she thrust it deep into the hole, pressing her face against the plaster. Black saw her body tense. She remained still for a minute, perhaps more. Then she withdrew, silently, her face alive with excitement. Black grabbed the light from her unresisting hand and crowded forward.

The feeble yellow gleam of the small flashlight could barely penetrate the murk within. But as he played it about, Black felt his own heart swell. *Everywhere the glint of gold.* . . . The yellow glimmer filled the kiva, winking and flashing everywhere, on the floor, on the stone banco that ran around the perimeter: the rich mellow shine of a thousand curvilinear golden surfaces.

Violently, Black withdrew his hand. "Break it down!" he cried. "It's stuffed with gold!"

"By the book, Aaron," Sloane said sharply, but the exhilaration in her voice belied caution.

He seized the pick and resumed working along the top of the doorway. Grabbing a second pick, Bonarotti stood beside him, driving it furiously into the adobe in time with Black's own blows. Soon, the hole grew to more than two feet square. Black stopped to jam his entire head into the opening, wedging his shoulders hard, trying to force his body through, swinging Sloane's flashlight back and forth. But their picks had roused so much dust within the kiva that all he could see were faint golden glimmers.

The flashlight beam failed and he pulled himself back out, throwing it down in disgust. "More!" he gasped.

Outside the city, another muffled crump of thunder punctuated the obbligato whisper of rain. But Black heard nothing except the sound of his pick on plaster, and the ragged hiss of his breath in the close air. Reality faded into a dream. A strange sensation filled his head, and he realized he could no longer feel his arms as they wielded the pick.

The dreamlike sense grew stronger, almost frighteningly strong, and he staggered back from the kiva, trying to clear his head. As he did so, he felt an overwhelming tiredness. He glanced first at Bonarotti, who was still swinging his pick in a regular, metronomic cadence; then at Sloane, waiting behind, her body still tensed with expectation.

There was a sudden crumpling of plaster, and Black swivelled his head toward the kiva. A large chunk of adobe had come free, breaking into earth-colored chunks on the rocks below. And now Black saw that the hole was definitely large enough to admit a person.

He picked up one of Sloane's lanterns and moved forward. "Get out of my way," he said, peremptorily shoving Bonarotti aside.

The cook staggered back, dropped the pick, then turned to face Black, his eyes narrowing. But Black ignored him, desperately trying to angle the lantern beam into the dusty hole.

"Step aside," came Sloane's voice from behind him. "I said, step *aside,* both of you."

Bonarotti hesitated a moment. Then he took a pace back. Black followed, surprised by the sudden cold edge to Sloane's voice.

Sloane came forward, taking another series of shots. Then she looped the camera around her neck, turned to Black, and took the lantern from his hands.

"Help me in," she said.

Black placed his hands on her hips, pushing upward as she scrambled over the rocks and into the hole. He could see her light striping wildly across the kiva's ceiling. Then, suddenly, it receded to a mellow glow. He followed quickly, scrabbling up the rocks, wriggling through the rough hole and sliding down the inner side, face-first, sprawling in an ungainly muddle, spitting out mouthfuls of dust. A distant part of him thought that this was not exactly how Howard Carter would have gone about it.

Sloane had dropped the lantern, and it lay on its side in the dust. Trembling with excitement, Black rose to his feet, grabbed the curved metal of the lantern's handle, and hoisted it upward. His arm ached with the motion, and electric pains went through his lungs each time he drew in breath. But he barely noticed: this was the moment of ultimate discovery; the defining moment of his entire life.

Bonarotti had climbed in beside him, but Black paid him no mind. Everywhere, from all sides, the gleam of gold sprang out of the murk. Almost snorting with excitement, he bent forward and seized the closest object—a dish, filled with some kind of powder.

Instantly, he knew something was wrong. The dish in his hand was light, the material warm to the touch: not like gold, at all. Tossing the powder from the bowl, he brought it closer to his face.

Then he straightened up, flinging the object away with a sob.

"What the hell are you doing?" Sloane cried.

But Black did not hear her. He looked around the Sun Kiva with a sudden, wild desperation: grabbing things, dropping them again. It was all wrong. He staggered, fell, then rose with an effort. The bottomless disappointment, after such feverish hopes, was more than he could comprehend. Mechanically, he glanced at his companions. Bonarotti stood motionless beneath the ragged hole, a thunderstruck look on his dust-caked face.

Then Black slowly turned his eyes toward Sloane. In his pain and unutterable dismay, he could not quite comprehend that her face, instead of despair, reflected shining, complete vindication.

57

I̲T WAS IMPOSSIBLE TO KNOW HOW MUCH TIME had passed before—at long, long last—Nora felt a cool gush of air stir the damp hair on her forehead. Slowly, the memory of where she was and what had happened returned. Her head throbbed mercilessly as she gulped at the fresh air.

There was a dead weight pushing against her back. She struggled, and the weight moved slightly, allowing a dim light to filter into the cavity. The roar in the canyon had now abated to a deep-throated, thunderous vibration that rattled her gut. Or perhaps it was just her water-clogged ears that were muffling the sound.

Uncramping her legs and turning painfully around inside the cavity, she saw that the dead weight against her back was Smithback. Now he was lying on his side, motionless. His shirt lay across his chest in torn ribbons. The light was very dim inside the cavity, but as she peered more closely she noticed, with horror, that his back was as lacerated as if it had been brutally lashed. The leading surge of the flood had passed over them while they were jammed in the rock shelter; Smithback had shielded her—and taken the brunt of the water's force—with his own back.

Nora gently laid her head on his chest, placing a trembling hand on his face as she listened. The heartbeat was faint, but at least it was there. Hardly knowing what she was doing, she kissed his hands, his face. His eyelids struggled open, the eyes beneath glassy and dull. After a moment, the eyes focused. His mouth moved soundlessly, his face screwing up into a rictus of pain.

Over his shoulder, beyond the lip of their little crawlspace, she could see the flood about five feet below them, now a smooth sheet of water, surging, falling, and surging again. It had fallen since the first intense rush. And yet Nora was surprised to see that the water seemed to be rising again, not falling. Rivulets were trickling down the sides of the canyon and dripping outside the mouth of the cavity, and she realized that it must be raining hard again in the upper watershed. It was not just their little space that was dark: it was growing dark outside, as well. She must have been unconscious for hours.

"Can you sit up?" she asked. At the effort to speak, a pain stabbed through her temples.

Smithback struggled, wincing and breathing hard. The movement brought small streams of fresh blood trickling down across his stomach and onto his thighs. As Nora helped him into a sitting position, she got a better look at the damage that had been done to his back.

"You saved my life," said Nora, squeezing his hand.

"It's not saved yet," he gasped, shivering.

Carefully, she peered out from their shelter, scanning the rock face above for some hint of handholds. It was polished smooth; there was no way to climb farther up. She looked back down, thinking. They had to get out of the crawlspace, that was certain. They could not spend a night in there. If the temperature continued to drop, Smithback might become hypothermic. And if the water rose farther—or if another flood surge came through—they could not hope to survive. But there was no way out.

No way, except to launch themselves into the current and hope for the best.

The current just beneath their shelter was fast but smooth,

a laminar flow that moved straight down the polished walls of the narrow canyon. She watched pieces of debris flashing by, all trending toward the center. If they could make it out into the middle of the current, they might be able to ride it through the slot and into the valley without being battered against the canyon walls along the way.

Smithback watched her, the lines around his mouth tightening as he followed her train of thought.

She returned the look. "Can you swim?" she asked.

Smithback shrugged.

"I'm going to bind us together," she said.

"No," he protested. "I'll only drag you down."

"You saved my life. Now you're stuck with me." Carefully, she peeled off the tattered remnant of his shirt, ripped off the sleeves, and twisted them into a short tether. Leaving as much slack as possible, she tied one end to her left wrist, and the other end to Smithback's right.

"This is a crazy—" Smithback began.

"Save your breath for the ride. Now look, we're only going to get one chance at this. It's getting dark, we can't wait any longer. The most important thing is to stick as much to the middle as possible. That won't be easy, because the canyon is so narrow. So when you find yourself getting too close to one of the walls, lightly kick away from it. The most dangerous moment will be when the flood drops us into the valley. Once we're there, we'd better head for the shore damn quick. If we get swept through into the far canyon, we're done for."

Smithback nodded.

"Ready?"

Smithback nodded again, eyes narrow, lips white.

They waited for a surge to subside. Then Nora looked at Smithback, their eyes locking as she took tight hold of his hand. There was a moment's hesitation. And then, together, they slid out into the flood.

Nora's first impression was of the water itself: mind-numbingly cold. The second was of the current: it was shockingly strong, infinitely stronger than it had appeared from the rock cavity. As they tore along, she realized there was no chance of controlling their descent: all she could do was struggle to keep from colliding with the murderous walls, blurring past sometimes a foot, sometimes mere inches away. The surface of the water boiled and churned, full of tiny particles of wood and plant material dancing hysterically around them. Deeper, a chaos of gravel and sand churning in the turbulence battered her legs. Smithback struggled beside her, crying out once when the gnarled root of a tree collided with his shoulder.

A harrowing minute passed. And then Nora saw light ahead; a vertical notch of gray amid the rushing darkness. The canyon wall came dangerously close, and she pushed it away with a desperate kick. Suddenly they were soaring out of the canyon, riding a huge hump of water that sailed over the scree slope and collapsed into a boiling pool. There was an angry roar and Nora felt herself tumbled under the waves. Jerking on the improvised cord, she frantically propelled them upward, breaking the surface. Looking around and spitting water, she was horrified to see they had already traveled halfway through the valley. Only a few seconds' ride ahead of them lay the narrow crevice at the far end of the valley, the flood boiling and sucking into it with a furious confusion of sound. Then they were briefly caught in a swirl that propelled them into the slacker water near shore.

As she thrashed, Nora felt a blow to her midriff, followed by a painful scraping. She reached down into the water, grasping for a hold, while they swung about in the current. She realized it was the top of a stiff juniper bush. She clawed her way across its top, groping downward for a thicker branch, feeling the current tugging at them, trying to tear them away.

"We're hung up on a treetop," she said. Smithback nodded his understanding.

Steadying herself, Nora glanced toward shore. It was only fifty feet away, but it might as well have been fifty miles for all the ability they had to swim across the current.

She looked downstream. There was another treetop, this

one sticking out of the flood, lashed and shivered by the water. If they let go, they could grab that one. As long as the roots didn't give way under the tug of the water, there was a third tree, a little farther downstream—and from that they could reach the slacker water near shore.

"Ready?" she asked.

"Stop asking me that. I hate the water."

She launched into the current, grasped the next tree, then the next, dragging Smithback along, his head barely above water. Suddenly her feet touched bottom, wonderfully solid after the flood. Slowly, she pulled herself up on the muddy bank toward the copse of cottonwoods, Smithback staggering behind her. They sat down heavily amid a whirlwind of splintered branches, Smithback collapsing in pain. Nora undid the twisted rag that bound them, then rolled onto her back, sides heaving, coughing up water.

There was a ragged flash of lightning, followed by the sharp crackle of thunder. She looked up to see that a second, smaller storm had covered the canyon with a counterpane of darkness. Her thoughts turned to the weather report. Clear skies, it had said. How could the report have been so wrong?

The rain grew heavier. Nora turned her face away from it, looking up the ruined bank toward camp. There was something strange about the camp that she couldn't quite put her finger on. Then she understood: it had been carefully set up again, the struck tents repitched, the equipment carefully tarped against the rain.

Makes sense, I suppose, she thought. No one was going anywhere for a long time; at least, not out the slot canyon.

And yet the camp was deserted.

Had the rest of the expedition sought sanctuary in Quivira itself? But if so, why would they still be there, now that the worst of the flood had passed?

She sat up and looked at Smithback, who was lying on his stomach, water and blood trickling together into the sand. He was hurt. But at least he was alive. Not like Aragon. She had better get him to the warmth and safety of a tent.

"Can you walk?" she asked.

He swallowed hard and nodded. She helped him to his feet; he staggered a little, took a few steps, then staggered against her again.

"Just a little farther," she murmured.

She half dragged, half carried him to the high ground of the deserted camp. Hauling him into the medical tent, she rummaged through the supplies, picking out a painkiller, antibiotic ointment, and gauze bandages. Then she paused to poke her head out of the tent and look around. Once again, she was struck by how deserted the place was. Had they all been swept away? No, of course not: someone had to have repitched the tents. And Sloane and Swire, certainly, would have known right away what was up. They would have made sure everyone got to high ground in time.

She opened her mouth, preparing to call out. But then she shut it again. Some vague instinct she did not understand told her to remain silent.

She withdrew into the tent and looked at Smithback. "How are you doing?" she asked quietly.

"Bloody great," he said, wincing. "So to speak."

Looking down at the wet hair plastered over his forehead, Nora felt a sudden welling of affection. "Can you stand moving again?" she asked.

He looked at her. "Why?"

She shook her head. "Because I think we should get out of here."

She saw the question in his brown eyes.

"There's something strange going on," she continued. "And, whatever it is, I'd rather learn more about it from a distance." She handed him a couple of painkillers, passed him a canteen, then began dressing the horrible lacerations on his back. He stiffened, but did not complain.

"How come you're not protesting?" she asked.

"Don't know," came the slurred response. "Guess I'm numb from the water."

He was shivering now, his forehead clammy. *He's going*

into shock, she thought. The rain outside was increasing steadily, and the wind had picked up, buffeting the sides of the tent. She realized, with a dull finality, that there was no way she could move him, at least not now.

"Keep that sleeping bag bundled close," she said, stroking his cheek. "I'm going to see if I can't get some hot liquid into you." Gently tucking the sleeping bag around him, she moved toward the opening of the tent.

"Nora," came the voice from beneath the sleeping bag, slow and dreamlike.

She turned. "Yes?"

Smithback looked at her. "Nora," he said again. "You know, after all that's happened between us . . . well, I'd really like to tell you how I feel."

She stared at him. Then, gliding closer, she took his hand in hers. "Yes?"

His lips parted in a feeble grin. "I really feel like shit," came the dry whisper.

Nora shook her head, laughing despite herself. "You're incorrigible."

She bent closer and kissed him. Then she kissed him again, a gentle, lingering kiss.

"Please, sir, I want some more," Smithback murmured.

She smiled at him for a moment. Then, drawing back, she crawled out of the tent, securing its front flap. Hunching her shoulders against the rain, she moved across the camp, heading for the supply cache.

58

SLOANE GODDARD STOOD IN THE MURK OF the kiva, gazing on the rows of gleaming pots. For a long time, she saw nothing else. It was as if the outer world of time and space had retreated to a vast distance, leaving nothing but this small space behind. As she stared, she forgot everything— Holroyd's death, the flash flood, Nora and the others, the creeping presence of the horse killers.

Only a few small sherds of black-on-yellow micaceous pottery had ever been found. To see them whole was a revelation. They were transcendentally beautiful, by far the most exquisite pottery she had ever seen. Each piece had been perfectly shaped and formed, and polished with smooth stones to a sensuous luster. The clay they had been made from fired to an intense yellow, but the color had been immeasurably enhanced by the addition of crushed mica to the clay. The resulting pottery shimmered with an internal light, and as Sloane stared at them—at the heaps of bowls and jugs, hunchbacked figurines, skulls, pots, and effigies—she felt they were *more* beautiful than gold. They had a warmth, a vitality, the precious metal lacked. Each piece had been decorated with geometric and zoomorphic designs of superlative artistry and skill: the entire pictographical history of the Anasazi people, laid out before her.

It was all here, as she had been certain it would be: the mother lode of micaceous pottery. It had been her father's pet project: over the course of thirty years, he had mapped each rare sherd, traced hypothetical trade routes, searched for the source. Because the number of discovered fragments was so small, he had theorized that this pottery was the single most prized possession of the Anasazi people, and that it was stored in a central, most likely religious, place. Eventually, after mapping the distribution points of all known sherds, he had come to believe its location would be somewhere back in the labyrinthine canyons. Briefly, he had entertained dreams of finding the source himself. But he had grown old and sick. Then, when word of Nora and her father's letter reached him, hope had sprung anew. Instantly, he realized that Quivira, if it existed, might be the source of the fabulous pottery. It was speculative, of course—much too speculative for a man of his position to publish, or even broadcast. But it was enough to launch an expedition, with his daughter on the team.

Sloane knew she was supposed to have discussed the matter privately, with Nora, if they ever found the city. But, of course, there was no way she would have cued Nora into the great discovery that lay ahead. Nora already had more than her share of the glory. How many times, on the trail to Quivira, had the thought wormed its way bitterly into Sloane's heart: there she was, taking orders from a second-tier, untenured academic, when by rights *she* should be the one in command. In the end it would be Nora, and by extension Sloane's father, who would get all the credit: just another example of her father's thoughtlessness, his lack of faith in her.

Well, things would be different now. If Nora hadn't been so selfish, so stubbornly dictatorial, it wouldn't have had to end this way. But as fate would have it, the discovery would be hers. *She* was now the leader of the expedition. Hers would be the name forever linked with the discovery of the fabulous pottery. Everyone else—Black, Nora, her father especially— would be subordinate.

Slowly, she came back to the present. From the corner of her eye, she saw Bonarotti, cloaked in silent disappointment, shambling on stiff legs toward the hole he had helped cut. In another moment, he had climbed onto the banco and vanished out into the cavern.

Her eyes swivelled away, over the almost unbelievable abundance of pottery, to a large hole in the floor she had not noticed before. It seemed, inexplicably, to have been freshly dug. But that made no sense: who else but themselves could have been inside this kiva in the last seven hundred years? And who would single-mindedly dig out a few pounds of dust, while ignoring one of the richest troves in all North American history?

But her jubilation was too intense to ponder this for long. Excitedly, she turned toward Black: poor Aaron Black, who had let his own boyish lust for golden treasure blind the mature archaeologist within. She had not tried to correct him, of course: no need to dampen his enthusiasm, when his support had been so important. Besides, once the initial disappointment and embarrassment was past, he would surely realize how infinitely more important the real find was.

What she saw of Black, in the murk of the kiva, shocked her. *He looks terrible*, she thought. The man's flesh seemed to have shrunk on his frame. Two red, wet eyes stared hollowly out of a face caked in pale dust that was turning to mud on his sweating skin. In those eyes, she saw a brief, terrifying vision of Peter Holroyd, paralyzed with fear and illness, in the chamber near the royal burial.

Black's mouth had gone slack, and as he stepped toward her he seemed to stagger. He took another step, reached into a bowl, and took out a necklace of micaceous beads, shimmering golden in the torchlight.

"Pottery," he said woodenly.

"Yes, Aaron—*pottery*," Sloane replied. "Isn't it fabulous? The black-on-yellow micaceous that has eluded archaeologists for a hundred years."

He looked down at the necklace, blinking, unseeing.

Then, slowly, he lifted it, placing it around her neck with trembling hands.

"Gold," he croaked. "I wanted to give you gold."

It took Sloane a moment to comprehend. She watched him try to step forward, teetering in place.

"Aaron," she said urgently. "Don't you see? This is worth *more* than gold. Much more. These pots tell—"

She broke off abruptly. Black's face was screwed up, his hands pressed to his temples. Sloane took an involuntary step back. As she watched, his legs began to tremble and he sank against the inner kiva wall, sliding down until he was resting on the stone banco.

"Aaron, you're sick," she said, a sense of panic displacing her feelings of triumph. *This can't be happening,* she thought. *Not now.*

Black did not respond. He tried to steady himself with outstretched arms, scattering several pots in the process.

Sloane stepped forward with sudden resolution, grasping one of his hands. "Aaron, listen. I'm going down to the medical tent. I'll be back as soon as I can."

She climbed quickly up through the ragged hole and out of the kiva. Then, shaking the dust from her legs, she half walked, half ran, out of the cave, through the Crawlspace and into the silent city.

59

KNEELING BESIDE SMITHBACK, NORA stuffed a flashlight retrieved from the drysacks into her pocket and helped the journalist swallow a small cup of steaming bouillon. Just outside the tent, the portable propane stove ticked and sputtered as it cooled. Taking the empty cup from his hands, she helped him back onto the sleeping bag, stretched a woolen blanket over him, and made sure he was comfortable. She had replaced his soaked shirt and pants with dry ones, and his shock seemed to be passing. But with rain still drumming on the tent, moving him remained pointless. What he needed most, she felt, was some sleep. She glanced at the field wristwatch that had been strapped around the head tentpole. It was after nine o'clock. And yet, inexplicably, nobody had returned to camp.

Her mind turned back to the flash flood. The storm that produced it must have been enormous, awe-inspiring. It seemed inexplicable that anyone standing atop the plateau could have missed it . . .

She rose quickly. Smithback looked up at her with a weak smile.

"Thanks," he said.

"You get some sleep," she replied. "I'm going up to the ruin."

He nodded, but his eyes were already closing. Grasping the flashlight, she slipped out of the tent into the darkness. Switching it on, she followed the cylinder of light toward the base of the rope ladder. Her bruised body ached, and she was as tired as she ever remembered feeling. A part of her half anticipated, half dreaded, what she might find in the ruined city. But Smithback had been cared for, and leaving the valley was now impossible. As expedition leader, she had no choice but to enter Quivira, to learn for herself exactly what was going on.

The raindrops flashed through the yellow beam like fitful streaks of light. As she approached the rock face, she saw a dark figure climb down the ladder and leap lightly to the sand. The silhouette, the graceful movement, was unmistakable.

"Is that you, Roscoe?" Sloane's voice called out.

"No," Nora replied. "It's me."

The figure froze. Nora stepped forward and looked into Sloane's face, illuminated in the glare of the flashlight. She saw, not relief, but shock and confusion.

"You," breathed Sloane.

Nora heard consternation, even anger, in her tone. "Just what is going on?" she asked, trying to keep her voice under control.

"How did you—" Sloane began.

"I asked you a question. What's going on?" Instinctively, Nora took a step back. Then, for the first time, she noticed the necklace that lay around Sloane's neck: large beads, obviously prehistoric, glittering yellow—*micaceous* yellow—in the glow of the light.

As Nora stared at the necklace, what had begun as a smoldering fear burst suddenly into fierce conviction.

"You did it, didn't you," she whispered. "You broke into the kiva."

"I—" Sloane faltered.

"You deliberately entered that kiva," Nora said. "Do you

have any idea what the Institute will say? What your *father* will say?"

But Sloane remained silent. She seemed stunned, as if still unable to comprehend, or accept, Nora's presence. *She looks as if she's seen a ghost,* Nora thought.

And then, in an instant, she realized that was precisely it.

"You didn't expect to see me alive, did you?" she asked. Her voice was steady, but she could feel herself trembling from head to foot.

But still, Sloane stood rooted to the spot.

"The weather report," Nora said. "You gave me a false weather report."

At this, Sloane suddenly shook her head vigorously. "No—" she began.

"Twenty minutes after you came down from the rim, that flash flood hit," Nora broke in. "The entire Kaiparowits drains through this canyon. There was a gigantic thunder head over the plateau, there had to be. And you *saw* it."

"The weather report out of Page is a matter of public record. You can check it when we get back . . ."

But as she listened, an image came unbidden to Nora's mind: Aragon, the flood shredding him to pieces as it pulled him along the pitiless walls of the slot canyon.

She shook her head. "No," she said. "I don't think I'll do that. I think I'll check the satellite images instead. And I know what I'll find: a monstrous storm, centered directly over the Kaiparowits Plateau."

At this, Sloane's face went dead white. Beads of rain were collecting on her wide cheekbones. "Nora, listen. It's possible I never looked in that direction. You've *got* to believe me."

"Where's Black?" Nora asked suddenly.

Sloane stopped, surprised by the question. "Up in the city," she said.

"What do you think he'll say when I confront him? He was up on top of that ridge with you."

Sloane's eyebrows contracted. "He's not well, and—"

"And Aragon is dead," Nora interrupted, speaking in a barely controlled fury. "Sloane, you were going to break into that kiva, no matter what the cost. And that cost was *murder.*"

The ugly word hung in the heavy air.

"You're going to jail, Sloane," Nora said. "And you'll never work in this field again. I'm going to make sure of that personally."

As Nora stared at Sloane, she saw the shock, the confusion, in her eyes start to turn to something else.

"You can't do that, Nora," Sloane replied. "You can't." Her voice was suddenly low, urgent.

"Watch me."

There was a flash of jagged lightning, followed almost instantly by a great peal of thunder. In that instant, Nora glanced downward, shielding her eyes. As she did, she saw the dull glint of the gunmetal tucked into Sloane's belt. Looking up quickly again, she saw Sloane watching her. The woman seemed to straighten up, draw a sudden breath. Her jaw set. In a face full of lingering surprise, Nora thought she saw a resolution begin to form.

"No," she murmured.

Sloane looked back at her, unblinking.

"No," Nora repeated, more loudly, backing up into the darkness.

Slowly, tentatively, Sloane's hand dropped toward the gun.

In a sudden, desperate movement, Nora snapped off her light and wheeled away, sprinting into the close, concealing darkness.

The camp lay a hundred yards off—no protection there. Sloane stood between her and the city. And the flood had cut her off from the other side of the valley. In the direction she was headed, that left only one option.

Her mind worked furiously as she ran. Sloane, she realized, was not the kind of person who could bear to lose. If she had refused to even leave Quivira without opening the kiva, was it possible she would allow Nora to take her back to civilization—in shame and humiliation—to face life in ruin? *Why did I provoke her like that?* Nora raged at herself. *How could I have been so stupid?* She herself had demonstrated to Sloane exactly how stark her choice was. Nora, effectively, had signed her own death warrant.

She dashed as quickly as she dared along the rocky base of the cliff, making for the landslide at the far end. Fitful tongues of lightning guided her way. Scrambling up the talus of broken boulders, she searched for a hiding place, not daring to use her flashlight for fear of betraying her position. Halfway up the slope she found a suitable hole: narrow, but still large enough to fit a human body. She wedged herself as far inside as she could and crouched in the darkness, gasping for breath, trying to sort things out, raging with frustration and despair.

She glanced around her hiding place. She had managed to crawl fairly deeply into the landslide. Still, it was only a temporary option: it would only be a matter of time before Sloane searched her out. And Sloane had the spare gun.

Her thoughts returned to Smithback, lying asleep in the medical tent, and her hands clenched in anger. He was a sitting duck. But no: there was no reason for Sloane to enter the tent and find him. Even if she did, there was a chance she would not kill him. Nora had to cling to that hope—at least, until she found some way to stop Sloane.

There *had* to be a way. Bonarotti and Swire were out there, somewhere. Unless they were part of the conspiracy, too . . . she shook her head, refusing to let herself follow that line of speculation.

Perhaps she could find a way to sneak back into the camp, steal away with Smithback. But that would mean hours of cautious waiting, and one way or another Sloane would certainly act before then. Nora knew she couldn't climb up to the rim and escape—not with Smithback behind, injured, in the valley. As she crouched in the darkness and turned over her options, it dawned on her, with a desperate kind of finality, that in fact there were no options at all.

60

BEIYOODZIN MADE HIS WAY ACROSS THE slickrock plateau, far above the valley of Quivira. The heart of a second, smaller storm was passing overhead now, and it was very dark. Beneath his feet, the irregular rock was slick with rainwater, and Beiyoodzin walked with great care. His old feet ached, and he missed the presence of his horse, tethered back in the valley of Chilbah. The Priest's Trail was impassable for all but the two-legged.

The trail markings were irregular and vague—a small, ancient cairn of rocks here and there—and the way was difficult to make out in the darkness. Beiyoodzin needed all his skill simply to follow it. His eyes were not as strong as they had once been. And he was all too aware that the single most difficult stretch lay ahead: in the tortuous, dangerous descent along the ridge of the narrow slot canyon at the far end of the valley.

He wrapped the sopping cloak tighter and moved on. Though his grandfather had hinted of it, Beiyoodzin had never believed that the Priest's Trail could be so demanding, or so long. After arrowing up the secret cut in Chilbah Valley, it followed a long, complex route across the high plateau, wriggling for miles through the stunted junipers, in and out of dry washes and steep little ravines. He urged his tired body to move faster. It was late, he knew; perhaps too late. There was no telling what might have happened, or what might be happening, in the valley of Quivira.

Suddenly, he stopped short. There was a smell in the air: a lingering smell of woodsmoke, damp ash, and something else that brought his heart into his mouth. He looked around, eyes wide to the darkness, letting the occasional tongues of lightning guide his way. There it was—in the shadow of a large rock, as he knew it would be—the remains of a small twig fire.

He looked around quickly, carefully, making sure he was alone; making sure the creatures who had made this fire were long gone. Then he crouched, sifting the ash with his fingers. He pulled the remains of root strips, burned and brittle, from the small pile, rubbing them appraisingly between his fingers. Then, brow furrowing, he began to sift more quickly, fingertips impatiently brushing the ash aside. One hand closed on something, and he drew in his breath sharply: the petal of a flower, limp and withered. He brought it to his nose. The scent confirmed his worst fears: beneath the heavy smell of woodsmoke, he could still make out the lingering odor of morning glories.

He stood up, brushing his fingers on his wet trousers in agitation. Once, as a child in the village of Nankoweap, he had seen a terrible thing: a very old man, a bad man, partake of the forbidden datura flower. The man had flown into a rage under the influence of the drug, lashing out violently at all in his path with several times his normal strength. It had taken half a dozen young men of the village to subdue him.

But this was worse. Much worse. Those he was tracking had taken datura in the ancient way, the evil way, mixing it with psilocybin mushrooms, buttons of the mescal cactus, forbidden insects. The unholy spirit would take possession of them, bring great strength to their limbs and a murderous frenzy to their minds; make them oblivious to their own pain, or the pain of others.

Kneeling, he said a brief, fervent prayer in the darkness. Then he rose again and continued down the trail with redoubled speed.

61

BONAROTTI SAT LISTLESSLY ON THE SMOOTH rocky ground of the Planetarium, his back against the unyielding wall, elbows resting on upraised knees. He stared out into the darkness, beyond the curving shelf that hid the great city. The valley was dark, lit infrequently by livid forks of lightning. A thin curtain of water fell across the entire length of the overhanging lip of rock, cloaking the entrance to Quivira. There was no longer any reason to leave the comfort of the dry city. In fact, there was no reason to do anything, except wait out the next several days with as much comfort and as little inconvenience as possible.

He knew that he should feel vastly more disappointment than he did. Initially—during the first minutes of his realization that the secret kiva held, not gold, but merely countless ancient pots—the feeling of dismay and shock had, in fact, been overwhelming. And yet now, here on the outskirts of the city, all he felt was a vast ache in his bones. The gold would not have been his, anyway. He wondered why he had worked so hard, gotten so uncharacteristically caught up in the excitement of the moment. Now his only reward were limbs that felt unnaturally heavy. The butt of the big revolver dug into his right side. Minutes before, he thought he had heard the quick patter of feet running across the central plaza, followed by an angry buzz of conversation in the valley below. But he had not been certain, over the annoyingly steady burble of rain. His ears felt clogged and painful; perhaps he had imagined the sounds. And he felt little interest in exploring further.

With great effort, he dug into his breast pocket for a cigarette, then sounded his trousers for a match. He knew that smoking was forbidden in the ruin, but at the moment he could not have cared less; besides, he somehow felt that Sloane would be more tolerant of such things than Nora Kelly had been. Smoking was about the only comfort he had left in this godforsaken place. That, and the secret cache of grappa he had secreted deep among his cookware.

But the cigarette proved no comfort. It tasted terrible, in fact: like cardboard and old socks. He took it out and peered at it closely, using the fiery tip for illumination. Then he inserted it once again between his lips. Each fresh inhalation of smoke brought stabbing pains to his lungs. With a cough, he pinched it out with his fingers and dropped it into his pocket.

Something told Bonarotti that the fault did not lie with the cigarette. He thought briefly about Holroyd, and how he had looked, in those agonizing minutes before he died. The thought sent a galvanic twitch to his limbs, and he rose instinctively to his feet. But the sudden motion drained the blood from his head; his body grew hot, and a strange low roaring sounded in his ears. He put an arm to the cliff face to steady himself.

He took one deep breath, then another. Then he tried putting one foot in front of the other, gingerly. The world seemed to reel around him, and he steadied himself against the wall again. He had only been seated for fifteen minutes; maybe half an hour, at most. What could be happening to him? He licked his lips, staring out into the center of the city. There was a painful pressure in his head, and the hinges of his jaws throbbed with a mounting ache. The rain seemed to be easing up, and yet its steady, monotonous drone was becoming increasingly irritating to his ears. He began moving toward the central plaza, lurchingly, without purpose. Lifting his feet seemed an act of supreme difficulty.

In the darkened plaza, he stopped. Despite its openness, he felt the three-story roomblocks crowding in on all sides, their blank windows like skeletal eyes, staring stonily at him.

"I feel sick," he said matter-of-factly, to nobody in particular.

The sound of the drumming rain was torture. Now, his only wish was to escape it: to find someplace dark and still, where he could curl up, and cover his ears with his hands. He turned slowly, mechanically, waiting for another slash of lightning to reveal the city. A blaze of yellow briefly illuminated the doorway of the nearest series of roomblocks, and he shambled toward it to the accompanying sound of thunder.

He paused in the entryway, a brief sense of alarm piercing the haze of sickness and discomfort. He felt that, if he did not lie down immediately, he would collapse to the floor. And yet the blackness of the room before him was so complete, so intense, that it seemed to be *crawling*, somehow, before his vision. It was a repellent, almost nauseating phenomenon Bonarotti had never seen or imagined. Or perhaps it was the sudden smell that nauseated him: the ripe, sickly sweet scent of flowers. He swayed where he stood, hesitating.

Then a fresh wave of lightheadedness overwhelmed him, and he plodded forward, disappearing into the gloom of the doorway.

62

SQUINTING AGAINST THE LIVID FORKS OF lightning, Sloane watched Nora vanish into the storm. She had to be heading for the rockslide: there was no place else to hide in the direction she was headed. As she stared after Nora, Sloane could feel the cold unyielding weight of the gun butt, pressing against her palm. But she did not draw the weapon, and she made no move to pursue.

She stood, hesitating. The initial shock of seeing Nora come walking up, *alive,* out of the gloom was wearing off, leaving turmoil in its place. Nora had called her a murderer. A *murderer.* Somehow, in her mind, Sloane could not think of herself as that. Playing back the accusation, remembering the look on Nora's face, Sloane felt a deep anger begin to smolder. Nora had asked for the weather report, and she had given it, word for word. If Nora hadn't been so headstrong, so stubborn, so insistent on leaving . . .

Sloane took a deep breath, trying to calm herself. She had to think things through, act with care and deliberation. She knew Nora was not an immediate physical threat: Sloane herself had the spare gun. On the other hand, Nora might stumble across Swire, or Bonarotti, out there in the night.

She drew the back of her hand across her forehead, scattering raindrops. Where were Swire and Bonarotti, anyway?

They weren't in the city, and they weren't in the camp. Surely, they wouldn't be standing around somewhere, in the darkness and pouring rain. Not even Swire was that mule-headed. It made no sense.

Her mind wandered back to the magnificent discovery they had just made. A discovery even more astonishing than Quivira itself. A discovery that Nora had tried to prevent. At this thought, Sloane's anger increased. Things had been going better than she could ever have hoped. Everything that she had ever wanted was up in that kiva, waiting for her to claim its discovery as her own. All the hard work was done. Bonarotti, even Swire, could be brought around. Sloane realized, almost with surprise, that things had gone too far to turn back: particularly with Aragon and Smithback dead. The only thing that stood in her way was Nora Kelly.

There was a faint cough in the darkness. Sloane pivoted, instinctively yanking the pistol from her belt. It had come from the direction of the medical tent.

She moved toward the tent, pulling her flashlight from a pocket and cupping its end to shield the glow. Then she stopped at the entrance, hesitating. It had to be Swire, or perhaps Bonarotti: there was nobody else left. Had they overheard Nora? Something close to panic washed over her, and she ducked inside, gun drawn.

To her immense surprise, there lay Smithback, sleeping. For a moment, she simply stared. Then understanding flooded through her. Nora had only mentioned Aragon's death. Somehow, both she and Smithback had survived.

Sloane slid to her knees, letting the flashlight fall away, resting her back against the sopping wall of the tent. It wasn't fair. Things had been working out so perfectly. Perhaps she could have found a way to deal with Nora. But now Smithback, too . . .

The writer's eyes were fluttering open. "Oh," he said, raising his head with a wince. "Hi. And ouch."

But Sloane was not looking at him.

"I thought I heard shouting just now," Smithback said. "Or was I just dreaming?"

Sloane waved him silent with her gun hand.

Smithback looked at her, blinking. Then his eyes widened. "What's with the gun?"

"Will you shut up?" Sloane snapped. "I'm trying to think."

"Where's Nora?" asked Smithback, suspicion suddenly clouding his face.

At last, Sloane looked back at him. And as she did so, a plan began to take shape in her mind.

"I think she's hiding in the rockfall at the end of the canyon," she replied after a moment.

Smithback tried to ease himself up on one elbow, then slumped. "Hiding? Why? What happened?"

Sloane took a deep breath. *Yes*, she thought quickly: *it's the only way.*

"Why is Nora hiding?" Smithback asked again, more sharply, concern crowding his voice.

Sloane looked at him. She had to be strong now.

"Because I'm going to kill her," she replied as calmly as she could.

Smithback gasped painfully as he again tried to rise. "I'm not following you," he said, sinking back again. "Guess I'm still delirious. I thought you said that you were going to kill Nora."

"I did."

Smithback closed his eyes and groaned.

"Nora's left me no choice." As she spoke, Sloane tried to detach herself from the situation, to rid herself of emotion. Everything, her whole life, depended on pulling this off.

Smithback looked at her. "Is this some kind of sick joke?"

"It's no joke. I'm just going to wait here for her to return." Sloane shook her head. "I'm truly sorry, Bill. But you're the bait. She'd never leave the valley without you."

Smithback made a mighty effort to rise, then collapsed again, grimacing. Sloane checked the cylinder, then closed the gun and snapped the cylinder lock back in place. The

weapon had no safety, and she cocked the hammer as a precaution.

"Why?" Smithback asked.

"Incisive question there, Bill," Sloane said sarcastically,
anger returning despite her best efforts. "You must be a journalist."

Smithback stared at her. "You're not sane."

"That kind of talk just makes what I have to do easier."

The writer licked his lips. "Why?" he asked again.

Suddenly, Sloane rounded on him. "Why?" she asked, the
anger rising. "Because of your precious Nora, that's why.
Nora, who every day reminds me more and more of my own,
dear father. Nora, who wants to control everything down to
the last iota, and keep all the glory for herself. Nora, who
wanted to just *walk away* from the Sun Kiva. Which, by the
way, contains an incredibly important find, a treasure that
none of you had the faintest conception of."

"So you did find gold," Smithback murmured.

"Gold!" she snorted derisively. "I'm talking about pottery."

"Pottery?"

"I see you're no smarter than the rest," she replied, picking up the disbelief in Smithback's voice. "Listen. Fifteen
years ago, the Metropolitan Museum paid a million dollars
for the Euphronios Krater. That's just one beat-up old Gre-
cian wine jug. Last month, a little broken bowl from the
Mimbres valley sold at Sotheby's for almost a hundred grand.
The pots in the Sun Kiva are not only infinitely more beautiful, they're the only intact examples of their kind. But that
doesn't matter to Nora. She told me that, when we get back
to civilization, she's going to accuse me of murder, see that
I'm ruined."

She shook her head bitterly. "So tell me, Bill. You're a
shrewd judge of humanity. I have a choice to make now. I can
return to Santa Fe as the discoverer of the greatest archaeological find of the century. Or I can return to face disgrace,

and maybe even a lifetime behind bars. What am I supposed to do?"

Smithback remained silent.

"Exactly," Sloane replied. "It's not much of a choice, is it? When Nora returns for you, she's dead."

Smithback suddenly rose on one arm. "Nora!" he croaked, as loudly as he could. "Stay away! Sloane is waiting here for you with a—"

With a quick movement, Sloane whipped the gun across the side of his head. The writer flopped sideways, groaned, then lay still.

Sloane stared down at him for a moment. Then she glanced around the medical tent. Finding a small battery lamp among the equipment, she snapped it on and placed it in the far corner. Picking up her flashlight and switching it off, she quietly unzipped the tent and slipped outside into the dark.

The tent was pitched near a low, thick clump of chamisa. Slowly, quietly, Sloane crawled into the chamisa, then turned around and lay on her stomach, facing the tent. The lamp within it gave out a subdued glow, cozy and inviting. She was completely concealed within the dark vegetation, and yet she had an unobstructed view of the tent. Anyone approaching it would automatically be silhouetted by the dim light. When Nora returned for Smithback—as Sloane knew she would— her silhouette would make a perfect target.

Her thoughts drifted briefly to Black, sick and alone, waiting for her back at the kiva. She tried to ready herself for what was to come. Once this business was done, she could quickly drag Nora down to the river. In seconds, the current would sweep her into the narrow meat-grinder of a canyon at the far end of the valley. And when Nora's body reached the Colorado River—eventually—there wouldn't be enough left for a postmortem. It would be the same as if Nora had been washed out by the flash flood in the first place—as, by all rights, she should have been. No one would know. And then, of course, she'd have to do the same to Smithback. Sloane closed her eyes a moment, unwilling to think about that. But there was no longer any choice: she had to finish what the flood had failed to do.

Resting both elbows on the ground, Sloane eased the pistol forward, balancing it with both hands. Then she settled down to wait.

63

AARON BLACK LAY IN THE KIVA, CONFUSED and horribly frightened. The fitful glow of the dying lamp still faintly illuminated the close, dusty space. But Black's eyes were shut fast against the darkness, against the overwhelming evidence of his failure. It seemed that hours had passed since Sloane had left, but perhaps it was only minutes: it was impossible for him to tell.

He forced his gluey eyes open. Something terrible was happening; perhaps it had been coming on for a while, and now that the fevered digging had given way to crushing disappointment, it was upon him at last. Perhaps the air was bad. He needed to get out, breathe some fresh air. He mustered the energy to rise, staggered, and with astonishment felt his legs buckle.

He fell back, arms flailing weakly. A pot rolled crazily around him and came to rest against his thigh, leaving a snake's trail in the dusty floor. He must have tripped. He tried to rise and saw one leg jerk sideways in a spastic motion, muscles refusing to obey. The lantern, canted sideways, threw out a pale corona, suffused by dust.

From time to time, growing up, Black had been tortured by a recurring nightmare: he found himself paralyzed, unable to move. Now, he felt that he was living that nightmare. His limbs seemed to have grown frozen, unwilling or unable to respond to his commands.

"I can't move!" he cried. And then, with a sudden terror, he realized he hadn't been able to articulate the words. Air had come out of his mouth, yes—an ugly splutter, and he felt saliva dribbling down his chin—but no words came. He tried again and heard once more the ugly choking rush of air, felt the refusal of his tongue and lips to form words. The terror increased. In a spasm of panic, he struggled unsuccessfully to rise. Weird shapes and writhing figures began crowding the darkness beyond his eyes; he turned to look away, but his neck refused to move. Closing his eyes now only caused the shapes to spring to greater definition.

"Sloane!" he tried to call, staring up into the cloudy dimness, afraid even to blink. But not even the splutter of air came now. And then the lantern flickered again, and went black.

He tried to scream, but nothing happened. Sloane was supposed to be bringing medicine. Where was she? In the close darkness, the hallucinations were all around him, babbling, whispering: twisted creatures; grinning skulls, teeth inlaid with bloody carnelians; the clinking of skeletons moving restlessly around the kiva; the flickering of fires and the smell of roasting human meat; the screams; the victims gargling their own blood.

It was too terrible. He could not close his eyes, and they burned with an internal pressure. His mouth was locked open in a scream that never came. At least he still recognized the shapes around him as hallucinations. That meant he wasn't too far gone to tell reality from unreality . . . but how unspeakably dreadful it was to not feel anything; not to know any longer where his limbs were lying, whether or not he had fouled himself; to lose some profound internal sense of where his body was. The panic of paralysis, that dream-fear out of his worst nightmares, washed over him yet again.

He couldn't understand what had gone wrong. Was Nora

really dead? Was he himself also dying, in the horrible darkness of this kiva? *Had* Sloane and Bonarotti really been inside the kiva with him? Perhaps they were going to Aragon for help. But no—Aragon was dead, like Nora.

Aragon, Smithback, Nora . . . and he had been as guilty of their deaths as if he had pulled the trigger. He hadn't spoken up, down there in the valley. He'd let his own desire for immortal fame, for that ultimate discovery, get the better of him. He groaned inwardly: clearly, nobody would come to help, after all. He was alone in the darkness.

Then he saw another light, very faint, almost indivisible from the darkness. It was accompanied by a rustling sound. His heart surged with fresh hope. Sloane was returning at last.

The light grew stronger. And then he saw it, through the film of his sickness: fire, strangely disembodied, moving through the darkness of the kiva, dropping sparks as it went. And carrying this burning brand was a hideous apparition: a single figure, half-man, half-animal.

Black fell into renewed despair. Not a rescue. Just another hallucination. He wept inwardly; he wailed in his mind; but his eyes remained dry, his body flexed and immobile.

Now the apparition was coming toward him. He smelled juniper smoke, mixed with the ripe, sweet scent of morning glories; he saw in the flickering light the glittering black of an obsidian blade.

Distantly, he wondered where such an image, where such an unexpected scent, could have come from. Some grotesque recess of his mind, no doubt; some dreadful ceremony that perhaps he'd read about in graduate school, long forgotten and now, in the extremity of his delirium, resurrected to haunt him.

The figure bent closer, and he saw its blood-stiffened buckskin mask, eyes fiery behind the ragged slits. Surprisingly real. The coldness of the blade on his throat was astonishingly real, as well. Only a person who was as gravely ill as he was, he knew, could hallucinate something so . . .

And then he felt the unyielding knife blade trace a hard cold line across his neck; felt the abrupt wheeze of his own air, the gush of hot blood filling his windpipe; and he realized, with transcendent astonishment, that it was not a hallucination, after all.

64

SLOANE WAITED, EVERY MUSCLE TENSED, LIS-
tening with rapt concentration. There was a break in the
storm, and the rain had slowed to an occasional patter. Cupping her watch to shield the glow, she briefly illuminated it:
almost ten thirty. The sky had broken into patches of light
and as tattered clouds swept past a gibbous moon. Still, it was
mostly dark—dark enough for a person to think she could
creep into camp unobserved.

She shifted, rubbing her elbows. Once again, she found
herself wondering what had happened to Swire and
Bonarotti. No one had appeared at the mouth of the city.
And they obviously weren't in camp. Perhaps they'd never
left Quivira in the first place, and were even now back in the
kiva, watching over Black. In any case, it was best they were
not around. Nora couldn't hide forever. Soon, she would be
coming for Smithback.

Sloane returned her gaze to the tent and its thin, small
glow, like a canvas lampshade in the center of the dark landscape. The camp remained still. Concentrating on dismissing
all irrelevant noise, she waited, ready to distinguish the sound
of Nora's approach from the distant rush of the swollen
creek. Ten minutes went by, then fifteen. The moon fell once
more behind ragged clouds. The rain came on again, accom-

panied by distant thunder. It was more difficult than she could have imagined, waiting here like this, gun in hand. She felt an undercurrent of rage: partly at Nora, but partly at her father. If he had trusted her, put her in charge of the expedition, none of this would have happened. She suppressed the sweep of dread that came over her as she contemplated what *was* about to happen—what she was being forced to do.

She forced her thoughts back toward the limitless wonders that awaited in the secret city. She reminded herself once again there was no other way. Even if she managed to beat Nora's accusations somehow, it would ruin her forever. And in his heart, her father would know . . .

It came at last: the crackle of a twig. The soft chuff of a foot, placed carefully in wet sand. And then another; at least, she thought she heard another, against the distant call of the river and the soft patter of rain.

Someone was sneaking up to the tent; someone exercising exceptional care.

Sloane hesitated momentarily; she didn't know Nora had such capacity for stealth. But nobody else, she knew, would be approaching the tent so cautiously.

She took a breath, opening her mouth as if to speak. For a moment, she considered calling out to Nora: to give her one more chance, to forget Aragon, the weather report, everything. But then she remembered the look on Nora's face— the word *murderer*, uttered between clenched teeth—and she remained silent.

With a slight pressure of her thumbs and middle fingers, she raised the muzzle of the .38, relaxing her hands to absorb the recoil. She was a decent shot; at this range, there was no chance of missing. It would be quick, and probably painless. Within two minutes, both Nora and Smithback would be in the river, moving inexorably toward the narrow slot at its far end. If there was ever any question, she could always tell the others she had been shooting at a snake.

She waited, barrel leveled steadily. The steps were so quiet, and spaced so far apart, Sloane could not tell if they were approaching or receding. And then at last a shadow interposed itself between her and the tent.

Sloane breathed out slowly through her nostrils. The shadow was too tall to be bandy-legged Swire, and too short to be Aaron or Bonarotti. It could only be Nora. The shadow deepened slightly as it glided around the side of the tent, hovering outside the door.

Carefully, Sloane aimed the gun, centering on the shadow. This was it, then. She suspended her breathing, timed the shot to the interval between heartbeats, and squeezed the trigger.

The short-barreled weapon jerked back violently in her hands as the shot reverberated down the canyon. There was a gasp; the sound of spasmodic kicking; a brief, retreating scrabble. When her eyes cleared, the silhouette had disappeared from the dim light of the tent and all was silent.

She crept out of the chamisa and rose to her feet. It was done. She realized she was shaking violently but made no attempt to control it. Snapping on her light, keeping the gun drawn, she came forward. She hesitated at the side of the tent, momentarily unwilling to see the destruction her gun had wrought. Then, with a deep breath, she stepped forward.

Instead of Nora's body lying before the tent, broken and bleeding, there was nothing.

Sloane's hands went slack in consternation, and she fought to maintain her grip on the gun. She looked down at the sand before her, horrified. How could she possibly have missed? It was practically a point-blank shot. Could the gun have misfired? She swivelled her light around, looking for something, anything, that could explain.

And then, in the sand at the far edge of the tent, the cone of light caught something. It was a thick gout of blood. And, beside it, a partial bloody footprint in the damp earth.

Sloane peered more closely. The print did not belong to Nora—or, it seemed, to any other human being. It looked, in fact, like a clawed forepaw.

She drew back and glanced around, swinging her flashlight

as she did so. There, caught in the beam behind her, was Nora, sprinting across the valley toward her and the camp. As the moon peered briefly through the rainclouds, Nora caught sight of Sloane, and stopped short; then veered away quickly, angling now toward the rope ladder that led up to the city. The shot had flushed her from the rock pile, but in the worst possible way.

Sloane raised the gun in her direction, then lowered it again. Nora had not approached the tent, after all. So what *had* she shot?

As she slowly circled the camp with her light, something resolved itself against the farthest row of tents. Sloane staggered in disbelief.

The cold light had fallen across a terrifying apparition. It stood, humped and ragged, staring silently back at her. Red eyes bored like dots of fire through holes cut into a buckskin mask. Wild painted designs of white along the legs and arms were spattered crimson with blood. Its pelt steamed in the humid air.

Instinctively, Sloane took a step backward, panic and disbelief struggling within her. *This* was what she had shot. She could see the great wound in its midriff, the blood shining black in the moonlight. And yet it remained standing. More than that: as its chest heaved slowly, she could see that it was very much alive.

Though the revelation took only a split second, to Sloane it seemed as if time had come to a standstill. She could hear her heart beating a frantic cadence in her ribs.

And then, with terrifying, deliberate malevolence, the creature took a step toward her.

Instantly, panic took over. Dropping the flashlight, Sloane wheeled and ran. For a moment, the kiva, the flood, everything was forgotten in her desire to escape this monstrous vision. *This* was the thing that massacred the horses, desecrated Holroyd's body . . . then she thought of Swire and Bonarotti, and suddenly her legs were churning even faster, the night air tearing in and out of her lungs.

Now she could barely make out Nora, climbing toward the city. Desperately, Sloane veered to follow, keeping her eyes locked on the ladder, running with reckless abandon, trying with all the power of her will to ignore the awful, low, flapping sounds of the pelted thing as it came racing up the darkness behind her.

65

NORA HEAVED HERSELF OVER THE RIM, scrambled to her feet, and sprinted away from the edge of the cliff. Vaulting over the retaining wall, she dashed across the central plaza into the deeper darkness beneath the shadow of the roomblocks.

She came to a stop, leaning against a wall, sobbing, sides heaving. As if from a great distance, she heard the steady beating of rain. She paid it no heed. A single, fleeting image was burned into her mind: Sloane, standing outside the door to Smithback's tent after the sound of that terrible shot. She had found Bill, and killed him. For a moment, the pain and despair were so overwhelming that Nora considered simply walking out into the plaza and letting Sloane gun her down.

A peal of thunder boomed, echoing again and again beneath the vast dome. Just being in the city made her feel sick. Her gaze traveled first to the far wall of the plaza, then back toward the roomblocks and the granaries. There, black upon black, yawned the maw of the Crawlspace. She flitted toward the rear of the plaza, careful not to raise any dust. Perhaps she could lure Sloane inside the Crawlspace, then ambush her, take the gun . . .

She pulled up short, breathing hard. This was stupid; she was panicking, making bad decisions. Not only was the

Crawlspace a potentially deadly bottleneck, it was loaded with fungal dust.

There was a fresh slash of lightning, and she turned back to see Sloane scramble over the top of the rope ladder, pistol in hand.

"Nora!" she heard Sloane call out wildly. "Nora, for God's sake, wait!"

Nora wheeled, diving away from the plaza, back toward the curved rear wall of the city.

Another tongue of lightning ripped the distant landscape, briefly illuminating the ancient city in indigo chiaroscuro. A second later, there was a crack of thunder, followed almost immediately by a second sound, shockingly loud in the close confines: the sound of gunfire.

Keeping to the darkest shadows, moving as swiftly as she dared, Nora crept along the stone wall toward the old midden heap. Careful not to trip over Black's tarps, she moved along the edge of the city, approaching the dark bulk of the first tower.

The sound of running footsteps rang out against stone. Nora shrank quickly behind the pole ladder propped against the tower, trying to make herself as inconspicuous as possible. In the darkness, it was impossible to tell where the footsteps had come from. She needed time to think, to determine a plan of action. Now that Sloane was in the city, perhaps there was a way for her to sneak back to the ladder, descend into the valley, get Smithback, and . . .

Footsteps again, much louder now; gasping breath; and then, coming around from the front side of the tower, was Sloane.

Nora glanced around in fresh desperation: the midden heap, the back alley leading to the Crawlspace, the benchland trail that led out to the narrow circuit above the valley. Every one was a dead end. There was nowhere left to run. Slowly, she turned back toward Sloane, steeling herself for the inevitable: the roar of the gun, the sudden lance of pain.

But Sloane was crouched at the base of the tower, peering

cautiously around its front edge. Her left hand was clenched against her heaving chest; her gun hand was pointed, not at Nora, but out into the darkness of the plaza.

"Nora, listen," Sloane gasped over her shoulder. "There's something after us."

"Something?" Nora echoed.

"Something *horrible*."

Nora stared at Sloane. *What kind of a trick is this?* she wondered.

Sloane remained crouched, gun pointed out into the plaza. She glanced back at Nora for a moment, and even in the darkness Nora could see fear, disbelief, nascent panic in the almond eyes.

"For God's sake, watch behind us!" Sloane begged, returning her own gaze to the plaza.

Nora looked quickly back down the direction from which she'd run. Her mouth had gone dry.

"Listen, Nora, *please*," she heard Sloane whisper, struggling to get her breathing under control. "Swire and Bonarotti have disappeared. I think we're the only ones left. And now, it's after us."

"*What's* after us?" Nora asked. But even as she phrased the question, she realized she already knew the answer.

"If we separate, we're dead," Sloane continued. "The only chance we have is to stick together."

Nora stared out into the darkness, past the midden heap, toward the granaries and the hidden maw of the Crawlspace. She struggled to keep the panic from clamping down and freezing her limbs. The woman at her back, she knew, had brought tragedy to the expedition; caused Aragon's death; murdered Smithback in cold blood. But right now, she could not afford to think about that. Now, she could think only of the dreadful apparition that, at any moment, could come scuttling toward her out of the black.

The city was full of recesses in which they could hide. But hiding in the dark was not the answer. It would be just a matter of time until the skinwalker tracked them down. What they needed was some defensible place where they could hold out for at least a while. Daybreak might afford a fresh set of options. . . .

In that instant, she realized that there was nowhere to go. Nowhere, except up.

"The tower," she said.

Sloane turned quickly to her. The question in her eyes disappeared as she followed Nora's gaze toward the structure that reared above them.

Grasping the pole ladder, Nora scrambled up to the small second-story rooftop. Sloane followed, kicking the ladder away behind her. They dashed through the low crumbling doorway and into the enfolding darkness of the great tower.

Nora paused within, digging out her flashlight and shining it into the rectangle of darkness above them. The sight was terrifying: a series of rickety pole ladders, balanced on ledges of projecting stone, rising into the darkness. To climb, she would have to place one foot on a series of projecting stones that ascended the inside wall, and the other foot on the notches of the poles. There were three series of ladders, one above the other, separated by the narrow stone shelves that ran around the inner walls of the tower. It had been deliberately designed to be the most precarious climb possible.

On the other hand, if they could just reach the redoubt at the top, they might be able to hold the skinwalker off. The Anasazi had built this tower for a single purpose: defense. Sloane had a gun. And they might even find a cache of stones at the top that could be lobbed down into the tower.

"Go on!" Sloane whispered urgently.

Nora checked her flashlight. Its beam was growing feeble. But she had no choice: they could not make the climb in total darkness. Sliding the lit flashlight into her shirt pocket, she reached for the first pole, testing its sturdiness. Taking a deep breath, she placed a foot in the first notch. Her other foot went on the first small stump of rock, projecting from the tower wall across from the notch. She hoisted herself up, spreadeagled over open space. She climbed as fast as she dared, trying not to think of the swaying of the pole under her weight, creaking with dry rot and shedding powdered wood. Sloane followed behind, her frantic climbing shaking the brittle structure still further.

Reaching the first platform, Nora stopped to catch her breath. As she crouched, gasping, she heard a faint clatter from outside the tower: the sound of a pole ladder being thrust up against adobe walls.

Instantly, Nora leaped for the second pole, Sloane following. She scrambled upward, vaulting up the swaying pole, listening to the crackling and splitting of wood beneath her feet. This ladder felt much less secure than the first. As she neared the top, she felt its supports beginning to give way. She threw herself onto the second shelf, gasping and crying.

Just then, she heard the patter of footsteps below. A dark form momentarily blotted out the dim rectangle of light at the entrance to the tower. Beside her, Sloane cursed under her breath.

For an instant, Nora found herself unable to move, as the choking terror of the encounter in the abandoned ranch house returned to her in full force. Then she was shocked back to the present by the deafening blast of a pistol shot. The echoes died crazily within the confines of the tower. Heart in her mouth, Nora angled the flashlight downward. The figure was swarming up the first ladder, swift and sure. Sloane raised her weapon again.

"Save your bullets for the top!" Nora cried. She urged Sloane onto the third and final ladder, its ancient geometry faint in the beam of her light.

"What the hell are you doing?" Sloane whispered.

But Nora simply pushed her up the ladder without a word. It was time to take a desperate chance.

Taking a firm hold on the stone shelf, she drew her leg back and kicked at the bracing of the second pole as hard as she could. She felt it shudder with the impact. She kicked at it a second time, then a third. Below, she could hear a desperate scrabbling as the figure rode the shaking structure. Summoning all her strength, Nora kicked at the pole once again. With a shriek of rending wood, the pole lurched outward about six inches, whipsawing itself into a notch of rock. Nora heard a muffled roar from below. Chancing another look down, she saw the skinwalker lose its grip and begin to fall away toward the base of the tower. Then, catlike, it lashed out, grasping a set of supports. It clung there for a moment, swinging in and out of the dying beam of Nora's light. Then, with careful deliberation, it began climbing toward her again. Nora kicked out once more, trying to knock the structure away completely, but it was now jammed fast.

She leaped for the third pole and climbed, arms and legs protesting, toward the third shelf and the hole leading to the redoubt at the top of the tower. Moments later she was onto the ledge. From the small room beyond, Sloane reached out a hand to help her in.

Crouching beneath the low ceiling, Nora swept her flashlight around the room. It was tiny, perhaps four by six feet. Above her head, a small ragged hole led up onto the roof of the tower. A disarticulated skeleton lay in a heap against one wall. Her heart sank as she saw there were no stones, no weapons—nothing they could use to defend themselves except a few useless bones.

But they still had the gun.

Shielding the flashlight, Nora leaned back out into the cool dark shaft of the tower. Two bobbing red eyes reflected the feeble beam: it was on the second ladder again, and coming inexorably closer.

She shrank back into the redoubt and looked at Sloane. A pale face stared back at her, drawn with fear and tension. Beneath it, the necklace of micaceous beads gave off a faint golden sheen. Nora cupped her hand over the light. A part of her could not fully comprehend what was happening: stuck here, with the woman who had caused the death of her friends, while a creature out of nightmare was climbing toward them. She shook her head, trying desperately to clear it.

"How many bullets?" she whispered, shining the veiled light toward Sloane.

Mutely, Sloane held up three fingers.

"Listen," Nora went on, hearing distinctly the quaver in her own voice. "There's no time left. I'll turn off the light, and we'll wait here in the opening. When it's close, I'll aim the beam, and you fire. Okay?"

Sloane suppressed a cough, nodded urgently.

"We'll only have time for one shot, maybe two. Make them count."

She snapped off her light, and together they moved toward the opening of the redoubt. As Nora inched out cautiously, she became acutely aware of every sense: the cool air rolling up from the darkness of the tower, the hard metal of the flashlight in her hand, the smell of dust and decay from the redoubt.

And the sound of scrabbling claws on wood, growing closer, ever closer.

"Get ready," she whispered.

She waited a moment, then another, hearing the hammering thud of her heart, the blood rushing through her veins. Then she snapped on the light.

And there it was below her, terrifyingly close. With an involuntary cry, she took in the petrifying image: musky wolf-skin; feral eyes; tortured, howling mask.

"Now!" she cried, even as the roar of the gun drowned out her voice.

In the faint beam, she saw the skinwalker jerk to one side, pelt flying wildly about him.

"Again!" she shouted, fighting to keep the dwindling pin-point of light on the twisting figure. There was another blast, superimposed by a muffled howl from below. As the light guttered out Nora saw the figure crumple in on itself and fall away, swallowed by the well of darkness.

She dropped the useless flashlight into the gulf and listened. But there was nothing: no groan, no rasping intake of breath. The faint glowing rectangle of doorway far below them betrayed no movement, no twisted shadow.

"Come on!" Sloane said, pulling her back into the redoubt and urging her toward the hole in the ceiling. Grasping the adobe framework, Nora pulled herself up onto the roof. She backed away from the opening as Sloane came up behind, gasping and coughing.

Here, far above the ruins of Quivira, it was cool, with a faint breeze. The dome of the alcove was only a few feet above her head, a rough, fractured surface. Nora stood motionless, emotionally and physically exhausted. There was no parapet on the tower; the roof ended in open space. Beyond it, the city lay stretched out below her feet. The moon was struggling to show itself behind an expanse of ugly, fast-scudding rainclouds, and there was the whisper of rain. The pale illumination, waxing and waning, gave the roomblocks, towers, and plazas a fleeting spectral glow. Moist air brushed her cheek, stirred her hair. She heard a faint flutter of wings, a low wind in the valley. Somewhere out in that valley lay Smithback's body.

She turned quickly toward Sloane. The woman was kneeling at the opening in the roof, gun drawn, staring intently downward. Nora came over, and together they waited in tense silence. But no sound or movement came from the darkness below.

At last, Sloane stood and backed away. "It's over," she said.

Nora nodded absently, still staring into the dark cavity, her thoughts clouded, her mind troubled.

For what seemed several minutes, they stood motionless, overwhelmed by the furious emotion of the chase. Then, at last, Sloane snugged the gun into her belt.

"So what now, Nora?" she asked huskily.

Nora looked up at her, slowly, uncomprehending.

"I just saved your life," Sloane went on slowly. "Isn't that going to count for something?"

Nora could not bring herself to speak.

"It's true," Sloane said. "I saw that storm. So did Black.

But I didn't lie about the weather report. You gave me no choice." There was a sudden flash of anger in the almond eyes. "You were willing to abandon everything, keep the glory to yourself—" A sudden racking cough cut short the sentence. Nora could see Sloane fighting to keep her voice calm.

"I'm not proud of what I did," she went on. "But it had to be done. People have died for far lesser causes than this. The *true* wrong was yours: walking away, ready to deprive the world of the most glorious pottery ever made by man."

"Pottery," Nora repeated.

"Yes. The Sun Kiva was full—*is* full—of black-on-yellow micaceous pottery. It's the mother lode, Nora. You didn't know it. You didn't even *suspect* it. But *I* knew."

"I knew there was no gold in that kiva."

"Of course there wasn't. Neither one of us ever really believed that. But all those ancient reports weren't totally fabricated—not really. It was a translational blip."

Sloane leaned forward. "You know the value of black-on-yellow micaceous. No intact examples have ever been found. That's because *they're all here*, Nora. They were the true treasure of Anasazi. And they're more than just pots. I've *seen* them. The designs are unique—they tell, in pictographic form, the entire history of the Anasazi. *That's* why they were made and hoarded here, and nowhere else: knowledge is power. They hold the answers to all the great mysteries of southwestern archaeology."

For a moment, Nora froze at these words. The horror and danger were forgotten as she thought of the magnitude of such a discovery. *If this is true*, she thought, *then it makes all of our other discoveries seem like . . .*

And then Sloane coughed, drawing the back of her hand across her mouth. The climb seemed to have drained all the energy from her: she seemed pale, her breathing rapid. Instantly, Nora returned to the present. *The sickness is coming on her*, she thought.

"Sloane, the entire back of the city—especially the Sun Kiva—is full of fungal dust," she said.

Sloane frowned, as if doubting she had heard correctly. "Dust?"

"Yes. That's what killed Holroyd. The skinwalkers are using it for corpse powder."

Sloane shook her head impatiently. "What are you doing—trying to distract me with bullshit? Don't change the subject. I'm talking about the greatest discovery of the century."

Sloane fell silent for a moment. Then she began again. "You know, we could keep the mistaken weather report between ourselves. We could forget about what happened to Aragon, forget the storm. This find is bigger than all that." She looked away. "You can't possibly understand what it means to me—what it *would* have meant to me—to be the sole discoverer. To have my name go down in history beside Carter and Wetherill. If it weren't for me, we would have left this place, the pottery undiscovered, ripe for looting by—"

"Sloane," Nora said, "the skinwalkers weren't *after* the pottery. They wanted to keep us away from it."

But Sloane put her hand up for silence. "Listen to me, Nora. Together, we could give this great gift to the world." She drew a ragged breath. "If I'm willing to share this with you, then surely you can forget what's happened here today."

Nora looked at Sloane, her tawny face dappled in the moonlight. "Sloane—" she began, then stopped. "You don't get it, do you? I can't do that. It's not about archaeology anymore."

Sloane stared at her, wordlessly, for a moment. Then she placed her hand on the butt of her gun. "It's like I told you, Nora. You leave me no choice."

"You always have a choice."

Sloane drew the gun quickly, pointing it at her. "Right," she said. "Endless fame, or a lifetime in disgrace? That's not a choice."

There was a brief silence as the two women stood, facing

each other. Sloane coughed once again; a sharp, ragged sound.

"I didn't want things to end up like this," she said, more calmly. "But you've made it clear it's either you or me. And I'm the one holding the gun."

Nora said nothing.

"So turn around, Nora. Walk to the edge of the roof."

Sloane's voice had grown very quiet. Nora stared at her. In the pale light, the amber eyes were hard and dry.

Her gazed still locked on Sloane, Nora took a step backward.

"There's only one bullet left in the chamber. But that's all I'll need, if it comes down to that. So turn around, Nora. Please."

Slowly, Nora turned around to face the night.

Open space stretched out before her, a vast river of darkness. Across the narrow valley, Nora could make out the dark violet of the far wall of cliffs. She knew she should feel fear, regret, despair. And yet the only emotion she was aware of was a cold rage: rage at Sloane, for her pathetic, misplaced ambition. *One bullet* . . . she wondered, if she threw herself to one side, whether she stood a chance in hell of dodging that bullet. She tensed, readying herself for sudden movement.

Sloane shifted behind her. "Step off the roof," she said.

But still Nora stood, eyes and ears open to the night. The storm had passed. She could hear the frogs calling from below, the hum and drone of insects going about their nocturnal business. In the intense stillness, she could even hear the blood as it rushed through her veins.

"I'd rather not shoot you," she heard Sloane say. "But if I have to, I will."

"Damn you," Nora whispered. "Damn you for wrecking the expedition. And god*damn* you for killing Bill Smithback."

"Smithback?" The tone in Sloane's voice was one of such surprise that, despite herself, Nora turned toward it. As she did, she saw a form suddenly emerge from the hole in the roof: a dark, matted shape, wolf pelt twisting around naked painted skin. Pale light glistened off a crimson patch of fur that stained the figure's midriff.

Sloane pivoted quickly as the thing rushed at her with a great howl of vengeance. There was a flash of moonlight on the gun, the arc of a knife, and both figures went down, rolling frantically in the loose dirt of the tower roof. Nora dropped to her knees and crawled crablike away from the edge, eyes riveted to the struggle. In the pitiless moonlight, she could see the figure, burying the horrible black knife again and again into Sloane's chest and stomach. Sloane cried out, twisting and thrashing her body, an agonized soprano keening. With a supreme effort, Sloane tried to pull herself away. She half rose, gun hand swiveling around desperately, only to be pulled down again. There was a terrible thrashing, another anguished cry from Sloane. The blade flashed down and the gun fired at last, blowing the knife into hundreds of glittering slivers of obsidian. With a howl, the dark shape flung itself upon her. There was a final thrash, a puff of dust: and then both figures were gone.

Nora rushed quickly to the edge, peering down in horror as the bodies, locked together, bounced off the retaining wall, flew apart, then rolled off the edge of the city into the valley below. Before the moon buried itself once again behind the clouds, it winked briefly off Sloane's pistol as it spun lazily, end over end, into the unfathomable night.

Trembling, Nora pulled herself back, sprawled across the floor, breathing hard.

They had not killed the skinwalker, after all. Using consummate stealth, it had hidden itself somewhere within the blackness of the tower, waiting for the right moment in which to strike. Then, it had attacked Sloane with a single-mindedness so furious Nora could barely comprehend it. And now, that skinwalker was dead. And so was Sloane.

But it was not the chase up the tower, or even the sudden, terrible encounter on the roof, that filled her with absolute terror. In the desperate struggle, one crucial fact had slipped

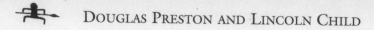

her mind. *Two* figures in wolfskins had assaulted her in the ranch house, on that clear Santa Fe night, barely three weeks before. And that meant only one thing.

There was another skinwalker, loose somewhere, in the valley of Quivira.

66

HER BREATH COMING IN SHORT, RAGGED gasps, Nora moved toward the hole in the tower roof. She lowered herself, as quietly as she could, into the small redoubt below. On hands and knees, she crawled toward the lip of the chamber, then looked slowly over the edge. It was pitch black in the tower; she sensed, rather than felt, the vast emptiness below her. She heard nothing save for the rush of water in the valley beyond—the maddening, unceasing babble that disguised other, stealthier, sounds.

Her arms trembled, threatening to freeze up in panic. The thought of descending, sightless, through the complex labyrinth of ancient wood was terrifying. Yet even more terrifying was the thought of remaining here, inside the tower, waiting for something to come for her. Now that she had no weapon—now that there was no possible way to defend herself—the tower had become a deathtrap from which she had to escape.

She struggled to regulate her breathing, to keep her mind from going numb. Extending one foot over the ledge, she swept it gingerly from side to side until she found the first notch of the topmost ladder. Moving carefully forward, she eased her weight onto the old framework, keeping one hand on the shelf until she knew she had a firm foothold. Then, with extreme caution, she began to descend, one notch at a time. She could feel a chill wind rising up from below, caressing her legs. The wind rose, and the tower creaked and ticked in response. Pebbles came clattering past her, their crazed echoing fall reminding her of the abyss that yawned below.

At last her foot reached the firmness of the second shelf. She paused for a second, trying once again to steady the wild rise and fall of her chest. But she could not remain here: poised between roof and floor, she was even more vulnerable. Groping in the darkness, fingers extended, she reached for the top of the detached second ladder. Once again, she began the descent, limbs balanced between the creaking wooden pole and the stone protrusions.

Just as she was about to reach for the next shelf, she suddenly froze. There had been a sound, she thought: the soft hollow sound of a footfall. She waited, listening, in the darkness. But there was nothing more, and with relief she slid down onto the safety of the shelf.

One more ladder. Steadying herself, she reached for it, tested it. Then, as carefully as before, she descended first one notch, then another, and then another.

Suddenly, she felt the pole give with a terrifying dry crack. The entire wooden structure seemed to shudder around her. Immediately, she pushed herself away from the pole and dropped the last ten feet, hitting the stone floor with a mighty impact. Needles of pain lanced through her knees and ankles as she scrambled to her feet and stumbled through the low doorway onto the adjacent rooftop. She glanced around, shaking with exertion and fear. But there was nothing: the city seemed perfectly silent and deserted.

She had to get to the valley. At least there, she might have a chance. Perhaps Sloane had been wrong. Perhaps Swire and Bonarotti were still alive. If she could hide until daylight, she'd have a better chance of finding them. There was safety in numbers. She might even be able to locate Sloane's gun, lying somewhere in the darkness of the valley floor. And there was always the hope, remote as it was, that Smithback's gunshot wound was not fatal . . .

Nora brushed her hand across her face with a sob. She could not allow herself to think about that; not now.

Keeping as low as possible, she crept across the roof and peered down the ladder that leaned against it. The way below seemed clear. Swinging herself over the edge, she descended as quickly as she dared, then paused to look around. Nothing.

Suddenly, she froze once again. The city seemed silent and asleep. The moon, alternately emerging from and disappearing behind the racing clouds, painted uncertain fingers of light across the roomblocks. And yet her instincts were screaming to her that something was wrong.

Cautiously, keeping against the wall of the tower, she moved around toward the front of the city and slowly peeked around the corner. One at a time, objects came into view, lit by the fitful glow of the moon: the retaining wall, the central plaza, the ghostly outline of roomblocks.

Once again, a sense of imminent danger washed over her, instincts ringing five-alarm. And this time she realized what it was: borne on the fitful midnight wind came the faint scent of morning glories.

Almost without knowing what she was doing, she fell back, away from the tower and into the darkness along the edge of the city. Galvanized into action, she found herself running with a desperate, reckless speed, heedless of obstacles. There was no plan in her mind. She felt simply an animal panic to get away: to race for the deepest, most secret place she could find. To stop, to delay, was simply to invite attack.

Dark alleys, low mounds of rubble, angular adobe structures flashed by in the faint moonlight as she ran. Suddenly, she caught herself short. To the right were the squat, low forms of the granaries. And directly before her, its low maw a rectangle of deeper darkness, was the entrance to the Crawlspace. Inside, she knew, the blackness would be complete. There might be a hiding place in there, perhaps inside the roomblocks of the secret city itself.

She began to move forward, then stopped. Pursuer or no, she would not allow herself to enter the Crawlspace, and its lethal payload of dust, ever again.

Instead, she turned and dashed into the alley alongside the granaries. Halfway down the alley's gentle curve, she stopped at a notched pole ladder, leaning against the rearward set of roomblocks. Grasping at the dry wood, she climbed as quietly as she could to the second-floor setback. Stepping onto the roof, she pulled the ladder up behind her. At least that would slow the skinwalker down, buy her a few more seconds of time.

She shook her head, forcing the panic away, trying to keep her thoughts clear. The clouds moved once again over the moon. Only the river spoke. Quivira was silent, watching, under a shroud of darkness.

She moved across the rearward set of roofs, past a long row of keyhole doorways. Bats flitted from the recesses of the city, flicking through the shadows on their way to the valley. Except for a few central roomblocks that ran from the front of the city to the back, most of the buildings were cul-de-sacs. She thought of hiding inside one of the roomblocks, then quickly dismissed the idea; out here, in the city proper, it would only be a matter of time until she was hunted down. Better to keep moving, to wait for an opportunity to descend into the valley.

She crept along the row of open doorways, then paused at the corner of the roomblock, listening.

A sudden footfall invaded the darkness. Nora looked around wildly; with the sound of the river echoing through the vault, it was almost impossible to tell where the sound had come from. Had the skinwalker followed her around to the granaries, and was it even now slipping up behind? Or was it lying in wait somewhere in the plaza, biding its time until she crept toward the rope ladder?

There was another noise, not as faint as the last. It seemed—she thought—to have come from below. Dropping to her stomach, Nora crawled to the side of the roof, and cau-

tiously peered over the edge into the pool of darkness.
Empty.

She rose to her feet, the smell of flowers stronger now:
overripe, sickly sweet. Her heart was hammering an overwhelming cadence in her chest. She backed away from the
parapet, and as she did so she heard the rattling sound of
the pole ladder being placed against its flanks. Quickly, she
ducked into the nearest set of roomblocks.

She pressed herself against the wall, gasping for breath.
Whatever she did, wherever she went, she was at a disadvan-
tage. The skinwalker was faster than she was, and far stronger.
It was at home in the dark. She realized, with a terrible sinking feeling, that it would never allow her to escape from the
valley.

There was only one possibility, remote though it was.
Somehow, she had to even the playing field, to minimize the
threat. And that meant finding a weapon.

Inside, the room was still and cool. Nora glanced quickly
around. A pile of war god masks stood in one corner, crimson mouths twisted and leering in the faint moonlight. The
air smelled of pack rats and mold. She crept through the next
doorway into another room, darker than the first, feeling
along the walls, letting her memory of the place guide her
steps.

Cautiously, she felt her way into the third room. A shaft of
pale light came through a crack in the roof, and there they
were: a stack of fire-hardened wooden spears, ending in
razor-sharp obsidian tips. She hefted a few, selected the two
lightest, and moved out of the room into a narrow passageway.

She felt her way along the wall, moving carefully toward the
next room in the block. Her memory of the location of the
spears had been more or less correct; she also recalled that this
system of rooms had an entrance at the front as well as the back.
But there were many hundreds of rooms in Quivira, and she
could not be certain.

Locating the doorframe, she ducked into the next room.

Here, gray light filtered from the far doorway. With a small glimmer of relief, Nora realized she must be close to the front of the structure. As quickly as she could, she moved into the darkest corner and waited, listening.

By now, the skinwalker would have followed her into the roomblocks. Nora rested the spear on her shoulder. It felt puny, insubstantial, in her sweaty fist. Perhaps it was the height of folly for her to think she could do anything to save herself. But the only other option was to do nothing, to wait in terror for the inevitable end. And she knew that—however diabolically quick and strong the skinwalkers were—they were also mortal.

She tensed at the faint sound of a footfall in the room beyond. The sound of the river was muffled here, inside the roomblocks, and she strained to listen. There was another faint noise. The reek of flowers grew overpowering. Struggling to keep her wits about her, Nora raised the spear. A ragged shadow, black upon black, seemed to fill the doorway. With an involuntary shout, she heaved the spear with all the strength she could muster. Immediately, she jumped away, running through the far door into the last room of the block. There had been no sound, no cry; but she thought she had heard the deep, flat sound of the spear sinking into flesh.

She stumbled forward, out the doorway and onto the flat roof along the front of the structure. Not daring to pause for a breath, she glanced about wildly for a way down.

There was a sudden scrabbling sound behind her, then a heavy weight fell across her back, forcing her violently to the ground. Crying out in pain and surprise, she tried to struggle away. A heavy pelt of fur, dank with sweat and the ghastly stench of rotting flowers, fell across her face. She looked up to see the masked head rear back over her, spear bobbing crazily from one shoulder. An arm raised up, obsidian knife flashing.

With a tremendous effort she pulled herself to one side. There was a searing pain in her calf as the knife struck a glancing blow. Without pausing, she tumbled headfirst off the roof of the roomblock. Landing in a pile of sand, she scrambled to her feet and ran into the protective shadow of the first-floor blocks. She was aware that she whimpered as she moved. Her leg throbbed, and she could feel the wet gush of blood running down around her ankle.

From behind came a heavy thump, as of a large body leaping to the ground. She ducked into the doorway of the nearest room, then half ran, half limped through a series of galleries to a small, dark chamber. Clouds had temporarily veiled the moon, but she knew that beyond this chamber lay the central plaza. She knelt in the close darkness, thinking furiously. A rancid smell of blood filled her nostrils: she must have been cut far deeper than she thought.

A brief running patter brought her to her feet. Any minute, and the moon would reappear from behind the clouds. It would be the work of thirty seconds to follow the trail of blood directly to her. And then, the thick smell of blood would be replaced by the wonderful, terrible, scent of flowers.

As if on cue, a ghostly aura crept across the walls of the room as moonlight slanted once again into the city. Nora tensed herself for what would be her final run across the plaza to the retaining wall. Deep down, she was well aware that she could never make it in time. But she could not bear to sit in this room, cornered like a rat, awaiting a brief, brutal end.

She took a deep breath, then another. Then she swivelled to face the doorway leading out of the room.

And froze.

In the far corner, illuminated by the sepulchral moonlight, lay Luigi Bonarotti. His glazed eyes were wide open in a sightless stare. In the dim light, he seemed bathed in an even deeper shadow of blood. Nora took in the outrageous, horrifying details: fingers cut off, unbooted feet torn away, head partially scalped. She fell to her knees and covered her mouth, gagging.

As if from a great distance, she heard the skinwalker moving in the alley behind the roomblocks.

She sat up quickly, her gaze returning to Bonarotti. There, still holstered around his waist, was the monstrous gun.

Without thinking, she leaped for it, fumbled with the catch, and pulled it from the holster. A .44 magnum Super Blackhawk, deadly as hell. She wiped the bloody grip on her jeans, then scurried back against the wall as another footstep sounded, closer.

Suddenly, with terrible speed, the skinwalker appeared in the doorway, thick pelt fluttering. The white spots along its midriff glowed blue in the moonlight, and red angry eyes staring at her from behind the slits in the buckskin mask.

For an instant, it eyed Nora silently. Then, with a low growl, it sprang forward.

In the confines of the small adobe room, the blast of the .44 was deafening. She closed her eyes against the blinding flash, letting her elbows and wrists absorb the mighty kick. There was a frenzied howl. Squeezing her eyes shut, she fired a second time at the sound. Ears ringing, she scrambled in the direction of the doorway, then tripped and fell sprawling out into the central plaza. Quickly, she rolled onto her back and pointed the gun toward the doorway. Incredibly, the skinwalker was framed within it, crouching, arms gripping its midriff. She could hear fluid pattering to the ground as terrible wounds in its chest and stomach overloaded the thick pelt with blood. It straightened, saw her, and leaped with a snarl of rage and hatred. She fired a third time directly into the mask and the force of the massive bullet stopped the figure in mid-air, jerking the head back, whirling the body sharply to one side. Raising herself to one knee, Nora fired again, then again, the mask disintegrating into wet shreds. The smell of blood and cordite filled the air. The skinwalker thrashed heavily in the dust, whirling and jerking in a frenzied dance, bone and matter glowing in the moonlight, small jets of arterial blood rising in an erratic cadence, a low furious cry gurgling in its throat. But still Nora pulled the trigger, again and again and again, the hammer falling on empty chambers with a click that could not be heard above her own cries.

And then, after a long time, came silence. Slowly, painfully, Nora raised herself to her feet. She took two steps toward the retaining wall, faltered, stepped forward again. Then she sank back to the ground, laying the gun aside. It was over.

There, at the stone doorstep of the ruined city, she wept silently.

67

AFTER SEVERAL MINUTES, NORA ONCE again rose unsteadily to her feet. The valley of Quivira lay bathed in a faint silver light. Dark jewels winked and played across the dappled surface of the quickly flowing river. Behind her, the bulk of the ancient city watched in stony silence.

Hesitantly, like a sleepwalker, she made her way to the rope ladder. She climbed painfully down, one rung at a time, mechanically, still in shock. Reaching the bottom, she turned to look toward camp. There was the medical tent, the beckoning orange glow now extinguished. Nora felt a sob rise in her throat. Walking up to that tent and looking inside was the most painful thing she could imagine. Still, she had to know the worst for herself.

She went a few paces, then stopped. There, a few feet away from the cliff base, was Sloane's body, lying broken and crumpled in the sand. Nora took a step closer. The amber eyes were black and sightless, overlaid with a dull sheen of moonlight. The sand around her was soaked in blood. Nora shuddered, then glanced away, looking automatically for the body of the skinwalker.

It was nowhere to be seen.

A sharp current of fear brought her fully alert once more. She looked around more carefully. There, in the sand half a dozen feet from Sloane, was a large, distorted hollow: a thrashed-out depression, smeared and sprinkled with blood. A silver concho lay in the sand beside it. But there was no skinwalker body. She took an instinctive step back, hand rising to her mouth, eyes searching the landscape. But there was nothing in the broad open area at the base of the cliffs.

Turning, she sprinted through the moonlight toward the camp, angling toward the medical tent, her torn calf protesting at every step. It was worse than she could have ever feared: the inside of the tent had been torn to ribbons, equipment and supplies strewn about, the sleeping bag shredded. There were spatters of blood everywhere. But there was no body.

Sobbing more loudly now, Nora backed away, staggering in the shimmering moonlight. "Damn you!" she cried, turning slowly in the darkness. "God*damn* you!"

And then she felt a thin, but incredibly strong, arm slide its way over her shoulders and clamp down across her mouth and neck. For a moment, she struggled frantically. Then she went limp, unable to struggle further.

"Hush," whispered the quiet, gentle voice into her ear.

The grip loosened and Nora turned, her eyes widening in wonder. It was John Beiyoodzin.

"You!" she gasped.

In the moonlight, the old man's braids seemed to be painted with quicksilver. He touched a finger to his lips. "I have your friend hidden at the far end of the valley."

"My friend?" Nora said, not understanding.

"Your journalist friend. Smithback."

"Bill Smithback? He's alive?"

Beiyoodzin nodded.

Relief and unexpected joy flooded through her, and she gripped Beiyoodzin's hands with newfound strength. "Look, there's somebody else still missing. Roscoe Swire, our wrangler—"

Something in Beiyoodzin's expression stopped her from continuing. "The man who watched your horses," he said. "He is dead."

"Dead? Oh no, no, not Roscoe . . ." She turned her head away. It was too much to bear.

"I found his body by the river. The skinwalkers got him. Now we must go."

He freed himself and began to turn away, gesturing for her to follow. But she put a restraining hand on his arm.

"I killed one of them up in the city," she said, forcing away the bitter tears, willing herself to be strong. "But there's another one. He's wounded, but I think he's still alive, somewhere in the valley."

Beiyoodzin nodded. "I know," he said simply. "That is why we must leave at once."

"But how?"

"I know a secret trail. The one the skinwalkers themselves use to get in and out of the valley. It is extremely difficult. But we must get you and your friend away from this place."

Beiyoodzin began moving rapidly and noiselessly through the dappled shadows, out of camp and back toward the overhanging cliff face. Using the darkness of the rock wall for cover, they made their way past the rockfall to the far end of the canyon, where the swollen river tumbled into the narrower slot canyon, disappearing in a violent waterfall. The sound of water was much louder here, and the entire mouth of the canyon was covered in the usual pall of mist. Without pausing, Beiyoodzin stepped through the curtain of spray and disappeared. Hesitating just a moment, Nora followed.

She found herself on a small, sloping ledge of rock. The trail, chiseled into the rock, started directly behind the curtain of spray and went down, a few feet above the roaring cataract. Here in the narrow canyon, the reflected moonlight was dim, and Nora moved across the slippery, moss-covered rock with care. A false step, she knew, would send her over the edge: into the rushing waters, the narrow labyrinth of knifelike stone, and certain death.

After a few moments, the trail flattened out onto a ledge. Billows of cold mist rose from the tumbling water, encircling her like a cloak. Here, the constant presence of moisture had created a bizarre microclimate of mosses, hanging flowers, and dense greenery. Moving to one side, Beiyoodzin parted a veil of lush ferns, and in the gloom beyond Nora could just make out Smithback, sitting, arms clasped around himself, waiting.

"Bill!" she cried, as he rose in astonishment, joy sweeping over his face.

"Oh my God," he said. "Nora. I thought you were dead." Embracing her weakly, he kissed her, then kissed her again.

"How are you?" she asked, touching the ugly welt on the side of his forehead.

"I ought to thank Sloane. That sleep did me wonders." But his weak voice, and the ragged cough that followed, belied his words. "Where is she? Where are the others?"

"We must keep moving," Beiyoodzin said urgently.

He pointed ahead, and Nora followed his gesture. She could make out the dim narrow trail leading upward along the canyon face, zigzagging through the clefts and pinnacles of rock, squirreling up crevasses. In the pale light of the moon, it looked terrifying: an insubstantial, spectral path, intended for ghosts, not humans.

"I'll go first," whispered Beiyoodzin to Nora. "Then Bill. And then you."

He looked at her for a moment, searchingly. Then he turned and began to climb, keeping his weight toward the wall of the canyon, moving up the slope with surprising nimbleness for one so old. Smithback grasped a handhold, and, trembling, pulled himself up behind. Nora followed.

They made their way slowly and painfully up the precipitous trail, careful to avoid the slippery moss and algae that clung to the ledges underfoot. The roar of the waterfall echoed up from below, a heavy vibration that churned the air. Nora could see that Smithback was barely able to pull himself up; each step required all his strength.

Terrifying minutes later, they were out of the microclimate. The slot canyon was narrowing, and the resulting loss of moonlight made progress even more difficult. Some distance ahead, at the limit of vision, Nora could see the trail make a sharp switchback and disappear around a corner. At the bend, a small parapet of rock led out over the roaring cataract below.

"How are you doing?" she asked Smithback.

He didn't answer at first. Then he gasped, coughed, and gave a thumbs up.

Suddenly, Beiyoodzin stopped short, raising a warning hand over his shoulder.

"What is it?" Nora asked as she stopped, renewed fear sending her heart hammering.

Then she, too, caught the sweet scent of morning glories on the freshening breeze. Wordlessly, she looked at Beiyoodzin.

"What is it?" Smithback said.

"He's following us up the trail," Beiyoodzin said. The years suddenly seemed to show on his lined, drawn face. Without another word, he resumed his climb.

They followed him as quickly as they could up the precipitous cliff face. Nora bit her lip against the pain of her wounded leg. "Faster," Beiyoodzin urged.

"He can't go any—" Nora began. Then she stopped short. *Ahead* of them, at the sharp bend in the trail, a shape had appeared: a clot of black against the dimly shining rockface. The heavy pelt steamed, and the fringe of fur along its bottom edge was caked in blood. It took a shambling step toward them, then stopped. Sick with fear and horror, Nora could hear the rasping breath being sucked in through the blood-soaked mask. Through the dimness, she thought she could make out red pinpricks of eyes, glowing with anger, pain, and malice.

Unexpectedly, Beiyoodzin moved forward. Reaching the outcropping of rock before the switchback, he stepped out onto it carefully. The skinwalker watched him, motionless. Digging into his clothing, Beiyoodzin drew out his medicine bag, tugged it open, and reached inside. Never taking his eyes from the skinwalker, he sprinkled a small, almost invisible, line of pollen and cornmeal onto the narrow ledge between them, chanting softly.

As Nora watched in silent dread, the skinwalker took a step forward, toward the line of pollen. Beiyoodzin spoke a word: *"Kishlinchi."*

The skinwalker stopped, listening. Beiyoodzin shook his head in sorrow. "Please, no more," he said. "Let it end here."

Still the skinwalker waited. Now, Beiyoodzin held an eagle feather outstretched before him. "You think evil has made you strong. But instead it has made you weak. Weak and ugly. Evil is the very absence of strength. I am asking you to be strong now, and end all this. This is the only way to save your life, because evil always burns itself up in the end."

With a growl of anger, the skinwalker unsheathed an obsidian knife. It took a step forward, breaking the line of pollen, and raised the knife, standing within striking distance of Beiyoodzin's heart.

"If you will not come back with me, then I beg you to stay here, in this place," Beiyoodzin said quickly, his voice cracking. "If evil is your choice, then stay with evil. Take the city, if you must." He nodded in Nora's direction. "Take these outsiders, if nothing else will satisfy your blood lust. But leave the people, leave the village, alone."

"What are you saying?" Smithback cried in outraged surprise. But neither the skinwalker nor Beiyoodzin seemed to hear. Now, the old man reached deeper into his clothes and pulled out another bag: much older, worn almost to a paper thinness, its edges trimmed in silver and turquoise. Nora stared from Beiyoodzin to the medicine bag and back again, feelings of anger, fear, and betrayal mixing within her. Stealthily, she placed a hand on Smithback's elbow, urging him to move slowly back down the trail, away from the confrontation.

"You know what this is," Beiyoodzin said. "This bag holds the Mirage Stone of the Fathers. The most treasured artifact of the Nankoweap People. Once, *you* treasured it, too. I offer it to you as earnest of my promise. Stay here, trouble our village no more."

Slowly, reverently, he opened the bag, then held it forward, his outstretched hands trembling, whether from fear or age Nora could not tell.

The skinwalker hesitated.

"Take it," Beiyoodzin whispered. The matted figure moved forward and reached for it, leaning outward.

Suddenly, with lightning speed, Beiyoodzin thrust the open bag toward the skinwalker.

A heavy cloud of dust erupted from within, flying up into the figure's mask, spraying in long gray lines across the bloody pelt. The skinwalker roared in surprise and outrage, twisting around, tugging violently at the mask, growing more and more off balance. With the agility of a cat, Beiyoodzin leaped from the outcropping of rock back onto the trail. The skinwalker kicked frantically as it struggled, teetering a moment at the edge of the precipice. Then it went over with a howl of fury. Nora watched the plunge into the violet, moon-drenched shadows: matted pelt flapping crazily, limbs scrabbling at the air, mask pulling free as the blood-curdling cry meshed with the roar of the flood beneath. And then, suddenly, it was gone.

There was a moment of stasis. Beiyoodzin looked at Nora and Smithback, and nodded grimly.

Painfully, Nora helped Smithback up the trail toward Beiyoodzin. He stood at the switchback, looking down into the abyss.

"I'm sorry to have scared you like that," he said quietly, "but sometimes, the only defense left us is to play the coyote, the trickster."

Still looking downward, he reached out and took Nora's hand in his. The old man's grasp was as cool, light, and dry as a leaf.

"And so much death," he murmured. "So much death. But at least the evil has burned itself out."

Then he looked up at her, and Nora saw kindness and compassion, as well as an infinite sadness, in his eyes.

For a moment, there was silence between them. Then Beiyoodzin spoke.

"When you are ready," he said, in a small, clear voice, "let me take you to your father."

EPILOGUE

Moving at a steady, easy pace, the four riders made their way up the canyon known as Raingod Gulch. John Beiyoodzin, atop a magnificent buckskin, led the way. Nora Kelly followed, riding abreast of her brother, Skip. The massive form of Teddy Bear padded alongside, his back almost grazing the bellies of the horses as he weaved in and out beneath them. Bill Smithback brought up the rear, his unruly hair imprisoned beneath a suede cowboy hat. The exhausting course of antibiotic treatment he and Nora had undergone ended two weeks before, but beneath the hat brim the writer's skin was still struggling to regain a healthy color.

The late August sky was sprinkled with light cumulus clouds, drifting over a field of brilliant turquoise. Wrens flitted about, filling the sweet little canyon with their bell-like cries. A merry stream, shaded by fragrant cottonwoods, ran sparkling across a bed of soft sand. At almost every bend in the canyon were small alcoves, Anasazi dwellings tucked inside them: none more than two or three rooms, but lovely in their humble perfection.

Nora let her horse keep its own pace, concentrating on nothing but the sun beating down on her denimed legs, on the murmur of water nearby, on the swaying of her mount. Every now and then, she smiled to herself as she heard Smithback behind her, leveling curses at his balky mount, who stopped frequently to nibble a patch of clover or bite off the top of a thistle, completely ignoring the dire threats and imprecations of his rider. The man just had no talent with horses.

She realized how lucky she was to have him here; how lucky she was to be here herself. Briefly, her thoughts returned to their struggle out of the wilderness a month earlier: Smithback weak, Nora herself growing steadily weaker as the fungal infection took hold. If Skip and Ernest Goddard had not met them halfway down the trail with fresh horses—and if there had not been a powerboat waiting at the trailhead, or helicopters idling at Page—they would probably have died. And yet, for a time, Nora almost thought it would have been easier to die than to tell Goddard the news: how their incredible discovery had turned into such a terrible personal tragedy for him.

Here, thirty-odd miles northwest of the ruin of Quivira, the countryside seemed built on a smaller scale: friendly, verdant, well-watered. John Beiyoodzin had paused in his long story—he had paused frequently during the ride, giving his narrative time to sink in.

As they rode on through the sunlit silence, Nora allowed her thoughts to move gradually from Goddard to her own father, and of what she had so far been able to piece together of his own last trip up this canyon. He had taken very little from Quivira. In fact, far from being a pothunter, he had carefully refilled what excavations he had made in a way that would have pleased even Aragon. But in doing so, he had exposed himself to a concentration of the fungal dust, and grown sick. Riding north in hopes of finding help, his sickness had worsened to the point where he could hardly sit his horse. Nora wondered how he would have felt. Would he have been terrified? Resigned? As a child, she remembered hearing him say that he wanted to die in the saddle. And he had done just that. Or almost: eventually becoming too sick to ride, he had dismounted. Then he turned his horses free and waited to die.

"It was my cousin who found the body," Beiyoodzin said, resuming his story. "It was lying in a cave at the top of a small rise. Seemed to have been there about six months. The coyotes couldn't reach it, so it hadn't been disturbed."

"How did your cousin find it?" Skip asked.

"Looking for a lost sheep. He saw some color in the rock-shelter, climbed up to take a look." Beiyoodzin paused to clear his throat. "Next to the body was the notebook—the one Nora has now. Sticking out of the front shirt pocket was a letter, stamped and addressed. And beside him was a satchel holding the skull of a mountain lion, inlaid in turquoise. So my cousin went back to Nankoweap, and he was a talker, and soon the entire village knew of the dead white man in the canyon to the south. And because of the turquoise skull, they also knew this white man had found the city we had kept secret for so many years."

His voice trailed away for a moment before returning, softer, more thoughtful. "This was not a city of our ancestors. Those few who had been there—my grandfather was one—said it was a city of death, of oppression and slavery, of witchcraft and evil. There are stories in our past of a people who came out of the south, who enslaved the Anasazi, and forced them to build these great cities and roads. But they were destroyed by the very god who gave them power. Most who went to the city came back with ghost sickness and soon died. That was many, many years ago. None of my people have returned to the city since. Until recently."

Beiyoodzin deftly rolled a cigarette with one hand. "The discovery of the body caused a problem for the tribe, because the secret of the city lay with the body of the man. To reveal the presence of the body would be to betray the secret of the city."

"Why didn't you just destroy the letter and notebook?" Nora asked.

He lit the cigarette, inhaled. "We believe that it is extremely dangerous to handle the effects of the dead. It is a sure way to get ghost sickness. And we all knew what the white man had died from. So, for sixteen years, the body lay there. Unburied. It just seemed that the simplest thing to do was to do nothing."

Beiyoodzin stopped his horse abruptly and turned toward Nora. "That was wrong. Because we all knew that the body in the cave had a family. That somebody loved him, wondered where he had gone and whether he was still alive. It was cruel to do nothing. Still, doing nothing seemed the easiest, safest course of action. But doing nothing caused a small imbalance. And this imbalance grew, and grew, until it ended in you coming here and all these terrible killings."

Nora reined in her own horse beside Beiyoodzin's. "Who mailed the letter?" she asked quietly. It was the question she had been burning to ask for many, many weeks.

"There were three brothers. They lived in a trailer outside our village with their alcoholic father. The mother had run off with someone years before. These were smart boys, though, and they all got scholarships and went down to Arizona for college. They were hurt by this contact with the outside world, but hurt in very different ways. Two of the boys dropped out and came back early. They were disgusted with the world they had found, and yet changed by it. They had grown restless, angry, eager for the kind of wealth and power that you can't come by in a village such as ours. They no longer fit in with the rest of my people. They began turning from the natural way of things, searching out forbidden knowledge, learning forbidden practices. They found an old man, an evil man—a cousin of the man who murdered my grandfather. He helped them, revealed to them the blackest of all the arts. The village began to shun them, and they in turn rejected us. In time, they turned to the greatest taboo of all—the ancient ruins—and eagerly picked up what dark hints of its history still remained among our village.

"The third brother graduated and came back home. Like the other two, there were no jobs here for him, and no hope of finding one. Unlike his other brothers, he had converted to the Anglo religion. He despised our beliefs and our fear of ghost sickness. He thought we were superstitious and ignorant. He knew of the body in the cave, and he felt that to leave it there was a sin. So he searched out the body, carefully arranged the man's possessions, covered the body with sand, planted a cross. And he mailed the letter at a trading post."

Beiyoodzin shrugged. "Of course, some of this is just my guess. I'm not sure why he sent the letter. He couldn't have known if it would ever reach its destination, sixteen years after it had been written. Maybe it was to atone for a wrong he perceived. Or maybe he was angry at what he thought were our superstitions. Perhaps he did the right thing, I don't know. But what he did caused a terrible break with the other two brothers. There was drinking, there was an argument. They accused him of betraying the secret of the city to the outside world. And the two brothers killed the third."

Beiyoodzin fell into another silence. He turned his horse's head and they resumed their slow journey up the canyon, the horses splashing across the stream at each bend. At one turn they surprised a mule deer, which ceased drinking and raced away from them along the bed of the stream, sending up crystal cascades of water that glittered and fell back through the sun-drenched air.

"Those two brothers rejected anything to do with the Anglo world outside. But they also rejected the good ways of the people. They saw the evil city as their own destiny. Based on the whispered stories of our people, they eventually found the greatest secret of all—the hidden kiva—and entered it. They would have broken inside only once—not for its treasures, of course, but for its lode of corpse powder. It would be their own weapon of fear and vengeance. Afterwards, they would have carefully resealed the kiva, in the proper manner." He shook his head. "They wanted to protect its secrets—the secrets of the entire city—at all costs. In all but name, they had already been transformed into *eskizzi*—witches. And with the killing of their brother, the transformation was complete.

In our belief, the final requirement in becoming a skinwalker is to murder someone you love."

"Do you think they actually had supernatural powers?" Skip asked.

Beiyoodzin smiled. "I hear the doubt in your voice. It is true that the forbidden roots they chewed gave them great strength and great speed, the ability to absorb pain and bullets without feeling. And I know the white people think witchcraft is a superstition." He looked at Skip. "But I have seen witches in Anglo society, too. They wear suits instead of wolfskins. And they carry briefcases instead of corpse powder. As a boy, they came and took me to boarding school, where I was beaten for speaking my own language. Later, I saw them come among our people with mining contracts and oil leases."

As they rounded another bend, the canyon gave way to a small grove of cottonwoods. Beiyoodzin halted, and motioned for them all to dismount. Turned loose, the horses wandered off to graze the rich carpet of grass along the stream. Teddy Bear leaped onto a large rock and stretched out, looking for all the world like a lion, keeping guard over his pride. Skip walked over to Nora and placed his arm around her shoulders.

"How are you doing?" he asked, giving her a squeeze.

"I'm okay," she said. "You?"

Skip looked around, took a deep breath. "A little nervous. But actually, pretty good. To be honest, I don't remember feeling better."

"I'll thank you to take your paws off my date," said Smithback, ambling over and joining them. Together, they watched as Beiyoodzin untied his medicine kit from the saddle strings, examined it briefly, then nodded toward a gentle path that led up the side of the hill to a small rounded shoulder of rock. Above, Nora could see the rockshelter where their father's skeleton lay.

"What a beautiful place," Skip murmured.

Beiyoodzin led the way up the path and over the last little

hump of slickrock. Nora paused at the top, suddenly reluctant to look inside. Instead, she turned and let her gaze fall over the canyon. The rains had brought up a carpet of flowers— Indian paintbrush, sego lilies, datura, scarlet gilia, desert lupines. After much discussion, the two children of Padraic Kelly had decided to leave the body where it lay. It was in the redrock country he loved so well, overlooking one of the most beautiful and isolated canyons of the Escalante. No other gravesite could provide more dignity, or more peace.

She felt Skip's arm around her shoulder again, and she turned at last to face the shelter.

In the dim light of the interior, she could make out her father's saddle and saddlebags carefully lined up along the back wall of the rockshelter, the leather cracked and faded with age. Beside them was the turquoise skull, beautiful yet vaguely sinister, even here, far from the evil pall of the Rain Kiva. Beneath a thin layer of sand lay her father's bones. In places the wind had blown the sand away, revealing bits of rotten cloth, the dull ivory of bone, the curve of the cranium; she could see that he had died looking down into the valley below.

Nora stared for a long time. Nobody spoke. Then, slowly, she reached into her pocket. Her fingers closed over a small notebook: her father's journal, taken from the body by the witch she had shot and restored to her by Beiyoodzin. She opened it and removed a faded envelope she had placed between the pages: the letter that had started it all.

The letter had been addressed to her mother, written just before he had entered the city. But the last entry in Padraic Kelly's journal had been addressed to his children, written after his discovery of the city, in this very rockshelter while he lay dying. And now, in the presence of both her father and Skip, Nora began to read his last words.

She stepped forward, stopping at the foot of the grave. The cross was still there, two twisted pieces of cedar lashed with a rawhide thong. She felt Smithback's hand come forward to grasp her own, and she returned the pressure gratefully. After the horror of the last days at Quivira, and even in his own sickness and pain, the writer had been a kind, quiet, and steady presence. He had accompanied her to Peter Holroyd's memorial in Los Angeles, where she had left his own battered copy of *Endurance* beside the stone marker that stood in the stead of a grave: his body had never been found. Smithback had returned with her for a memorial service for Enrique Aragon on Lake Powell, when they boated out to the site where, beneath a thousand feet of water, Aragon's beloved Music Temple lay.

In time, she knew, they would return to Quivira. A hand-picked team from the Institute, armed with respirators and environmental suits, would make careful video documentaries of the site. Sloane's discovery—the micaceous pottery of transcendent beauty and value—would be carefully studied and documented back at the Institute, under the direction of Goddard himself. And perhaps, in time, Smithback would even write an account of the expedition—or, at least, the part of the expedition that would not bring unendurable pain to Goddard.

She sighed deeply. Quivira would wait for her. There was no chance of its location ever being divulged, or becoming public knowledge—the poisonous dust would make sure of that. Almost all those who knew of its location—with the exception of the Nankoweap—were now dead. Those who lived, she knew, would keep its secret.

Nora watched as Beiyoodzin leaned over the skeleton, untied the little buckskin bag, and bowed his head. Pinching out some yellow cornmeal and pollen, he sprinkled it on the body and began a soft, rhythmical chant, beautiful in its simple monotony. The others bowed their heads.

When the chant was done, Beiyoodzin looked at Nora. His eyes were shining, his creased face smiling. "I thank you," he said, "for letting me put this to rest. I thank you for myself, and for my people."

It was Skip's turn. He took the letter from Nora, turning it over and over in his hands. Then he knelt down, gently smoothed the sand away, and placed it into the pocket of his father's shirt. He remained kneeling for a moment. Then he slowly stood up and returned to Nora's side.

Nora took a deep breath, steadied her hands. Then she turned to the final entry in her father's journal and began to read.

> *To my dearest and most wonderful children, Nora and Skip,*
>
> *By the time you read this, I will be gone. I have been stricken with a disease, which I fear I contracted in the city I discovered: the city of Quivira. Although I cannot be sure this will ever reach you, I must believe in my heart that it will. Because I want to speak to you through this journal one last time.*
>
> *If it is within your power, let the great ruins of Quivira lie undisturbed and unknown. It is a place of evil; I know that now, even from my own brief exploration. It may well be the cause of my death, though I do not understand why. Perhaps some knowledge is better left alone, to die and return to the earth, just as we do.*
>
> *I have just one request to make each of you. Skip, please don't drink. It runs in the family, and, I promise you, you won't be able to handle it. I could not. And, Nora, please forgive your mother. I know that in my absence, she may blame me for what has happened. When you are grown, forgiveness will be difficult for you. But remember that, in a way, she was right to blame me. And—in her own way— she has always loved you deeply.*
>
> *This is a beautiful place to die, children. The night sky is filled with stars; the stream splashes below; a coyote is sounding in a distant canyon. I came here for riches, but the sight of Quivira changed my mind. In fact, I left no mark of my passage there. And I have taken one thing only from it, and that was meant for you, Nora, as proof your father really found the fabled city. For it was there that I*

learned, for the first time, that I had left my real, my true successes—the two of you—far behind in Santa Fe.

I know I have not been a great father, or even a good father, and for that I am truly sorry. There is so much I could have done as a father that I didn't. So let my last act as a father be to tell you this: I love you both. And I will love you always, forever and ever, from eternity to eternity. My love for you burns brighter than all the thousands of stars that carpet the sky above my head. I may die, but my love for you never will.

Dad

Nora fell silent and closed her eyes. For a moment, the entire canyon seemed to drop into reverential silence. Then she looked up, shut the notebook, and carefully placed it on the ground beside her father. She turned and gave Smithback a tearful smile.

Then the four of them made their way down the faint path, to the waiting horses and home.

AUTHORS' NOTE

The archaeology of this story is speculative in places. However, it is grounded in fact. The history of the Anasazi, the mystery of the Chaco collapse and the abandonment of the Colorado Plateau, the long-sought evidence of a Mesoamerican connection, the use of radar to locate prehistoric roads—as well as the cannibalistic and witchcraft practices described herein—are based on actual research findings. In addition, one of the authors, Douglas Preston, has traveled and lived among southwestern Indian peoples, as recounted in his nonfiction work *Talking to the Ground.*

The authors made use of information from a number of other publications, the most important of which include: Clyde Kluckhohn, *Navaho Witchcraft*; Blackburn and Williamson, *Cowboys and Cave Dwellers*; *Basketmaker Archaeology in Utah's Grand Gulch*; Crown and Judge, eds., *Chaco and Hohokam: Prehistoric Regional Sytems in the American Southwest*; Kathryn Gabriel, *Roads to Center Place: A Cultural Atlas of Chaco Canyon and the Anasazi*; James McNeley, *Holy Wind in Navajo Philosophy*; David Roberts, *In Search of the Old Ones*; George Pepper, *Pueblo Bonito*; Hester, Shafer, and Feder, *Field Methods in Archaeology*; Lynne Sebastian, *The Chaco Anasazi*; Levy, Neutra, and Parker, *Hand Trembling, Frenzy Witchcraft, and Moth Madness*; Mauch Messenger, ed.,

The Ethics of Collecting Cultural Property, Chris Kincaid, ed., *Chaco Roads Project, Phase I: A Reappraisal of Prehistoric Roads in the San Juan Basin*; Tim D. White, *Prehistoric Cannibalism at Mancos 5MTUMR=3246*; Christy Turner, *Man Corn: Cannibalism and Violence in the Prehistoric American Southwest*; and Farouk El-Baz, "Space Age Archaeology," *Scientific American*, August 1997.

It should be noted that the Nankoweap tribe is wholly fictitious, as is the Santa Fe Archaeological Institute. The witchcraft practices and beliefs described herein are not intended to negatively depict or portray the beliefs of any existing culture. All the characters, events, and most of the places portrayed in this novel are also entirely fictitious products of the authors' imaginations.